'Hamer's strength is in the slow, considered revelations that pepper the novel, making it difficult to put down ... *After The Party* forces the reader to confront uncomfortable questions like, How far would you go to protect a child? How clear is the line between right and wrong? And, what does it truly mean to be a good mother?' —Mamamia

'Everything I love in a novel – jam-packed with intrigue and humour. *After the Party* will keep you turning the pages into the early hours.' —Rachael Johns, bestselling Australian author

'I guarantee you will recognise your child, your neighbour, your partner or yourself in this story ... light-hearted and heart-warming ... I can see it being passed from sister to sister, or from girlfriend to girlfriend, with a knowing look, an exasperated sigh and a genuine giggle.' —Cass Moriarty, author of *The Promise Seed* and *Parting Words*

'... blending the relatable with the extraordinary, Cassie Hamer hits the sweet spot with her debut novel, *After The Party* ...' —*Daily Telegraph*

Cassie Hamer has a professional background in journalism and PR, but now much prefers the world of fiction over fact. In 2015, she completed a Masters in Creative Writing, and has since achieved success in numerous short story competitions. *After the Party* is her first novel. Cassie lives in Sydney with her terrific husband and three mostly terrific daughters, who still believe piñatas are a fun and effective method of lolly distribution. She is working on her second novel, but always has time to connect with other passionate readers via her website—CassieHamer. com—or through social media. You can follow her on Facebook, Instagram and Twitter.

after
the
party

CASSIE HAMER

First Published 2019
Second Australian Paperback Edition 2020
ISBN 9781489280992

Published by
HQ Fiction
An imprint of Harlequin Enterprises (Australia) Pty Limited (ABN 47 001 180 918), a subsidiary of HarperCollins Publishers Australia Pty Limited (ABN 36 009 913 517)
Level 13, 201 Elizabeth St
SYDNEY NSW 2000
AUSTRALIA

A catalogue record for this book is available from the National Library of Australia
www.librariesaustralia.nla.gov.au

Printed and bound in Australia by McPherson's Printing Group

For Sam

CHAPTER ONE

Lisa Wheeldon yawned but kept her eyes shut. It was so cosy under the doona. So relaxing, and the semi-erotic dream she'd been having had left her with a warm, fuzzy feeling between her thighs.

Under the doona, she reached for her husband's leg and squeezed it. 'This is nice, isn't it?'

'Mmmm,' he murmured and placed his hand over hers.

Usually they woke to a prod in the back from Ava or Jemima, or both. Their two daughters had rendered all alarm clocks utterly useless. Mostly, they were up well before the sun, except for today.

Lisa stroked her husband's thigh. 'I was just having the hottest dream—'

'Yes?'

'About Max from Max's Garage. He came to me with his receipts—'

'Go on.'

'And they weren't in the bag.' At sixty-five, Max Ingall was her oldest client. Wizened as a sultana, his idea of book-keeping involved chucking receipts into a plastic bag, and handing them over. It drove the order-loving Lisa insane.

'No bag?' Scott knew how much she hated the bag.

'He came to me with folders.' She paused. 'Colour coded.'

'Oh, god.' Scott moaned appreciatively.

'I know, right.'

Lisa rolled onto her side and took a second to appreciate her adorable husband, with his smile lines and greying hair around the temples. Men were lucky in the way they slid so easily into middle age.

Yep. My Scottie has still got it.

With a speed she hadn't mustered in years, Lisa launched herself onto her husband's chest and kissed him full on the mouth. Encouraged by the equally rapid response of Scott's groin, Lisa started kissing him down his chest.

'Nice to see you so relaxed about the party,' he murmured.

The party.

Oh goodness, the party.

Lisa blinked madly and looked at the alarm clock.

8.36 am.

'Why didn't you tell me?' She leapt off Scott and out of the bed, sending her pillow flying. Quickly, she grabbed it off the floor and threw it back onto the bed, accidentally hitting her husband in the head.

'Ow.'

Lisa wrenched open the doors of her cupboard. 'Why didn't you wake me?'

'Because I was asleep.' Scott rubbed his eyes while Lisa clutched at the first article of clothing she could find—an ancient white (now over-washed grey) T-shirt, and a tatty pair of light (intentionally) grey yoga pants, complete with faded bolognaise stains and a big hole in the knee from too much crawling on the floor with the girls.

'Of all the days, of course today would be the one where they slept in,' she muttered, roughly pushing her feet into ugg boots.

'Get up,' she hissed at her still-groggy husband, before skittering out the door and down the stairs. In less than ninety minutes—one hour, twenty-three minutes now, to be precise—there would be thirty-two children between the ages of four and six arriving on her doorstep for Ava's fifth birthday party.

Thirty. Two. Children.

'You've managed accounts for hundred-million-dollar companies, you've got this,' she whispered to herself, while trying to visualise the spreadsheet she'd drawn up yesterday on her laptop—with things already done in the green column, and those outstanding in the red. Spreadsheets made her feel so much better about life; Microsoft Excel was her yoga. But there was no time to fire-up the computer. From memory, she had to:

- Make fairy bread (no crusts, gluten-free bread)
- Cut fruit (star shapes, as per Ava's request)
- Collect sushi from shop
- Blow up balloons (find balloon pump so as not to collapse from dizziness)

- Put up streamers
- Sweep the back deck for possum poo
- Get the girls dressed
- Clean the toilet (the girls treated the flush button like a bomb detonator—something to be feared and avoided at all costs, regardless of smell emanating from the bowl)
- Decorate the cake (a princess castle, completely beyond Lisa's abilities)
- Set up tea cups and saucers for the adults
- Heat up the frozen sausage rolls (homemade was now out of the question)

At the bottom of the steps, Lisa stopped. On the couch in the lounge room, the girls were curled up shoulder-to-shoulder under a rug and watching Sunday morning cartoons. A familiar twinge went off in Lisa's ovaries and despite the gargantuan nature of the to-do list in her head she couldn't help gazing on the yawning space next to Ava and Jemima that seemed to cry out for an extra body.

Two children was sensible, she and Scott had agreed. A third child would leave them outnumbered.

Can you imagine? Three mini-Mussolinis screaming for cuddles and only two sets of hands to provide them?

Still, Lisa couldn't quite quell the feeling that her family wasn't complete.

'Mummy! It's the party!' Ava and Jemima squealed as Lisa startled from her momentary reverie and scooted past them towards the kitchen.

'How long have you two been up?' she shouted and started flinging open a variety of cupboard doors, not exactly sure what she was looking for but certain that if she opened enough doors it would come to her.

'We've been up for ages, Mummy,' said Ava, bouncing on the couch.

'Since before the sun,' added Jemima.

'We were too excited.' Ava clapped. 'I'm having a party. I'm having a party,' she chanted.

'You've been up since dawn? Why didn't you come and get me up?' said Lisa, still wrestling with cupboard doors.

'We did, but you just rolled over and said something about folders.'

'But normally you poke me until I open my eyes.'

Ava stuck her head up over the couch. 'You've told us not to do that.'

'Yes, but you never listen to me!' Lisa banged some oven trays down on the bench and started lobbing sausage rolls onto them before quickly realising it would be faster if she upended the entire container onto the tray, which she did, and sent pastry crumbs flying everywhere. Now, in addition to all the food she had to prepare, the floor would also have to be vacuumed.

'Aren't you proud of us, Mummy? For not poking you?' This time, it was Jemima's worried face that peered up over the couch, like a soldier inching their head over the parapet.

Lisa thought for a second. It was one of those trick parenting questions that always seemed to stump her. On the one hand, they had done exactly what they were *told* to do. On the other hand, they had done exactly what she did not *want* them to do. In her experience, young children did not understand nuances or semantics or double entendres and the frustration she felt in that moment would be better served by being hidden by a cloak of maternal pride.

'Yes, my darlings. Of course I'm proud of you for letting me sleep. It's just that Mummy has rather a lot to do today for Ava's party, which begins in,' she checked her watch, 'approximately seventy-nine minutes.' Dread made Lisa's stomach drop. There was no way she could possibly get everything done.

'Mummy, do I have to have breakfast, even though it's my party?' Ava turned back to the TV.

Lisa poked her head out of the freezer from where she'd retrieved the bread. 'Yes, you do.'

'Then I want it now,' demanded Ava.

'Me too,' added Jemima.

Lisa dropped the loaf on the counter and slammed the sausage rolls in the oven, whizzing the temperature dial up to maximum. 'Manners, girls.'

'Pleeeeease,' they said in unison.

Where was Scott? There was some clumping going on upstairs, but it wasn't what one would call *speedy clumping*. It was clumping of the regulation kind. Slow and plodding, as if it was just another ordinary Sunday morning.

'Scott,' Lisa shouted up the stairs. 'Scott, the girls need their breakfast. Are you coming down?' *Like, today?* she added mentally.

'Coming, coming,' said Scott, sauntering down the stairs and casually pulling a T-shirt over his bed-ruffled hair.

'You make the girls' breakfast. I'll do the fairy bread.'

Scott picked up the loaf of bread on the counter. 'Gluten-free?'

'Don't touch that, it's for the fairy bread.'

'But this stuff tastes like cardboard, doesn't it?'

'Well, it'll have to do. One of the children has irritable bowel and can't eat wheat.'

'I thought only fifty-year-old women got that?'

'No, Scott.' She turned to him, wielding a large knife. 'It can be a very serious and debilitating condition for a five-year-old, not to mention embarrassing.' Lisa started slathering butter. 'Hermione's mother says it's as serious as a nut allergy.'

'Poor Hermione,' Scott murmured, moving methodically about the kitchen to set up bowls and cereal for the girls.

'Hey, don't move that.' She tapped Scott's hand as he reached to move an empty plate on the bench. 'That's part of my assembly line.'

'Are you making kids' party food or a car?'

'Very funny. But this is no time for jokes, Scott. This is an emergency.'

The next seventy minutes were a whirlwind of fairy bread, balloons and vacuuming up crumbs. The food was ready. The house was ready. Everything was ready, except for the cake. The girls were outside helping Scott with the last of the decorations. At least *he'd* had time to shower and shave. Lisa was still dressed in her grey trackies.

She wiped her hands with a tea towel, then mopped her brow with it and checked her watch: 9.55 am and already she was sweating in what she knew was an unattractive fashion. Long pants and ugg boots had been completely the wrong choice for a sticky, late-February day. But there was no time to change. She had five freaking minutes to build a castle that would make Walt Disney proud. She took a deep breath.

You've got this.

Everyone would be at least ten minutes late which gave her fifteen minutes to make Disney magic out of two rather pale, flabby and possibly crunchy (thanks, eggshell!) hunks of vanilla cake that she and the girls had made yesterday.

Diving into the kitchen drawer she ripped open the new piping set, bought especially to create piped rosettes as per the pictures in the book. Inside the pack was a device with ten different nozzles and a plastic barrel that looked like a comedy syringe.

Lisa's heart sank. Who was she kidding? This was the culinary equivalent of a Rubik's Cube. This was no time for puzzles. She needed results! Impact! Bulk icing! Stat!

She hauled the mixmaster out from under the bench, hurled icing sugar and butter into the bowl and set it to 'high'. Had the girls been present for the resulting explosion of white powder into the atmosphere, they would no doubt have cheered at the impressive creation of fog, almost like snow! But in that moment, Lisa found it impossible to feel anything but devastation. Icing required icing sugar. Preferably in the bowl, not misted across the kitchen. She leant over the still-whirring beaters to inspect the fallout. Was there enough icing sugar in there? She peered more closely. Closer and closer …

Suddenly her head was being pulled towards the beaters. Oh god! Her hair was caught and with each passing second more and more was becoming entangled. She felt around for the 'off' switch and pressed it. The beaters whirred to a standstill with her hair still firmly tangled in the beaters, and her face a matter of centimetres from the bowl.

'Scott,' she yelled. 'Scott! Help me. I'm stuck.'

Lisa could hear running footsteps but couldn't yank her head far enough to turn it to see who they belonged to.

'What the hell!'

Scott. Thank goodness.

'Mummy, why is your head in the bowl?' Ava stood at the door, hopping from one foot to the other, while Jemima just stared, her three-year-old brain trying to process why Mummy had stuck her head in a mixer.

'What happened?' Scott leant over and started untangling Lisa's hair.

'I was just looking at the icing, and suddenly my hair caught. And now the icing is ruined!'

With a final tug, Scott freed Lisa from her mixmaster-imposed imprisonment. 'There. All done.'

Lisa stood and surveyed the icing, which was now littered with her fine, brown, curly hairs. 'Oh god, it's ruined.' She clutched the bowl as Scott peered into it.

'Hey, it's okay. We've still got time. Let's start a new batch. I'll help.' He looked around the kitchen. 'What do we need? Flour?'

Oh god. He doesn't even know the ingredients!

The doorbell rang.

Lisa felt her legs giving way, her lips trembling. 'Oh no. They're here.'

Scott took her by the shoulders. 'Hey, c'mon, Lise. It's just a party. It's not like anyone's died.'

She raised her eyebrows. Scott knew that at some point today, probably when the girls were asleep, she would let herself have a good cry. She did it every birthday, since Ava was born, for as joyous as the celebration was, it was always tinged by the absence of her parents. They would have adored their granddaughters, of that she was sure, and the girls would have adored them. They had all missed out.

'Sorry,' said Scott. 'Poor choice of words. I know these days are hard for you.' He kissed her on the forehead. 'I'll take all the kids down the side passage and out to the back-yard. You keep working on the cake.' He squeezed. 'You can do this.'

'I can't.' Her voice quavered.

'You can,' he called over his shoulder and strode towards the front door with Ava and Jemima in tow. 'You have to.'

CHAPTER TWO

In two minutes, Lisa had the mixer going again with a fresh batch of icing, free of brown hairs thank goodness.

Scott was right. She had no choice but to make this birthday cake work. This was what parenting was. One foot in front of the other. Just keep going. Children rendered choices impossible. There was only moving forward. No standing still. No going back to the life they had before children. Being a mum was showing up, every day, even in a crisis.

Lisa stopped the mixer and started spooning huge, white pillows of icing onto the slabs of cake. As she spread it, a drip of sweat fell into the cake. Lisa stopped. *Oh bugger bum.*

She didn't have any infectious diseases, but still …

Lisa looked around. No one watching. She started smoothing down the icing again and within a second, the extra liquid had dissolved.

Salt is flavour after all.

After five minutes, the cake resembled something akin to a castle, albeit a very cheap, very pre-fabbed one with lopsided turrets and a general Pisa-like lean. Lisa stood back and wiped sticky hands on her pants.

Dreadful! Why is cooking such a dark art?

This was why Lisa loved accounting. The order. The predictability. Sure, running her own bookkeeping business wasn't quite as exciting as accounting for Lawson and Georges. But that was the choice she'd made when Ava was born.

From outside, she heard Scott yelling at one of the kids. 'Not in the face! Not the face! Legs. Legs. Nooooooo! Not like that.'

He needed her, quickly. One adult versus thirty-two children was a disastrous equation. She needed to reach him quickly, or a child would get hurt, maybe worse. A child who wasn't theirs, no less. She swivelled towards the backyard, and in so doing her hip caught the edge of the cake board.

Splat.

The cake landed at her feet like a pile of sludgy, cakey, crumby, melting snow and Lisa's insides dropped to the floor alongside it.

There was no saving the castle now. It was gone. A splattered, irretrievable mess. There would be no cake today.

No cake? *It's a fifth birthday party. Cake is compulsory.*

Lisa couldn't move. The destruction was mesmerising in its comprehensiveness. Frankie trotted to her side.

'Oh, puppy, what have I done?'

Frankie's tail thumped the ground appreciatively. 'No, Frankie. No eating!' She held a finger up and started to scoop the worst of the mess straight into the sink.

The doorbell rang.

'Scott! Scott! Can you get the door?' But there was only shrieking from outside. He was needed out there.

'Frankie, no eating!' As Lisa waggled a finger at her tail-wagging dog, the doorbell rang again. Three angry jabs.

'I'm coming. I'm coming.' Lisa ran her hands under the tap, dried them on her trackies and scurried towards the front door, briefly checking her reflection in the hall mirror. The grey pants had been smeared by white streaks of icing and her hair was a sticky, matted monstrosity.

I'm a homeless zebra.

At the door, she smoothed her icing-crusted hair and pasted a smile on her face.

She swung it open. 'Hello and welcome to Ava's party.' Lisa knew she sounded like she'd been snorting icing sugar, and the woman before her confirmed it by stiffening and recoiling.

'Hello,' said the woman formally.

Lisa knew her only as Mrs Glamazon—the mother who always looked immaculate at the school gate, and this morning was no exception. From the razor cut of her skinny jeans, to the fur-trimmed vest that hinted at perfect breasts, the woman was stunning and so was the little girl beside her, presumably her daughter, dressed in the biggest, frothiest tutu Lisa had ever seen.

'Hi. It's Savannah-Rose, isn't it?'

'I'm Savannah-Rose Bingley-Peters.' The little girl put out her hand and Lisa shook it.

'That's a big name for a little girl.'

'And I can write it all myself.' The little girl retracted her hand and primly held onto a handbag emblazoned with the words *Baby Dior*.

Lisa had never been within touching distance of a Dior handbag, let alone one made for a child. 'Savannah, all the kids are out the back, do you want to join them?' She pointed down the hallway.

'Yes thank you,' and she took off at lightning speed, reminding Lisa of a bounding poodle as she tore down the hallway and called over her shoulder, 'It's Savannah-Rose. Not Savannah. Bye, Mum.'

'Bye-bye, darling.' Mrs Glamazon held up a perfectly manicured hand before turning her attention to Lisa. 'Well, I'll be off then.'

'Wait. Won't you come in for a cuppa?'

'No, thanks. See you at twelve!' called the exotic woman over her shoulder as she strode away down Lisa's front path with her pert little bottom not daring to bounce behind her.

'Wait, wait!' Lisa scurried behind, slowed down by her ugg boots. 'What about Savannah-Rose? Don't you want to stay in case she, you know, needs you?'

The glamazon pirouetted on wedge sneakers and removed her oversized tortoise-shell sunglasses. 'Hon, Savannah-Rose is nearly six. She can more than handle herself.'

I'll bet she can.

'But I've got sausage rolls,' Lisa pleaded.

The woman made a face. 'I'm fully paleo, babe.' She patted her thighs. 'No carbs. No grains.'

No fun.

'All right then.' Lisa stuck out her hand. 'Well, I'm Lisa, by the way.'

'I'm Heather.' She quickly pulled her hand away from Lisa's and wiped it against her slim thighs. 'Hon, why don't you just go inside, pour yourself a champers, sit back and let the entertainer do all the work.'

'Oh, I haven't got an entertainer,' said Lisa airily. 'I was just going to do it myself.'

'You're going to entertain thirty-two children, dressed like that?' Heather looked Lisa up and down, sliding her eyes over the icing-smeared tracksuit pants. 'Is there some hobo-clown craze I didn't know about?'

Lisa's eyes were suddenly hot and itchy. She sniffed and rubbed at them. Everything had gone wrong. The cake was ruined, the kids were running riot and she looked like a total mess. This was Ava's first party at St John's! Her first chance to make a good impression. Lisa had to make it work or the kids would go home and tell their parents how hopeless it was and the Wheeldons would become the social pariahs of the school. Forever!

Lisa rubbed her nose and sighed. 'It's been a bad morning,' she said quietly. 'The kids didn't wake me, then my hair got stuck in the mixer and now there's cake all over the floor and the kids will be scarred for life if I perform balloon tricks looking like this.'

Heather peered at her. 'You need to pull yourself together, hon.'

'I don't know if I can. I'm usually so organised,' Lisa whispered, bewildered. 'I just wanted everything to be perfect.'

'It still can be,' said Heather in an unconvincing tone. 'Possibly.' From a snakeskin tote, she whipped out an impossibly sleek mobile phone and tapped out a number, her black polished nails skimming lightly over the screen. 'Arabella? Are you free, sweetie? I have a … a … an acquaintance who has a party emergency. We need you now … The Wonder Woman act … You can? Wonderful. I'll text the address. Bye, sweetie.'

Using her T-shirt, Lisa wiped her eyes. 'Who was that?'

Heather tapped out a text message as she spoke. 'My nanny moonlights as a party entertainer. She'll be here in fifteen minutes, dressed as Wonder Woman and armed with a bag of tricks.' Heather put the beautiful phone back in her beautiful bag and strode through the door and down the hallway. 'Now, let's see this cake problem.' As she marched into the kitchen, her nose wrinkled. 'Something's burning.'

'Oh no! The sausage rolls!' Lisa raced ahead to find smoke billowing from the oven. Fanning furiously she wrenched open the door to find her golden orbs of pastry transformed to nuggets of charcoal.

Heather sniffed. 'No loss there. Full of trans fats. Now, cake. What exactly is the issue?'

Having dumped the sausage rolls in the bin, Lisa scanned about the floor for the remains of the cake. But all she could see was a staggering Frankie, barely able to lift his head.

'How old is that thing?' Heather recoiled as Frankie sniffed forlornly about her denim-clad legs.

'He's only two.'

'Are you sure? Looks to me like he's about to drop dead.'

Lisa scanned the kitchen floor again. When she left, there'd been a huge pile of dropped cake right next to the bench.

'Oh god, I think the dog ate it all,' she whispered. 'He's in a sugar coma.'

Heather sniffed, went to the sink and slowly leant her head over it. 'I think a child's been sick in here.'

Lisa joined her. 'No. That's the rest of the cake.'

'Ugh. Well, just as well it got destroyed I suppose.' As the dog moaned and whimpered, Heather whipped out her phone again. 'Pierre? It's Heather, darling. *Mwah. Mwah.* I need one of your iced, flourless, dairy-free chocolate cakes immediately. As in, yesterday.' She covered the receiver. 'Dairy gives Savannah-Rose the runs,' she whispered to Lisa before returning to Pierre. 'You've got a spare? Fabulous … All right, darling. There in a jiffy. Ciao, my strudel super-hero,' she tinkled before hanging up.

Before Lisa could say thank you, Heather was sailing back down the hallway while talking over her shoulder. 'Arabella will be here in a minute and I'll be back in half an hour with the cake.' At the front door, she smoothly slid the sunglasses back over her eyes. Whenever Lisa did that, she always got a hair snagged.

'Thank you for helping me.' She clutched the doorknob for support.

'Anything for the children.' Heather pursed her lips. 'I think Savannah-Rose quite likes your daughter.' Her voice was baffled, like she couldn't work out why Savannah-Rose would deign to spend *any* time in the company of a child with such incompetent parents. She gave Lisa a final look up and down and sniffed. 'I'll be back soon.'

'Please! I mean … uh … thank you!'

With the smell of Heather's perfume still wafting through the hall, Lisa wandered back into the kitchen in a daze and pondered just how close she'd come to disaster. A memory pinged in her brain. What was it that Jamie had said in her email—the one where she checked off Lisa's party spreadsheet.

The only problems you'll face are the ones you never see coming, so just try to relax. It's a five-year-old's party. How bad could it be? Ha! Maybe Jamie understood corporate cocktail schmooze-fests, but she had zero clue about the complexities of kids' shindigs. Speaking of which, where was her sister? She was supposed to come early to help. It was there in the spreadsheet that she'd ticked off. *Jamie—arrive 8.30 am to help with set-up.*

It wasn't like her to be late. Where could she be? Was she okay? Why hadn't she called? It wasn't like her not to call. Not a day passed without them talking at least twice a day, once in the morning and again at night, and it had been that way ever since the accident. After all, they were the only family each other had.

Lisa collected her phone, and started dialling. By the third ring, her nerves had re-doubled. Jamie always answered by the second. The phone was like an extension of her arm, thanks to her job. At the sixth, Lisa's stomach somersaulted into her throat. Something must be seriously wrong.

'Yeah, hello.'

Her sister's voice was slurry, almost drugged sounding.

'Jamie! Where are you? Are you okay? You're supposed to be here for the party.'

There was scrabbling in the background. 'Shit, sorry, Lise. No, I'm fine.' More scrabbling. 'The stupid alarm didn't go off. I'll be there quick as I can.'

'You only just woke up?'

'Yeah, look, I don't know what happened. I'm so sorry.'

'As long as you're okay …'

'No, I'm good. Are you, though? You sound a bit strange.'

Lisa sighed. Where to begin. Her own sleep-in? The ruined cake? The total disorganisation? 'No, I'm good. Just wanted to check where you were. I'd better get back to the party.'

'I'll be there soon.' Jamie paused. 'I'm sorry if I made you worry. I'm really fine.'

Lisa took a breath. Jamie was thirty-five years old. Well and truly an adult, and usually a highly responsible one.

You're her sister, not her mother. No guilt-trips.

'Seriously, it's good. Just come when you can.'

'Will do.'

Lisa dismissed the niggling sense of irritation that urged her to tell Jamie to hurry. Her sister was okay, that was the main thing. The party, on the other hand, sounded like it was getting wilder by the minute. Lisa returned the phone to her pocket and headed towards the shrieking.

She stopped at the doors, the scene of utter chaos before her rendering her muscles immobile. In one corner of the garden, two little boys had armed themselves with plastic bats (meant for the piñata) and were smashing the heads off Lisa's beloved roses. In another corner, a group of five was industriously constructing a completely precarious tower of little plastic chairs atop one another near the fence, as if staging a great escape. In the middle of the garden, Ava was locked in a tug-of-war style battle with two other children over the skipping rope. 'It's mine,' she hollered. 'And I'm the birthday girl!' Near the BBQ, a small crowd had formed as one boy pushed desperately at the gas hob. 'I can make fire!' he boasted. 'Just watch.'

Where were the parents? Where was Scott?

Finally, she spotted him, emerging from underneath a pile of children. He tried to stand, but it was virtually impossible, with no less than eight children trying to drag him back down to the ground, two attached to each limb. 'No more jam sandwiches!' he protested weakly. 'Jam sandwich' was a game he sometimes played with Ava and Jemima where they piled on top of each other, usually with Scott at the bottom, which was all well and good with two rather petite little girls, but almost deadly with the wild and oversized mob currently attacking him.

Putting two fingers into her mouth, Lisa summoned the biggest whistle her lungs would allow.

The effect was immediate. The kids were like statues. Thirty-two pairs of eyes turned to her.

What now? *Think, Lisa. Quick, or they'll start killing each other again.*

'Pass-the-parcel,' she called. 'Everyone sitting here in a circle.' She gestured to the grass beneath her and nearly got knocked off her feet by the immediate flood of children.

'Get the music going, quick,' she hissed to Scott as he passed her, still trying to re-tuck his shirt and smooth down his crazed hair.

'Okay, everyone. Let's start with you.' She pointed randomly at a little boy with jet black hair and wide blue eyes. 'What's your name?'

'Mummy says I shouldn't talk to strangers.'

'I'm not a stranger. I'm Ava's mummy, Lisa.' *And if your mum is so worried about strangers, why has she dropped you and run?* 'But sweetie, you don't have to tell me your name if you don't want to. Just take the parcel and pass it on.'

Scott started the music. For the first minute, it was fine. Calm even. It was like a tennis match, with the kids' eyes glued to the parcel as if it were a ball. The music stopped. A little girl looked at Lisa with her head cocked to the side.

'Yes, darling. It's you. Open the first layer.'

The little girl started tearing. The kids inhaled and leant in as one. The wrapping was off. The girl turned the parcel over, and over again. 'Where's the treat?'

'Oh, there's a few more layers to go until we get to the big prize,' said Lisa gaily. 'Let's keep going.' She made eye contact with Scott and nodded. 'Ready please, Mr Music.'

The little girl held tightly to the parcel. 'But there's supposed to be a prize,' she said plaintively.

'At the end, sweetheart. I promise.'

Reluctantly, she passed it along. This time, the music stopped on a boy in a checked shirt, navy pants and what appeared to be some type of gel in his hair, given its unnatural spikiness. With gusto, he ripped, and kept ripping.

'No, no, darling. Just one layer.' Lisa moved closer. But what could she do? She couldn't just wrench the parcel out of his hands. 'Please. Just one.' She got close enough to gently tug it away.

'You mean there's no prize till the very end.' The boy stood and kicked at the ground. 'This is boring.'

'Yeah, this is boring,' murmured some of the others.

Ava caught her gaze. Her face was as sad and confused as Frankie's in the sugar coma.

'All right, then. Let's do the piñata!' Lisa clapped her hands together. 'Everyone line up behind me.'

A scrum quickly packed down behind her of jostling, pushing five-year-olds.

'I wanna go first.'

'No, me!'

'You got the parcel first.'

'Kids!' Lisa raised her hand, the way she'd seen the day care teachers do when they wanted attention. One by one, Ava's buddies followed suit until there were thirty-two raised hands, and absolute quiet. It was like magic.

In front of them, Scott took a step away from the rainbow unicorn he'd just finished tying to the clothes line. 'All ready to go.' He nodded at Lisa.

'You get one bash, then you hand it on.' She handed a plastic bat to the first kid in the line, a little boy wearing a ninja T-shirt.

He stepped up, eyes drilled into the unicorn, his mouth set in a determined line.

'Go, Cooper! Get 'im,' called another little boy from the line.

Cooper nodded grimly, raised his bat, and what proceeded to unfold was the most frenzied and violent attack on an inanimate object that Lisa had ever seen.

On and on he went. Thwacking and hacking. Beating and slicing.

Lisa felt a little body throw itself around her legs.

'Mummy, Mummy, why is Cooper hitting the unicorn? Make him stop. Make him stop,' wailed Ava. 'I don't like this. He's hurting the unicorn.'

'It's okay, honey. It's just a cardboard unicorn. It's not actually feeling anything.' Lisa knelt down to comfort her daughter while signalling frantically for Scott to *do something*! Halt the attack. Or no other kid would get a go at demolishing the mythical beast.

But removing the bat from Cooper's vice-like grip was easier said than done. Scott just couldn't get close, not unless he wanted to risk losing an eyeball, or a hit to the genitals.

Ava buried her head into Lisa's thigh and sobbed harder, while Lisa admonished herself for not having thought to explain the concept of a piñata to her. But who would have thought it necessary? Hadn't her daughter seen one before? Sometimes, it was the smallest, most unexpected things that most tripped her up as a mother.

'Cooper, stop, mate,' Scott called lamely, swatting at the bat as it swished past him. 'Time to give someone else a go.'

But Cooper had no intention of stopping, that much was clear, not until he'd dismembered the unicorn, which was now hanging at a very odd angle from the clothes line.

HURRAY!

The roar went up as the horned-horse fell to the ground and the kids descended on it like a pack of hungry wolves, intent on feasting off the carcass. All Lisa could do was stand back and shield Ava from the ensuing violence as shards of cardboard and bits of streamers emerged, flung out of the scrabbling mob in their desperate hunt for the inner treasure.

Cooper stood up and looked at Lisa accusingly. 'Where's the lollies?' He held up his hands, a rubber ball in one and an eraser in the other. 'It's just this stuff. My mum calls it junk.' He made a face and dropped the offending prizes, as if they contained a deadly virus.

'There'll be lollies later. Plenty of them,' said Lisa brightly. 'But only prizes in the piñata. Too much sugar is bad for us, remember?'

Cooper shot her a look that Lisa could only describe as pure disgust. 'I don't like this party.' Jamming his hands in his pockets, the boy sloped off to the back of the garden.

She felt her hand being tugged. 'Mummy, I don't like this party either.' Ava looked up at her, eyes brimming and Lisa felt her heart shrivel a little. She wanted this to be perfect! Or at least, moderately enjoyable.

'Oh, darling. Don't say that. It's going to get better, I promise. This is just the beginning.'

She checked her watch. Only 10.17? Her heart shrivelled a little more. How had she forgotten that minutes passed like dog years at a child's party.

Where was Heather? Where was the Wonder Woman she'd promised?

Only a superhero could save this party now.

CHAPTER THREE

'Mummy, are you coming in with me?'

Ellie was wide-eyed and wriggly as Missy removed her keys from the ignition and folded her daughter's wormy fingers into her own. 'No, El. I won't come in but I'm going to walk you right to the gate.'

For the past fifteen minutes they'd sat in the car and watched a procession of shiny-shoed and glossy-haired children stream through the front gate to the Wheeldons' house. While the children were beautifully primped and preened and trotted happily down the side path to the backyard, their parents looked harried. Un-brushed hair. Un-ironed shirts. It was the weekend, after all. None of them stayed inside the Wheeldons' for long. Just a drop-and-go, and out they hurried with a little glint in their eyes that said, *Yes! Two hours to read the newspaper and have a coffee in peace.*

Missy sighed and her stomach did its thousandth revolution for the morning. The thought of what she was about to do made her feel sick. Sicker than even the drive over to the party. It was strange, to be behind the wheel again and she spent the entire journey checking the rear-view mirror. *Please, no police*, she'd prayed. Getting caught driving without a licence could ruin everything.

Missy played with Ellie's braid. The end of it was like a soft-bristled paintbrush and she stroked it gently across her cheek.

'Ellie, we talked about this.'

The child nodded miserably. 'But I won't know anyone at the party!'

Missy reached over the gearstick to pat her daughter's leg. 'I have a plane to catch, remember? So, I have to drop you now.'

She hated lying to her daughter and what shocked her was how readily Ellie accepted the untruths. She had full faith in her mother, and Missy hated herself for exploiting it.

'Honey, the Wheeldons are a lovely family. They'll take care of you, I promise.' Missy took her daughter's finger and crossed it over her chest. 'Cross my heart. You're going to love staying with them and this is going to be the best party you've ever been to.'

Missy could say that with full confidence, for it was also the only party Ellie had ever been to. There had been no choice. It was the only way of keeping her safe. Stay detached. Never get close to anyone. Never let them know who you really are.

'Will there be a cake?' Ellie asked, wiggling her finger out of Missy's grip.

'For sure! The most delicious cake you've ever eaten, and there'll be games and ...' As Missy described every child's fantasy party, she visualised Lisa Wheeldon, floating serenely about her home, a beacon of calm and organisation. Having watched her closely over the past few weeks (undetected, obviously) Missy had come to realise that the perfect mother did, indeed, exist. Her name was Lisa Wheeldon and Missy knew that any party organised by this woman would be perfect as well.

'Can I go in now?' Ellie tugged at Missy's sleeve and pulled at the door handle. 'I don't want to miss anything.'

Missy's speech had done the trick. The fear in her daughter's eyes had been replaced with excitement.

She looked at her watch: 10.20. All the party guests would have arrived by now. Missy double-checked out the window. The street was quiet. Perfect. 'For sure. Let's go.'

She let Ellie out of the car and walked her across the road, gripping her hand a little more tightly than usual and feeling for her daughter's knuckles. Only eighteen months ago, it would have been impossible to feel the bones. At the age of five, Ellie's knuckles had been nothing but starbursts of chubby flesh. All squish, and no hardness. But her daughter was six going on seven now. Lengthening out, developing angles, and losing the softness that Missy had never imagined her losing.

They stopped at the gate.

'This is a nice place, isn't it, Mummy?' Ellie looked around at the giant fig trees that overhung the street, providing a cool canopy on a day that was shaping up as another hot one.

'It is a nice street, El.'

'Nicer than ours.'

'I agree.' She leant down. 'But I think you'd better go inside before you miss too much of the party.'

'Okay, Mummy. I'll see you soon,' said Ellie happily, her arms not quite reaching all the way around her mother.

'Bye-bye, my Elle-belle.' Missy squeezed hard and swallowed back the tears forming in her throat. 'I hope you have the best time ever.'

'I will,' she said confidently, one hand swinging the bag that held the gift and the other clutching her little overnight bag which contained a toothbrush, some clothes, and her favourite books.

'I love you so much.' Missy hugged her daughter again.

'I love you too. More than you love me.'

Missy laughed. 'That's not possible.'

'Yes, it is,' said Ellie over her shoulder as Missy opened the gate to let her through. Down the side passage she could hear high-pitched squeals of delight. Ellie paused once more and looked to her mother for reassurance.

'Off you go, hon.'

The little girl raced away. 'Enjoy your trip, Mummy,' she yelled.

Missy watched as Ellie ran towards the Wheeldons' backyard, heels and plaits flying. Then, she was gone and Missy slumped against the gate.

She allowed herself a thirty-second cry and pulled herself together. The plan would never work if she allowed herself to fall apart.

Ellie was safe. For now. That was all that mattered.

CHAPTER FOUR

Jamie hung up the phone, threw off the sheet and cursed herself. Poor Lise. Her voice—so tight and stretched. She sounded completely overwhelmed, despite her claims to the contrary. Why hadn't the alarm gone off? Damn phone! Of course Lise would have freaked at her non-appearance. Jamie sat for a moment, fiddling with the settings as if discovering the cause of its failure might rid her of the guilt. She prided herself on always answering within the first couple of rings. 'Call me, any time, and I'll answer,' she always told her clients, and she did. She was renowned for it. Even at two o'clock in the morning, which is when the worst PR crises always tended to happen. Her football-playing clients had proved it time and again. But that was okay, it was her job, and a little lost sleep was a small price to pay for being a senior account manager at Spin Cycle—the hottest PR agency in Sydney.

'Oh good, you're awake! Here you go.' Jamie's boyfriend, Jared, set a coffee on her bedside table.

'Thanks, babe, you're a lifesaver. I've gotta move.' She took a sip. Strong and hot, just how she liked it.

Jared grinned and stood in front of the bed, hands on hips. 'Like the new gear?'

Jamie rubbed the crust out of her eyes to get a better look. Jared was a great-looking guy—blond hair, tall, muscly without being scary, hazel eyes—but when he wore his cycling gear, he reminded Jamie of a pork sausage, all squished-in and likely to burst at the first sign of heat.

'You look great, J.'

Jared turned on the spot to give her a better view of all his angles. 'Pretty cool, huh. It's the latest kit from Clincher.'

'They're one of my clients, aren't they?'

Jared looked sheepish. 'Angel sent it to me. She knows I cycle.'

And she'd be drooling right now, to see you in your skin-tights.

Jamie's boss, Angelica (Angel for short) was a complete workaholic and assumed everyone who worked for her was as well. But she was also an unabashed cougar. She'd had two marriages and one child (and famously answered a few work emails while in labour) and wanted no more of either, thank you very much. 'Marriage is sooooo last century,' she would say when any of the girls at Spin got engaged. 'Why don't you just bonk until you're sick of each other and move on to the next one? Hmmm?'

Jamie drew her knees up. 'Please don't get too close to Angel. You know it makes it hard for me.'

Jared put his hands on his hips. 'Sorry, babe. Should I send it back?' He gave a sweet, mournful look that made

Jamie feel like she'd just yelled at a puppy. How could he help it if people, like Angel, loved him? He was so cute! So what if he made the occasional mistake and urinated on the floor, or accepted gifts when he shouldn't. You couldn't love someone for their sweet appeal, and then punish them for it. Jared was the same age as her—but he was a young thirty-five. He'd grow up, eventually, and ask her to marry him, hopefully.

Staring at him, she allowed herself to follow her thought trail—proposal, marriage, a house, babies, first birthdays ...

Oh shit! Ava's birthday. She really needed to get moving.

Jamie leapt up, sending her precious mobile flying. 'What time is it?' she said, scrabbling round on the floor to find it again.

Jared checked his watch. 'Just gone 10.30. Why?'

'Ava's party.' She checked her phone again. A text from her assistant, Ben. How had she not heard it? *Just reminding you that Ava's party is at 10.* That's right. It'd been such a crazy week at work she'd joked to Ben that she was in danger of losing the 'Best-Aunt-Ever' status by forgetting her niece's birthday.

'I won't let that happen,' Ben had replied seriously.

But that was exactly what was about to happen if she didn't get her butt moving ASAP. Jamie started opening drawers as Jared sat on the bed, watching her. She stopped. 'Aren't you coming to the party?'

Jared's face fell. 'The party's today?'

'I did tell you, didn't I?'

'I don't think so.' He shook his head. 'And you know I'd love to come ...'

'Never mind,' Jamie sighed. It was only her niece's birthday party. Not worth causing a fight over. She resumed drawer opening. Her wardrobe was full of naughty-but-nice pencil skirts, peek-a-boo camisoles and sharp blazers. Not exactly fifth birthday party attire.

'I'm actually meeting up with Tom to talk about Dubai,' said Jared.

'What about Dubai?' Jamie held up a pair of bleached jeans. The designer tears in them sat a little high on the thigh, but nothing that would totally scandalise a kindy kid or their parents.

'You remember, don't you?' Jared reclined on the bed. 'There's a job coming up that I applied for.'

Jamie stopped. 'You applied for a job in Dubai and you didn't tell me?' She let the jeans drop to the floor.

'I did tell you.' Jared put his hands behind his head. 'But I think you were texting someone.'

'Then I didn't hear you!'

Jared rolled off the bed and clattered in his cleats towards the bathroom.

Jamie followed him. 'Shouldn't we talk about this?'

'We did talk about this.' He started peeling off the cycling gear. 'I told you about the position, and you said "Go for it". So I did, and I'm pretty sure I've got it.'

'Wait! What? A minute ago you said you applied for it. Now you've got it?'

'It's about ninety per cent certain. The CEO just has to sign off.'

So tight was Jared's cycling top, his head was now stuck inside it, which meant Jamie couldn't see his face. 'What about me?'

'What do you mean?'

Jamie strode towards Jared, yanked roughly to free his head, grabbed his chin and looked him directly in the eyes. 'Am I supposed to come with you, or stay here?' A chill wrapped around her stomach as Jared's eyes dropped to the floor.

'We're not breaking up, are we?' she asked in a quavering voice.

It couldn't be happening. After all these years of waiting, he could not be leaving her now. She was too old to start again with someone new. Just last month when Jamie was renewing her contraceptive prescription, the doctor had gently suggested that if she was thinking about having babies she needed to start putting thought into action. After thirty-five, a woman's fertility didn't just go into decline, it fell off a cliff. Right now, that's how Jamie felt, like she was falling, with no safety net beneath her.

Hearing the tremble in Jamie's voice, Jared snapped his head back to meet her gaze. 'I just assumed we'd do the long-distance thing.' He turned away again to put on the shower taps. 'The contract is only going to be for a year. Two years max. I didn't think you'd want to leave your job. I know how much it means to you.'

Jamie sat on the toilet seat. Her job. She worked hard at it, that's for sure. But did she really love it? Occasionally, when she bought her double-shot cappuccino from the cute barista at the entrance to her office building she experienced a momentary sense of doom. A feeling that she was actually walking into a prison. Once she was in, it wasn't so bad. In fact, she loved it. Maybe it was a case of Stockholm Syndrome—that thing where prisoners fell in love with their captors. Maybe keeping busy was her way of deluding herself into pretending to love the job, when in actual fact, Angel was simply her captor, albeit one in Jimmy Choo shoes.

Jamie leant against the basin. 'You know what? I think I'm ready for a change. I've been at Spin for eight years now.'

And if I wait for you for two more years, I'll be thirty-seven before we can even get a start on having a baby!

A fabulous thought popped into her head. 'Maybe I could set up my own consultancy in Dubai? There's got to be plenty of companies there who need a little PR help.'

'Sure.' Jared closed his eyes and lathered shampoo into the blond curls that Jamie so loved. 'But I think the company only pays for spouses to relocate. And there's the cultural thing too. I think it helps in those countries if you're married.'

Jamie had another fabulous thought. 'We could get married!' Certainly, they had discussed marriage, albeit in an abstract kind of way, as something they both wanted at some indefinable time they referred to as *in the future* ...

But that conversation was at least two years ago, so Jamie figured *the future* probably had arrived.

'We could get married,' said Jared in a neutral voice, as if weighing up dinner options. *We could have Thai ... or we could have Japanese.* In the end it was usually Jamie that decided. But this was bigger than dinner. This was marriage! She needed to know how he really felt.

She paused. 'Do you want to get married?'

Finally, he turned off the tap and looked at her through the shower screen, still spattered with tear-like drops of water. 'You know I want to get married.'

Ugh! It was like a poker game, with Jared still refusing to show his hand even though Jamie's cards were already on the table. Time to call his bluff. 'Then why don't we just go ahead and do it? As long as it's what you want.'

Jamie offered him a towel. Jared took it and started rubbing it through his hair for what seemed like minutes, but was possibly only a few seconds. Finally his head emerged. 'I think that's an awesome idea.' While Jamie squealed and clapped her hands, Jared flashed her a quick smile and a wink. 'It would have to be quick, though. The job's supposed to start in six weeks, assuming I get it.'

'Six weeks?' Jamie stopped clapping.

'Yup. Tenth of April.'

Jamie started scrambling together a list in her head— venue, invitations, cake, flowers, dress, photographer, music … Her mind went on, tripping and tumbling over itself in excitement. It was crazy. Impossible. Weddings usually took eighteen months to organise. The best venues booked out usually two years in advance. But hey! She was a PR professional. If there was one thing she could do in a hurry, it was organise a fabulous party. That's what a wedding was, wasn't it? A fabulous party where you signed a very important piece of paper that bound you for life to your partner. For life! How amazing! They'd have babies but how many? It wasn't something they'd discussed in concrete detail. Hopefully he wouldn't want any more than three. Two seemed sensible. Maybe three if they were financially secure. They'd call the first one Henry if it was a boy, and maybe Charlotte for a girl. She'd always loved those names. *Wonder what names Jared would like?* He'd probably go along with whatever Jamie wanted. He was pretty good like that, letting her have and do what she wanted. Maybe he was a little too good at it. Sometimes, she wondered if anyone could really be that easygoing—or if maybe he just didn't care? No, of course he cared. After all, he was willing to marry her.

'Your smile is starting to scare me.' Jared was now out of the shower and towelling himself down in front of the vanity. He watched Jamie in the reflection, leaning against the shower screen and grinning like a goofball.

'I'm just thinking about baby names.'

'Whoa! Hold on there, babe. We haven't even worked out if we're getting married yet.'

'But you said—'

'I said that if we were going to get married, we'd have to do it in less than six weeks.'

'I can do that!' She circled her arms around Jared's waist and kissed his strong, soapy smelling neck. 'You do want babies, don't you?'

'Sure. Eventually.'

'Great! Let's do this.' She squeezed his waist and squealed. 'We're getting married!'

Jared disentangled himself from her arms. 'You really are happy, aren't you,' he mused.

'Of course I am. This is, like, the biggest thing ever.' She grabbed his hands and drew him in for a deep kiss.

'Oooh, I like it when you're happy,' he murmured, letting his towel slip to the floor.

'Me too,' she breathed back as her hands explored the muscles she knew so well, and now seemed even more of a turn-on to her. Jared led her towards the bed, but as he went to lay her down, Jamie felt her head touch something hard. Her phone.

'Oh shit! Ava's party. I've gotta run or Lise will kill me! She's probably stressed out of her head right now.'

She pushed Jared away.

CHAPTER FIVE

'Oh, thank goodness you're back!' Lisa nearly fell into Heather's arms as she stalked up the side passage, arms filled with a cake box and what looked like a bottle of champagne.

'Excuse me, but I think I'm needed.' It was Wonder Woman, brushing past them both and heading straight for the backyard where the children had resumed their various, frantic activities, with Scott and Lisa hovering close by to ensure no serious or permanent injury occurred.

In the middle of the lawn, Wonder Woman settled a black suitcase by her side, and raised her hand. 'Who wants to see me produce a rabbit out of this empty suitcase?' she announced loudly. 'The first child to sit quietly in front of me will get to pat it.'

Not another word was needed. In seconds, Wonder Woman had all thirty-two children seated calmly, goggle-eyed as she knelt down in her knee-high red leather boots to unclip the suitcase.

'I think we can leave her to it.' Heather touched her arm. 'Let's crack this one open, shall we?' She gestured to the bottle under her arm. 'It's the only way to make these things bearable.'

Back in the kitchen, Heather popped the cork while Lisa searched about in a few cupboards before locating two champagne flutes.

'We don't drink much,' she admitted, blowing a thin layer of dust off the glasses and handing them over.

'Really? And you call yourselves parents!' Heather poured generously and raised her champagne glass. 'Chin-chin.'

Lisa clinked, put the glass to her lips and paused. 'Should we be doing this?' She checked her watch. 'It's not even midday.'

Heather gave her a look and kept drinking while Lisa took a small sip. It was deliciously sweet. Not at all like the normal champagne which tended to make her wince. This stuff was delicious! And pink! Like fizzy, alcoholic cordial. And what was it called again? Moscato? She'd never even heard of it.

'Don't worry, sweetie. It's low-alcohol, and it's the best way to survive these things.' She touched her nose. 'Mummy's little helper.'

Actually, mummy's *big* helper, given the amount of moscato Heather was currently consuming. She'd already finished one glass and was busily pouring herself another. She held out the bottle to Lisa. 'Top-up?'

Lisa put her palm over the glass. 'Not for me. Don't want to be rolling round on the floor when the other parents turn up.'

Heather sighed. 'Don't think there's much chance of *that*.' Grabbing the bottle, she marched over to the couch and flopped into it gracefully. 'May as well stay here, now that the party's half over.'

'Yes, of course. Please stay. Apart from the sausage rolls, I also made a whole slab of zucchini quiche for the adults. Would you like some?'

Heather looked at Lisa as if she'd suggested eating a yak's placenta. She patted her non-existent stomach. 'Errr … I think I'm good for zucchini quiche, thanks all the same.'

'Carrot stick then?' Lisa held up the tray of cut-up veggies and hummus she'd prepared for the kids who, of course, had ignored all the healthy stuff and gone straight for the chips.

'No, really. Nothing for me. Why don't you just relax? Sit down.' She patted the couch next to her. 'Kick off your …' Heather looked disdainfully at Lisa's tattered ugg boots. 'Those sheepskin things.'

But Lisa remained standing, shifting her weight from foot to foot. 'I feel like I should be out there doing something.' Children's birthday parties were like cyclones—torrid, occasionally violent, and seemingly never-ending, but actually quite quick in hindsight. Right now, Ava's party seemed to have entered an eerie eye of the storm. Heather's babysitter had cast a spell over them. There they were, sitting on the lawn and quiet as mice, staring open-mouthed as Wonder Woman twisted balloons into bunnies and horses and then made good on her promise by producing a real live rabbit out of her seemingly empty suitcase. Scott was as enraptured as the kids, though that was possibly due to the tightness of Wonder Woman's leotard and the low-cut nature of her top. Arabella truly was a wonder woman. A wondrous woman. Even Heather seemed entranced, watching through the French doors and sipping at the bubbly.

'She has quite a way with the kids, doesn't she?' Lisa settled on the armrest of the couch and followed Heather's gaze.

'Arabella? Oh yes, she's absolutely amazing. A total star. Just ask any of the mums.' Heather smirked.

'What do you mean?'

'Well, I probably shouldn't tell you this but,' Heather leant in so close that Lisa could smell the alcohol on her breath. 'Our little Arabella may have had a little *liaison* with one of the school dads last year.'

'Which one?' Lisa drew back, horrified.

Heather waved her arm. 'Oh, don't worry. It was a parent from Year Four. Nothing to do with kinder.'

'But ... but ...' stammered Lisa. 'It's a Catholic school!' she finally blurted.

Heather laughed, but when Lisa didn't join in, her laughter petered out. 'You're serious?'

'Yes! It's so immoral!'

Heather finished her champagne thoughtfully. 'I suppose.' She put the glass on the coffee table. 'Anyway, she's saved your bacon.'

'I suppose,' said Lisa gloomily, now seeing Wonder Woman in a new and very unflattering light. Right at that minute, Arabella had finished making a very phallic balloon-sword. She ended her act by striking a ninja pose with Scott leading the applause as Wonder Woman took a coquettish bow.

'You owe her three hundred bucks,' said Heather.

'What?' Lisa nearly spat out the moscato, which was starting to taste sickly rather than sweet in her mouth.

'That's what she charges for a party.'

'Gosh, that's a better hourly rate than a ... Than a ...'

'A what?'

Fortunately, Lisa was saved from answering the question by the stream of five-year-olds now stampeding inside towards the birthday cake. As Ava led the charge, Lisa clenched her fingers. Pierre's cake was nothing like the castle Ava had chosen three months ago from the cake book. What the patissier had failed to mention on the phone was that his 'spare' cake had been intended for a boy's twenty-first birthday (the party was cancelled when word of it being 'gate-crasher-friendly' leaked onto the socials). The cake itself was moulded in the shape of a champagne bottle with sparklers and sugared stars exploding out of the cork. For a twenty-first birthday party, it was quite spectacular. For a five-year-old, it was entirely inappropriate. Heather and Lisa had managed to scrape away the *Happy 21st Blake*. But there was no covering the fact that it was a cake in the shape of a champagne bottle, which made Lisa very nervous indeed. Not only was there her own personal aversion to excess alcohol consumption, there was also the fact that Ava could be quite finicky when she wanted to be—sandwiches had to be denuded of crusts before she would even look at them, and Lisa wouldn't dare contemplate serving her breakfast without her special froggy spoon.

So, as Ava ran towards the bottle-shaped cake, Lisa took a breath.

'Now, darling.' She leant over to whisper in her daughter's ear. 'I know it's not quite what you—'

'Mummy! Mummy! It's the best cake ever.' Ava turned to Lisa, beaming. 'It's like a bottle you'd find washed up on a beach with a secret message in it.' She leant closer to the cake. 'Is there a message in it?'

'Who knows, darling,' said Lisa gaily, feeling the knots in her stomach starting to loosen. 'How about we sing "Happy Birthday" and find out.' She stood up again. 'On my count. One, two, three. Happy birthday to you …'

After the singing died down, Arabella called the children outside for another game—a version of Duck, Duck, Goose, which she'd renamed Batman, Batman, Robin. As Lisa started slicing up the cake and giving pieces to Heather to distribute, Lisa felt a kiss on her cheek.

'I'm so sorry I'm late.' Jamie squeezed Lisa's shoulders. 'Surviving? It sounded quiet from out on the street.'

'I could have used some help earlier. I was worried,' said Lisa, hacking at the cake.

'I understand, Lise, and I'm sorry,' began Jamie. 'But— and I say this with love—you don't have to worry about me. You've got enough on your plate.'

'I'm never going to stop, you know,' said Lisa in a low voice.

'I know. And I love you for it.' Jamie squeezed again. 'But please try. For your sake, and mine.'

'I am,' Lisa muttered. One day, her sister would understand, perhaps when she had her own children. Maternal instinct was primal. Instinctive. Not something that could be easily switched off, once it was flicked on, as it had been for Lisa the night the police came knocking on their door. Was it, what? Nearly twenty years ago now. Yes, nearly twenty. Lisa, only four months from turning eighteen. Jamie, just fifteen. Too young to live by themselves. Who could they stay with, the police asked?

At first, the question of where to live was just another to add to the pile of other, equally substantive questions—who would kiss them goodnight? Who would bring them toast and flat lemonade when they were ill? Who would edit Jamie's essays on Jane Austen? Or Lisa's on *Macbeth*? And put smiley faces in the margins when they made a good point? Who would one day walk them down the aisle? Go shopping with them for a wedding dress? Bring packets of marshmallows for the grandchildren? In the confusion of grief and loss that Lisa and Jamie experienced in the days after the crash, all these questions remained unanswered, along with the more immediate issue of who could put a roof over their heads. Family services were firm. They couldn't stay at home, at least not until Lisa was eighteen and old enough to apply for permanent guardianship over Jamie. Until then, adult supervision was required. There had to be someone else? A relative?

Well, actually, no. Their mum and dad were only-children. Their own parents had long since died. No grandparents. No aunts and uncles. Not even a cousin, at least none they knew of. Their dad had been transferred to Sydney only two years earlier, not even long enough to establish close friends—or at least, not the sort of closeness required to take the girls into their own homes. While Lisa understood her parents to be organised and sensible people, their wills were conspicuously silent on the matter of custody in the event of their deaths, as if they simply couldn't countenance the idea that one rainy Saturday night they would go out for dinner and a movie, only never to return. Not when there was no other family to replace them.

Jamie doesn't get it. Not yet. Once a parent, always a parent.

Lisa resumed cutting forcefully, channelling the remainder of her anxieties into the cake.

With a slight wobble, Heather joined her side and took another glug of moscato. 'Four more pieces required, then we're done, thank goodness.' She looked Jamie up and down.

'Heather, this is my sister, Jamie.' Lisa addressed Jamie. 'Thankfully, Heather here was able to stay and help me.'

'You're Lisa's sister.' Heather frowned. Her eyes were glassy. 'I would never have guessed.'

Lisa took a brief survey of what Jamie was wearing—artfully slashed jeans, sky-high platform sandals in silver, and an off-the-shoulder grey sweatshirt, very *Flashdance* circa 1983. It was vintage-Jamie: an eclectic mix of the glamorous and the everyday that somehow seemed to work on her. The only thing the sisters shared was their curly hair: Lisa's, dark brown verging on ebony, Jamie's, dirty (bottle) blonde.

'It's nice to meet you.' Jamie thrust out her hand. 'It sounds like you've been a wonderful help.'

'It was looking rather desperate at one stage, but we made it through.' Heather's eyes swivelled towards the moscato on the benchtop. 'Thanks to this.' She picked up the bottle. 'Now, where's my glass.' She hiccoughed, then rubbed her stomach. 'Actually, I'm not feeling so well. Forgot to have breakfast, again, unless you count that aspirin I took. You know how it is with children. Busy, busy, rush, rush, headache, headache,' sang Heather.

Lisa and Jamie exchanged glances.

'Why don't we sit you back down on the couch?' Lisa took Heather by the shoulders and started steering her towards the lounge room. 'Jamie here will look after you.'

'You're so pretty,' said Heather. 'And—well-dressed.' She touched Jamie's top in wonder. 'Cashmere?'

Jamie took over the steering and led Heather to the couch. 'How about we sit here.' The cushions sighed as the two women collapsed onto them.

Heather yawned and looked around. 'Might just rest my head for a minute ...' Her voice trailed off as her head sank into Jamie's lap. And stayed there.

Lisa peered at her face. 'Oh god. I think she's passed out.'

'I met her one minute ago and now her head's in my lap.' Jamie held her hands up, as if frightened to touch her. 'What's been going on here?'

Lisa sat on the coffee table opposite the now-snoring Heather. 'You have no idea.' They fell silent for a minute, listening to Heather moaning softly. 'She saved my life.'

'She's passed-out drunk!'

Lisa folded her arms. 'Well, it's partly your fault,' she said in a loud whisper. 'You were supposed to be here at eight-thirty to help set up. Where were you?'

Jamie rested one hand gently on Heather's forearm and the other on the armrest. She smiled. 'I've got news.'

Lisa's heart twinged. She clenched her pelvic floor, and felt her maternal sensibilities stir.

'What? What's your big news?'

Lisa went through a quick mental list of what she hoped it might be:

1) That Jamie had quit her job
2) That she'd broken up with Jared
3) That she'd quit her job AND broken up with Jared.

'Well,' Jamie began, the smile again tip-toeing across her face. 'I'm getting married!'

Lisa's stomach rolled. 'To Jared?'

'Of course to Jared. Who else?' Jamie said crossly, trying to fold her arms but stopped by Heather's snoring head.

'It's just …' Lisa paused, and a vision of Jared climbing a tree flashed into her head. It's what she recalled most of their first meeting—a 'meet-the-family' picnic in Centennial Park, organised by Jamie when Ava was just a baby. Midway through lunch, Jared had abandoned his sandwich to climb a tree he'd spotted in the distance. *He's obsessed with climbing*, Jamie told them as Jared scampered from branch to branch. At the time, Lisa had found it sweetly endearing that her sister's new boyfriend still had such ready access to his inner-child. But as the years went by, and Jared's obsessions moved from climbing trees, to frisbee-football, then slacklining, Lisa realised there was a difference between childlike and childish. Her sister deserved a husband who was her equal, her partner in life, not a man who would never quite grow up. There had to be a way to talk her out of it.

'It's quite quick, isn't it?'

'We've been together for five years.'

'But only living together for a couple of months.'

'You and Scott didn't live together at all before you married.'

'True,' she said miserably.

'And we're probably moving to Dubai.'

'No!' This time Lisa couldn't stop herself. While her head was tactful, her heart always tended to win out in these matters.

'Jared's gone for a promotion in the firm's Dubai office, and he thinks he's got it.' Jamie paused. 'And the job starts in six weeks.'

'What? You can't organise a wedding in that time.'

Jamie raised an eyebrow. 'Lise. C'mon. I could organise a wedding in five minutes. We don't *all* need five tastings to decide on a wedding cake.'

Lisa cringed. She'd been atrocious at planning her own wedding. It wasn't that she was fussy, she was just frightened of making the *wrong* decision. Would people prefer chicken or lamb? Caramel mud cake or chocolate? French champagne or Australian? There were just so many decisions! And everything was so expensive. She didn't want to waste her inheritance because of bad decision-making. This was when a person really needed their parents. Her mother would have known exactly what to do. In the end, Jamie, who seemed to have inherited their mum's organisation capabilities, had taken over and the wedding had gone beautifully. Lisa couldn't even remember the flavour of the cake now, only that it was delicious and when Scott fed her the first mouthful, she had been laughing so hard that some of it spilled out and left a rather unfortunate brown smear on her dress, which made Lisa laugh even harder. Now, it was her little sister's turn to plan her own wedding for which Lisa should have been happy. Only one problem—she was sure Jamie was marrying the wrong guy.

'But what about your job?' said Lisa.

'You mean the one you're always telling me to leave?'

'Yes! You love that awful job.'

Jamie stretched and clasped both hands behind her head. 'I'm going to set up my own business, like you did. This move is exactly the push I needed.'

Lisa's shoulders slumped. Earlier, when she dropped the cake on the floor, she had thought the day couldn't get any worse.

She was wrong.

'But I'm going to miss you too much.'

'We'll still talk every day.' Jamie put her arm around Lisa. 'And it won't be forever. One year. Two max.' She squeezed her sister's shoulder. 'Please be happy for me, Lise. This is what I want. Truly … And maybe it will be good for us to have a little more distance.'

Before Lisa could reply, a tornado of five-year-olds whirled in from the back deck. 'Lolly bags! Lolly bags!' they chanted and crowded around the kitchen bench expectantly. Wonder Woman strode towards Lisa with Scott hanging off her shoulder like a little puppy dog.

'I said they could have their lolly bags if they cleaned up the backyard. Hope that's okay?' Arabella checked her watch. 'The parents should be here at any moment.'

Lisa leapt off the coffee table. 'Oh no! The lolly bags.'

'I'll get them, Lise. Where are they?' said Scott.

Lisa clapped a hand to her forehead. 'I completely forgot. I was supposed to do them this morning, but then we slept in, and the cake fiasco, and—'

Arabella held up her hand authoritatively and Lisa immediately shut up. No one could disobey Wonder Woman. 'I've got a plan.' She clasped her hands together. 'We'll make it into a challenge.' She pointed at Scott. 'You go scatter lollies around the backyard.' She pointed at Lisa. 'You give out the empty bags to the kids. We'll tell them it's a treasure hunt.'

'And what should I do?' Jamie asked.

'You,' Arabella pointed at Jamie, 'keep looking after Heather. I'll drive her home later.' She gave Lisa and Scott a look. 'For an extra fifteen bucks.' They gave a silent nod of agreement. 'Okay,' said Arabella assertively. 'Ready, team?'

Lisa was half-tempted to spin around, Wonder Woman-style. Instead she muttered a yes and hurried towards the cupboard while Arabella announced the 'challenge' to the kids, who hooted and hollered like they'd been told they'd never have to eat broccoli ever again, instead of being told to go make their own lolly bags.

Ten minutes later, it was all over. The party ended as quickly as it had begun, the parents slinking in and out with such haste that Lisa began to worry. What was it with these people? At Ava's pre-school parties, the parents had been so friendly and attentive to their children, sticking around to make sure they didn't run riot or have a little wee-ing accident or eat potato chips and nothing else. Had Lisa missed the memo which said that once a child hit the age of five they were considered perfectly able to fend entirely for themselves at a complete stranger's house? They were still so little! But here were these parents, treating them like the next step was a driving licence.

'Thank you, Arabella. You were wonderful.' Lisa handed her a cheque.

'Nothing to it,' said the girl nonchalantly as Heather, who had now roused herself into consciousness, slid on her sunglasses and smoothed down her hair.

'And thank *you*, Heather. I couldn't have done this without you.' Lisa gave her a warm kiss. The woman smelt of stale champagne and wobbled slightly.

'Yes, well. That's probably true. Goodbye, Lisa.' Heather turned. 'Come along, Savannah-Rose. Say your goodbyes.' Savannah cuddled Ava like it was her last hug on earth and skipped out the door, shouting, 'Thanks for the party,' over her shoulder, before running ahead of Arabella, who was still holding tightly to the slightly unsteady Heather.

'She really saved the day, didn't she?' Scott murmured in Lisa's ear.

'Who?'

'Arabella, of course.'

'But it was Heather who organised her, and the cake.'

'Two Wonder Women, then.'

Lisa turned to see Scott's eyes following Arabella's blue lycra-encased bottom up the garden path. 'Hey! Eyes up, buster.'

'What?'

'Your eyes are glued to Arabella's bum!'

'Now there's a visual,' Scott laughed, pulling Lisa in for a hug. 'You know you are the only Wonder Woman for me.'

Lisa buried her head in his shoulder, feeling, as she always did in this position, that she was home. Safe, warm, and loved.

'That party was such a disaster.' Lisa let out a muffled wail.

'No, it wasn't.' Scott stroked her hair. 'The kids absolutely adored it. Ava told me it was the best ever.'

'Really?'

'Really.' Cupping her face in his hands, Scott leant in for a kiss. It was gorgeous. Gentle and soft. Lisa was enjoying it, so much so she didn't quite realise that it was deepening into something quite different from a peck on the mouth. She broke away.

'I think we better do some cleaning up before we, you know ...'

'Get dirty?' Scott smiled, before trudging towards the front gate to remove the balloons which were now hanging limp and tired.

Lisa could relate. Having a child tug on you all day was exhausting.

Back in the kitchen, Lisa's ears buzzed from the quiet. Ava and Jemima had disappeared into the bedroom with Jamie to de-brief over the party and fill her in on all she had missed.

Lisa picked up a garbage bag and surveyed the backyard.

Was it a party or a ransacking? was Lisa's initial thought. The outdoor furniture had been upended and one chair appeared to have lost a leg. Admittedly, it had been wobbly before the party, but still. The roses had no heads and the lawn was covered in a confetti of white and pink petals. The rickety side-fence now had a more pronounced lean to it and the washing line had been reduced to a tangle of knots. Under one of the bushes was a pair of children's underpants, covering a stash of lollies.

What were Scott and Arabella thinking, to let them get away with all of this? What happened to the clean-up?

Lisa pocketed the undies and unwrapped a lolly. Its tangy sweetness prompted a tidal wave of saliva in her mouth. She needed the sugar hit. Anything to help confront the disaster before her. She started collecting the rubbish—burst balloons, streamers torn down from where they'd swung festively from the trees, and a general array of little plastic trinkets that had been hidden in the piñata.

At the sound of hulking, heaving retches, Lisa stopped in her tracks.

The dog.

Round the side of the house, she found him standing over a pile of green vomit—the same colour as Ava's champagne bottle birthday cake. Lisa twigged. There'd been leftovers. She hadn't had time to put them in the fridge. With golden retrievers there was never enough time. Frankie's speed over the five metres from the back door to his dog bowl would rival a cheetah's.

His head hung low. Was he ashamed? Or contemplating eating the chunder?

'Poor Frankie puppy,' she crooned. 'That's what you get for eating two cakes.'

Lisa gave him a forgiving pat and fetched the hose. The puke broke up into algal-coloured rivulets and the dog wandered forlornly towards its kennel.

This time it was a yelp that made Lisa pause from cleaning. A human yelp. And a flash of red from inside Frankie's kennel.

Lisa took a few, cautious steps towards it. 'Anyone in there?' She waited. Inside the kennel Frankie moaned softly then quietened. The thump of his tail registered through the wooden slats of the kennel. Someone was patting him.

'Hello. Is anyone in there?' Lisa took a few more steps towards the kennel. The dog barked. A little voice whispered, 'Shhhhh.'

Feeling slightly nervous, Lisa leant over the entrance to the kennel to find two pairs of eyes staring back at her. Round and glassy as marbles. One set belonging to Frankie and the other to a little girl Lisa had never seen before. As her eyes accustomed to the dark, she could see the girl was wearing a beautiful red tulle dress with a sash at the waist, her dark hair braided into the most precise plaits Lisa had ever seen.

'Don't be scared. Frankie won't hurt.' Lisa sat on her haunches. 'He's too sick and sorry for himself at the moment to think about anything much.'

'He's very soft,' said the little girl in a low voice.

'Would you like to come out of there?'

The plaits moved like whips as the little girl shook her head.

'What's your name?'

The girl, pale and ghostly, kept her hand on Frankie. 'My name is Ellie,' she whispered.

CHAPTER SIX

Missy gazed around the granny flat one last time to make sure she hadn't left anything. The place was bare. Soulless. Not that the converted garage had ever been a particularly characterful place, but it was functional as granny flats tended to be. Just two rooms—a bedroom big enough for a double bed and little else, plus a living room with kitchenette. But that was all Ellie and Missy required. To Ellie, who didn't know any better, it was the perfect home. To Missy it was a simple solution to her problem. What had sold her on the place was that the owner, an elderly Russian man, would take cash for it. A little envelope with $180 in it that she left in a post office box every Monday, marked *Mr Ivanov*. They'd met just twice, in person. His English wasn't great but when Missy had introduced Ellie his eyes had lit up. 'I have granddaughter,' he said haltingly, using his hands to indicate a height similar to Ellie's.

The place was theirs. No paperwork required. Electricity, water and furniture included. He also owned the main house but chose to keep it empty. When Missy had peeped through the blinds there had been nothing to see, just rooms of furniture covered in white sheets. 'You have car?' he'd asked. No, Missy didn't. 'Ah, good. You use this one. You keep it running.' He raised a grey tarpaulin to reveal a small, white Fiat. Fairly old, given the boxy shape. Missy demurred—she didn't even have a licence, a fact she kept to herself—but Mr Ivanov pressed the key into her hand anyway. Where Mr Ivanov lived, what he did, whether he was married, what his first name was—Missy had no idea. Once, she'd run into him near one of her work places and he'd seemed as shocked as she was. 'My work,' she explained, pointing at the hair salon. He'd simply nodded and looked as though he was about to move on, but he stopped again. 'Your daughter? How she does?'

'Ellie? Oh, she's fine. Just great.'

'The car. You use?'

'Not really, but I turn the engine over every week to make sure the battery doesn't go flat.'

At that, he'd nodded and moved on without a word. Old Mr Ivanov was as concerned with maintaining his privacy as Missy was with hers—and that suited her just fine. Every day, she thanked her lucky stars for the little note she'd spotted on a telegraph pole, advertising a granny flat for let. It had given them three years of stability. A place to call their own. A place where Missy could decorate the walls with Ellie's paintings of rainbows and pink elephants, and fill their bookshelf with tales of elves and fairies.

Now, all of that was gone. Packed away into candy-striped storage bags that still smelled of the Chinese factory in which they were made. Their whole life, in three bags.

In her last rental payment, she had written a note to thank Mr Ivanov for allowing them to rent his flat, and telling him they were moving on. She would leave the key to the flat and the car in the post office box, if that was all right with him.

There had been nothing back.

Missy checked one last time under the bed. A thorough check this time, on hands and knees.

There, hiding in the far back corner, something grey and furry caught her eye. She wriggled under until her hands reached the softness. Ellie's old rabbit Mr Snuggles—the toy she'd had since birth and still slept with every night, even though he was now missing an eye and half his ear thanks to Ellie's chewing.

Missy's stomach contorted as she buried her nose into Mr Snuggles' tatty fur. Her beautiful girl. What would she be doing right now? Would she be scared? Or brave as Missy had told her to be? How would she survive without her favourite toy?

Missy let her tears flow into Mr Snuggles' fur until the rabbit was a sodden and matted mess. Then she walked through the flat a final time, put Mr Snuggles into one of the storage bags and closed the door behind her, feeling the sense of a happy chapter being closed and a highly uncertain one beginning.

CHAPTER SEVEN

Lisa took Ellie's hand and walked her towards the house from where they could now hear screaming. Two little high-pitched voices, fighting like tomcats on the prowl. The little girl's grip tightened on Lisa's hand.

'It's all right, sweetie. Nothing to be frightened of.'

But Ellie gave her a doubtful look and at the French doors she pulled back on Lisa's wrist to stop her from going inside. For a moment, they stood at the doors and watched.

On the coffee table, a Barbie doll was in the process of being decapitated. Jemima was clenched to the legs, her little face turning puce with the effort of yanking the doll out of her sister's hands. Ava was fighting just as hard, her finger-tips turning white from circulation loss, so entwined were they in the Barbie's ratty blonde hair. Leaning over the table with her hands in a karate-chop position was Jamie, making a lame effort at separating the two kittens-turned-wildcats.

'She's mine,' shouted Ava. 'Saffron gave her to *me*!'

'Nooooo.'

As Jemima threatened to separate the doll's hair from its head, Lisa dropped Ellie's hand to step inside the doors. 'What's going on here, girls? Jamie?'

'Ava won't share,' whined Jemima.

'She's my doll!' shouted Ava.

'Jamie?' said Lisa. 'Tell me who's in the wrong here.'

Jamie held up her hands defensively. 'I'm Switzerland in this. I am not taking sides.' She took three steps away from the coffee table.

'All right, then no one can have the doll.' Lisa forced Ava's and Jemima's sticky hands from the tortured Barbie. 'Until you can learn to play nicely with her.' She put the doll on the highest level of the bookshelf as the girls huffed and folded their arms.

'Who's she?' said Ava, shrugging a shoulder towards Ellie.

'You know Ellie. From school. She's in your class, isn't she?'

Ava looked blank. 'But the party's over.'

Why is she acting so strange? Must be all the sugar. 'Her mummy's just a bit late,' said Lisa brightly. 'Now you little ladies are all sticky and messy and I think the only solution is for you to hop in the bath.'

Ellie started rubbing at the dirt on her knees.

'Do you want to join them, Ellie?' said Lisa. 'You can if you're quick. Your mum might be here any second.'

Ellie nodded.

Her mum won't mind, will she? Bathing with virtual strangers?

'Aunty Jamie, will you come and watch us in the bath?' asked Ava.

'Sure, kiddo.'

The five of them trooped into the bathroom. Lisa ran the bath while Jamie helped the girls undress.

'Hey, where's the rest of your finger?' Ava pointed at Ellie's hand, which was raised above her head as Jamie helped her out of her dress.

'Ava, don't be silly.' Lisa switched off the tap.

'But look. She's missing her pinkie.'

Ellie pressed her hands to her chest.

'Ava, you know we don't make silly comments about the way people look. I'm sure there's nothing wrong with Ellie's hand.' Lisa smiled reassuringly. 'Nothing at all.' But Ellie's frown caused doubt to tip-toe into Lisa's throat. The little girl had now hidden her hands behind her back. 'And even if there is, I'm sure there's a simple explanation, which Ellie does not need to provide to us.' Lisa kicked off her ugg boots. 'None of us are perfect. Look at my second toe. See how it's joined to my big toe. Very odd, isn't it?' Six young eyes peered at her toe.

'Poo. Your feet smell.' Ava crinkled her nose and waved her hand in front of her nose. Jemima and Ellie looked at each other and giggled.

'Well, the point is, none of us are perfect.'

'I've got an outie bellybutton,' Jamie volunteered and raised her top. 'You can touch it if you like.' The girls crowded round her and Jemima poked at the little thumb of skin.

'Oooh,' she giggled. 'It looks like a boy's ding-dong.'

'Need any help in here?' At the sight of Scott, leaning against the doorway, Jamie dropped her top while Ellie hugged herself to cover as much of her naked body as her little hands and arms would allow.

She's scared.

The idea stilled her. That anyone could be scared of her darling husband was just bizarre. Still, Ellie wasn't to know that he was the kind of man who would rather catch and release a spider than tread on it. These days, children were taught to be wary of strangers, particularly male ones, and with good reason, Lisa concluded. There were some truly terrible individuals out there; her time in the group home had taught her that.

For her and Jamie, the home had been a stop-gap—a welfare-agency cottage not far from their own house where they could live with a few other teens under adult supervision for a couple of months until Lisa turned eighteen and could officially apply to become Jamie's legal guardian. For the other kids there, the group home was a refuge—a place where they came because of terrible experiences in foster care. For the largely sheltered Lisa, the stories were shocking. Wandering hands, strange and cruel punishments, and an ambivalence bordering on neglect. The *idea* that an adult could hurt a child was something her seventeen-year-old self had never before contemplated. Her own parents had been so loving, so kind, so normal. She'd assumed that's the way all families were. How wrong she was. How sheltered she'd been.

Lisa brushed off a shiver. 'No, we're fine, thanks, hon. Just comparing weird body parts. Why don't you go and pour Jamie a glass of wine?'

'Okay.' He gave her a look and disappeared into the kitchen. Lisa heard a bottle being unscrewed and the glug of wine being poured.

In the bath, she and Jamie soaped the girls' bodies until they shone like pearls. Without making it obvious, she took a look at Ellie's pinkie. Where the nail should have been, there was just a bald stump. It was all she could do to stop herself from staring. Instead, she averted her eyes and kept soaping, her mind working overtime. *Was she born that way? Was there an accident? How does a child simply lose a fingertip? Why is her mum running so late?*

Lisa shook her head to snap herself out of thinking of Ellie's poor, stubby finger. 'Now, I want you to do your own faces and fannies.' She handed out three washcloths. 'Faces first, thank you very much. Fannies second.'

Ellie wiped her forehead. 'My mummy doesn't call it a fanny. She calls it a vagina.'

The word pinged through Lisa like an electric shock. Jamie looked at her with raised eyebrows.

'What's affa-gina?' Ava screwed up her face.

'It's just a different word for your fanny,' said Lisa.

'But a boy's thing is called a ding-dong. Isn't it, Mummy?' Ava looked up from the bath, so innocent, clean and pure that it made Lisa want to cry.

'No. It's a penis,' said Ellie, matter-of-factly.

'But Mummy, you call it a ding-dong,' said Ava accusingly.

Lisa inhaled. 'Ellie is correct. It's called a penis, but as none of us have them, we don't have to worry too much.'

'Daddy has one,' said Ava.

'Yes. Our daddy does have a ding-dong.' Jemima nodded seriously. 'Does your daddy have one?' She tugged on Ellie's arm.

'Girls!' said Jamie and Lisa at the same time. They exchanged looks of dismay. As different as Jamie and Lisa were, they could virtually read each other's thoughts.

'My daddy's dead,' said Ellie quietly.

'Is he dead forever?' asked Ava.

Ellie hung her head.

'Ava!' said Lisa sharply. 'I think we've had enough time in the bath.' Lisa stood and squeezed Ellie's shoulder. 'Are you okay, sweetie?' she said quietly as Ava and Jemima squabbled over who would release the plug.

Ellie nodded. 'He died before I was born.'

Lisa felt a pang in her heart and, as much as she wanted to, she resisted the urge to wrap the little girl in her arms. After her parents' death, far too many near-strangers had thrown themselves over her and Jamie, assuming that because they were, strictly speaking, children, they needed to be swaddled in affection, when what they really wanted was their mum and dad back.

She winced at the memory of it and handed the bath towel to Jamie. 'Could you dry them off? I'll go get some clothes.'

But instead of going to the bedrooms, she headed to the kitchen. Scott's head was still in the fridge but on the counter were two glasses of wine.

'God, I need one of these.' Lisa took a gulp. She really wasn't a wine drinker. She would have liked to be. How often had she seen friends' updates on Facebook showing a delicious, pale-as-straw glass of white, with condensation pooling elegantly on the glass. *Ahhh, welcome to Friday afternoon.* When you were a 'mumpreneur' there really was no such thing as Friday afternoon, or weekends for that matter.

Every day carried just as much responsibility and labour as the rest.

Scott poked his head out of the fridge. 'Hey! They're for me and Jamie. I didn't think you wanted one.'

'Sorry! But—' She held up a hand and took another sip as Scott stood at the fridge, hands on hips. 'Ahhhh,' she exhaled. 'I needed that.'

'What's going on?'

'Nothing.' Lisa felt the oozy warmth of the alcohol in her legs. The upside of being a non-drinker was that it only took a miniscule amount to make her feel pleasantly weak. 'Just a slightly confronting conversation in the bathroom.'

'About?'

'Genitalia and death.'

'Ah. I see. A rabbit-hole conversation.'

Scott understood. Of course he did. Parenting was full of rabbit-hole conversations—discussions that started in one place and ended in an entirely different and unforeseen one. How was it that a conversation about shoes could end in questions about how the sky was formed? Or a request for Ava and Jemima to brush their teeth lead to a discussion about whether Santa was real? Talking to children tested logic to the extreme as they leap-frogged from thought to thought with only the barest of links between each one.

Scott leant against the bench beside her. 'Who's the scared kid in the bath?'

'Name's Ellie. Her mum's running late.'

'Bit weird.'

Lisa shrugged, trying to look unconcerned. Scott had warned that inviting the entire class into their home after only three weeks of school was possibly *not* the best idea, in the same way that giving the kids red cordial after 6 pm was possibly not the best idea, that is, unless they *wanted* the joy of putting two demented circus clowns to bed. But Lisa had gone ahead with the party anyway. It was easier to suffer Scott's mild protests, compared with Ava's complete devastation.

'Maybe her car broke down. Or she got lost. I don't know. I gather Ellie's dad has passed away,' said Lisa.

'Poor kid.'

'Poor mother, doing it all on her own.'

Scott touched her arm sympathetically and Lisa patted it. 'I'm fine. I'm sure it's nothing sinister.'

'I guess, but wouldn't she call you if she was running late?' said Scott.

Yes, Lisa wanted to say. *Why hasn't she called!* But saying that would make the situation sound real and a bit frightening, so instead she put her arm around Scott. 'Hon, not everyone is like us. In fact, I'm starting to think that none of the parents at this school are like us.'

'In what way?'

'Like today. They just dropped off their kids and ran and I had all this food ready.'

Scott shrugged. 'I wouldn't take it personally.'

'But we have to spend the next seven years of our lives with these people!'

'No, we don't. It's Ava who has to make friends. Not us. We can be as hands-off as we like. Just drop her off. Pick her up. Stick to ourselves.'

Lisa looked at him. 'That sounds dreadful.' She folded her arms. 'I don't want to be the sad parent who doesn't know anyone and has no friends.'

Scott sighed. 'You sound like a teenager. Who cares what other people think of us. Aren't we past that?'

No. Lisa was not past that. In fact, she was right back in that mindset of needing to impress. Certainly Ava was the one wearing the uniform, but Lisa was the one experiencing all the anxiety that came with starting school. No one had told her how she would be reduced to a quivering, nervous mess at the gate. For Ava's benefit she outwardly maintained her composure, offering words of comfort and reassurance which were perhaps more for Lisa's own sake than Ava's, for her five-year-old daughter would no sooner reach the entry than she would be off running towards the classroom without so much as a backward glance. Lisa should have been pleased, she supposed, that her daughter was so confident. So independent. But a little part of her would have preferred it if Ava had clung to her for a day or two, drawing a little sympathy from the other mums and perhaps a glance of admiration that she was so clearly adored by her daughter. But no. Ava was as sentimental as a rock. She was like the kid who dived headlong into a pool, while Lisa was the one who squirmed on the side, feeling like she needed a wee.

Now, standing in front of Scott, Lisa crossed her legs nervously. Facing his admonishment was almost as bad as facing the school drop-off. 'I just want them to like me. I want a *community*.'

Scott patted her shoulder. 'They will. Just give it a chance. It's only week three. You've got another two hundred or so to go, remember.'

Seven years of primary school. Forty weeks a year (thank goodness for the long holidays). Ten drop-offs and pick-ups a week. Goodness, that was nearly three thousand, friendless, visits to the school.

'How depressing,' she muttered, taking another tiny sip from the glass.

'PRESENTS!' A whirlwind of towels, wetness and slick little bodies bowled into the kitchen with Jemima making a beeline for one of Lisa's legs, while Ava clung to her other.

'Aunty Jamie says I can open all the presents now. Can I? Can I?' clamoured Ava.

A bedraggled Jamie emerged from the doorway, trailed by Ellie. Clearly, things had got a little out of hand in the bathroom, for Jamie was a sodden mess. 'Sorry,' she apologised. 'But presents were the only way I could get them out.'

Lisa gave her daughter a squeeze. 'Of course you can open them, darling. But let's get you dressed first.'

'I'll make some popcorn,' Scott volunteered.

With the children clean and dressed, and a pen in hand to take note of who gave what (she would write thank you notes later, a perfect chance to reach out to the other parents!) Lisa finally relaxed as her daughter opened her giant haul of presents. For each one there was a squeal of delight, a hurried inspection, and a short negotiation between Ava and Jemima outlining the terms of use. *You can use it for two minutes after me. But I'm taking it to bed.* Children were so easily pleased, really, when it came to presents. For a start, they had no clue about price or value. To Jemima, the $5 hairbrush was just as thrilling as the $25 Barbie doll.

Finally, they were down to the final gift. Ellie's. She had asked specifically for hers to be the last one opened and had sat hunched over the pink-wrapped box, watching carefully as Ava opened her haul. Wider and wider her eyes had grown, until she reminded Lisa of a little frog—completely still but ready to leap at any moment. Solemnly, Ellie handed the gift to Ava. 'Happy birthday,' she said seriously.

'Thanks!' Ava started tearing at the paper as if it were the first gift she'd opened, not the thirty-second. Or was that the thirty-third? Lisa had lost count. Her notes just a mess of scribble.

'Card first, Ava,' Scott reminded her.

'Sorry, Dad.' Ava paused, chastened, before ripping into the card with as much gusto as she'd torn into the present. But as she opened the glittery pink envelope, a piece of paper floated out of it and drifted gently to the ground.

'Hey, Ava, you missed something.' Jamie pointed.

'Thanks, Aunty Jamie.' Ava picked it up and held it to her nose. 'But I can't read it.'

'Pass it here, hon.' Jamie outstretched her hand. Lisa sat poised with her pen, ready to write. Ellie's mum was now nearly two hours late! Where could she be? Maybe Lisa had written the wrong time. Maybe she wrote 2 pm instead of 12 pm. It was entirely possible. On one child's invitation, she'd put the date of the party and the RSVP as the same date, causing great confusion (and a little sense of glee it seemed to Lisa) for the child's mother.

'Oh, Mummy,' breathed Ava. 'Look at these.' She held up a pair of sparkly, fire-engine red ballet slippers. 'They're the best shoes I've ever seen.'

Lisa sucked in a breath. The shoes were gorgeous. Every little girl's dream. The brand was a good one too. They would have cost at least $50.

'Let's hope they fit!' said Lisa with forced gaiety.

Ava slipped them on. 'They're perfect. Thank you, Ellie.' She wrapped the other girl in a spontaneous hug.

'That's an extremely generous gift. Thank you, Ellie.' Lisa started collecting torn wrapping off the floor.

'Ummm … Lise.' Jamie's face was white. 'I think you'd better read this.'

Lisa took the paper, noting the neat elegance of the handwriting and the thick, creamy quality of the paper and the way the black ink had bled just a little into the rippled texture. An ink pen, not biro.

She started reading.

Dear Lisa,

I'm sorry. Please know this, above all else. I am truly sorry to put this responsibility on you but I have been left with little choice.

My daughter, Ellie, is more precious to me than anything else in the world. To keep her safe, I will do whatever I have to. For the moment, that means giving her to you to look after. To love as your own.

Ellie thinks I have gone away to work for a few weeks. That's not true. I would never leave her for something so unimportant but it was the only thing I could think that wouldn't scare her. You do not know me, but I know you and your family, and I know you are a wonderful, loving mother who would do anything for her children. Once I have worked things out, I will be back for her. You and your family are not in danger. Please do not call the police. If you do, they will take her and put her into care, and I know you wouldn't want that for her.

Xx Ellie's mum

Lisa's body felt heavy. Drained of energy. Weak and limp. She leant on Jamie's thigh and looked up at her. 'Is this some kind of sick joke?' she whispered.

Jamie squeezed Lisa's shoulder and leant down so the kids couldn't hear. 'I don't know what the fuck is going on.'

'Mummy.' Ava tapped her leg. 'Mummy, look.'

Lisa sniffed and raised her head. The red shoes sparkled like rubies at the end of Ava's sparrow-like feet. 'Beautiful, darling,' she said in a strangled voice. 'Why don't you take your new skipping rope outside and test it out?'

'Can I wear my new shoes?'

'Sure.' Lisa couldn't think straight.

'Yeah! C'mon, Jems. C'mon, Ellie. You guys can swing the rope for me.' Like a mother hen (or a mini-Maggie Thatcher) Ava rounded up the two girls and dragged them outside. At the door, Ellie paused and looked back at Lisa. She looked anxious. Uncertain. Perhaps she knew what was in the note? Surely not. This was all some kind of giant, weird misunderstanding. There would be a simple explanation. Surely. Things like this didn't happen to Lisa. She was a bookkeeper, for goodness sake!

'Ah, peace and quiet.' Scott put his feet up on the coffee table, leant back and closed his eyes. Jamie and Lisa looked at each other.

'Hon, you need to see this ...' Lisa stood and relocated herself next to Scott. She needed to be near him. He would know what to do. He would comfort her and tell her everything was all right and that it was all probably some bizarre initiation joke on behalf of another parent. A prank or something. (Maybe they should consider moving Ava to a different school?)

'This note is a bit ... strange.' Lisa held the folded paper in her hands.

Scott opened his eyes. 'What do you mean?'

'Here, read.'

She watched him skim it quickly, eyes narrowing as he progressed down the page.

'Holy shit. What the hell is this?'

'It's seriously fucked-up, that's what.' Jamie folded her arms.

'We need to call the police.' Scott sprang off the couch and moved towards the phone.

'Wait!' Lisa caught his arm. 'The note says not to.'

'I don't care what it says. The woman is clearly crazy.' Scott angrily waved the note in the air like a lawyer presenting evidence of insanity.

In that moment Lisa felt real fear. Anger was such a rare emotion for her darling husband. Generally he had the temperament of a puppy dog—easily pleased and eager, and with a tendency to fall asleep quite a lot. Getting Frankie had been his idea. Lisa had supposed it was so he could have a like-minded soul (and another male) in the house. But at this moment he was furious, more viper than puppy.

'Let's just calm down and think this through.' She patted the couch. 'Come and sit down, Scott.'

The three of them sat in silence, though Scott seemed to be breathing more heavily than usual and his leg jiggled uncontrollably. Lisa put what she hoped was a calming hand on it.

'Why don't you talk to Ellie?' said Jamie.

'She thinks her mum's gone away for work. I don't want to frighten her.'

'We can at least find out what her mother's name is. Check her phone number on the class list.' Scott ran an anxious hand through his hair. 'Ring her up. Try and talk to her. Work out what the hell is going on.'

'All right, I'll go and find out.' Lisa rose from the couch. Outside, Ellie and Jemima sat on the grass, providing an attentive audience for Ava who was trying desperately to co-ordinate hands, feet and rope.

'Muuuum!' she wailed. 'I can't do it!'

'Practice makes perfect, sweetie,' she said with false bravado, and sat next to Ellie.

'Ellie, honey. Your mummy's running a little late and I'm wondering if we should call her to see where she is.'

The little girl looked at her, eyebrows raised. 'You know where she is.'

'No, darling. I don't.'

'She's gone away to work. It says so in the note.'

Lisa's stomach crunched. Ellie knew about the letter! What more did she know? 'What else does the letter say, sweetie?'

'You've read it.'

'I have but I'm not sure I quite understood it correctly. Maybe you could tell me what you think it says?'

With her eyes glued to Ava, Ellie spoke. 'It says she's had to go away for work and that while she's away I have to stay with you.' She looked at Lisa. 'I have to stay with you,' she repeated.

Sucking in a breath, Lisa resisted the urge to bury her face in her hands. 'Honey, what's your mummy's name?'

'It's Missy Jones.'

'Missy Jones. Okay, you wait right here.' Lisa scrambled to her feet and half-ran, half-walked back to the house. Inside, she brought up the class list on her phone, the one that another school mum had collated and emailed out at the start of the year. Scott and Jamie crowded around her.

'Jones, Jones ...' She trailed her finger down the list. Harkness, Hooper, Huang, Jakes, Jeffrey, Jiggens, Joss, Karl, Karim ... Wait. No Jones? She re-read the list.

'Where the hell is it?' said Scott.

'I don't know. I don't know.' Lisa checked the list again.

'She's not there,' breathed Jamie.

'No, no, she must be on the list.' Lisa scanned the names again and tried to ignore the growing sense of dread filling her stomach.

'We've all checked it, Lise. And unless we're all going blind, she's not there.' Scott started pacing.

'All right, then, there must have been an admin error. Maybe it's incomplete. I'll ring Heather. I'm sure she'll know this Missy Jones.' She headed down the hallway to get away from Scott and Jamie's doubting eyes. She had the sense they somehow thought this was *her* fault.

Was it her fault? After all, she was the one who did the school pick-ups and drop-offs and generally managed things on the home front. As far as domestic disasters went, this could be classed as an epic fail on her behalf.

'Heather speaking.'

'Heather, it's me, Lisa Wheeldon.'

'Naughty Lisa Wheeldon.' Heather sounded miffed. 'You've managed to get me into quite a bit of trouble with my husband.'

'What do you mean?'

'Alcohol at a five-year-old's party? I mean, what were you thinking! Henry and I are supposed to be going to the opera tonight but now I have a crushing headache all thanks to that cheap plonk you made me drink!'

For a moment, Lisa marvelled at Heather's complete revision of history but then thought better of taking her to task over it.

'Yes, right, gosh, I'm so sorry. Forgive me.'

'Apology accepted.'

'Wait, Heather. Before you go I need to ask you a question.'

'Yes?'

'Do you know a parent by the name of Missy Jones?'

'Missy who?'

'Jones. Missy Jones. Mother of Ellie in kinder.'

'Never heard of her. Who's asking? What's she done?'

'Well, nothing ... yet,' Lisa stammered. 'It's just that Ellie's here at our house and her mother hasn't come to pick her up.'

'Oooh, slack mummy. I've never met one of those at St John's. How dreadful!'

'I'm sure it's just a misunderstanding.'

'Probably, darling. But it really has been the party from hell, hasn't it?'

'The kids enjoyed it,' said Lisa mildly.

'Of course they did. Of course they did. Though Savannah was a touch disappointed by the lack of party bags. Anyhoo, let me know how you go finding this mysterious Missy Jones.'

'I will.'

After five minutes and four more calls to fellow class mothers who denied all knowledge of Missy Jones, the dollop of dread in Lisa's stomach had grown into a huge boulder. Where could this woman be? Who could she be? And as one of the mothers had brusquely pointed out, was Missy her real name or a nickname?

She trudged back down the hall to Jamie and Scott's expectant faces.

'Nothing,' Lisa said miserably. 'No one's ever heard of Missy or Ellie. It's like they appeared out of nowhere.'

'Just so strange.' Scott scratched his chin while Jamie's gaze turned slowly from Scott back to Lisa. She held up her finger.

'Wait right here!' Jamie ran to the French doors. 'Ellie, babe. Can you come here for a moment?'

Obediently, Ellie trotted to the door and Jamie put a reassuring hand on her shoulder.

'Hon, what school do you go to?' Jamie bent down to look into her eyes.

'I don't go to school,' said Ellie simply.

'Okay, sweetie.' Jamie paused. 'Have you ever gone to school or pre-school?'

'Nope.' Her eyes brightened. 'But I want to. I can read and everything,' she said proudly.

'Well that's impressive,' Jamie squeezed her shoulder.

Ellie doesn't go to St John's? Why didn't Ava say so? How was it that a five-year-old could recite all the character names from their favourite TV show but not even know their own classmates?

Lisa felt her knees weakening. If Ellie didn't go to St John's, how did she know about the party? Lisa had printed precisely thirty-three invitations—thirty-two for the class and one for Jamie. Who was this girl? Where had she come from?

As if reading her mind, Jamie knelt down. 'Hon, can you tell me where you live?'

'I live at 64 Abner Road, Daceyville,' Ellie recited.

Lisa knew the street, it was only a suburb away from their place. Where Randwick still boasted a few character homes, Daceyville was slightly newer. A little more industrial. Fewer trees, but otherwise a perfectly normal place to live.

'Clever girl, Ellie.' Jamie gave her a quick hug. 'Now, how about you go back and play with the girls?'

'Okay,' said Ellie and off she trotted into the backyard where Ava was still trying to master her new rope.

'I'm taking her home,' said Scott, striding towards the sideboard where his car keys were normally kept.

'Hon, let's just think this through,' said Lisa.

'What is there to think through? We know where she lives, let's take her back there.'

'But we don't know what we're taking her back into.'

Scott stood with his hands on his hips. 'Then let's call the police.'

'Not yet,' said Lisa.

'Then what?'

Lisa tried to think clearly but her brain was a muddle of thoughts and feelings. What would make a mother do this? Why had she chosen them? How must poor Ellie be feeling? And how had Ellie's father died? He must have been quite young. Is that why Ellie had reacted so strangely to Scott in the bathroom?

'I'll take her.' Lisa said the words with more confidence than she felt.

Scott shook her head. 'Lise, I don't think that's a good idea. You yourself just said that we don't know what we might find over there.'

'He's right, you know. You don't know what kind of crazies these people might be,' said Jamie.

'I'll be fine. *We'll* be fine,' Lisa corrected herself. 'That note sounded to me like a mother who loves her daughter very much.'

'Enough to abandon her?' snorted Jamie.

'Jamie, if there's one thing I know about parenting it's that a mother would never willingly leave her child. Never.' Lisa's eyes started growing hot at the very idea of a total stranger taking Ava or Jemima by the hand, feeding them, bathing them, kissing them goodnight.

In caring for Jamie, as her guardian, she'd had a taste of how it felt to be responsible for another human being. But Jamie was fifteen, able to (largely) fend for herself. When Ava was born, the midwife had placed her into Lisa's outstretched hands and whispered 'There you go, Mum'. In that instant, Lisa realised that she was, in a way, lost forever to a love that would have no bounds. Parenting her own child was a more intense thing altogether. This was her own flesh and blood. Entirely defenceless and vulnerable. Metaphorically and literally, she could never let go of this little human, so much so that in the early months Scott had complained, jokingly, that he would never be able to tweeze his eyebrows as they were the only feature by which Ava would be able to recognise him. With a start, Lisa realised it was true. Scott was always hovering at her shoulder, eyebrows waggling, waiting his turn for a cuddle. But there was something so primal and instinctive in the way she loved her girls. She loved them because they were hers. And Scott's, of course. No one else could ever love them or care for them in the same way, because they were not theirs. It was as simple and complicated as that. Now, she had been asked by another mother to care for a child who was not her own. It could be done, but should it? This woman had to be incredibly desperate. Perhaps there was another way in which Lisa could help.

'I'll take her back.' She rubbed her eyes. 'It was me she wrote to.'

'I don't think that's a good idea,' said Scott.

'I have to do this.' Lisa clasped Scott's hand. 'For whatever reason, Ellie's scared of you—' Scott went to speak but Lisa squeezed his hand. 'I know it's unwarranted, but put yourself in her position. She's only five.'

'Actually, she's six.' Jamie put her hand up, attracting a glare from Lisa. 'She told me in the bath. She'll be seven in September.'

'Well, she's still very little and no doubt very afraid and I think it has to be me that takes her home.'

Scott paused and looked at the floor. 'I don't like this.'

'I don't either,' said Jamie. 'And didn't you just have a glass of wine?'

'Only a sip,' Lisa protested. 'I'm fine to drive.'

'I'll come with you then.' Jamie moved to collect her bag.

'No, you stay with Scott. He might need an extra pair of hands if anything … you know, happens here. I'll be fine. Seriously.' She nodded at both of them in a way that she hoped was reassuring. 'I'll take my phone and ring you as soon as I get there.'

Scott reached for the keys in his pocket and dropped them into Lisa's hand. 'As soon as you get there—I mean, before you're even out of the car—I want a call from you and then you leave your phone on as you walk into that place. I want to hear everything.'

CHAPTER EIGHT

In the car, Ellie was subdued but Lisa filled the silence with chatter about tooth fairies and TV shows that the little girl might have seen. Lisa's best conversations with her daughters tended to happen during car journeys. It was probably something to do with the lack of eye contact and the fact that Lisa was usually distracted by the act of actually driving to pay too much attention to what they were saying. True to the contrariness of children, the half-heartedness of the whole situation seemed to spur them into dropping the occasional gold nugget of information. But not Ellie. She answered Lisa's questions politely but offered nothing beyond what was being asked. Yes, she had lost a tooth. And yes, the tooth fairy had come and left her $2. No, *Tinkerbell* was not her favourite TV show. She didn't really like television. Actually, they didn't even own a TV. Or an iPad.

No TV and no iPad. The mind boggled. Though Lisa hated the idea of filling her children's sparkly brains with mush, she couldn't really imagine life without it—so powerful was its hold over the children with its ability to settle fights (*If you don't give Jemima the Barbie, there'll be no iPad for a week!*), offer comfort (*There, there. Will your ouchy feel better if we turn on the TV?*) and generally provide Lisa with a few minutes of peace and quiet each day. She was careful to follow the recommended 'doses' (no more than two hours' screen time per day) but couldn't quite imagine getting rid of it altogether. Was Ellie's mum one of those enviable women who never tired of Play-Doh and Barbies? Oh, how Lisa would have loved to be that perfect mother! She resolved to cut back Ava and Jemima's screen time to thirty minutes per day.

'This is it.' Ellie sat up in her seat and craned her neck to get a better view out of the window. They were in front of a maroon-brick bungalow that had an air of benign neglect. Two-foot high weeds sprouted from the front wall, which had developed a drunken lean. The blinds were drawn, like closed eyelids. Lisa's heart sank. Either the house had not been lived in for a long time or its occupants had lost the will to administer basic maintenance.

'Are you sure this is it, honey?'

'Yes. We live out the back in the granny flat.'

With the unclicking of the seatbelt, Lisa felt her spirits rise. There was still hope. Perhaps the house was suffering neglect but that didn't mean the granny flat was too.

'It's up here.'

Lisa followed Ellie's pale legs up the driveway. The child moved quickly, matching Lisa's own rising excitement levels.

Out the back was a double garage, in the same auburn brick as the house. It had clearly been converted—the roller door removed and replaced by two rectangular window frames, all in fairly decent condition compared to the house. Ellie stopped and turned to Lisa. 'Mummy said she was leaving today, so I don't think she'll be here.'

'Let's check anyway, shall we?'

Ellie knocked. 'Mummy, Mummy. It's me. I'm back from the party.'

Silence.

This time Lisa knocked. 'Hello, is anybody in there? It's Lisa Wheeldon. And I have your daughter, Ellie.'

Silence. So much silence that Lisa felt sure she could hear her own heart pounding. Remembering Scott's insistence that she call, she reached in her pocket for her phone.

Damn. Empty.

She knocked again and waited. Never had she wanted so much for a door to be opened. For a face, any face, to greet her and tell her that everything was okay, that it was all a misunderstanding. That she, Lisa Wheeldon, had not been caught up in what was starting to feel like one of the strangest experiences of her life, second only to the night the police had come knocking on their door to break the news about her parents.

'I told you she wouldn't be here,' said Ellie neutrally. 'Let's just go back to your place.'

'Hold on, honey. Let's check through the windows.'

Ellie sighed. 'There's nothing in there. We packed it all up last night. Mummy says we'll live in a new place when she comes back.'

Lisa felt a cold chill wrapping around her stomach.

'Let's just see, shall we?' Even to herself, Lisa's voice sounded falsely bright. She took Ellie's hand and led her to the window where, thankfully, the curtains had been left open.

The place was empty. Lifeless. So clean that it was almost creepy, as if Ellie's mother had tried to remove all evidence of their existence.

Ellie stood on her tip-toes and balanced against Lisa. 'See. I told you. Can we go now?' She slipped her hand into Lisa's and started pulling her away. But Lisa's eyes remained glued to the window and she resisted Ellie's pull. It was as if she was witnessing a car crash. Time had slowed. Everything was beyond her control. It was like that dream she sometimes had, where she was in the car with her mum and dad as it slipped off the road and careered towards a towering gum tree, the trunk of it appearing as a headless ghost in the glare of the car's headlights.

'Just one more minute, darl.' She gently pulled Ellie to the window again. She blinked hard and took another look, hoping this time that she would see chairs, a table, pictures on the walls, a kettle and maybe a toaster.

Nothing. Her eyes had not deceived her. There was truly nothing to see.

They trudged back to the car.

'Who lives in the house, honey?' Lisa paused with her fingers at the lock.

'No one. It's empty.'

This time Lisa didn't even bother to check, for she knew the little girl to be telling the truth.

CHAPTER NINE

The pub was cranking and Jared couldn't wait to get out of there. It was seven hours since he'd left Jamie, and his morning coffee with Tom had somehow turned into lunch, which had become Sunday afternoon drinks with a bunch of their workmates. The young, single ones. Now, pooling in Jared's stomach was an uneasy mix of coffee, salt and pepper squid, beer and something else that he'd been struggling to put his finger on. Something he rarely felt. Guilt.

'Oy, Silver, your round, dickhead.' Tom held up his empty beer glass.

'I got the last one.' Silver (real name: Sterling) protested. 'It's Cinders' turn.'

Cinders (real name: Ashley. Ash. Cinders. Geddit?) nodded glumly. 'Um, fellas, I'm a bit short this week.'

'Mate, you're a lawyer in a top five firm. You ain't short. You're tight.' Tom grabbed Cinders by the collar. 'Admit it, you're a tight-arse.'

'All right,' said Ashley in a tone of resignation. 'I'll go to the bar. Same again?'

'Yup. Four schooners, mate. None of that cheap middy crap,' said Tom.

I really should leave now.

Jared had been here so many times before. Many, many more times than these boys. It was that point in proceedings where things slipped from being fun and jocular, into being messy and drunken. Besides, he really needed to see Jamie. Really, really needed to see her. There was something nagging at him. Something he needed to tell her.

He checked his phone. No messages. No calls.

'Oi, big J, put that away. You're not going anywhere so don't even think about it,' ordered Tom.

'What? I'm just checking my messages!'

Tom shook his head. 'You attached people are all the same. Always checking up on each other.' He put his hand on his chest. 'If I ever get a girlfriend who checks up on me all the time, please shoot me.'

'I think that's highly unlikely,' said Jared.

'Damn straight.'

'Because you'll never get a girlfriend.'

Tom was an idiot, which is why he was still single. And he was completely off the mark about Jamie. She didn't keep him on a tight leash. That was something Jared really dug about her. She never checked up on him at all. She was cool like that. He felt a sudden urge to be near her.

Under the table, he tapped out a message.

Hey, are you still at your sister's? J

'So what's your missus think about the Dubai situation?' Tom took a swig from the fresh beer that Cinders had placed before him.

'She's cool with it.'

'She going to go with you, or will you do the long-distance thing?' Tom sniggered. 'Like that ever works.'

Actually, we're getting married.

'We haven't worked it out yet.'

Why couldn't he say it? Maybe it was because he was still getting used to the idea. This morning, he had woken with no idea that by the end of the day he would have a fiancée. But there it was. He felt good about it. Basically pretty good. Maybe he acted cool, but the lawyer in him did feel its significance. This was a commitment, a contract they were entering into.

Quite frankly, he'd expected her to choose her job over him. Not that he wanted to break up. Not at all. Jamie was an awesome woman, smart as a whip and smokin' hot as well. Occasionally, a small part of him wondered what she saw in him. But that was only a small part, and the thought was relatively rare. He knew he was a decent catch as well. Or, he could be.

'You know what, boys? I'm going to call it a day.' Jared stood from the table amid cries of protestation.

'Don't go now ...'

'Geez, you're a softie ...'

'You've still got half a beer.'

Jared drained his drink. 'It's been fun, boys, but I'll see you at work tomorrow.'

'See ya, J,' they chorused as Jared slipped into the crowd.

'You're going to fucken love Dubai,' Tom shouted after him.

As Jared stepped out of the pub into the narrow Paddington street he breathed a sigh of relief. The quiet was a welcome contrast to the din of inside. Either he was getting old or pubs were getting louder. Neither was great.

Jared's phone bleeped.

Hey hon. Still at Lise's. Been a bit of a hiccup here, so might be a while. Xx

Jared thought for a second before typing.

Can I come over?

The reply was almost immediate.

Of course! Love you to.

Jared slipped on his helmet and started up his Vespa. Jamie called it his 'mid-life crisis motorbike'. But Jared was only thirty-five, and most of the time felt no older than twenty-five, that is, until he hung out with actual twenty-five-year-olds like Tom and Ash and Sterling. It was then he realised he really was growing up, and it kind of sucked.

Jared whizzed through the streets of Paddington, past the rows and rows of little terraces. It really was a great place to live, with a pub on almost every corner and work only a five-minute scoot away in the guts of the CBD.

So why did he feel so restless?

On paper, everything was great. His job was satisfying, his girlfriend was smart and gorgeous and they lived in the coolest suburb in Sydney. Why was he trying to get away from it all by moving to Dubai? It wasn't like he *had* to apply for the promotion.

Jared gunned the accelerator and the scooter fish-tailed as he took a tight corner. He was on Anzac Parade now, just passing the stadium. The city was fading behind him and flapping overhead was the city's bat colony, making its sunset migration into Centennial Park. Ahead lay the sub-urbs where Jamie's sister and her family lived. Single-storey homes. Backyards with pools and lawns that would need mowing—a far cry from the tiny courtyard that constituted the entire outdoor space of the terrace he shared with Jamie.

Jared took a left-hand turn off the main drag, and then a right, and another right. The street was empty and riding down it, he had the sensation of being watched by the squat houses with their big front windows, like unblinking eyes. He noted the trampolines, the abandoned kids' bikes in front yards. The whole thing had the air of an abandoned fun park.

He parked the scooter and took off his helmet. This was his future. After the Dubai secondment, he and Jamie would return to Sydney. She would probably want to start a family. Have a baby.

A baby. Even though the afternoon was still warm and slightly sticky, Jared felt a chill run through his bones.

He was sure Jamie would understand. After all, it had happened well before they met. That it had never come up in conversation before was somewhat surprising. He knew most women tended to grill their boyfriends about previous girlfriends. Not Jamie. She was too self-assured for that. But entering into a marriage, even an engagement, was like entering into a contract—it was only fair that both parties do their due diligence, and in that light, it was only fair that he share with her, before they made it official. It wasn't like he'd held *material* information from her, but he conceded that a woman may see it differently.

Squaring his shoulders, Jared strode up the front path and rang the bell.

'Jared! Congratulations! What a surprise! A wedding. So exciting. So … surprising!' Jamie's sister, Lisa, kissed and hugged him warmly.

Oh shit! Jamie had already told her about the engagement. Of course she would. Mentally, Jared face-palmed. That's what women did. They shared these things. But he wasn't quite ready for this. It felt like he'd turned up to court without his briefcase.

'Thank you. I'm still—' he searched for the words '—I'm still getting used to the idea.'

Lisa gave him a funny look. *Oh shit. Not quite the right response.* 'But I'm very happy of course. Jamie's a great girl.'

'She sure is.' Lisa hugged him again. 'We know you'll do the right thing by her.'

Was that a statement, or a warning?

She stood aside from the door. 'Come in. Come in. Jamie's inside. Did you find your way here okay?'

Was that another dig at him? About finding his way to the house? In their years of dating, Jared had successfully avoided most Wheeldon family functions, a fact he was sure wouldn't have gone unnoticed. *Nah.* Jamie's sister was too nice to make snide remarks. He dismissed the thought. Still, there was something a little odd about Lisa today. She was even more bright-eyed than usual. Perhaps a little manic.

In the kitchen, Lisa's husband was drinking a beer and frowning. Both unusual activities for him. Scott was a genial fella. A little on the boring side and rubbish taste in beers, but that wasn't his fault.

'Hey, mate.' Jared reached out his hand.

'Hi, Jared.' Scott shook it. 'I hear congratulations are in order,' he said in a subdued voice.

'Yeah, yeah. It's all happened pretty quickly.'

'Would you like a beer, Jared?' Lisa busied herself about the kitchen.

'Umm ...' He thought about saying no, but there was a tension in the air to which he didn't want to add. 'Sure.'

Silence. The only sound in the room was the hiss of the cap being pulled from the beer bottle. What the hell was going on? These two were usually the chattiest, happiest couple Jared knew. But right now, the room was stretched tight as a drum with the quiet.

'Uh, where's Jamie?' Jared swigged his beer.

'She's in our bedroom.' Scott's mouth was set in a line. 'Ava and Jems are in bed, asleep. Been a big day. You know how it is.' He gave a weak smile.

'Sure.' Actually, Jared had no idea how it was. The last kid's birthday party he'd been to was his own, when he was eleven.

'We had a little ... problem. At the party.' Lisa was still playing with the bottle opener, twisting it nervously this way and that.

'Let me guess. The piñata didn't break,' Jared joked. No one laughed. What the hell was wrong with these two? It was a five-year-old's party for god's sake. It couldn't possibly have been *that* disastrous.

'One of the mothers didn't turn up to collect her child,' said Scott evenly, his arms still folded and the beer resting in the crook of his arm. 'And she left a note.'

'Right.' Jared still wasn't following. What was the big deal about a mum running late?

Silently, Lisa passed him a piece of paper. As he read, Jared's eyes widened.

'You really don't know this woman?'

Lisa shook her head as Jared handed her back the note.

'We went around to the little girl's flat. But there's nothing there. It's been completely emptied out.' Lisa's voice was high-pitched. 'And now we don't know what to do.'

Scott and Lisa looked at Jared expectantly.

'Shit. Don't look at me. I've got no idea.' This was too fucking strange. The sooner he and Jamie got out of here, the better. They had enough on their plate without having to deal with some weirdo woman who'd decided to leave their kid with a bunch of strangers, even if the strangers happened to be Jared's future in-laws. Lisa and Scott were good people but Christ—it didn't matter how nice they were, it wasn't right to leave a kid on their doorstep without any warning or pleases or thank yous.

'So Jamie's in with the kid now?' asked Jared.

'Yes. They're reading stories together while we work out what the hell to do next.' Scott raked his fingers through his hair.

The guy was completely stressed out. Even Jared could see that.

'I might go and say hi.' Jared left his beer bottle on the bench as Lisa showed him to the stairs.

Jared climbed slowly and with a growing sense of doom. This had been a strange day. A very strange day. There were too many fucking secrets in the world. Well, there was about to be one less. Jared would come clean. He would tell Jamie everything. At least that would be a little of the weight lifted from his shoulders.

From behind the bedroom door, he could hear low murmurings. He opened it quietly to find Jamie stretched out on the bed beside a little girl whose face was hidden behind a large picture book.

'Knock, knock,' said Jared, not wanting to scare them.

'Hey, babe.' Jamie rolled off the bed and stood to kiss him. She clasped her hands around his neck. 'I'm so glad you're here.'

'So am I,' he whispered into her ear. 'There's something I really need to tell you.'

'Jamie, could we please finish the book? I really want to know what happens to the pig.' The voice was sweet and young.

'Sure, Ellie. But first I want you to meet my fiancé, Jared.' Jamie led him towards the bed.

The little girl lowered the book and locked eyes with Jared. 'Hello,' she said. 'I'm Ellie.'

Jared blinked, and blinked again. Then rubbed his eyes.

'Jared? What is it? What's wrong?'

Jared shook his head. What the hell was going on? Half-formed thoughts tripped over themselves in his head. The hair, it was just like … And the shape of her face, he knew that pointy little chin anywhere. And those blue eyes, that particular shade of cornflower blue that was exactly like … And that little ski-jump nose, the one he used to …

Trembling, Jared stepped away from the bed. This was too weird. He thought he was cool with his past. After all, what was done was done. But maybe it wasn't. Maybe what he *thought* was done, was not done at all. Maybe it was here, sitting in his future sister-in-law's bedroom.

'What is it, hon? What's wrong?' Jamie caught his arm.

'Nothing. No. Nothing,' he stuttered and shook his head. 'I forgot. A work thing. I've gotta go. Sorry.' He rushed out of the room and took the stairs two at a time. Near the bottom, he stopped and leant his head against the cool wall.

Upstairs, he heard the bedroom door closing. 'Don't worry about him, Ellie. Men can be a little bit funny sometimes.'

Jared made a fist and ground it into the wall. *Fuck. Fuck. Fuck.*

He wiped his sweaty palms against his pants and re-entered the kitchen, where Scott and Lisa stood with their heads bowed together, talking quietly.

'Hey, guys. I just remembered there's something urgent I have to do at work.' Jared collected his keys from where he'd put them on the bench.

'On a Sunday night?' said Lisa doubtfully.

'Yep. Has to be done before Monday. Should have done it on Friday, but hey, you know how it is. Just slipped my mind.'

He gave Lisa a quick kiss on the cheek and from the hallway he waved at Scott. 'Can you guys just say sorry again to Jamie for me?'

'You're not even going to say a proper goodbye?' asked Lisa, following him down the hall.

'Nah. She's reading with ...' He couldn't even say her name. 'She's reading a book with the kid and I don't want to interrupt again.'

Jared couldn't get out of the house quickly enough. As Lisa closed the front door behind him, he paused on the step and breathed as if surfacing from a deep dive. The street was now bathed in a golden glow from the setting sun, and in the distance, the lights of the city were starting to come on.

Jared jumped on his scooter and sped towards them.

CHAPTER TEN

'Ellie, honey. We thought you might like a little snack, seeing as you didn't eat much dinner.' Lisa padded into the bedroom holding a cup of milk and Scott followed behind her with a plate of bickies.

'Ooh yum. Choc-chip is my fave.' Jamie leant off the pillow to take a biscuit, and then passed another one to Ellie. 'Here you go.'

'Thank you, Jamie.' Ellie started munching. 'Hmmm ... yummy. Thank you, Lisa. Thank you, Scott.'

The girl's manners were impeccable. She was such a sweet little thing, which made what Lisa was about to do all the more difficult.

'Ellie, I know we've already asked you a lot of questions. But we just want to ask you a few more because we really want to find your mummy and tell her you're okay.'

The little girl nodded and Scott cleared his throat. 'Ellie, does your mum have a job?'

Ellie nodded again. 'She calls it the panelbeaters.'

'So, she's a mechanic?' said Scott with a rising inflection.

'A mechanic?' Ellie looked at Jamie.

'Someone who fixes cars.'

'I don't think it's that.' Ellie said quietly. 'I don't really know.'

'When she goes to work,' said Lisa, 'who looks after you?'

Ellie's face brightened. 'Joanna's my babysitter. She takes me to the park and the library and she teaches me lots of things. Reading and writing, stuff like that.'

'And where does Joanna live?' Scott leant forward.

'She's gone back to her home. I think it's called Iceland.' Ellie screwed up her face.

'Ireland?' Jamie offered.

'That's it,' agreed Ellie. 'She went back last week cause her knees-up was finished.'

'Knees-up?' said Scott quizzically.

'I think she means visa,' said Lisa, who considered herself fluent in child-speak. 'She must have been an au pair.'

On they went, asking Ellie every single question they could think of that might lead to a name or a phone number. Yes, Ellie's mum had a mobile phone—one of those little flip ones—and Ellie liked to look at photos, but the screen was tiny and no, she didn't know the number. No, she didn't have any cousins or aunties or uncles or grandparents that she ever visited. Yes, she liked sports and dancing, but no, she never took classes. She and Mummy just played ball at the park and did ballet around the kitchen.

After nearly an hour of questions, Ellie's bottom lip began to quiver. 'I'm sorry I don't know,' she whispered, as a fat tear slid down her cheek. 'Am I in trouble?'

'No, darling, of course not.' She paused. 'Would you like a hug?'

Ellie nodded and Lisa pulled the little girl into her lap. Resting her chin on Ellie's head Lisa looked at Scott, who shook his head sadly. His skin was grey and there were shadows forming under his eyes. He mouthed a single word. 'Police.'

With a large knot forming in her throat, Lisa squeezed Ellie even more tightly. 'It's going to be okay, honey.'

Gently, Lisa closed the bedroom door and followed Scott back downstairs to the kitchen.

'You know we need to call the police. It's the right thing to do. It's our only choice.' He drummed his fingers on the benchtop.

'The letter specifically said we shouldn't.'

'So now we're taking orders from a woman we don't know?'

'I'm just saying we should think about it.' Lisa took Missy's note from her pocket and unfolded it.

You and your family are not in danger. Please do not call the police. If you do, they will take her and put her into care, and I know you wouldn't want that for her.

'She's right, you know. If we call the police and say we have an abandoned child, they'll take her into emergency foster care.' She re-read the last line, silently.

I know you wouldn't want that for her.

'How do you know that about me?' said Lisa, under her breath.

'Maybe foster care is where she belongs. It sounds like her mum's in a bad place right now.'

Lisa gave him a look. 'Even after everything I've told you about the group home that Jamie and I went into? Those kids were scarred for life by foster care.'

'That was twenty years ago. Things have probably changed since then.'

'For the worse, if anything. Remember that doco?'

It was appalling. The reporter had nearly been in tears, interviewing kids who'd been removed from abusive homes, only to be put into the hands of other abusers in foster care. Lisa had turned it off, halfway through. It was all too triggering.

'But I'm sure not all carers are like that? There must be some good ones out there.'

Lisa nodded. 'You're right. I'm sure there are plenty of kind and loving foster homes out there, but there are also some that aren't, and the thing is, we have no idea of which kind Ellie would be placed into. We could be putting her into the hands of an angel, or a monster. If this was Ava or Jemima, would you really be willing to take that risk?'

'Maybe we are taking a risk, by accepting this child into our home. The mother says we're not in danger, and usually when people tell you there's no danger, it's because there actually is!'

'Ellie's a child. A sweet child from what I can see. To be honest, I think the risk of something bad happening to her in foster care is far higher than anything happening to us if we take her in.'

'What's that about risk?' Jamie had joined them in the kitchen. 'Ellie's out like a light in your bed,' she explained. 'Emotionally exhausted.'

'I know the feeling.' Scott ran a hand through his hair.

'He thinks we should call the police and get Ellie into emergency foster care.' Lisa folded her arms.

'Haven't you told him?' said Jamie.

'Of course I have!'

'You can't call the police.' Jamie locked eyes with Scott. 'Seriously. If you knew what went on in some of those homes …' She shuddered.

'So, what are we supposed to do?' asked Scott, mildly.

'We keep her,' said Lisa simply. 'Look after her, and keep trying to find her mum.'

Jamie nodded. 'I'm happy to help.'

'Isn't that some form of kidnap? To keep a kid you don't actually know? You're not suggesting we hide her here.'

'Well, her mother seems to know us.' Lisa held up the letter. 'We have this, and it proves that we haven't taken Ellie against her will. It's just like asking a friend or a relative to look after your child. If anyone asks, which I doubt they will, but if they do, that's what we'll tell them. She's a friend's child that we're looking after while she's away on work.'

'What about Heather, and the other mums that you rang? *They'll* know,' said Scott. 'What if they tell the authorities?'

'They won't,' said Lisa, with more confidence than she actually felt. 'They're mums too. They'll get it. They might even help me try and track down this Missy Jones.'

'Really? Weren't you the one saying before how unfriendly they all were?' Scott raised his eyebrows.

'This is different,' said Lisa firmly. 'This is a child's welfare at stake. They'll understand.'

'And what about Ava and Jemima? How will they feel about having someone new in the house? They might get jealous.'

'It'll be good for them. They'll love it. They're always asking to have their friends for a sleepover.'

'But this isn't just one night, is it? What happens if she doesn't come back? The mother, I mean?' Scott folded his arms. 'We can't keep Ellie indefinitely.'

Jamie walked around the kitchen island, closer to Lisa. 'How about we set a time limit? Say, six weeks from now—if we haven't found Missy by then, we go to the police.'

'Six weeks!' Scott exclaimed. 'That's way too long.'

'It's a maximum, and I suspect we'll find this woman well before then,' said Jamie evenly. 'But it gives us something to work towards.'

'So what's that—early April? Isn't that when you're getting married?' said Lisa. 'You won't have much time to help us look.'

'I'll make time,' said Jamie fervently. 'Sound like a deal. Scott?'

'Okay.' He sighed and scratched his head. 'I hope you two know what you're doing.'

'We do.' Jamie gave first Lisa, then Scott a kiss on the cheek. 'I need to get going, but I'll call you in the morning.'

Once Jamie had left, the house fell into silence. Scott and Lisa set about making up the trundle bed in Ava and Jemima's room. They both agreed it would be nicer for her to wake with familiar faces, rather than in the isolation of the study. Once it was ready, Scott gently collected Ellie off their bed and carried her carefully down the stairs and along the hallway to Ava and Jemima's room. Lisa pulled back the covers and the little girl stirred briefly, before settling back into a peaceful sleep, her eyelids purple with fatigue. Lisa kissed her forehead and retreated to the door. She paused.

Through their window, she had a view out to the street. Most of the homes were in darkness now but, as always, she gave herself a moment to think about what was happening behind those closed doors. Were there parents fighting? Violence? Kids frightened? Maybe going to bed on an empty stomach? There would be all those sorts of terrible things and more; her time in the group home had taught her that.

Leaning on the doorframe, Lisa allowed her body to relax for the first time in what had proven to be a crazy day. In turn, she looked at each one of the three little girls before her. Safe, warm, clean, well-fed and loved. Exactly how it should be.

CHAPTER ELEVEN

There was no way Missy would sleep that night and she had no idea why she was bothering to try. She kicked off the cheap, scratchy sheets and flicked on the bedside lamp, casting the sheets into a tone best described as 'aged-yellow'. The hotel was a complete dive, but they took cash and when Missy said she had no identification the manager hadn't batted an eyelid.

Since her check-in, there'd been a procession of trucks roaring in and out of the car park, headlights flashing into Missy's room and footsteps that sounded a lot like stilettos. Thank goodness she hadn't brought Ellie here. It was no place for a child.

She padded into the bathroom for a glass of water. At the tap, she gripped the sides of the basin and leant in. She'd never spent a night away from Ellie. Never spent more than a few hours away from her, except for work. Missy angled her head one way, then the other. Who was she in this gaping silence? What had she done? Could she still call herself a mother?

She leant out. Her hair was limp and unwashed. So long since it was cut, nearly grazing her hip now. She should cut it. Dye it. That's what people did in her situation, didn't they?

She twisted it up into a knot. Maybe not yet. Her hair was long, but thin. She could hide it under a cap, something she'd need to wear anyway, just to be sure

Emotionally and physically, she was spent. For most of the day, she'd discreetly staked out the Wheeldons', almost sick with fear that the police would turn up at any moment.

They didn't.

There was hope.

Watching from behind the low brick wall of a seemingly vacant home, Missy had watched Lisa leave and then return a short time later with Ellie, her arm slung over the child's shoulders. Missy knew exactly where they'd been. The granny flat would have been the first place she'd go too, if she'd been in Lisa's position. Question was—what would Lisa do next?

Minutes had become hours. Missy watched the clouds and made pictures out of them, something she did with Ellie. She had seen the bloke on the Vespa arrive but didn't catch a look at his face, because of the helmet and the approaching sunset. He'd left pretty quickly as well. Missy presumed he was no one special.

Then nothing. Maybe the letter would be enough? Maybe Lisa would intuitively understand the desperation of the situation? Maybe she would prove to be the loving, wonderful mother that Missy believed her to be? Her plan was to stick close for a couple of days, just to make sure Ellie was safe, and that Lisa Wheeldon had no intention of passing her into the hands of the authorities.

Missy had trusted the police, once. She'd believed their promises. Taken them at their word and put her life in their hands, confident in their powers to keep her and Ellie safe. After all, they were the people that caught the crooks and stood up for justice. They were the people you were told to trust, as if the uniform gave them special powers.

But they were just human beings. She knew that now. Trusting them had made her and Ellie vulnerable. There were good ones and bad ones—just as there were in all walks of life. Policing was, after all, a job. It wasn't, necessarily, who you were. It wasn't even necessarily for life. Not like being a mother. That's why Missy had chosen Lisa. A loving mother would do more to protect a child than the police ever would.

At least, that's what she hoped.

CHAPTER TWELVE

Jamie stood before her wardrobe and surveyed the array of clothes before her. Normally, she loved the process of getting ready and going to work. Even on a Monday. There wasn't a part of it she didn't enjoy. From deciding which combination of skirt and heels to wear, to catching the bus with everyone smelling of perfume and expensive aftershave, to getting a coffee and buttery raisin toast from her favourite barista downstairs, to then seeing Benny's smiling but slightly nervous face already at his desk, ready to talk her through the day, share any office gossip he'd heard, or be a welcome listener for any woes that Jamie cared to dump on his shoulders.

But today she was nervous and tired, and casting an eye over her wardrobe she tried to suppress a huge yawn. She'd had a terrible night's sleep, with her thoughts tumbling between Ellie and the police, and her upcoming wedding to

Jared. Six weeks to organise a wedding! Could she really do it? In the end, she'd slept fitfully and dreamt of the police interrupting the wedding mid-vows, to snatch Ellie, acting as flower girl, from her side.

Quickly, Jamie settled on her new black Chanel, fit-and-flare mini, matched with a wine-coloured, pussy-bow blouse from a high street chain (head-to-toe designer was *so* nineties) which was just see-through enough to allow for a tiny peek at the black lace bra beneath. She capped it off with her scariest Jimmy Choos—black, shiny, and pointier than a dagger—murder to walk in, but sexy as hell.

Jared wolf-whistled as she made her entrance into the kitchen. 'Big meeting on today, babe?'

'Oh, nothing too special.' She offered her cheek for him to kiss so she wouldn't smudge her red lipstick. She wouldn't mention Ellie, or the wedding. Last night, Jared had been acting funny about both.

Jared dumped the bowl in the sink and started tying his tie.

Pointedly, Jamie took the bowl, put it in the dishwasher, slammed it shut and told herself to breathe. It was just a bowl, after all. She needed to let it go. If he hadn't changed his ways after her asking him three thousand times to put his damn bowl in the dishwasher, he wasn't going to. And what did it matter? It was just a bowl.

Her phone bleeped. A text from Lise.

I'm going crazy. Can't stop thinking about Ellie's mum! Are we doing the right thing?

Jamie tapped back. *Yes. Definitely. Who knows what would happen to her if you went to the police …*

Poor Lise. What a weird experience! That poor little girl, to be abandoned by her own mother, and she seemed such a lovely kid. But the note. It was odd. Was there a chance that in doing the right thing by Ellie, Lisa was putting her own family in danger?

'It's very weird,' said Jamie, not realising she'd spoken out loud.

'What's weird?' said Jared.

Jamie paused. Should she level with him? Share her concerns? Yes, he'd seemed a bit strange about it all last night, but if they were taking their relationship to the next level, maybe it was time she started confiding in him. *Really* confiding in him.

She took a deep breath. 'That whole thing last night with little Ellie. I mean, why would a mother do such a thing?'

Jared straightened his tie and checked his watch. 'Babe, I'm running late as it is.'

Why are you acting so strange about all of this?

'See you tonight.' He kissed her so quickly that it was more like a lip-swipe, and then he was gone, leaving only the smell of his aftershave to keep Jamie company. She hated how he did that—how he got out of bed after her, showered after her, ate his breakfast after her, yet managed to leave the house first. It wasn't fair. When Jared lived on his own, he was a model of domestic godliness. So when they moved in together and he suggested that the last person to leave the house should ensure its tidiness, she readily agreed, never for a minute thinking that Jared would always be first to go. Unlike her, he was terrible at going to work. Moaned about it. Put the alarm on to snooze at least twice. Never ironed his shirt till the last minute, yet he still managed to scoot away first.

Fuming, Jamie quickly wiped down the bench where Jared had left splodges of milk and checked the bathroom where she knew he wouldn't have bothered to hang up his towel. She wasn't dressed for this, she thought, careful not to get her Jimmy Choos wet in the damp bathroom. It was like having a child. Poor Lise. Having to do this all day, every day.

If I get pregnant straight away, maybe I can have the baby in Dubai and employ maids and nannies to help me out.

Yes! It would be perfect.

With a spring in her stiletto steps, Jamie swept out the door, leaving behind a cloud of Jiff, and dreaming about the great, big diamonds she would lust after in her lunch break. Engagement ring shopping would surely take her mind off things.

Jamie flung her handbag onto the desk and gratefully accepted the toast and coffee being offered to her.

'Benny, you're a lifesaver.' She planted a big, lipsticky kiss on his unsuspecting cheek, causing it to flush nearly as red as the lippie. Secretly, she enjoyed unnerving the poor man. He was so cute when he blushed. He was usually so collected. So together. So neat. It was fun to see him brought a little undone at the seams. 'Oops. I've lipsticked you. Let me get a tissue.' He couldn't meet her eyes as she held his chin in one hand and dabbed at his cheek with the other. Gosh his aftershave smelled good. Gucci, at a guess. They always made the best. Deep and woody. She closed her eyes for a millisecond and inhaled. When she opened them, Ben was staring and Jamie felt something twinge in her groin. His eyes were like little pots of hot chocolate, deep and creamy brown. His boyfriend, whoever it was, was a lucky man. Not that Jamie actually knew for sure that he was gay; Ben was too discreet about his personal life, but she just assumed. After all, he was so neat, so sensitive, and he tended to wear pink shirts a lot. Yes, it was a superficial judgement, but they *did* work in PR after all, where superficial appearances and actuality were interchangeable. A company *was* its image.

She stopped dabbing. 'Right, that's it then. All clean.' Ben was staring at her oddly; maybe she'd gone too far? Jamie broke the moment by briskly settling into her chair and drawing it into the desk.

'Righto. What mess do we have to deal with today?' She fired up the computer and brought up a very blank looking diary on the screen. 'Why is it empty?'

'Hang on a sec.' Leaning over her, Ben swept and clicked her mouse. 'Here it is,' he murmured, tickling her ear.

'Thank you,' said Jamie curtly, as another twinge went off. 'Now, can you please sit down? I can't talk properly if you're behind me.'

'Sorry.' Ben hurried round to the other side.

'No, I'm sorry.' Jamie sighed. 'I had quite the weekend. Kind of a good news-bad news type weekend.'

'What happened?'

'The bad or the good.'

'Start with the bad.'

She filled him in on Ava's party, and Ellie, the little lost girl. As she described her, Ben's frown deepened.

'That poor kid. And your poor sister, and you too,' Ben added. 'Traumatising for all of you, really, given what you went through with your own folks.'

'Exactly,' Jamie agreed. 'I mean, obviously I think about Mum and Dad all the time, and the group home was pretty awful, but I don't know, I think Lise shielded me from so much of it. She made it bearable, and she was always born to parent, which helped.'

'Maybe the other mother knew that.' Ben had picked up a pencil and was now chewing on it thoughtfully.

'How? Lisa doesn't even know this woman, so how could she know anything about Lisa?'

'I don't know.' Ben paused. 'What about the good news?' he prompted. 'You said you had bad news *and* good news.'

'Oh, yes, right.' Jamie took her eyes off the screen and felt a flutter of nerves. *Why am I so worried? It's just Ben, after all!*

She exhaled. 'I'm engaged.'

'To Jared?'

'That's what my sister said!'

'It's just,' Ben waited a beat. 'You've always said he wasn't really the marrying kind.'

'That's what all women say when they're waiting to be asked.' Didn't Ben know anything?

'Well, congratulations then. He's a very lucky guy …' Ben trailed off as Jamie waved away the compliment and started looking through her appointments.

'Nine am, 9 am,' she murmured to herself, trying to find the right spot.

'You're happy, right?' Ben leant in closer and seemed to hold his breath.

'Yes, yes. Of course. Ecstatic. Who wouldn't be?'

'So when's the big day?'

'Early April.'

'Seriously?' Ben's eyes widened. 'What's the rush?'

Jamie explained Jared's job promotion and the move to Dubai.

'So you're quitting work as well?' Ben slumped in the chair, as if he'd been punched.

Jamie leant in, a finger to her mouth in the shushing position. 'Please keep it to yourself,' she whispered. 'Angel will make my life hell if she knows I'm leaving.'

Ben nodded slowly and looked out the window. 'I don't want you to go.'

Jamie looked at him. The poor man. She'd just downloaded a whole lot of trauma onto his shoulders, not thinking how heavy the burden would be. He was a sensitive soul. He took things to heart. She should have thought about that before she opened her mouth. Of course he would be a little worried. After all, her move to Dubai would mean a new boss for him. A new boss who might not want Ben as an assistant.

'Don't worry, Benny. I'll put in an extra-special good word for you when I submit my resignation,' she said quietly. 'This might be good for you. It might mean a promotion.'

'It's not that—'

'Uh-uh,' Jamie interrupted, shaking her head and putting her finger to her lips as a tornado of grey curls and hi-tops spun its way towards them.

'My little minions,' Angel cried, blowing air-kisses at Ben and Jamie as she stood over the desk. Angel only ever air-kissed, but not for fear of lipsticking other people (she never wore lippie—said it was ageing for a woman of 'certain years') but because of the hygiene. The woman never got sick and put her rude good health down to a strict regimen of air-kissing, fish oil and an unhealthy addiction to sanitising gel. Once, in the wake of an office-decimating cold virus, Angel had called a staff meeting to instruct them in the correct use of the stuff: *You're all too stingy. Use with abandon, my darlings. Lather it on, my sweets. Your immune system will thank you for it!* Mid-lather, Jamie had facetiously suggested Angel buy shares in the product, which in typical Angel-style, had spun off a totally new business idea—ecologically sound, sweet-smelling, alcohol-free hand sanitiser.

The product was in development. Jamie would manage the launch when it was ready.

I want this gel in every woman's handbag. I want it to be bigger than perfume! No pressure, then.

As Jamie slapped her cheek in acceptance of Angel's blown air-kiss, a happy thought crossed her mind. *I won't have to launch the sanitiser! I won't be here.* Dubai was sounding better and better all the time.

'Any news, my sweets? Hmm? Hmm?' she said expectantly, looking from Jamie to Ben. You had to hand it to her. Angel was like a bloodhound when it came to gossip, sniffing it out wherever she went. Come to think of it, she did have a habit of walking around with her chin up and nose in the air. Jamie had put that down to Angel's refusal to be distracted, but maybe it was about keeping her nose to the wind.

Ben cleared his throat. 'I think Jamie has something to tell you.' He looked at her, challenging.

I'm too scared to tell her I'm leaving. Jamie looked at Ben in alarm. *I thought you were my friend.*

'Well, my little head minion,' said Angel, checking her watch. 'Out with it. We haven't got all day.'

'Well, I'm …' *Moving to Dubai. Moving to Dubai. Just say it. Rip that bandaid off in one hit.*

'Getting married,' Ben supplied with a rueful smile.

Getting married. Of course. Why do I keep forgetting that part?

'What? To Jared?' asked Angel, sounding genuinely confused.

'Of course, Jared. Why does everyone say that?'

'Men like Jared do not marry,' declared Angel, resting two hands on Jamie's desk and leaning over it as if issuing a business directive.

'Well, he wants to marry *me*.' Jamie stared back at the screen. Why couldn't anyone believe that Jared wanted to marry her? Was it because he was too good-looking for her? Too successful? In the air above her head, she felt Angel and Ben exchange glances.

'*If* Jared was going to marry anyone, of course it would be you, darling. You're gorgeous.' Angel patted the air above her shoulder. 'Let's have a little office shindig this afternoon to celebrate. Benny'll organise the champers, won't you, my sweet?' She gave him a dazzling smile and flounced off towards the hallway.

'Angel,' Jamie called after her. 'There's just one more thing.'

'More?' She stopped at the doorway. 'That sounds ominous.'

'Ben, would you excuse us for a minute?'

Giving her a grateful smile, Ben fled the room and Jamie closed the door behind him.

'Would you like to take a seat, Angel?' Jamie pulled out a chair.

'No, I would not. You know I detest sitting,' said Angel, folding her arms.

Jamie silently rebuked herself. Of course Angel would stand. The woman had a treadmill in her office and it wasn't unusual for her to conduct entire meetings from it, convinced that 'computers will kill us all, one day'. At first, Jamie had found it distracting, trying to talk serious business over the sounds of a whirring machine and a woman huffing and puffing. But after a while it became second nature. What Jamie had come to learn was that Angel only ever made sense when she was talking business. In most areas of her life, exercise included, she was quite nuts. But her business acumen was undeniable. While she couldn't sustain a long-term personal relationship to save herself, she excelled at client relationships and had an uncanny knack of keeping her customers in a state of ecstatic bliss. The money was pouring in.

Jamie leant against her desk. Nutty or not, her boss deserved the full truth. 'Well, Angel, the thing is ...' She paused. 'Jared has secured a job promotion in Dubai and he moves there in six weeks.'

'Well, good on Jared. But I have to say it doesn't sound like the ideal way to start a marriage. Him overseas and you here.'

Trust Angel to assume I couldn't possibly be leaving.

'The thing is, Angel—'

'Will you please stop saying "the thing is".' Angel put her hands on her hips. 'Just say the thing.'

'I'm moving to Dubai with Jared.' Jamie took a breath. 'I'm leaving Spin.'

Angel's eyes narrowed. 'No you're not,' she said in a steely voice.

'I'm afraid I am.'

'You can't.'

'Look, I really am very sorry, Angel. You have been wonderful and I appreciate all the opportunities—' Jamie stopped. Angel had flopped into the chair. 'Are you all right?'

'No,' she said in a puzzled voice, as if not quite believing she had actually sat down. 'I'm not all right. I was going to retire and let you run the business. Make you Executive Director and sign over a 20 per cent equity stake. The works.' She splayed her hands. 'But now you want to leave me.'

'Angel, why didn't you tell me what you were planning?' Jamie was shocked. Angel was so devoted to Spin and she was the youngest 62-year-old Jamie had ever met. Retirement simply wasn't a word she'd ever associated with her.

'Why didn't you tell me what *you* were planning?' said Angel in an accusatory tone.

'Jared only told me on the weekend.'

Angel grunted, considered the neon orange lacquer on her fingernails, then fixed Jamie with her gaze. 'So what are you going to do over there in Dubai?'

'I was thinking of starting my own consultancy.'

Angel snorted. 'You don't know the first thing about that place.'

'I can learn.' Jamie stuck out her chin. She could handle Angel's disappointment, but not her insults.

Angel leant forward. 'But think about it, Jamie darling. I'm giving you your dream. The top job at Sydney's best PR agency. I thought we'd moved on from the days where women had to throw away their careers for a man. I mean, aren't you even going to *think* about it?'

This was the closest to begging that Jamie had ever seen Angel come. What she was offering *was* a dream come true. She'd worked so hard and given so much of herself, was she really going to throw it all away simply because Jared had been given a job that might last only one year, two at most?

Angel was still staring at her and Jamie couldn't meet her gaze. 'I can see you're thinking about it.'

'I am tempted,' admitted Jamie. 'It's a very generous offer.'

'I tell you what.' Angel placed her hands on the armrests. 'I'll give you one week to come up with two business plans. One for this place. And one for your new business in Dubai. You present them to me and I'll give you my honest opinion about which one I think you should pursue. And I think you know that if nothing else, I am always honest.'

Jamie looked out the window. As eccentric as Angel was, she did make sense when it came to business-related matters. The idea was a good one. After all, it was no good running off to Dubai without a proper plan in place. This way, she'd get to assess the true viability of the idea, while also keeping alive the possibility of taking over at Spin.

'All right, Angel, we have a deal.'

At Jamie's outstretched hand, Angel sniffed and rose from the seat. 'Darling, you know I never shake unless I absolutely have to.' She shuddered. 'All those germs.' And out she swept from Jamie's office.

CHAPTER THIRTEEN

Ava and Lisa approached the front gate to St John's and Lisa reached for her daughter's hand.

'You know, darling, it's all right to feel a little nervous on a Monday, after the weekend and all.' She squeezed Ava's fingers, enjoying the softness of her little fingers.

'I'm fine, Mummy.'

Wish I could say the same.

Lisa had to talk to Principal Valentic and while she wasn't looking forward to it, she knew the conversation was necessary. School was the only way Ellie's mother could have found out about the party. Maybe the principal could shed light on how it might have happened? She also needed to raise the idea of enrolling Ellie into the school, temporarily. Her mission was to make the little girl's life as normal and stable as possible and to Lisa's great relief, it had started well, with Ellie waking happily and eating a tonne of Weet-Bix for breakfast. She was even quite happy to stay and play with Jems and Scott while Lisa dropped Ava up to school.

Ava dropped her mother's hand. 'You're all sweaty, Mummy.' She wiped it on her uniform. 'Yuck.'

'Sorry, darling.'

They walked side by side, Lisa's hand aching with emptiness and her stomach like a cement mixer of nerves, rolling over and over.

They were inside the school grounds now, surrounded by arrivals and drop-offs. 'Hey, Sienna!' Ava charged off in the direction of another little girl whose face had lit up with recognition when she saw Ava's.

'Wait, you haven't said goodbye. And you forgot this,' Lisa called out and held up Ava's backpack.

But her daughter had already melted into the sea of oversized royal blue hats, checked uniforms and black leather shoes.

Lisa located Ava's locker—the one with the ladybird sticker—deposited the bag and returned to the playground. There weren't many parents around now. Most had retreated back to their cars or to the front gate where a regular group that Lisa had dubbed 'the exercisers' congregated every morning, talking in furiously hushed voices before bouncing off, presumably to the gym. The fitness levels of the St John's mothers were really quite extraordinary. By Lisa's estimate, approximately 90 per cent of them were involved in some kind of daily exercise routine. Why else would they turn up to every pick-up and drop-off in a uniform of leggings, natty vests, high ponytails and sleek runners?

She suspected Principal Valentic did not entirely approve of such casual attire. There she was, near the monkey bars, with fishnet stockings poking out from beneath her fluoro-yellow high-vis vest. The headmistress was unlike any school principal Lisa had ever met. For a start, she wore fishnet stockings on a regular basis, not in a tarty way but in a very grown-up, chic sort of way. She wouldn't have been out of place in Jamie's office, but here in the schoolyard she was like a Thai orchid in a field of carnations. Almost sculptural.

Lisa approached slowly. 'Ah, Principal Valentic?'

'Call me Jane,' boomed the exotic flower, turning on her stiletto to face Lisa. 'Who are you?'

Lisa swallowed. Her throat was suddenly dry. 'I'm Lisa Wheeldon, mother of Ava Wheeldon in KV.'

The principal took a step closer. 'Talk to me,' she demanded.

'Well, um, everything's fine with Ava. She's very happy and has made some lovely little friends—'

'Excellent, excellent,' Principal Valentic cut in. 'I think you'll find the parents of St John's generally have a very high level of satisfaction, particularly with our kindergarten program.'

'Yes, yes. It's all great.' Lisa paused.

'Yes?' intoned the glamorous giraffe.

'It's just that … something a little strange happened at Ava's party over the weekend and I thought you could possibly help me to figure out how it occurred.'

From there, Lisa went into her rehearsed speech about the party and the additional child (without mentioning Ellie by name) and wondered aloud how someone might have managed to get a copy of the invitation when they had only been distributed within the school grounds.

'So, I guess I'm just wondering if it's possible that some-one, you know, took an invitation from one of the children's bags, or—'

'A security breach?' Principal Valentic folded her arms. 'Not possible. Our front gates are locked every morning at 9 am, and they do not reopen until 3 pm.'

Lisa shifted weight, nervously. 'Well, is it possible that there was a student who left earlier in the term? Like, maybe the child came for the first couple of weeks, got the invita-tion, and then left the school, but came to the party anyway?'

'No, Mrs Wheeldon. It is not possible. The year began with thirty-two students in kindergarten and that's how it has remained. How many children were invited to this gathering?'

'Uh … The entire class. All thirty-two.'

'Thirty-two invitees? I mean, really!' she huffed. 'A little over the top, don't you think, Mrs Wheeldon? Here at St John's, we pride ourselves on our three core values of sim-plicity, modesty, and—' The principal's face went blank, but the slip in the mask was temporary. 'And those values inform all that we do,' she said firmly.

'I was just following the school's inclusive party policy,' Lisa said meekly.

'Yes, well, that policy is currently under review.' Principal Valentic shifted her gaze to a melee of four boys, scrabbling on the ground. 'Cooper O'Connor,' she barked, the scrum dissolving as a little crew of scraped knees and untucked shirts picked themselves up dejectedly from the artificial grass. 'In my office at recess. And tuck those shirts in.'

The boys cowered next to Lisa, who felt like giving them all a hug. Thankfully, the bell started to chime and the playground mayhem reached a new pitch as children raced from all directions to find their spot in the line-up.

Lisa took another breath. She'd also practised this part with Scott, mostly because it involved telling a lie. 'Uh, Principal Valentic. Just one more thing. I have a friend who's had to go … go away to … um … look after her … ah … her sick mum.'

'What's wrong with her?'

'With who?'

'Your friend's mother.' A flicker of irritation crossed the principal's face.

Oh bugger.

She and Scott hadn't thought to think up a particular *type* of illness. Lisa's eyes dropped to the principal's chest, drawn to the merest hint of a neon pink bra poking cheekily from beneath her blouse.

'Oh … ah … she, um, has cancer. Breast cancer.'

The principal met Lisa's gaze, her eyes softer. 'I had an aunt who died of breast cancer.'

'I'm so sorry. That's terrible for you.' Lisa's left eye start to twitch. She hated lying.

'Olivia Bryant! Step away from that skipping rope. You nearly took an eye out.' The principal was back to business mode, eyes roving like heat-seeking radar over the chaos of the playground. 'Tell me, Mrs Wheeldon, what can we do to help?'

'Well, I'm looking after her child, a six-year-old, Ellie, turning seven in September, and I was wondering if she could attend St John's for the next six weeks or so.'

'A temporary enrolment? We've had a few of those before. Parents on secondment, that sort of thing.' The principal held up a hand. 'See the office. Fill out the forms. Seven in September did you say? Right, then she can go into Year One where we do have a couple of spaces. She can begin on Wednesday at the athletics carnival.'

'Oh, gosh, thank you, I didn't think—'

But the principal was already striding away. 'Generosity!' she called over her shoulder. 'That's the other core value at St John's. We help those in need.'

Lisa left the playground quickly, handbag clutched to her chest in a defensive gesture against the children swarming about her like clouds of midges. She had given up on the idea of giving Ava a proper goodbye involving a hug and kiss. If Lisa escaped the playground with her life, she would be happy. At the admin office, she collected the enrolment forms and at the front gate, she exhaled, aware that she'd been holding her breath since the abrupt end to her conversation with Principal Valentic. What a scarily confident woman! No wonder the school did so well academically. The woman ruled with an iron fist. A child dare not do badly.

Lisa leant against the school gate, exhausted. She'd been sure Principal Valentic held the key to discovering the truth about Ellie, but their conversation had left her just as confused as before, and the principal now seemed to have her pinned as a troublemaker. At least she'd agreed to let Ellie attend the school. Thank goodness for the school's core values!

The usual crowd of exercisers was still there and the huddle tightened as Lisa approached.

'That's the one I was telling you about,' one of them whispered, before she felt a tap on the shoulder.

'Lisa, I was hoping to catch you,' cried Heather, flicking her ponytail. Lisa hadn't noticed her in the group, but the scrum was so tight and everyone looked so identical it wasn't surprising. 'What an exciting weekend. Tell me, whatever happened to the poor little abandoned girl at the party?'

Lisa felt the other exercisers edging closer, ears positively flapping. Oh god. Now she was the talk of the entire school.

'Well, she's still with us.'

'Still with you? Oh, how traumatic!' At that point, the exercisers moved in en masse, murmuring consolingly and surrounding Lisa in what she presumed to be a supportive gesture but, from the outside, might also have been mistaken for a murder of crows descending on a carcass.

'You must join us for coffee.' Heather clutched Lisa's arm.

'But aren't you all off to the gym?'

'No, no, no,' she laughed gaily. 'We hate gyms. Can't stand them.'

'For a walk, then? Or a jog?'

'Hon, I haven't exercised since the nineties. We just wear this stuff cause it's comfy.'

The other women giggled. 'Seriously,' said one of them. Lisa thought her name was possibly Kimberly. 'You should get some. They're the most gorgeously comfortable things you'll ever wear.'

But tracksuits are comfy. Why not them?

'I'm not quite sure they're me,' Lisa muttered.

'Of course they are.' Heather linked her arm through Lisa's. 'Now we're going to take you for the best coffee in the suburb. You're free? No little one around?' Heather stopped and looked down and around as if Jemima might appear around their ankles at any minute.

'She's home with Scott. Let me just check with him that it's okay for me to take a bit longer.'

It's my chance to ask them for help! Maybe discover a clue as to who this Missy Jones could be …

Lisa pulled out her phone as Heather bounced off down the street.

'I'll go ahead and save us a seat.'

Lisa knew the café. She passed it every day on her way to the school but she'd never thought to go inside. Speakeasy featured a graffitied exterior with old gin crates out the front that served as both stools and tables. At first, Lisa had assumed it to be a bar, until one day she took a closer look at the menu and discovered the place was unlicensed. No alcohol at all.

Oh, of course! Irony.

Speakeasy was the kind of place that served its food on planks of wood, rather than proper plates. So impractical for things such as poached eggs which tended to run like yellow rivers, forcing one to eat quickly before the inevitable spill. Plates and their practical 'lips' were far too underrated these days, in Lisa's view.

On the way down to Speakeasy, the exercisers talked companionably with her about the amazing coffee they served. Single origin. Sourced from Lake Kivu in Rwanda. Had Lisa heard of it?

Lisa hadn't—her knowledge of emerging coffee-growing regions was not what it could have been—but she was happy to try!

Within thirty seconds of arriving at the café, Lisa understood it wasn't just the coffee that attracted the women of St John's.

'The usual, ladies?' The barista had a curled, 1920s moustache, with Brylcreemed hair and khaki-green eyes. It didn't take much to imagine him in a tuxedo, and the visual was extremely pleasing. Perhaps the modern term might have been 'hipster', but in Lisa-language he was a dreamboat. A modern-day matinee idol.

'I see we have a new member.' The barista winked at Lisa. 'What will it be, hon?'

'A cappuccino, please,' she said with more confidence than she felt.

'Almond? Rice? Cashew?'

'Uh … just the normal. From a cow.'

The barista smiled, and the lines around his eyes crinkled in a way that made Lisa feel a little breathless. 'And are we eating this morning?'

The menu. Right. She tore her eyes from the gorgeous man before her and quickly scanned the clipboard, feeling her confidence return as she noted the familiar rollcall of eggs, smashed avocado and bircher muesli. 'Just some banana bread, thanks.'

She felt the table collectively inhale. Was banana bread the wrong thing to order?

'Good on you,' whispered the lady on her left, distinguishable for being the only other one at the table with brown hair. 'No one ever orders food.'

Never ate at a café? Never exercised in their gym gear? Lisa clearly didn't understand these women but she wanted to like them and she wanted them to like her. After all, between Ava and Jemima she would be spending the next nine years of her life at St John's.

Heather leant forward and cut in above the chatter. 'So, Lisa, the girls are dying to hear about the party.'

'Oh, yes, right … well …' she stammered.

'Oh, don't be shy, Lisa,' Heather cajoled. 'Maybe they can help?'

Lisa took in the six sets of eyes all trained on her. 'All right. Well, it's quite simple really. My daughter had a party on the weekend, and a little girl turned up who, it seems, hadn't actually been invited.'

'No, no, no. That's only the half of it.' Heather wrung her hands. 'Tell them about the note.'

Reluctantly, Lisa summarised the contents of the letter, emphasising the fact that Ellie's mum sounded very much like a mother who adored her child but had found herself in a difficult situation.

'See!' said Heather to the rest of the group.

'Ugh! That's dreadful,' said the brown-haired lady.

'It doesn't make sense.' Kimberly frowned into her coffee before raising her gaze to meet Lisa's. 'You need to talk us through it again. Everything you know. One step at a time. Tell me like I'm a five-year-old.'

'Kimberly's a lawyer at one of the top firms in Sydney,' explained Heather. 'Part-time, because of her two daughters— Xanthe in kindy. Madison in Year Five.'

'Oh, yes. Ava loves Xanthe. She was there yesterday, right? I'm sorry we didn't get a chance to chat. I was a little … er … busy,' said Lisa apologetically.

'My husband did the drop-off,' said Kimberly. 'He said it was a madhouse but he didn't say anything about a gate-crasher. That's appalling.'

Lisa flinched. 'I wouldn't call her ...' She began again. 'I don't think there's much more I can tell you.' She took a weary sip of the coffee which, despite its exotic provenance, didn't even taste very nice to her admittedly-naïve-but-usually-receptive tastebuds.

'Just one more time,' said Heather, folding her arms on the table and leaning forward eagerly. 'Step by step.'

She looked at the expectant faces around her. These women were her best shot. Maybe one of them knew this Missy Jones?

Resolved that the exercisers were motivated more by charity than voyeurism, Lisa went through her disastrous day minute by minute, from the accidental sleep-in to the dropped cake, the piñata debacle, the visit to Ellie's house and, finally, their decision to keep Ellie at home, and keep the authorities out of it, at least for the moment.

'Something happened to my sister and I ... when we were teenagers.' The women leant in. 'We were orphaned.' A collective intake of breath. Hands to chests. 'And we had to go into care for a little while, and it was ... well, it wasn't too bad for us but we heard some awful stories from the other kids, about foster care. I can't let that happen to Ellie.'

Five out of the six heads nodded with understanding. Only the lawyer—Kimberly was it?—was shaking hers in disapproval.

'You really should call the police,' she admonished. 'I know I would if it was my family under threat.'

'Under threat?' enquired Lisa.

'This woman invaded your family! Lord knows what else she knows about you—or what she'll do next.'

Suddenly, all the ponytails were nodding gravely and the gin crate beneath Lisa started to feel unsteady. Maybe they were right? Maybe her family was under threat? Her precious family who meant the world to her. Perhaps Missy would prove to be some kind of insidious and destabilising presence in their lives. How had she not realised that everything she cherished was at stake? A stranger had invaded their lives, via a child, no less! Certainly, it seemed no real harm had been done. Not yet, unless of course you counted poor darling Ellie. But who knew what could happen next? The women were right. She needed to do something. Quickly.

'You need to help me,' she said weakly, sweat erupting from her forehead. Her fingers were clammy. The gin box creaked and swayed.

'But how?' enquired Heather.

'I don't know,' whispered Lisa.

There had to be something, anything! Who else could have known about the party? A thought leapt into her head and Lisa put the coffee down before she wobbled a little to stand from the crate.

'Excuse me, ladies, but I've just thought of something I need to do.' Lisa grabbed her handbag and set off down the street without waiting for their goodbyes.

'But what about your banana bread?' called one of them after her.

'You eat it!' she called back.

But she knew from the cackles behind her, they wouldn't.

CHAPTER FOURTEEN

Lisa pulled down her cap. She didn't usually wear hats as her neck was a bit short and they made her look like a mushroom. But for this particular mission, she did not want to be recognised by anyone and if she needed to look like a vegetable to ensure her anonymity, that's what she would do.

'Can I help you?'

Lisa jumped at the long face standing over her. She'd been in this store at least twenty times before and no one had ever approached to offer assistance.

'No, I'm fine,' she stammered. 'Just browsing, thanks.'

'Let me know if I can help.'

You can tell me who Ellie Jones is, thought Lisa as the man in the blue polo shirt sauntered away to frighten some other poor unsuspecting customer. This place was renowned for its lack of customer service. Lisa only shopped there because of the array of home-office supplies that promised order and organisation. Plus, it was a cheap source of craft supplies for the girls and an excellent rainy-day time-waster. The girls could spend hours trawling its aisles of stickers, textas and paper. It also had the added bonus of offering a printing service for photos and invitations.

Lisa clutched the hurried list she'd made in the car after the coffee at Speakeasy. She was supposed to be reconciling bank statements for Suzie the seamstress, one of her sweetest clients, but her mind was too full of what the school mums had said about Ellie's mother.

A woman capable of abandoning her own child might yet be capable of much, much, more.

Lisa had to find her.

Always methodical, she'd started with a list of all the people who'd known about Ava's party. There was, of course, all the children from Ava's class. How was she going to check with all thirty-two? Make each person produce their invitation? They'd probably chucked them into the recycling by now. Then again, maybe Missy had worked at the school? As secure as Principal Valentic made it out to be, there had to be any number of comings and goings.

She wrote it out in large letters—SCHOOL—and circled it. The options out of this one word were endless and overwhelming. St John's alone was a whole world of possibilities. She shook her head. What was that saying about eating an elephant? You did it one bite at a time. School was like eating the entire elephant torso in one hit. There had to be a smaller chunk. A tail, for instance.

Who else knew about the party?

She bit the pencil. There was that party entertainer she'd emailed, Magic Paul, who'd come highly recommended from a mother's group friend. But Magic Paul and his rabbit Booboo were already booked for the day for another child's party. Could he be the link?

Hmmm … unlikely. I never even gave him our address or the time.

She scratched Magic Paul off the list, along with the butcher who supplied the hotdogs and the balloon lady who, while she worked in the party shop, was a cranky woman with very little time for children which made her choice of occupation very odd indeed. Once, when Ava had gone particularly feral among the fairy dresses and refused to take off the wings unless she got a chocolate, the woman had sighed at Lisa and declared that working in a party shop was a better contraceptive than any pill you could buy.

No, Missy Jones wasn't masquerading as the party shop lady.

It had to be someone who'd seen the invitation and knew exactly the time and place of the party.

STATIONERY SHOP.

Over that one, she paused.

The stationery shop. Her brain twanged. It was a possibility. Yes, a definite possibility. After all, they'd not only printed the invitations there but they also regularly printed her family photos. Lisa was a conscientious printer of family photos and collator of albums. Where was the romance in gathering around a computer screen to look through old memories? And what happened if someone stole your computer? Or you got a new one? Or the computer died? The concept of relying on digital devices for the preservation of one's life memories was riddled with potential disasters and risks that Lisa was not prepared to take.

Anyway, the print shop was a possibility. Had her mania for printing put her family under threat? Did Ellie's mother work there? Had she spied the invitations and formed her plan around them? With a flicker of hope in her chest, Lisa had turned the key in the ignition and high-tailed it to the shops.

Now, here she was, wandering through the aisles, not exactly sure who or what she was looking for, but confident she would know it when she saw it.

After half an hour of perusing staplers and leafing through empty exercise books, Lisa had narrowed her search down to two suspects. The first was a young woman stacking shelves in the Office Supplies aisle. Deeply tanned with platinum blonde hair, she looked nothing like Ellie, but then again Ava and Jemima were little clones of Scott with their blonde hair and button noses. There was no biological law that said little girls had to look like their mums. The shelf-stacker was a possibility. Lisa sidled up to her and cleared her throat.

'Um … excuse me. I'm looking for … um … I'm looking for …' Lisa looked around in desperation. She was the queen of pre-planned conversation. How could she not have planned this one?

'Yes?' The woman cocked her head. Actually, she was more girl than woman, Lisa could see now. There was a stud in the top of her ear, so tiny it could have been mistaken for a blackhead, and on her neck a dragon tattoo breathed fire beyond the collar of her blue polo.

'Um … I'm looking for …' Lisa spotted a sign for computers. 'A mouse pad! Yes, a mouse pad. Desperately need one for my … you know … mouse, before it gets all scratched and um … un-mousy. They're supposed to roll around all smoothly and easily, you know, scamper about, I suppose. Anyway, my husband had a big clear-out last year and threw out our mouse pad, and I was saying to him this morning I must go to the shop and get a new one … And he said, "Yes, before the desk gets all scratched and"—'

Lisa was aware she was babbling but she couldn't stop herself. It was what she did when she was nervous.

The girl yawned.

'Well, if you could just show me the mouse pads that would be great.' Lisa clasped her clammy hands together.

'Your computer must be pretty ancient.' The girl started walking down the aisle. 'Don't get many people asking for mouse pads. But if we have them, they'll be here.' She gestured to a wall of computer accessories and squinted, running her eye over the shelves. 'Here you go.' She reached up on tip-toes and retrieved a mouse pad from the top shelf.

'Oh, thank you.' Lisa clutched it to her chest. 'That's wonderful.'

'No problem.' The woman started to walk away. She was walking away and Lisa hadn't had a chance to ask her anything!

'Wait!' she shouted and the shop assistant turned. 'Sorry, I didn't mean to scare you but I really did want to thank you again. My husband is very particular about his computer. You know, the children are always getting onto it and using the mouse, and rolling it around roughly, and well, you know how it is with children.'

The woman stared at her blankly.

'Do you happen to have children?' asked Lisa in what she hoped was a casual voice but suspected actually sounded rather high-pitched and shrill.

'I'm nineteen,' the woman said in a bored voice and started walking again. Nineteen! Oh dear. Lisa had always had a poor radar when it came to guessing people's ages and it was seemingly getting worse. This girl couldn't be Ellie's mum.

But she might know who was.

'Wait! Please!' said Lisa in a raised voice.

The girl stopped again and scowled in the way teenagers did when an adult was causing them maximum annoyance. Did they really have to breathe the same air as such morons?

'What about your colleagues? They might understand. That lady on the cash register, for instance. Does she have children?' Lisa had spotted her on the way in. Her colouring was similar to Ellie's—pale skin, dark hair.

'I dunno. Ask her.' And then, the dragon-tattoo girl was gone.

Lisa was trembling. This detective business was hard. Not to mention stressful. She trudged over to the office furniture area and slumped into one of the chairs, which swivelled unexpectedly and caused her to wobble violently. She caught hold of a desk to steady herself, and waited for the dizziness to pass.

This was a nightmare. This was not her. Lisa Wheeldon didn't go around in disguise, snooping into other people's lives and chatting up unsuspecting shop assistants.

Damn this Missy Jones!

Maybe she hadn't meant any harm, but she was already turning Lisa into someone she didn't want to be. This was what the school mums had meant. A person could still cause harm, even if they didn't mean to. Even if you didn't quite know who they were!

Lisa lay her head down on the desk, enjoying the dark and quiet cave she had created with her forearms. She was tired. Oh so tired. Exhausted. She'd barely slept a wink last night. Instead, her mind had endlessly replayed the events of the tumultuous party. An utter disaster from start to finish that she couldn't help but feel was mostly her fault.

Lisa yawned. It was quite pleasant here, surrounded by folders and files and so many products designed to keep life ordered and organised. Such a relief from the chaos! She would take just a moment to have a brief rest before resuming her mission. Just a short break. Very brief …

'Excuse me, ma'am.'

There was a tap on her shoulder and Lisa's head flew up off the desk. Where was she? What time was it? What day?

'Ma'am, are you all right?' The question came from a police officer, one of two standing before her. Both women. A short, older one, and a taller but younger-looking one. Grave-faced and resolute.

'Yes, yes I'm fine … I'm sorry. I just put my head down for a minute and then … and then I was asleep. I don't know what happened,' Lisa spluttered.

'Ma'am, we've had a complaint about you,' said the short, older one, clearly the boss of the pair.

'A complaint? About me?'

'The store phoned us. You've been asleep here for nearly an hour.'

Lisa checked her watch. Nearly 11 am! 'Oh, goodness. I've got to go.' Scott had clients at twelve, which meant she needed to get back to Ellie and Jems. Lisa leapt up and wobbled on her feet as the blood rushed to her head.

The younger one put her hand out. 'Have you been drinking? Or taken something?'

'No, no, of course not! I mean, I had a coffee after school drop-off, but that's it. Nothing else, I promise.'

'Could you please remove your hat and sunglasses.'

Lisa meekly obeyed.

'What's your name?' The shorter of the two policewomen took out a notebook.

'Lisa Wheeldon. W-H-E-E-L-D-O-N.'

The police officer wrote it down and snapped the notebook shut. 'So, Ms Wheeldon—'

'It's Mrs, actually,' Lisa interrupted.

'All right, Mrs Wheeldon,' said the police officer, emphasising the *Mrs* in a way that showed Lisa she wasn't used to being interrupted. 'What are you doing here then? The shop assistant said you were going on about a mouse or something.'

'Oh, yes! I'm so sorry,' she said in her most conciliatory tone. 'I really was just looking for a mouse pad, then I sat down, and I fell asleep. That's the honest truth. I've had a crazy couple of days,' she sighed. 'I think it all just caught up with me.'

'Everything all right at home?' The older officer raised an eyebrow.

An image of the note from Ellie's mother jumped into Lisa's mind.

Please do not call the police.

'Yes,' she said in a bright tone. 'Just life with two little girls. A husband who insists on having mouse pads. You know how it is.'

The officers exchanged glances. 'Mrs Wheeldon, is there something you're not telling us? If there's a problem at home, there are ways we can help. Put you in touch with domestic violence services, for instance. Or we can talk to your husband, if you think it might help,' said the older of the pair.

'Oh god, no. Please. You've got it all wrong.' Lisa's heart hammered. 'Really, it's nothing. I'm fine. My husband's the loveliest man. He'd never hurt a fly. He's a podiatrist.'

'Mrs Wheeldon, I've been in this job long enough to know that it takes all types. Even podiatrists.'

'No, honestly. My husband is the kindest. He watches YouTube video tutorials on French-braiding so he can do our daughters' hair! He gives me flowers every Friday. He adores us. You're really barking up the wrong tree.'

The policewoman nodded. 'All right then, Mrs Wheeldon. If you're certain we can't help, then you need to move along.'

'Yes, of course I will. Thank you!'

But I haven't ruled out all my suspects yet! The cashier!

The police officer nodded approvingly. Then, Lisa had a brainwave. 'But I just need to buy a roll of that sticky bookcovering stuff. My daughter's just started school and—'

'You mean contact paper?'

'Yes. That's it!'

'Aisle two.' The police officer gave her a tight smile. 'I have two children myself.'

'Right, of course. You know all about it then.' Lisa kept up the chit-chat as the officer led her directly to the right spot, and she was still at her elbow as it came time to pay. Lisa made sure she got in the queue for the lady cashier, the one she'd spotted earlier. Perhaps there'd be some clue. A photo at the cash register. A wedding ring. Anything to hint as to a connection with Ellie.

Lisa handed over the contact paper.

'That'll be $4.95 thanks.' The cashier put the roll of contact into a plastic bag.

'Oh, don't worry about a bag, I'm happy to carry it.'

The cashier handed it back and Lisa gave her a ten-dollar note. The younger police officer was back and talking quietly to the older officer, who'd finally moved away from Lisa's side.

'Beautiful day, isn't it?' said Lisa as the cashier rang through the sale.

'Yes.'

'A lovely day for the park, actually. I might take my daughters there after school. What about you? Do you have children?'

'No.'

'Oh, just as well ... sensible really when you consider how much work they are,' chirped Lisa.

The woman's face reddened. 'I ... can't ... have ...' She choked over the words and a sob entered her voice.

'Oh, gosh. I didn't realise. Oh, I'm so sorry.' Lisa clapped a hand over her mouth, as the older officer returned to her side and gave her a look that said *Look at what you've done.*

'I'm so, so sorry,' said Lisa, patting the lady's arm. 'I didn't mean to ... You know there are lots of treatments ... I had a friend who ... oh, never mind ...' When Lisa saw the officer's raised eyebrows, she stopped babbling. She was only making things worse. The policewoman took a step back. *Your mess, you deal with it*, said her frown.

'I think it might be best if I just leave now,' said Lisa meekly, turning for the exit.

'Your change,' croaked the cashier as Lisa hurried for the door, with the officer striding alongside her.

Outside, the officers gave Lisa a final talking to. 'Mrs Wheeldon, please go home and get some sleep. And it might be best to stay away from here for a while. The staff think you're a bit strange.'

'I'm really not. I'm actually quite normal, I promise.'

The officers gave her a disbelieving look.

'But that's fine. I'll steer clear.' Lisa scurried down the street, head down. At the car, she stopped and checked over her shoulder. The policewomen were still there, waiting for her to leave. Lisa cursed herself. Not only had she failed to get any closer to finding Missy Jones, she'd also earned herself what sounded like temporary expulsion from her daughters' most beloved source of stationery supplies.

The school mothers were right, this Missy Jones was already affecting her family, making her into someone she wasn't, and depriving her children of cheap textas and pencils. There had to be another way to find her.

CHAPTER FIFTEEN

At 3 pm, when swathes of purple silk started going up in the glass conference room, Jamie had an inkling that something special was about to happen and it was exactly what she needed. All day she'd been unable to concentrate on work, and the confirmation was in her browser history. She'd done web searches on everything from wedding cakes, to the current state of the Dubai economy and the name 'Missy Jones'—a search that returned nearly twelve million results. While she'd been able to narrow it down to three million by adding a few extra search terms, she felt no closer to finding out the truth about Ellie.

At 6 pm, Angel came to her desk and ordered her to shut down her laptop. When Jamie said she needed one more minute, Angel shut it for her, and sat on it—actually causing it to creak. Only when she was sure Jamie wouldn't try to reopen the computer did Angel frog-march her down the hallway. 'Happy engagement,' she trilled theatrically as she stepped aside the door to the meeting room.

Jamie stopped and gasped. It was extraordinary, like opening a treasure chest. Gone was the sterile conference table and chairs and in their place were oversized jewel-coloured cushions, scattered across luxurious Persian rugs and around low wooden tables. The room glowed with the flickering of hundreds and hundreds of tea lights (electric— Angel didn't mind paying for the party but drew the line at forking out for fire damage) and the ceiling was draped in purple silk and strings of fairy-lights. This was exactly what she needed to take her mind off Ellie and get it focused on her engagement.

'Do you like it?' said one of the junior girls excitedly. 'It's straight off Gwyneth Paltrow's blog. She did the gypsy theme for her kid's eighth birthday and I thought it just looked ah-mazing! Ah-mazing!' To put more emphasis on the point, she clapped her hands together.

'It's gorgeous,' Jamie replied honestly. 'I love it.'

Then the food started coming, platters and platters of dolmades, dips and warm flatbreads, mini pastries oozing with cheese and to finish, sweet, syrupy mouthfuls of baklava, topped with melt-in-the-mouth Persian fairy floss.

The girls, and Benny, had outdone themselves. While Angel was tight with the everyday office essentials (no-name tea bags, powdered instant coffee and scratchy toilet paper, thank you very much) she knew how and when to loosen the purse strings. She was like a see-saw, tipping the balance to and fro, but this party had certainly tipped the balance in favour of staff spending.

Jamie's champagne glass was never empty, receiving refill after refill from the hot, young waiter, who was dressed in harem pants, a turban and nothing else. After the third top-up, Jamie had discovered that his name was Dean and that any sense of objectification he may have felt at being topless was being easily diminished by the $60 an hour that Angel was paying him to be there, half-naked. With that assurance, Jamie started to eat and drink guilt-free. Hell, you only got engaged once! (Or four times, in Angel's case.)

For the first time at an office party, Jamie let her hair down. She resolved to break her usual office rule of one-drink-per-function and really cut loose. What did it matter? There was a strong chance she'd be leaving in six weeks. Even though she'd promised to consider Angel's offer of taking over Spin, she was still leaning towards Dubai. So what if she was sacrificing her career for Jared? She was running out of time. All her friends were having babies and if there was one thing Jamie really hated, it was being left behind.

But as she looked around the room at her co-workers cackling and chewing and sipping, she felt a pang of sadness. These girls really knew how to have fun. They were like sisters in a way. They worked hard and played hard. They had each other's backs. When people discovered she worked in a nearly all-female work environment, they always asked about the bitchiness. But the assumption of cattiness rankled Jamie. These girls had her back. She'd go to war with them, though the idea of them clattering their way to the front lines in Jimmy Choos and pencil skirts made her giggle. The point was—it was a genuinely great place to work. The camaraderie was palpable. At some stage, all their menstrual cycles would sync up, Jamie was sure. The idea of leaving them was hard to stomach.

She felt a tap on her back. 'Consulted the cards yet, my dear?' Angel slung a caftan-sleeved arm around Jamie's shoulders. Her silver turban had slipped to a rakish angle, giving her the appearance of a tipsy gypsy. Angel never missed an opportunity to rig up in fancy dress, though her bird-of-paradise caftan was actually a piece from her every-day wardrobe. The turban was a new development, just for the party Jamie supposed.

'You know I don't believe in that rubbish,' said Jamie airily.

Angel inhaled loudly and closed her eyes. 'I will not let the tarot gods hear such blasphemy.' Jamie went to speak but Angel held up her finger and stabbed the air. 'No! I will not hear another word. Get thee to the corner. And get thee in touch with thine own spiritual self!' With a flounce of her caftan, Angel whirled off towards the topless male waiter with her champagne glass outstretched.

Jamie glanced at the corner of the room where the tarot reader was sitting cross-legged on the floor and watching her. Most of the girls had already had their reading and most had come away satisfied. Money, love, success— apparently it was all just around the corner waiting for them.

The woman's glance hadn't deviated and Jamie felt herself being reeled towards her like a freshly hooked fish.

The tarot reader nodded as Jamie tried to sink gracefully into the red-velvet cushion, but instead half-collapsed into it with a little champagne spilling onto the rug.

The psychic remained serene. 'Lady of the moment.' She bowed her head.

'That's me!' Jamie held up her champagne glass.

'My name is Seraphina, which comes from the Latin word for Angel.'

'Of course it does.'

Typical Angel, hiring a psychic named after herself.

'I see you are a sceptic.' Seraphina delivered the sentence in a neutral tone. Her voice was low and resonant and reminded Jamie of a viola, the instrument she'd played throughout her schooling because it was a little bit different but not *too* different. Not like the French horn, which is what Lisa learnt, honking away morning after morning until Dad begged her to stop.

Jamie cleared her throat. 'I'm happy to be proved wrong.'

'Do you have a question, my lady, that you would like the cards to answer?'

She tried to think quickly, but her brain felt as jellied as the Turkish delight now being handed around. 'Umm … nope.'

'An open reading then.' Seraphina kissed the large purple crystal hanging around her neck and started shuffling a deck of cards. Jamie felt herself becoming mesmerised by the ease and fluidity with which Seraphina's hands moved. The way in which she whipped and snapped the cards was positively hypnotic. As she laid out three of them, Jamie's eyes narrowed on the images and the rest of the party seemed to fall away, the sounds of the drinking and carousing fading into a gentle backing track.

'Past, present and future,' said Seraphina, gently placing a finger on each card as she spoke.

Jamie swallowed hard as she read the word on her 'future' card.

Death.

Seeing Jamie's troubled look, Seraphina patted her knee. 'This tarot does not predict but seeks to explain.' She pointed to the Death card. 'This is not the one you fear.'

Jamie sipped her champagne to get rid of the lump in her throat.

'To the past.' Seraphina tapped the first card, a picture of a moon, frowning down upon a yelping dog and a howling wolf. 'The tame and the wild both cry to the moon but what do they cry for? It is only light. A trick of the eye, controlling little more than the tide.'

'I don't understand,' Jamie whispered.

'It means—all is not what it seems. Perhaps you are deceiving yourself. Perhaps you have been deceived. You must look within yourself. Be open. Overcome any sense of denial that may be preventing your heart from opening to the truth.'

An image popped into Jamie's mind. Ellie. Her face as pale and large and frowning as the moon on the card. Why had she thought of the little girl? Ellie had nothing to do with her past. Or did she? When Ellie had fallen asleep on the bed at Lisa's, Jamie had studied her face. There was something in the little girl she felt she recognised, but simply couldn't put a finger on.

'The present.' Seraphina placed her finger on the second card. The Lovers.

Jamie gave a wry smile. 'I think I understand this one.'

'The lovers are naked, yes. But their nudity stems not from sexual desire but from a desire for vulnerability. To know the other fully. They stand, palms open to the sky, to the winged figure of Raphael, clothed in robes and therefore unknowable. Raphael is a figure of healing. But healing for what? Is this love truly your heart's desire?'

Jamie burped and felt the burning ferment of stale alcohol in her mouth. Did she love Jared? They enjoyed each other's company, certainly. They had fun together. Laughed at the same things, mostly. Took great holidays. Never made demands of each other. Only fought over silly things, like Jared's domestic slackness. But did she really know him? Did she really love him? How could she even be asking the question? Of course she loved him; she must love him if she wanted to spend the rest of her life with him!

'I think I've got the love bit covered,' she said. 'This is my engagement party, after all.'

'Of course,' Seraphina nodded. 'And now the Death card.' She tapped the ominous third card. A picture of a skeletal knight, riding a white horse into battle. Jamie couldn't wait for Seraphina to spin it into something positive. If she could do that, she could spin anything and Jamie would recommend Angel hire her straight away. After all, PR was the art of transforming negatives into positives, which was a kind of alchemy in its own way.

'Note the flowers, here,' Seraphina pointed, 'being offered by the child as Death rides by, on his way to battle. Death is not an end but an intense change and we must embrace it as the child does, putting aside our deepest-held fears and offering ourselves joyfully and with open hearts.'

Was Seraphina talking about her move to Dubai? Certainly that would be an intense change, though it wasn't one Jamie was particularly frightened of. If anything, she was excited. So was that the change the cards were referring to? Or was it something else entirely? Something Jamie hadn't even considered? Why couldn't the cards be more obvious!

'I can see you were seeking more concrete guidance.'

Goodness, maybe she really is a mind reader?

'But this is not the way of the tarot cards.' As Seraphina placed her hand on Jamie's knee, she felt the palm burning through to her bone. 'You must search your heart.' The woman leant in. 'Search deeply, my lady.'

'I will,' said Jamie in a low tone, placing her hand over Seraphina's.

'Fancy a top-up?' The topless waiter broke into Jamie's reverie by putting a champagne bottle under her nose.

'Why not! You only live once.' Jamie held out her glass. 'Unless you believe in reincarnation.' She tilted it towards Seraphina.

'Still no reason to reject champagne,' said Seraphina brightly, putting forward a glass that must have been hiding under her robes during the reading, for Jamie had not seen it beforehand. 'Just a mouthful, thanks, hon.' She beamed at the waiter. 'I'm sure Angel wouldn't mind, would she?'

'No, of course not,' Jamie murmured. Who was this chirpy woman? And what had she done with the floaty mystic who'd just reached into Jamie's heart and touched her soul?

Seraphina pulled back the jewelled sleeve of her robe to reveal a chunky, rubber, Casio watch. 'Whoops! Time's up. My daughter's netball practice finished ten minutes ago.' She downed the champagne in a single gulp and started peeling off her robes to reveal jeans and a T-shirt underneath. 'Hope you don't mind, hon,' she said apologetically.

'I usually change in the loo. But, you know—needs must!' She scooped up her cards and crystals and shoved them quickly into a plastic bag, along with her robes. With that she was gone, scurrying through the beaded curtain and pulling at the head scarf that had kept her maroon curls in check.

Jamie followed her to the doorway and would later question whether she actually saw what she saw, or whether it was a product of the champagne. Either way, it was shocking. As Seraphina pulled off the scarf from around her head, the maroon curls came with it. It was a wig! Covering a blonde bob! What a fraud! Jamie resolved on the spot to forget everything the woman had told her.

'Everything okay?' It was Ben, standing behind her. 'Who's the soccer mum?' he asked, following Jamie's gaze.

'That,' said Jamie dramatically, 'was the amazing, incredible, all-seeing, all-knowing, Seraphina.'

'Oh, right,' said Ben thoughtfully. 'She looks a lot like Angel's tennis partner, Susan.'

'Well, whoever she was, she reckons I'm in for some very scary, very exciting changes in my life.'

'I guess that's one way of looking at marriage.'

'Oh, it's all just psychic mumbo-jumbo, Benny. I've never believed in it and I'm not about to start,' said Jamie airily and gave him her most dazzling smile. 'C'mon, Benny. Let's find that topless waiter and get truly sozzled together.'

By 9 pm, everyone else had gone and it was just the two of them, Ben and Jamie, sitting with their feet up on the conference table. All the girls had kissed Jamie wistfully on the cheek as they clattered off into the night, no doubt wondering when it would be *their* turn to be feted by Angel with an impromptu party. Not an engagement one, necessarily, because marriage spelt babies and children. Virtual career suicide, basically, at least at Spin Cycle where Angel expected 24/7 access to your life.

The conference room was nearly back to its normal, bland self, save for the beaded curtain still strung up around the doorway. Jamie had promised Angel she would take it down when she left. There was an 8.30 am meeting with an IT company happening in the conference room. 'They're far too straight for the likes of this,' Angel had commented as she tripped through the doorway and tangled herself in the sparkly spaghetti strands.

'Leave it, Angel. Please, you've done so much. Ben and I will take care of it.' Jamie had crossed her heart. Actually crossed her heart like a five-year-old. 'Promise.'

'All right then, you two.' Angel stopped at the door. 'Don't get up to mischief.' She waggled her finger at them and turned off the lights, plunging the room into complete darkness. Ben and Jamie giggled.

'Why did she turn off the lights?' said Jamie.

'Because she's had twenty million glasses of champagne.'

'I heard that,' came a voice from down the corridor before the elevator pinged at their floor. Angel was getting into the lift. There was the hiss of the doors closing, then silence.

Ben and Jamie collapsed into raucous laughter. Jamie guffawed so hard she took her legs off the table and crossed them to save her bladder from bursting.

Eventually, their laughter slowed to giggles, and petered out into sighs and silence.

'It's nice in here like this,' said Jamie.

'I can't see my hand in front of my face.'

Jamie heard the scratching sound of Ben pulling his phone from his pocket. He switched it on, providing a dim light source, then disappeared under the table and re-emerged with a couple of tea lights that had been overlooked in the clean-up.

'That's better,' he said, switching them on. 'At least I can see your face, now.'

'And I can see my glass.' Jamie reached for her champagne.

'Refill?' Ben held up the last bottle, three-quarters empty.

'Last one.' She offered her glass for him to fill and sat back in the chair. It had been a great party. One of Angel's best. She'd even made a lovely speech about Jamie and how indispensable she was to the business and, obviously, to Jared as well. This kind of praise was rare. Unexpected. Maybe it was a subconscious pitch to get Jamie to stay, but whatever the intention, she didn't mind. It had been a great, great night. And now she was here with her best work friend, enjoying the silence and the French champagne.

But it wasn't silent for long.

Ben was always up for a chat, and with the tea light flickering across his face he launched into a hilarious recount of the latest *Real Housewives* episodes. Jamie had missed a couple and Ben was more than happy to fill her in.

After half an hour, her stomach was sore from too much laughter and her champagne glass was finally empty.

Ben yawned.

'Is that a subtle way of telling me it's time to go,' said Jamie.

He covered his mouth. 'No, no. Of course not. I love being with you.' He added hastily, 'Here. At work. Chatting I mean.'

Jamie nodded. 'I know what you mean.' She put both hands on the armrest. 'But I think we both need our beauty sleep.' She rose, wobbled and reached out for Ben who grabbed her under her arms and pulled her up to his chest.

'Whoa, sorry,' said Jamie, blinking. 'That champagne really goes to your head.'

'Sure does,' he murmured, still holding her close. His breath was warm on her cheek and he was close enough for Jamie to see the flecks of green in his deep brown eyes.

'You've got tadpoles in your eyes,' she giggled.

'What do you mean?'

She leant in. They were now nose to nose. 'Little green bits in your eyes. They're like—'

Suddenly, Ben's mouth was on hers. So warm and so wet. The shock of it made her legs buckle and she threw her arms around Ben's neck as he manoeuvred her to the wall, pressing her against it, leaning the weight of his body into hers and kissing her in a way she'd never been kissed before. His fingers massaged her head and he pressed his knee between her thighs. Their tongues met gently and the touch caused Jamie's insides to cave.

Finally, a thought entered her head.

'Ben,' she whispered, and turned her face to the side. 'This is not right.'

Now he was kissing her neck.

'I'm your boss.'

'I know.' He kept kissing her.

'And I'm engaged.' Still no pause in the kissing.

'And you're not straight.'

Ben pulled away. 'What did you say?'

What could she tell him? That it was because of the way he dressed? The fact he worked in PR? That he enjoyed *Real Housewives*? That he'd been so secretive about his relationships? Not that there was any reason to be. Half the clients at Spin were homosexual. It was just the nature of the industry.

'Well, I just assumed you were gay. You are, aren't you?' Jamie started smoothing her skirt. 'Actually, no. You don't have to answer that. It's extremely unprofessional of me. I'm sorry.'

Ben put his hands on his hips, taking them away from where they'd been caressing Jamie's body in a totally gorgeous but terribly inappropriate way. 'You think just because I like crappy reality shows and work in PR that I'm gay? As a matter of record, I'm actually straight.'

Jamie felt her cheeks flush. 'But didn't you just break up with someone?'

'Yes. A woman.' He looked at the floor. 'Her name was Karen,' he said quietly.

Jamie felt her knees starting to give way again. She would tell herself later that it was simply the shock of the news. And the kiss. Ben wasn't the man she thought he was. They worked so closely, she thought she knew everything about him. But in among the feelings of shock and surprise, there was something else she felt. Something she didn't want to admit.

Elation.

She reached for the table to steady herself.

'Whoa there.' This time, Ben's arms encircled her waist. 'I think we better sit you down.' He helped her back into an office chair.

Jamie lay her head on the table, thoughts flying like butterflies in her head, flitting about too fast for her to catch. 'I need to go home.'

'I'll call you a cab.'

She heard the chair creak as Ben rose out of it, but she didn't look at him as he walked out the door to make the call. She had kissed a man who wasn't her fiancé. The shame of it swept over her and dampened the fizz in her stomach. Would she have to tell Jared? How could she? They'd been engaged for little more than twenty-four hours. It wasn't exactly a promising start to the next phase of their relationship. What would she want if *she* were Jared? Honesty had to be the bedrock of any solid relationship. But was it always the best policy? If Jared had a drunken pash with a co-worker that meant nothing and led nowhere, would she really want to know?

But that kiss with Ben did mean something, said a little voice inside her head.

Jamie pushed the thought aside. Until five minutes ago, she'd never considered Ben in that way. Sure, he was sexy and funny and had impeccable dress sense. But he was her junior. He was off-limits. That hadn't changed. His sexuality wasn't the issue at all. It shouldn't change how she saw him.

She half-opened an eye to look at him, standing in the gloom just outside the conference room. Always so considerate. So attentive to her needs. He'd unbuttoned his shirt collar and was rubbing his neck, the part where Jamie's hands had just been. It had felt too good.

She couldn't be attracted to him. Surely not. And he wasn't attracted to her. She'd never had that vibe from him.

A couple of times she'd caught him staring at her but she'd passed it off as part of his devotion to the job. He was simply waiting for her to speak, discuss the next steps, outline what needed to be done.

The kiss was meaningless. It was the alcohol. Nothing more. They'd both been too tipsy to know better. In the morning they'd laugh about it, be embarrassed for a moment and then move on. It would all be fine.

Jamie sat up as Ben came back into the room.

'Taxi's on its way.' He stood at the table. 'I'll walk you down.'

'Do you want to share it?' she said, trying to sound casual.

'No, I've got a little more work to do.'

She put her hand on his forearm. 'Ben, it's late. Do it tomorrow.'

'No, it's something for Angel and she needs it first thing.'

'Okay then.'

She took the hand that Ben had outstretched to help her out of the chair. Down the hallway, into the lift, and out onto the street, he didn't let go, but not once did he look at her.

When the cab came, she kissed him chastely on the cheek. 'Thank you.' She paused. 'For everything.'

He said nothing but nodded.

As the cab turned the corner, Jamie could still see him standing on the street with his hands jammed into his pockets, watching after her.

All Jamie wanted was to slip into bed unnoticed by Jared, drift off into a dreamless sleep and wake in the morning to a fresh new day in which she could start planning her wedding.

But as the cabbie turned the corner into their back lane, Jamie saw a glow of light coming from their courtyard. Quickly she paid the driver, hopped out and swung open the back gate.

Involuntarily, she gasped. The courtyard was covered with tea lights. Real ones, judging from the scent of melting wax in the air, and in the middle of the candles was a gorgeous white, canopy tent, the kind of thing a Bedouin would be happy to call home. Under the tent was a sleeping Jared, sprawled over wine-coloured cushions and a Persian rug. Surrounding him were platters of luscious fruits, oozing cheeses and jewel-toned bowls of dips. A Middle Eastern feast.

What was going on? First Angel's party and now this? Had she entered some kind of alternate universe where everywhere she went, she would be greeted by a scene more familiar to a wandering Bedouin than a high-powered PR professional?

She sat down and gently stroked Jared's forehead. He was so handsome in his sleep. Childlike. The humidity had caused a few stray curls to become plastered to his forehead. Jamie touched them gently, releasing the hair from the skin and allowing the curl to bounce back into shape.

He stirred and opened his eyes. 'You're home,' he said sleepily.

'I'm home,' she whispered, lying down in front of him in the spooning position. She pulled his hands around her tightly.

'You missed the party,' he murmured into her hair.

Jamie stiffened at the mention of the word *party*. Over the last two days, she'd attended two of them and both had ended strangely. 'I'm sorry.'

'It's okay.' He paused. 'I'm sorry I didn't propose to you the right way and I wanted to make up for it.'

'It's okay,' she crooned. 'Just go back to sleep.'

'I did this for you.' He kissed her hair. 'Dubai in Paddington.'

'It's beautiful.' Jamie fought back tears. He'd done this all for her. He loved her. He must. Why else go to all this trouble? And she had betrayed him by kissing Ben. Jared deserved better. Guilt settled like oil in her stomach.

'I bought you a ring.'

Jared disentangled his arm and Jamie felt him reaching into his pocket. In front of her eyes appeared a small, black box.

'Open it,' he said sleepily.

She did. It was gorgeous. The most perfect, square-cut diamond solitaire Jamie had ever seen.

'I love it; it's perfect.' But as Jamie turned to kiss Jared on the cheek, she could see from the stillness of his eyelids that he'd already gone back to sleep, and relief washed over her like a shower of rain at the end of a hot summer day.

She needed to be alone with her thoughts and her guilt and work out what the hell she was going to do next. About Jared, about Ben, about Dubai and about Angel's offer.

CHAPTER SIXTEEN

From the start, Lisa's gut told her the playground was a bad idea. Why hadn't she listened to it? Her stomach rarely lied, except when it consumed chocolate and told her brain that it was fine to eat the whole block.

But it was rarely wrong about other matters, especially those relating to her children. And if she'd chosen to ignore her stomach, she could at least have paid some attention to her heart, which sank to the ground when Ava and Jemima announced in the car home from school on Tuesday afternoon that they very much wanted to go to the playground.

'What about you, Ellie? What would *you* like to do?' Lisa had asked via the rear-view mirror.

'I like the playground,' said Ellie simply.

'Yay,' chorused Ava and Jemima. 'Playground, playground, playground,' they chanted.

It had been a good day for Lisa. She'd almost managed to forget yesterday's brush with the law by busying herself with getting enrolment forms and a school uniform sorted for Ellie, not to mention Suzie-the-seamstress's bank reconciliations. Now all she wanted was to go home and huddle over her little girls like a mother hen brooding over her chicks. Besides, she was secretly a bit tired of swings and slippery dips and see-saws. People spoke of 'playground politics' as if it was something solely for the children to navigate but in Lisa's view, the kids' bust-ups were small-fry compared to the adult power-plays. A child had yet to learn a grudge in the way of a parent—a lesson Lisa had learnt when Ava was ten months old and playing happily in a sandpit until an older child started throwing sand in her face. Ava had cried loudly, making her feelings clear in no uncertain terms, but the little monster continued to throw sand at her until Lisa caught his arm. 'Darling, I'd prefer if you not do that, thank you.'

'Okay,' said the boy happily, and Lisa had thought little of it until a shadow came over her, cast by a very angry, very tall and, heretofore very invisible, mother.

'How dare you touch my child!' she'd exclaimed, wrapping up the previously happy little boy in such a breath-constricting hug that he started to cry.

'I'm sorry but he was throwing sand in my daughter's face.'

'You're new at this, aren't you?' The mother's eyes had narrowed until it looked like she would fire bullets from them.

'I guess so,' Lisa had said meekly.

'Next time you lay a finger on my child, I'll call the police.' And with that, she'd stomped out of the sandpit and over to another group of mums whereby there was much gesticulating and pointing of fingers and dirty looks towards Lisa.

Sadly, she had since had the misfortune of running into the same woman several times over. Mothers and playgrounds were like emperor penguins and their breeding grounds; they had a habit of returning to the same one time after time.

Therefore, when the girls suggested a trip to the playground, Lisa gently countered the idea by suggesting they go home and watch *Charlie and the Chocolate Factory*. With popcorn as well!

'But Mummy, my teacher says it's not healthy to watch television all the time,' said Ava.

'Yes, but you don't watch TV *all* the time. You've been at school all day and Jem's been at kindy, remember?'

They weren't convinced, and as Lisa hated being the constant naysayer—parenting tended to be nine parts 'no' to one part 'yes'—she gave in.

Now they were here, and as Lisa robotically pushed Jemima on the swing all she could think about was Missy. Where was she right now? What was she doing? She looked about the playground. Mothers pushing and pulling their kids, others trying strenuously to ignore them.

Could one of them know Ellie's mum? The playground wasn't far from where they lived. Maybe she should talk to some of the mums? See if they knew of her?

'Higher, Mummy, higher,' shouted Jemima, swinging her little chubby legs completely out of time with the rhythm of the swing.

'Okay, darling.' Lisa summoned the energy to push her child towards the heavens.

Who was she kidding? The other mothers would think her a nutcase if she randomly started up a probing conversation with them. After the stationery store incident, she couldn't afford to draw attention to herself again. Lisa kept swinging and let her mind turn to what they might have for dinner that night. Steak and veg, or sausage and veg? Maybe spaghetti bolognaise? That would be the easiest. The kids liked that the best and tended to eat it in five minutes flat. Anything with vegetables took at least half an hour.

Her phone bleeped.

You still okay to meet in the morning? Xx

Ugh. That's right. Jamie had an early pre-work appointment to try on wedding dresses at some exclusive boutique which was usually booked out for weeks.

Yes! Can't wait. Xx

Definitely the bolognaise then. One less thing to worry about.

'Mummy, I want to get off.' Jem swivelled in the seat, nearly toppling off the swing.

'Whoa, hang on, darling. Two hands, remember.' Lisa scooped her off and set her down gently. 'Now, where's your sister? And Ellie?'

Jemima screwed up her face. 'Don't know.'

'Okay, well let's go find them.' Lisa took Jemima's sticky hand in hers and headed towards the sandpit, which tended to be Ava's favourite place at the playground.

No sign of the girls.

She dismissed the little flutter of fear that always accompanied the first sensation that her daughter may have disappeared.

Ava always turned up. Always.

Lisa sauntered over to the slippery dip and checked underneath. No Ava there, just a cheeky little boy who poked his tongue out at her. She checked the trees that Ava had been known to climb. Not there either. Her pulse quickened. The monkey bars! Of course. She loved the monkey bars.

Nope. Not there either.

Now, Lisa was running, with a vice-like grip on Jemima's hand.

'Owwww, you're hurting me.' Jemima yanked back on Lisa's arm.

'Darling, please.' Lisa knelt down and brushed the hair from her daughter's eyes. 'We really need to find Ellie and your sister. Where did you last see them?'

Jemima screwed up her face and put a finger to her chin. 'In the car.'

Lisa sighed. 'C'mon.' She scooped Jemima up into her arms and held her daughter's head close to her shoulder to stop it from bouncing as she ran from parent to parent, asking if they'd seen two little girls—one with ash-blonde hair, wearing a school uniform and the other with dark hair, navy dress. Mostly they shook their heads with a regretful but slightly smug smile as if to say *You loving-but-hopeless mother*.

'They'll turn up,' offered one. 'They always do.'

But what was that saying—that to lose one child could be considered a misfortune, but to lose two, including one that wasn't her own, would be considered careless in the extreme.

Now sweating with panic, she felt Jemima's head lift off her shoulder. 'There they are!' Her daughter's body twisted in the direction of the gate and Lisa swivelled. Ava! Ellie!

Hallelujah! But why were they walking in the other direction, and holding hands with a third person? Who was it? The trees between them obscured Lisa's view.

'Ava! Ellie!' Lisa started running awkwardly, juggling Jemima on her hip with one hand, and waving her free arm wildly. 'Come here.'

But Ava was too deep in conversation with the companion to hear anything, so Lisa shouted again and Ava turned slowly, smiling at first and then frowning upon the realisation that her mother appeared very cross indeed.

Now, Lisa was close enough to see the other person, the one who was holding Ava and Ellie's hand.

A child.

Relief and confusion soaked through Lisa's veins and she rushed towards them. Now, they were all within her grasp—Jemima, Ava and Ellie—and she thought her heart would explode with relief.

'I thought I'd lost you,' she cried, kissing Ava on the head.

'I was playing with Ellie in the sandpit, and then we started playing with—' She screwed up her face and looked at the third child. 'What's your name again.'

'I'm Isla and I'm six years old,' said the little girl softly.

'Pleased to meet you, Isla. Now where's your mummy, sweetie? She might be worried about you too.'

'She's not here,' Isla whispered.

Lisa leant down. 'Who are you here with, darling?'

'That lady over there.' Isla pointed to a grey-haired woman sitting on a park bench, so engrossed in a book she was oblivious to the commotion happening less than twenty feet away.

'Is she your grandmother?'

'No,' said Isla. 'She's my carer and I don't like her. Her house smells of potatoes.'

Lisa felt an ache starting to rise behind her eyes. 'Let's go and introduce ourselves, shall we?' A couple of feet from the bench, she cleared her throat. The woman didn't look up. Isla looked at Lisa as if to say *See what I mean*. Lisa squeezed Isla's hand.

'Excuse me.' She touched the woman gently on the arm and the woman jumped as if she'd received an electric shock.

'Oh dear lord Jesus, you nearly gave me a heart attack.' The woman recoiled and flung her hand to her chest. 'I was just getting to the good part.' She held up the book. 'I never go anywhere without my Stephen King.'

'I'm sorry.' Lisa took a step back. 'But I lost my two girls, momentarily and then found them playing with Isla here. I wasn't sure if you knew where she was, so I thought I'd just check. I understand you're looking after her.'

'Correct, I'm the *emergency* foster carer.' She stressed the word as if announcing herself as a member of the royal peerage and Lisa took in the woman's tightly cropped hair, pleated navy slacks, white blouse and sturdy black shoes. It was an outfit that screamed 'former nurse'. A matron, most likely.

'Someone needs to give that one a good talking to.' The woman clutched her arm and Lisa smelt mothballs. '*Demanded* we come to this park, even though it's miles from where I live. *Demanded* it, or she said she'd run away. I tell you, children these days,' she huffed.

'Yes, well, they can be challenging,' Lisa muttered.

The woman checked her watch and beckoned to Isla. 'Nearly teatime. Say your goodbyes, my little miss.'

Lisa checked her phone. 'But it's only four o'clock.'

'Dinner at 4.30. Bath at 5.30. Bed at six.' The words came out of the woman's mouth like rounds of rapid gunfire. Not to be argued with, unless you valued your life.

Lisa decided to be brave. 'But it's still broad daylight at six.'

'The room has lovely heavy curtains. Black as pitch once they're closed.'

'You surely don't expect them to sleep from six?'

'Sleep. Don't sleep. I don't mind what they do in that room. I just know that the door shuts at six and reopens at seven in the morning.'

Lisa could barely spit out the words. 'You don't *lock them in*, do you?'

'Of course not,' the woman scoffed. 'The children are free to use the bathroom.' She raised her finger. 'But that's all. Or it's plain toast for breakfast. No butter. No jam, and certainly no vegemite.' She stretched her lips into a thin, mean smile. 'I make no apology for running a tight ship. Some good old-fashioned discipline is precisely what these sorts of children need.' She inclined her head. 'Time to go, Missy. Say goodbye to your friends.'

The name pinged in Lisa's mind. How odd, that this woman would use that name—the very same as Ellie's mum.

'No,' came the small but defiant voice. Lisa felt Isla cowering into her. 'You can't make me.'

'See what I mean.' The woman clicked her tongue. 'Come now, Missy.'

Lisa flinched again.

'I've had just about enough trouble from you.' The old woman outstretched a scrawny, blue-veined hand. 'Time to go.'

Reluctantly, Isla let go of Lisa's hand and slipped her small fingers into the carer's vice-like grip.

You can't let her go with that woman.

But Lisa stood still, muscles quivering, watching. At the car, the old lady opened the door and ushered the girl inside, leaning across to make sure she was carefully strapped into the seat. Then she handed Isla a small packet of biscuits. Lisa felt her anxiety ebbing. Maybe the woman was a dragon, but she would at least feed and clothe the little girl, and keep her safe. From what she'd learnt at the group home, foster carers could be worse. Far, far worse.

You can't save all the children.

She felt a tug on her hand. Ava. 'Mummy, can we have an ice-cream. Pleeease!'

She looked down at three little faces, filled with hope.

'Yes. Yes. Let's have an ice-cream.'

Ava and Jemima bolted ahead, while Ellie slipped in beside Lisa and trod carefully over the grass.

'Who was that woman? The old lady with Isla?'

Lisa put her arm around Ellie's shoulders. 'Don't worry about her. She's no one, darling. At least, no one you need to worry about. I promise.'

As they walked towards the gate, Lisa felt her resolve building with each step. She would go back to the beginning. Back to the school. Tomorrow was the athletics carnival. It had to be an opportunity to scope out more of the parents and teachers. But she needed help. Someone who knew the school intimately. Someone unafraid to dig. Someone who liked meddling.

She knew exactly who that person could be.

Lisa pulled out her phone and started dialling.

'Heather, it's Lisa Wheeldon.'

A slight pause. 'Lisa. So glad you rang. I was just thinking about you.'

'You were?'

'Yes. Now don't worry about Kimberly. The woman is a certified b-i-t-c-h.' Lisa heard her covering the phone. 'No, Savannah, I did not just spell out the B word. How about you go and find the iPad. Mummy's on the phone.' The sound became clear again and Lisa visualised Heather uncapping the speaker. 'Sorry, Lisa. Those children—never listen when you're speaking to them, and suddenly develop the hearing of an owl when you use inappropriate language. Anyway, as I was saying, after you left today, the other mothers and I had a chat.' She paused. 'We want to help you find Ellie's mother.'

Silently, Lisa did an inner squeal. 'That's amazing. That's exactly why I was ringing you.'

'Savannah-Rose Bingley-Peters,' roared Heather, causing Lisa to hold the phone away from her ear. 'I did NOT say you could go onto YouTube. You have ten seconds to get onto the Reading Eggs. OR ELSE! One, two, three ... Good.'

Lisa brought the phone back to her ear. 'Is this a bad time? Maybe we could talk later? Are you going to the carnival?'

'Of course I am. All the parents are.'

'Excellent. How about we get together and come up with a bit of a plan?'

'Leave it to me, Lisa Wheeldon. You leave it to me.'

CHAPTER SEVENTEEN

It was only 8 am and Jamie felt like she'd died and gone to tulle-heaven. Sitting on the velvet banquette in the middle of the bridal shop was like sitting on a cloud, surrounded by textures and shades of white, ranging from the softest of soft pinks to the most delicate hues of grey, the colours accentuated by the golden light starting to filter into the shop. The tulle was everywhere—veils, overskirts, underskirts and general swathes of it, coating everything like a fine, gossamer web.

Jamie took a sip of her takeaway coffee to stop herself from sighing out loud. The boutique was a childhood dream come true.

As an eight-year-old, Jamie had hankered to do ballet for the sole reason of wanting to float ethereally about the stage in the end-of-year concert as a snowflake perhaps, or a winter fairy, or whatever involved the wearing of a frothy white tutu. But when the roles were assigned, Jamie thought she'd misheard. Mouse? They wanted her to be a mouse? But mice didn't wear fluffy white tutus! There had to be some mistake?

There wasn't. For the production of *Cinderella*, the seven- and eight-year-olds were to play the mice that were magically transformed by the fairy godmother into footmen for Cinderella's coach. Jamie had cried but her mother was firm. If she wouldn't wear the brown leotard with matching furry tail, they would have to tell Santa, and Santa may decide she didn't deserve any presents.

Jamie was stuck. She had to go on stage, so she did and was the sourest mouse ever seen. The home movie of her performance was family folklore. It never failed to make Jamie cry with laughter, but a part of her also winced. She was still in love with the romance of white tulle. Always would be. Such a different aesthetic to her normal chic and sharp attire. In fact, her penchant for white netting frightened her a little. Tulle was very nineties. And, in the hands of the wrong designer, so naïve. She needed someone to save her from herself. Someone with impeccable taste. Someone who understood the difference between romantic and schmaltzy, chic and too-sharp, sexy and slutty. Normally, that someone would have been Ben. But after their kiss at the party, she had thought better of it. Yes, she'd been a little drunk and perhaps they had become too close, but that's all it was. Jamie had mistaken familiarity for intimacy, nothing more. What they needed was a little distance.

In the end she'd asked Lisa to attend the early appointment. Admittedly, her sister had an entirely different aesthetic to hers, if you could even classify denim skirts and

T-shirts as an *aesthetic*. As a corporate accountant, Lisa had displayed a style that Jamie would have categorised as 'classic with a twist'. Smart, slightly dull clothes brought into the realm of 'interesting' thanks to bold accessories—chunky beaded necklaces, dangly earrings, hand-painted scarves, and the like. Her streak of style was discernible, if modest. But since having Ava and Jemima, which necessitated the move into self-employment and 'mumpreneuring' her sister's sense of fashion had taken a decided step backwards. It was as if the sudden leap into true maturity (the care of another human being) must necessarily be countered by a corresponding sartorial reversion back to the clothing of childhood. Shorts and T-shirts. Flat shoes. Socks! And not just with sneakers! Jamie understood the practicalities that dictated Lisa's wardrobe; one could not crawl about the floor in Manolos. But she had hoped for at least a little resistance to the inevitable pull of practicality and comfort. If Jamie ever had children, she would find a way to pull it off fashionably. That was non-negotiable. But before children, there was a small matter of a wedding to organise.

In a little over forty-eight hours, Jamie had booked the reception venue (a private waterfront home with stunning views of the harbour that few people knew was available for hire) and a caterer. Because the date was so close, she didn't have the option of endless choices and had settled for a Saturday morning ceremony and lunchtime reception. She'd barely bothered to check anything with Jared. The transfer to Dubai was now official, which meant Jared had to finalise his own projects, organise the handover and also get a feel for what would be needed over there. Jamie hadn't told him about Angel's business offer and she wasn't quite sure why.

She didn't want him to doubt her, perhaps? Still, no harm in covering all bases. No reason she couldn't start secretly working on the Spin business plan, as well as the Dubai one. In between the flurry of wedding calls and business plans, she'd also made a little time to dig further into the mystery of Missy Jones—PR professionals were nothing if not exceptional at multi-tasking. So far, she'd checked the official police Missing Persons' website and plenty of unofficial sites established by relatives and friends to spread the word about missing loved ones. But with only a name to go on, and no photo, the search was virtually pointless. And it was also very depressing—all those people, simply vanishing off the face of the earth and leaving their loved ones bereft.

Sitting in the dress shop alongside her sister, Jamie felt the exhaustion of the previous two days, and everything that lay ahead, catching up with her as she took another large sip of her coffee.

'You don't know the week I've had, and it's only Wednesday,' Lisa sighed.

'Actually, I have a feeling I probably do,' said Jamie.

'Oh look at us. Two tired sad-sacks. This is crazy.' Lisa turned to Jamie. 'This should be fun. It's your wedding dress!' She patted her arm and beamed. 'Let's forget our difficult days and enjoy it, okay?'

'Okay,' Jamie agreed as a petite woman in black started to buzz about them with a kind of nervy, scatty elegance.

Cici: Design Consultant, read her name badge. *Shop assistant*, Jamie mentally corrected as Cici stood before them with hands clasped and heels together in a way Jamie recognised. She knew a frustrated ballerina when she saw one.

'Are we thinking modern or traditional?' asked Cici.

'Modern,' said Jamie and Lisa together.

'Fitted or floaty?'

'Fitted.' Again Lisa chimed in, beaming, as Jamie gave her a look.

'Your sister knows you well.' Cici nodded approvingly. 'Always helpful to have a matron of honour who's on the same page. Sleeves or no sleeves?'

'Sleeves,' they said together. Lisa giggled.

'Sorry.' She covered her mouth, but her cheeks were still stretched wide so Jamie knew she was smiling.

'I'll be back in a jiffy.' Cici held up a finger and scurried out of the room, presumably to another room where there was a stack of fitted, sleeved, modern gowns.

'What is wrong with you?' Jamie hissed, clutching her sister's forearm.

'I'm just trying to make this fun!'

'Well, it's annoying.'

'I'm sorry.' Lisa looked wounded. 'I'm not myself at the moment. I just can't stop thinking about Ellie.'

Jamie nodded. 'I've been thinking about her too but trying to find Missy Jones is like looking for a needle in a haystack.'

Lisa looked pensive. 'Yesterday at the playground, I had a run-in with an old woman, a foster carer I think. Anyway, she was being a bit horrible to this sweet little girl and she kept referring to her as *Missy*.'

'And?'

'It just took me back to our time at the group home, and it made me wonder if maybe Ellie's mum knew us from there?' Lisa sat up on the velvet banquette.

'You think? I mean, it's a bit of a stretch. That was such a long time ago ...'

'We did meet a fair few kids. I'm not even sure I remember them all now. It was such an awful time.'

Jamie looked into the bright lights of the chandelier. 'Hang on, I think Ellie told me something on that first night. She didn't know her mother's exact birthday but she did know she was twenty-six—a fair bit younger than us.'

'And all the others at the group home were about our age,' sighed Lisa. 'So it can't be from that.'

A disappointed silence settled over the pair. 'I've still got the school mums to look into.' Lisa shifted her knees. 'Some of them have offered to help actually. You remember Heather from the party?'

'The drunk one?'

'We're going to chat at the girls' carnival today.'

'I don't think I'd be pinning all my hopes on her. She seems slightly unstable.'

'At least she's willing to try,' Lisa said defensively, then stopped and clutched her sister's arm. 'Look.'

Jamie followed Lisa's gaze to Cici, who was back in the room and holding aloft the most exquisite gown Jamie had ever seen. White and shimmery, long and lean, it was the kind of gown a mermaid would wear, albeit if mermaids had legs and wore dresses with sleeves. It was magical. Ethereal. Jamie couldn't speak.

'Oh my gosh,' breathed Lisa. 'It's gorgeous.'

'Would you like to try it on?' asked Cici.

Jamie nodded. For a minute, thoughts of Ellie receded into the back of her mind. The beauty of the gown had rendered her mute. And now she got to actually try it on. It was too much!

In the dressing room, Cici kept up an endless prattle about the designer, the hand-beading, the flattering way the gown fitted to the knee and then flared, and the fact that several Sydney A-list celebrities had worn similar designs to their nuptials.

Jamie heard none of it. She was too busy holding her breath, feeling the liquid touch of satin against her skin and the slight scratch of the lace-tulle sleeves as they passed over her knuckles. Tulle sleeves! The dress was her dream come true, albeit two sizes too large.

'This is a twelve,' Cici explained as she inspected the hundred or so fabric-covered buttons that trailed down the back of the gown. 'You're an eight on top, ten in the hips, yes?'

The question was more of a statement and in any case, Jamie was too stunned by the dress to respond.

Using bulldog clips Cici cinched in the waist so that the gown now clung to every inch of the body that Jamie had worked so hard in the gym to create.

'There.' Cici stood back—the coryphée looking enviously at the prima ballerina. 'You're so lucky.'

The words were so quiet that Jamie wasn't sure she heard them at all. She spun around to face Cici. 'I'm sorry, did you say something?'

The shop assistant was flustered and wrung her—ringless, Jamie now noticed—fingers together. 'I meant that your fiancé is so lucky. You look beautiful.'

Jamie turned back to her reflection. She'd been in this position so many times, critiquing and surveying herself in the mirror, and usually she was marginally displeased by

what she saw. But for the first time—possibly in her life—
Jamie actually believed the words Cici had uttered. She
believed them of herself. She felt beautiful and she knew
for once that objectively, she also looked beautiful. Not just
that the dress was gorgeous, which it obviously was, but that
she was gorgeous in it.

'Let's show your sister, shall we?'

Cici swept aside the curtain, drawing a gasp from Lisa
who immediately leapt to her feet and clapped her hands
together. 'Oh my gosh! It's so beautiful.' She paused, eyes
widening and shining, looking Jamie up and down as if she
were an apparition. 'I can't believe it … I mean, don't get
me wrong Jamie, you're always beautiful, but that dress is
just … it's just … stunning.' Lisa was always effusive with
her praise—so much so that Jamie occasionally doubted
its sincerity—but this wasn't her normal, enthusiastic I've-
just-patted-a-cute-puppy tone. There was an edge to her
voice that verged on incredulity, as if she couldn't actually
believe what she was seeing.

Cici helped Jamie over to the small, raised podium in the
middle of the store, surrounded on three sides by mirrors.
Instead of being intimidated by the multiple reflections,
Jamie revelled in them, twisting this way and that to confirm she wasn't being deceived. But from whichever angle
she looked, the dress was still perfect.

'Oh my gosh,' Lisa squealed behind her. 'The first dress,
and it's THE ONE.'

'Maybe,' said Jamie over her shoulder, trying to sound
casual but failing to quell the tremble in her voice.

'Wait right there.' Cici held up her finger as if she'd had
a bright idea, and scuttled out of the room. When she

returned, her arms were again full of beaded netting. 'The veil,' she announced, stepping up to the podium.

As the tulle went over Jamie's head, she instinctively closed her eyes. When Cici was done, she opened them again. The world was white. Everything was blurred. Glowing. How it might look if it were snowing. Magical. Jamie regarded herself in the mirror. Where before she had simply been wearing a beautiful, white gown, she was now a bride. The veil had transformed her. This is how she would be presented to Jared. How she would take his hand and promise to be his wife forever. No turning back. No chance to kiss anyone else ever again.

Lisa sighed. 'Oh, I wish Mum were here to see you.'

Jamie's palms broke out in a sweat. Her eyes felt hot and itchy. 'I don't like it,' she said in a steely voice.

'What? The veil? Let me take it off.' Cici reached for it.

'No, no,' said Jamie, waving her away. 'All of it. The dress. Everything. It's not right.'

'Are you kidding?' Lisa was again incredulous, but this time in an I-don't-believe-what-I'm-hearing kind of way.

'No, I'm not,' Jamie snapped, stepping down off the podium and turning her back on the mirrors. 'Take it off me,' she ordered Cici.

'Jamie, there's no need to be rude about it,' said Lisa.

'I'm sorry, Cici,' Jamie sighed. 'But would you please help me take this off?' She started pulling at the clips on her back.

'Of course.' Cici hurriedly released the clasps. 'But perhaps there's something else you'd like to try? We have many, many beautiful gowns.'

'No, no. I don't think there's anything here for me.'

Lisa was agape. 'What are you talking about? You're not going to try anything else? We've got a bit of time.' She checked her watch. 'Another half-hour at least. Why not try on something else?' Her tone was pleading.

'I don't want to,' said Jamie.

'Cici, could you give us a minute?' asked Lisa.

'Certainly.' Cici gave a little bow before retreating from the room.

Lisa squared Jamie by the shoulders. 'What is going on with you? This dress is gorgeous. If I were you, I'd be running around this fitting room doing a happy dance right now.' She squeezed. 'You've found it. You've found the one! Remember what a nightmare it was shopping for my dress?' Lisa groaned.

Jamie did remember. She'd tried to forget because it *was* a nightmare. A nightmare that lasted for weeks and weeks. Six weekends in a row, Lisa and Jamie traipsed all over Sydney, from shop to shop in search of 'the one'. It wasn't so much that Lisa was picky. Quite the contrary. She would have been quite content with the first strapless Cinderella-dress she tried in a horrible little shop on Parramatta Road. But Jamie wouldn't have it. She was determined to do better than a meringue for her lovely-but fashion-backward sister. To twenty different shops they went until finally, almost out of exhaustion, Jamie conceded defeat and allowed Lisa to buy a strapless, Cinderella-number, almost exactly like the one she had first tried on. As much as she wanted her sister to resemble something other than a cake-doll, she found it was actually the right silhouette for Lisa as it accentuated her tiny waist, boosted her small bust and totally camouflaged her trouble area—the thighs. But what Jamie most remembered from the entire experience was Lisa's joy—not so much over the dress—but over the idea of becoming Scott's wife. Through the interminable hours of try-ons, it was what kept them both going—the notion that all their hard work was worth it, because it was the frock in which Lisa would finally declare herself as Scott's wife.

Jamie couldn't meet Lisa's eyes. With her head bowed to the floor, the first of her tears rolled down her nose and into the lush cream carpet at her feet.

'I did something,' she whispered.

'What?' Lisa whispered back.

'I kissed someone.'

'Who?'

'Ben.'

'Your gay secretary?' Lisa squinted, puzzled.

'Turns out he's not so gay after all.'

'Oh,' said Lisa thoughtfully. 'And how do you feel about that?'

Lisa had done an online course in amateur psychology where she'd learnt about open and non-judgemental questions. It frustrated the hell out of Jamie, who generally liked quick, judgemental responses to her momentous disclosures.

'How do you *think* I feel about that?' Jamie snapped.

'Confused? Guilty, I imagine—'

'I feel happy,' Jamie broke in and slumped to the ground with her bottom on the podium. Lisa took up the spot next to her.

'What do you mean?'

'I liked it when he kissed me. I don't know. It's like I woke up or something.'

'It was probably just lust. You know, after a few years with one person, you sort of forget what that feels like. Lord knows, if you've seen a man floss his teeth, it's hard to imagine him as a wild animal in bed, if you know what I mean. And maybe Ben reminded you of that pre-flossing, passionate stage.'

'I think it's more than that.'

'You have feelings for him?'

Jamie nodded. She couldn't speak. All through Tuesday, she'd avoided Ben and told herself that the nerves in her stomach were simply related to the anxious excitement she felt about the wedding. But how could she explain the multiplication in butterflies when she thought about the kiss? It was glorious. But it meant nothing, she told herself repeatedly, because she knew that if she stayed *on-message* and said it often enough, she would believe it. Her infatuation with Ben was simply some strange expression of excitement about the wedding, she told herself, and it was what she had kept telling herself until she was standing on the podium wearing a veil.

At that moment it hit her.

This wasn't just a gown for a big party she was organising. This was the dress in which she would commit herself forever to the one man.

But was Jared the right one?

The moment she had asked the question, the tulle had begun to itch furiously on her arms. The veil was stopping her oxygen flow. The bulldog clips were cutting off her circulation. She needed it all removed. Straight away.

What would she do? She'd spent her best years with Jared. Invested time and effort into a relationship she thought would be forever. That wasn't something to simply throw away. Jared was a good man. Ambitious and hard-working. Most women would kill to be with a guy like him.

She felt Lisa's arm slipping around her shoulder. 'Whatever you decide to do, I'll support you.'

Jamie lay her head on Lisa's shoulder. 'Thanks, Lise. I'm glad you're here.'

They were quiet for a few moments. Jamie closed her eyes and into her head flashed images of Ben and Jared, circling each other. She opened them again and noticed Cici half-hiding behind a curtain.

'Cici, I'm so sorry for my behaviour.' Jamie rose and adjusted the beautiful gown around her hips. 'This is gorgeous, but it's been a tough couple of days and I'm just feeling a bit overwhelmed by everything at the moment.'

'I understand completely.' She inclined her head conspiratorially. 'You're not the first bride to have dropped their bundle in this dressing room.'

'No?'

'I've seen it all. Brides walking out. Mothers of the bride walking out. Bridesmaids throwing hissy fits about their dresses. You name it, I've seen it.'

Brides who are in love with their supposedly-gay-but-apparently-straight secretary?

'Thank you for your understanding,' said Jamie, stepping gingerly towards the dressing room.

'Yes, you've been marvellous,' chimed in Lisa.

Five minutes later, Jamie emerged in her jeans and flats, which had never before felt so comfortable. Even the air in the bridal shop seemed more fresh.

'Hey, do you have time for another quick coffee,' said Jamie, linking arms with Lisa as they walked out of the shop with Cici waving after them.

'I've got to get the girls to school and introduce Ellie to her teacher.' She checked her watch. 'But I can probably squeeze in a quick one. Maybe a sneaky churros as well. I saw a place down the street.'

Jamie pulled a face. 'I'm supposed to be watching my weight for the wedding, remember?'

'You mean you're still going to—'

'Yes, of course. I'm sure all of this is just pre-wedding jitters,' she said lightly. 'I know you get it. You're the queen of having second thoughts.'

'True,' Lisa conceded. 'Mostly about Ellie at the moment.' She looked up. 'I just hope we've done the right thing.'

'You have.' She tugged Lisa to cross the road. But as they weaved in and out of the traffic, it struck her. All their lives, Jamie had been the risk-taker, while Lisa took the safe option. Now, it seemed the roles had been entirely reversed.

CHAPTER EIGHTEEN

Was this a primary school running carnival, or the Olympic trials?

Lisa stood at the entrance to the sportsground, a little overwhelmed. She had fond memories of her own school athletics carnivals. Hazy, but fond. Tramping down to the local oval where a few chalked lines had been painted over the grass. Mums and dads with picnic rugs and deckchairs set up on the hill. The sports teacher interrupting every so often with a squealing loud hailer that never seemed to work properly. Spending 50c on a bag of mixed lollies at the little concrete kiosk.

It was nothing like this. This appeared to be some kind of sports stadium. Was this really the right place for the St John's carnival? Lisa pulled out her phone and double-checked the notification from the school. Yes, this was it. Perhaps there was a little patch of grass behind it?

Lisa joined the stream of parents filing into the ground. At the turnstile, she stopped and took a breath. There was a grandstand! And it was a proper athletics track, with that bright red, all-weather surface—the kind you saw at the Olympics. In the centre of the ground, she spotted a team of adults, adorned in high-vis vests, apparently setting up a range of events for the children. High-jump, long-jump, discus, and ... oh, surely not javelin? They wouldn't let the little ones near a spear, would they? There'd be no telling what Ava would do with it!

Was this one of the twenty-first century skills that Principal Valentic had warned them about at the orientation session? While Ava had been off learning where the toilets were and how to say the school prayer, the principal had sat the parents down for 'a chat'.

'School of today is not the school you remember,' she boomed. 'Do not bother asking your child where they sit or who they sit with in class because they will not have their own desk or chair. We want agile brains and agile bodies. Constantly on the move.' She'd actually banged the lectern, to reinforce the point. 'Your generation had the three "Rs"— reading, writing and arithmetic.' She gave them a sympathetic smile that read 'you poor fools'. 'Here at St John's, we teach the four "Cs".' She counted each one off with a finger: critical thinking, creativity, communication and collaboration.

Lisa had come away perplexed. Was the school aiming to produce literate children, or the next Bill Gates? The three 'Rs' had seemingly been good enough for her. Since when had school become so *professional*? And why?

Did the children really need an Olympic-standard sports-ground for their carnival? Surely none of them would be threatening the ten-second mark for 100 metres? And it obviously wasn't a space issue, for the parents were gathered into one small section, like a tiny bait-ball. Albeit, a very colourful one. Looking at them from afar was like peering into a packet of M&M's—all primary-coloured in blues, reds, greens and golds.

Lisa stopped, and mentally face-palmed. Of course. They were dressed in the colours of their child's sports team. She checked her own outfit. White T-shirt. Blue jeans. White joggers. At least she'd remembered to dress Ellie and Ava in red T-shirts.

After the bridal shop and a speedy churros with Jamie, Lisa had raced home to take them to school and introduce Ellie to her new teacher, Mrs Booth—friendly but a little flustered as she coordinated the children into lines for the short bus ride to the ground.

They'd be here by now, judging by the lines of children starting to stream into the ground. Lisa squinted, trying to pick up either Ava or Ellie in the crowd. But it was almost impossible under those oversized sunhats the children were made to wear. She would catch up with them later, after she'd found Heather. How exactly did she plan to help her find Missy Jones, Lisa had pondered, alone in the car on the drive to the carnival. But she knew better than to question. Heather Bingley-Peters wasn't a woman to be pushed, but as her behaviour at the party had suggested, she was certainly a woman of *action*.

Lisa scoured the crowd. Someone was waving at her. Someone wearing the brightest, neon-yellow shirt that she'd ever seen. Was it Heather? Lisa scurried closer. Yes, it was. The shirt was knotted at the waist and she'd matched it with denim shorts and a chic straw visor such that the overall effect was of having just stepped off the beach in Biarritz, rather than having been thrown into a blender with Big Bird.

Lisa couldn't help herself. 'You look lovely!'

Heather angled her face to allow Lisa to get in under the visor to kiss her cheek. 'Where's *your* coloured T-shirt?' she said accusingly.

'I didn't know it was a thing, for parents to dress up.' Yet another one of those unwritten school rules for parents, like the one about not tooting anyone to hurry up in the car line. The kids were lucky. At least *their rules* were spelt out clearly.

'I wish *I* had no idea,' Heather grumbled. 'In my next life, I hope to return as a slightly hopeless but very likeable person, a bit like you, but less … denim, perhaps. You have no idea how hard it is to make yellow'—she spat out the word in disgust—'look good. I really should see about getting Savannah transferred to the blue team. So much easier,' she sighed and adjusted the knot.

'Heather,' Lisa began hesitantly. 'Thank you for offering to help me find Ellie's mum. I've had a couple of ideas overnight and—'

Heather held up a hand. 'It's not just me. I have recruits.' She tapped the two women next to her, deep in animated conversation, which stopped immediately. 'You remember Louise and Jayne from the café.'

Lisa nodded with relief. Thank god it wasn't that Kimberly woman, the lawyer. She was frightening. Hopefully their paths wouldn't cross again.

'Thank you for doing this,' said Lisa gratefully. 'I'm sure you appreciate the delicacy of the situation.'

'Louise here is a beautician who specialises in genitalia-waxing so there is quite literally nothing she hasn't seen.'

'It's amazing what people will tell you when you have hot wax in one hand and their penis in the other.' Louise's lips were the most brilliant shade of cherry red (to match her T-shirt) and she broadened them into a smile.

'And she is the soul of discretion,' said Heather knowingly. 'Believe you me. I wouldn't trust my lady-privates to anyone else.' She turned her focus to the other woman, wearing a blue T-shirt. 'And Jayne here works in IT. She's told me at least twenty times what she does but I still have no idea.'

'For the twenty-first time,' Jayne smiled indulgently, 'I develop test systems to automate medical software and I help software engineers to integrate test protocols and script development.' She smiled and offered her hand for Lisa to shake. 'In shorthand, I'm a computer nerd.'

'Exactly!' Heather said triumphantly. 'She's the IT guru of St John's. Valentic adores her.'

'She's trying to get funding for a full-time ICT. But until then, I'm kind of it.' Jayne shrugged her blue shoulders.

'Which is good news for us because today—' Heather paused as if waiting for a drum-roll '—she's operating some new whizzbang computer thingy to collect all the times and results for the children.' Again, she waited, as if expecting applause.

Lisa frowned. 'I don't quite follow.'

Heather glanced in irritation at Louise and Jayne as if to say *See! See what I'm working with here?* 'So, she'll have the laptop which has a record of names and addresses for every child in the school!'

'And the teachers, because there's a race for them too,' added Jayne. 'So, I can at least confirm if anyone from that Daceyville address has ever attended the school, either as an employee or student.'

Lisa's jaw dropped. 'That's amazing ... but are you sure it's ... legal?'

Heather gave her a look. 'Do you want to find this woman or don't you?' The three women turned to her—yellow, red and blue—it was like being grilled by the Wiggles and Lisa had the most terrible urge to giggle inappropriately, which is something she sometimes did when nervous.

Instead, she cleared her throat. 'I don't want anyone to get into trouble.'

'It's fine,' Jayne waved her hand dismissively. 'I know how to cover my tracks.' And with that, she was off. 'I'll let you know how I go,' she called over her shoulder, jogging down the steps towards a marquee around which most of the high-vis vests had congregated.

'Thank you, Heather,' said Lisa fervently. 'For arranging that.'

'But wait! There's more!' She waggled a finger. 'I've managed to obtain a physical description of this Missy Jones.'

This time, Lisa actually did clap her hands together. 'How did you? I mean, we've obviously asked Ellie but all she says is that her mum is very pretty and reminds her of a sparrow.'

'Well,' Heather began. 'Last night, I remembered that my brother-in-law has a relative who's a ...' She leant in and whispered. 'He's a postman ... A postman of all things, in that neck of the woods.' She leant out. 'He's a relative by marriage. We don't spend much time with that side of Henry's family, but I figured this was an emergency,' she said darkly. 'He remembers Ellie and Missy because Ellie used to wait by the letterbox. She was desperate to get some mail, and never did. Not a scrap.' Heather whipped out a piece of paper. 'According to him, Missy is about 172 centimetres tall, slim build, Caucasian appearance, with long brown hair and either hazel or brown eyes, he can't quite remember.'

Lisa looked about in despair. 'But that could describe about 80 per cent of the women at this carnival.'

'No! Wait!' Heather's eyes shone and she crinkled the paper between her fingers. 'She has a nose piercing, a ring.'

Louise whistled. 'Well, if she's still got it in she's going to be super-easy to spot in this lot.' She gestured around at the other parents. 'I'm tipping most of them have never even smoked a joint.' She shared a conspiratorial grin with Heather. 'So square.'

But marijuana is a gateway drug! Not to mention the schizophrenia link.

Instead, Lisa winked. 'Like we haven't all smoked a few weeds before.'

Louise and Heather looked at her strangely.

Oh god, did I say it wrong?

'So, I guess the plan is that we spread out and see if we can find this pierced weirdo?' She kept her tone light and jokey.

Heather nodded. 'I'll take the field; Louise, you take grandstand north.' She pointed to the emptier end. 'And Lisa, you take south.' The busy end. Lisa's face fell and Heather's softened in response. 'Look, it won't be a definitive search, but it's a start. I mean, if you dumped your kid on complete strangers, you'd probably stick around for a day or two to make sure everything was working out, wouldn't you? If she's got Ellie under surveillance, there's a good chance we'll find her here.' She patted Lisa's hand. 'And if we don't, I've got a plan B up my sleeve. Heather Bingley-Peters always has a plan B.'

Lisa didn't doubt it. There was probably a plan C, D, E and all the way to Z.

'What's the back-up plan?'

Heather patted her shoulder. 'Never mind that now. Let's just complete the reconnaissance, and see what Jayne comes back with. Then we'll reassess all options.' Heather stood, and Lisa imagined for a moment that she was going to ask them to put their hands together and shout some kind of sporting psych-up chant.

Three-two-one break!

Instead, she threw air-kisses to both Lisa and Louise, and dissolved into the crowd, like a neon-yellow Berocca capsule.

Louise set off for her section of the stand and Lisa walked slowly up the stairs. Where to begin? There were faces everywhere and more brown hair than her eyes could compute. She headed towards the smell of coffee. No harm in getting one. The kiosk *was* in her designated area and it would give her a chance to scope out some of the parents while in the queue.

She took a place in the line. Just backs of heads. This was pointless. She needed to see noses. The piercing was their undeniable smoking gun.

Lisa groaned quietly and the woman in front turned.

'I know what you mean.' She gave a sympathetic smile. 'Some days, I just want an intravenous caffeine drip. Children! So exhausting!'

'I didn't even drink coffee until I had children.' Lisa leant in. Brown hair? Check. Slim build? Check. One hundred and seventy-two centimetres? Definitely possibly. Nose piercing? Seemingly not, though she did have a few faint freckles on her nose. Were they freckles? Maybe a piercing hole, disguised as a freckle?

The woman touched her nose. 'Do I have something on my face? My nose?' She looked at Lisa enquiringly. 'It's probably a bit of vegemite from this morning. I was in a bit of a hurry and ate the kids' leftovers. You know how it is.' She wiped furiously and Lisa took a step back.

'No. No. You're fine. I was just … um … admiring your freckles.'

'My what?'

'Your … um … freckles.'

She gave a brittle laugh. 'Two treatments, they said. Two treatments and we'll get rid of them for you. Zap. Just like that. Magic laser. Well, they should try it! Hurts like a mother—' The line moved forward and the woman's attention turned back to the kiosk.

Silently, Lisa edged away. Who was she kidding? She wasn't cut out to play Miss Marple; the experience at the stationery store should have told her that. Lisa Wheeldon wasn't covert, she was overt. Wore her heart on her sleeve, the sleeve that today should have been swathed in red to support the girls. The girls! Where were they? She didn't want to miss their races. She'd promised to film them. There had to be another way of finding Missy Jones. Heather had mentioned a plan B. Lisa would find her, and ask what it was. Anything had to be better than skulking around and looking up people's noses!

'Lisa Wheeldon! Just the person I need.' It was Principal Valentic, dressed in her usual uniform of high-vis vest and leopard-print blouse. Though, Lisa noted, she had made some concession to the day and ditched the fishnets in favour of tailored jeans and wedge sneakers.

'How can I help?' Lisa stammered. 'I was actually on my way to do something …'

'Not too busy to help the school out of a minor crisis, I suppose?' The principal folded her arms.

Lisa bowed her head. 'Of course not.'

'Good. Our timer for lane six has failed to show up and I need someone to take her place. Immediately!' Before Lisa could answer, the principal was shoving a vest and a stopwatch into her hands and guiding her down the stairs to the field. 'Now, it's very straightforward. You press *start* when you see smoke from the starter's gun. Don't wait for the sound, go with the smoke. Then you press *stop* when the child's chest crosses the finish line. Not their head. The chest. At the end of the race, you will give your time to the official timekeeper for recording.' She glanced over to the marquee and Lisa followed her gaze to the desk where Jayne was tapping away at a laptop. At that moment, she looked up from her computer and caught Lisa's eye.

Nothing, she mouthed. Lisa's heart sank. Strike one.

'Right, now the next race is about to begin. Get ready, Mrs Wheeldon.'

Lisa squinted down the track to where a line of children was crouched, ready to jump. A puff of smoke wafted into the air. Lisa's finger pressed *start* as the gun fired. The boy in her lane reminded her of a baby giraffe—gangly arms and legs flying in all directions. Year five, at a guess. At the end, he doubled over near Lisa.

'How did I go?' he panted.

'You did brilliantly, sweetie. Fifteen point two-two seconds.'

The boy scrunched up his face. 'Point two off a PB. Did I get a place?'

'I don't know, darling. I just record the time. I didn't see who won.' Out of the corner of her eye, she spotted a teacher by the side of the track holding a stack of blue, red and green ribbons. 'Look, here comes the teacher. She'll know.'

'First—lane two,' announced the ribbon-lady. 'Second—lane four. And third—lane seven.'

The little boy's shoulders slumped. 'I didn't get anything.'

'You did your best and that's what counts.'

He shot her a look of disdain and Lisa stiffened.

You're too young to be jaded and disappointed! That's what the teen years are for.

But there was no time for comforting. The starter had raised his arm again. *Bang* went the gun and *click* went Lisa's trigger finger.

Got it right on the gun, she thought with satisfaction and looked down at the stopwatch screen. No! Wait! What was happening? The numbers weren't moving. She clicked, and clicked again. She hadn't reset. Frantically, she pressed and pressed. The race was nearly over now, and it was a close one too. This time the child in her lane was no giraffe, she was a gazelle, running with a herd of other gazelles by the looks. Smooth and graceful, Lisa's gazelle pushed out her chest to cross the line, and promptly fell to the ground with a last-gasp lunge at the finish.

'Are you all right?' Lisa touched her shoulder and the little girl wheezed and nodded.

'Timers,' barked the ribbon-lady. 'No clear visual on that race. Too close to call. We'll have to go off the stopwatches.'

Lisa's stomach plummeted. Five point three-four seconds said her stopwatch. That obviously wasn't right. She cringed as the teacher approached.

'Lane six?' She looked at Lisa expectantly.

'Umm ... I ... ah ... had a technical problem,' she said quietly. 'The stopwatch didn't fire.'

The teacher glared, steely. 'Did anyone get a visual on the result? I repeat, did anyone get a visual on the result?'

Lisa felt seven pairs of eyes drilling into her as the other timers looked up from their stopwatches. No one spoke.

'All right,' said the teacher. 'I believe it was between lane four and lane six. Hands up, who believes it was lane six?' Three hands went up, including Lisa's who really had no idea who'd won but felt terrible at the idea of having failed the child. 'Lane four it is.' She held out the blue ribbon.

'Wait! Wait!' A blonde woman was running towards the finish line, holding up her phone. Oh blast. It was Kimberly from the café. 'Wait! What are you doing? It wasn't lane four, it was six. My Madison clearly crossed the line first. Look! The timer must have got it wrong. Where is she?'

With a sinking feeling, Lisa tried to saunter discreetly to the side of the track. Meanwhile, Kimberly stood over the teacher, phone thrust into her face. Eyes roving about the track, her gaze finally settled on Lisa and she shot her a look of disgust. 'Some people just shouldn't be placed in positions of responsibility,' she huffed.

Was she talking only about the timing? Or about Ellie as well? Lisa felt a chill settle in her stomach.

'All right.' The teacher finally looked up and passed the phone back to Kimberly. 'Having reviewed the video I'm going to reverse my decision. First place to lane six. Second to lane four. Moving along, everyone.'

The rest of the carnival passed in a daze. So focused was Lisa on not stuffing up the timing again, she barely registered the house cheers, or Ellie coming first in her race, or Ava coming third.

'A green ribbon!' she crowed, holding it up. 'My favourite colour. It's like I won.'

Lisa's congratulations were perfunctory—a quick hug, then Ava sent on her way. She had the next race to worry about!

Finally, it was over. The children swarmed back onto the buses while the teacher collected stopwatches from the timers and thanked them for a *near*-seamless day. Lisa headed slowly back to the grandstand, head thumping and bladder nearly bursting. She hadn't even had a wee break. After the fiasco with Kimberly's daughter, she hadn't dared.

Back in the grandstand, she found Heather, Jayne and Louise where she'd left them. They were chatting easily, laughing, and eating off what appeared to be a cheese platter. Lisa sat down heavily as Heather placed a piece of brie on a cracker and offered it to her.

'What happened to you?' she said crossly. 'You were supposed to be on reconnaissance, not timing. We had Jayne looking after that side of things, remember?'

'I didn't get a choice,' said Lisa wearily. 'I need a wee.' She chomped slowly. 'How did everyone go? Any success?'

Jayne shook her head. 'Nothing at all for that address in the system.'

Heather and Louise exchanged glances.

'I thought I saw someone. Her hair was in a cap, but I think she had the nose ring,' said Heather slowly. 'By the time I'd called Louise to back me up, she'd gone.'

Lisa felt energy from the food starting to enter her veins. 'Did you follow her?'

'I tried. But it was like she disappeared into thin air. Poof.' Heather snapped her fingers.

'Could you narrow down what she looks like? Draw a picture? Maybe I'd know her if I saw something more specific.'

Heather rolled her eyes. 'Hon, even Savannah-Rose thinks my stick figures are terrible. It'd be a total waste of time.'

'So, that's it then?' said Lisa. 'I can't just give up.'

'No one's suggesting you give up.' Heather patted her arm. 'I told you I had a plan B.' She stopped. 'You need to hire a private investigator.'

'A private investigator,' Lisa shook her head. 'No, no, Scott would never agree to that and even if I could get him to agree, I wouldn't even know where to *begin* to get a private investigator.'

Heather smiled. 'Lisa, Lisa, Lisa, you know I wouldn't suggest a plan unless I knew how to carry it out. I've got the perfect person to help you.'

'You know a PI? How?'

'Henry *travels* a lot for work.' She used air-quotes around the word. 'I just like to be sure that it's strictly for business, and not funny-business.'

Louise and Jayne nodded approvingly.

'But how much will it cost?'

'No more than a few hundred dollars. A thousand at most.'

'I don't know, Heather. I don't think Scott would like me spending—'

'Gosh, if I let Henry dictate all my purchases my shoe cupboard would be practically empty,' she laughed. 'A woman's got to have *some* say over the finances. Besides, can you really put a dollar value on reuniting a little girl with her mother?'

Three cocked faces turned to Lisa.

Scott would understand. He never begrudged any of her purchases. Then again, this was different. It felt dangerous, and a little bit seedy. It was a bit like the time she'd dressed up as Julia Roberts from *Pretty Woman* for a friend's thirtieth. Nothing really inappropriate about it, such a gorgeously romantic movie after all, but as a friend pointed out, she was a prostitute and Lisa had spent the rest of the night feeling a bit wrong and uncomfortable.

But Heather had a point. She couldn't just give up because that would be giving up on Ellie.

'All right, let's call him.' She swallowed hard. Maybe this man would be her Richard Gere.

CHAPTER NINETEEN

Missy tightened her grip on the suitcase and took a seat on the bench where a few others had settled in to wait for the train. At two o'clock in the morning, Central Station was all but deserted, except for the homeless who took refuge under its various eaves and porticos. There seemed to be more of them than there were actual passengers. Who would bother with a long-haul train journey in this day and age of cheap domestic airline fares? Only the truly desperate, people like her, who either didn't have a car or couldn't afford the rigmarole of airports and their incessant need for identity checks and all-seeing cameras.

She looked up and took in the small collection of people around her—all hunched shoulders, eyes to the ground, hands clutching at plastic bags and fast-food containers. There was one exception. A little girl, slightly smaller than Ellie, sitting on the bench near Missy. In the dim light, her pupils were the size of blackcurrants and she kept a tight grip on her Dora the Explorer wheelie bag.

Missy winked at her. 'Going on a holiday?'

'We're going to Coffs Harbour to see dolphins,' the girl said solemnly.

'Are you? Well, that's exciting.' Missy remembered the dolphin aquarium. Her mum had taken her for her tenth birthday. There was a photo, somewhere, of the dolphin kissing her cheek. The Pet-Porpoise Pool, it was known as back then. But it had changed to something else now. Dolphin Marine Magic rang a bell.

'And we're going to the Big Banana, too. Aren't we?' She tugged on her mum's hand and the woman turned to her wearily.

'I don't know, Layla. We'll see when we get there.' The woman didn't meet Missy's gaze. The little girl lolled against her, a stained and too-small T-shirt riding up over her bellybutton.

'I think a dolphin's skin would feel slimy. My friend Alice touched one when she went to Queensland.'

'Did she?'

'Layla, be quiet,' said her mother sharply. 'We don't all need to hear you yabbering on.'

'Sorry, Mummy.' The little girl kissed her hand. 'I love you.'

'I love you too,' she sighed.

'To the moon and back?'

'Further.'

This time, the mother gave a weak smile and Missy noted the bruise, blooming in the socket of her left eye. The woman turned away quickly.

With a hiss, the doors of the train slid open. It was ready for them. Layla jumped up and her mother followed, her steps laboured.

But Missy's feet wouldn't move.

This was wrong. This was all wrong. She needed to be with Ellie. It was madness, leaving her with the Wheeldons. What was she thinking? She should turn around right now, go back, tell them it had all been a mistake and she'd changed her mind. Of course she wasn't leaving her daughter, the sunshine of her life. How could any mother do that?

Her phone bleeped with a text message.

He's definitely out. He came by today.

Missy flinched. Her stomach contracted. The confirmation of it was like an electric shock. She'd known this was coming—but that didn't protect her from the hurt of it, or the fear.

She tapped the screen.

I'm coming.

Ellie will be okay, she told herself. *You saw her at the carnival. She's happy. She's safe. Lisa Wheeldon is doing everything you would do. Maybe more.*

She flipped the phone shut and stepped forward into the carriage.

CHAPTER TWENTY

Sitting in the café and sipping a cappuccino, Lisa could almost pretend it was a normal Thursday afternoon. Except that it wasn't, because any minute, she was expecting her private investigator (even the *idea* of it made her choke a little on the froth) to turn up, and that made it a galaxy away from being a normal Thursday afternoon.

She tugged on her shirt. 'Do I look all right?'

Heather rolled her eyes. 'This isn't a job interview. *You're* asking the questions, not him.'

'But, seriously, is it okay?' She loved this shirt. Midnight blue, with faint white stripes, it was one she'd worn when she used to work in the city, before Ava. It was her 'client' shirt—the one that made her feel crisp, and efficient for external meetings. Now, it was too tight across the boobs and one of the buttons seemed perilously close to popping.

Heather looked more closely and put her head to the side. 'You look like a naughty secretary. The whole button-popping thing is a little bit sexy, in a Benny Hill kind of way.'

'Mummy, I'm thirsty. Where's my babycino?' Dramatically, Jemima spread herself across Lisa's lap. Heather flinched at the touch of the little girl's fingertips against her black lycra-clad thigh.

'Don't you have an iPad or something?' she said irritably.

'Scott and I have decided to limit their screen time,' said Lisa, trying desperately to minimise the piousness in her voice, but ultimately failing as she battled to stop Jemima from up-ending the table with her feet.

'Oh, here. Give her my phone. If your husband finds out, you can blame me.' Heather handed over the sleek device. 'Don't drop it, kid.' She held her finger in front of Jemima's face and the little girl cowered. With her oversized sunglasses, all-black exercise attire and long arms and legs, Heather resembled a human-sized blowfly.

'I won't,' she promised, and located a game with a speed that both appalled Lisa and made her feel slightly vindicated.

So much for the people who say children need a device so they don't get left behind.

Heather drummed the table. Speakeasy was different at this time of day, 2 pm, just before school pick-up. There was no dreamboat barista for a start, just an older woman who seemed more interested in cleaning down the coffee machine than actually making any coffee with it.

'Ah, here he is.' Heather beamed.

Lisa had been expecting someone shadowy, slick. Maybe with a hat. Perhaps not a trench-coat—that would be a little too clichéd—but someone with at least an *element* of danger or intrigue about them. Not this guy, with his white linen pants and baby-blue shirt. He was more Miami Vice than James Bond.

'Hey, gorgeous, great to see you.' Jeff kissed Heather easily on the cheek and sat down. 'How's Henry?'

'Oh, you know. Still travelling.' Her laugh had a high trill.

'I can cover him again, just say the word?' Jeff raised his eyebrows. 'Anything for my favourite client.'

Lisa looked from Jeff to Heather. What was going on here? The last thing she'd expected was a flirtatious PI! If anyone had reason to worry about infidelity, it was surely Henry! An investigator was supposed to clarify matters, not muddy them.

'So, Jeff, as I explained on the phone, Lisa here is looking for a woman who goes by the name of Missy Jones.'

'Jones?' Jeff raised his eyebrows.

Lisa chimed in. 'That's what her daughter calls her. But you're right, we don't actually know for sure. I have a physical description, and her address written down for you, along with Ellie's date of birth, or what she thinks it is.' She passed over the piece of paper on which she'd conscientiously typed out everything they knew. 'And I also have this.' She handed him the letter from Missy.

'Can I keep this?' He held it up.

'No, I need that back, just in case.'

Jeff pulled out his phone and snapped a photo of Missy's letter. 'Never had a case like this before,' he mused, studying the writing.

'Do you think you can find her?' Lisa put her elbows on the table.

'Of course I can. Just ask Heather here. She knows all about what I can do.' He gave Heather a wink and Lisa got the distinct feeling of being more unnecessary at the table than a fifth leg.

Her bag was vibrating. Lisa fished out her phone while Jeff and Heather continued to make eyes at each other.

'Mrs Wheeldon. It's Jane Valentic.' Principal Valentic?

Lisa covered the mouthpiece. 'I have to take this,' she whispered urgently, knocking the table in her haste to get up.

'Is everything all right? The girls? Are they okay?' The words tumbled out of Lisa's mouth.

'Ellie and Ava are fine, but there has been … an incident, relating to behaviour.'

'What kind of incident?'

'It would be best if we discussed that in person.'

'Of course, I'll be there in a minute.'

Lisa hung up and threw the phone into her bag. 'C'mon, Jems. Time to give Heather's phone back to her.'

'Nooooooo … I don't want to.'

'Jemima! Now!' said Lisa sharply.

'What's happened? What's the great emergency? We're in a meeting, remember.' Heather placed her hand on Lisa's arm.

'Something's happened at school. I don't know what … Something about their behaviour. That was Principal Valentic on the phone.' Lisa was breathless, trying to get the words out.

Heather nodded efficiently. 'I'll finish up here. You go on ahead.'

'Thank you.' Lisa offered her hand to Jeff. 'I'm sorry to go … It sounds like you know what we need. Send me your invoice when you can ... and ... um ... I can't think of anything else.'

'Leave it with me, Lisa,' he said in a deep, reassuring voice. 'A couple of weeks. I'll find her.'

As Lisa tried to stride towards the school gates, Jemima clung to her leg like a limpet. 'Carry me, Mummy. Pleeeeease. I can't walk. My leg hurts. See.'

Lisa fought the urge to snap at her daughter and instead leant down to inspect.

'Darling, I can't see anything.'

'There.' She pointed to a blemish-free piece of skin and Lisa leant in more closely. 'There's BLOOD!'

Finally, Lisa spotted it. A tiny scratch and a speck of blood so miniscule that even the strongest microscope would have struggled to detect it.

'Darling, I think you'll survive,' Lisa said solemnly.

'I need a bandaid,' Jemima moaned.

Lisa felt in her pockets. They were normally a treasure trove of children's detritus—hair bands, tiny plastic figurines, a bandaid or two (her daughters had unquestioning faith in the healing powers of a sticky-strip). Of course, today, they were empty.

'I'm sorry, darling. I don't have a bandaid.'

'Then carry me.' Jemima lifted her arms weakly.

Lisa sighed. Carrying her youngest born was like carrying a wriggling baby elephant. And she didn't have the energy.

'I can't carry you, darling. Mummy's feeling a bit sick.' True. Sick with worry. Lisa went to stride away.

'Nooooooo!' Jemima attached herself to Lisa's leg.

'All right, honey.' She hoisted Jemima onto her hip and scurried towards the school gate, with her daughter's hair tickling her neck.

Nearing the school reception area, Lisa spotted Ava and Ellie, arms slung about each other and heads bowed.

Like sisters already.

But as she shifted Jemima onto her other hip, she could see that both girls were crying. Ellie seemed to be the most upset, with Ava talking to her animatedly.

'What's wrong, my darlings? What happened?' She leant down and Jemima immediately climbed out of her arms to cuddle Ellie's leg.

'Xanthe was being mean to her all day.' Ava patted Ellie's shoulder and Ellie nodded sadly in confirmation.

'She says my mummy doesn't love me and that's why she left me.' Ellie hiccoughed as a crack opened up in Lisa's heart.

'Darling, you know that's not true. Come here.' Lisa opened her arms and Ellie fell into them, sobbing.

'She says I don't even have a real mummy.'

Lisa squeezed her even harder, wishing desperately in that moment she had some magical power that could conjure Missy Jones out of thin air.

'Sweetheart, you know you have a mother.' Lisa took Ellie's hands and looked her directly in the eye. 'And she loves you very much. She's just had to go away for work, remember? That's all. You're just staying with us until she comes back, and we're so happy that your mummy chose us to have you. Now!' Lisa turned her attention to Ava. 'Honey, did you do something to Xanthe?'

Ava nodded. 'I bit her on the arm.'

Lisa gasped. 'Oh, no. Darling, we never bite people. Even when they've done something really, really bad.' Biting was the biggest playground crime a child could commit. She knew from experience that mothers tended to completely freak out, as if the bite might carry a rabies infection. Everyone knew there was only one thing worse than being the victim of a chomp—it was being the mother of the chomper. The guilt was extreme.

'Is this your child?' The voice came from a blonde woman. A woman Lisa recognised. Oh no! What was Kimberly doing here? It must be *her* Xanthe. Oh bugger bum!

'Yes, this is Ava, and I'm Lisa, if you remember from the other day ... from uh ... the café, and the carnival.' She thrust out her hand, hoping the friendly approach might defuse the situation. 'You're Kim, right?'

'It's Kimberly, as a matter of fact.' She stood with her hands on her hips. A little girl, her face bookended by pigtails, peeped out from behind Kimberly's legs and poked out her tongue.

Like mother, like daughter.

'My apologies, Kimberly. I'm so sorry but it seems we have a little problem between our girls.'

'You call biting a little problem? I call it a big one. Your Ava drew blood. Look!' Kimberly thrust forward Xanthe's arm and pointed at it. Lisa peered in the direction of her finger. The 'injury' on Xanthe's arm was as microscopic as Jemima's leg graze.

'Hmmm ... I see,' said Lisa noncommittally.

'I demand your daughter apologise.' Kimberly folded her arms.

'Well, I'm sure Ava's sorry for what she did,' Lisa said neutrally, 'but she was somewhat provoked by what Xanthe said to Ellie.'

'All she said was the truth,' Kimberly spat out. 'The child,' she pointed at Ellie, 'has a mother who dumped her. Now what does that tell you?'

Lisa clapped her hands over Ellie's ears and felt pure, hot anger rising into her throat. How could a woman, another mother no less, say such horrible things in front of a poor, innocent child like Ellie? Let alone put her at risk by saying them within earshot of the principal!

'Now, you listen to me.' Lisa shook her finger. 'Ellie's mother has more love in her heart than you'll ever know and just because she's not around to show it at the moment doesn't even matter, because I'll tell you what. I AM!' Lisa roared.

'Ladies, ladies. What's going on here? Lower your voices. Please!' Principal Valentic put herself between Lisa and Kimberly, stamping her stiletto. 'My office. Now!'

In the corridor outside the principal's office, Lisa rested her aching head against the cool cement. Following Heather's lead, she'd given her phone to the girls, who were happily watching a video of an American woman opening toys and playing with them. It was quite bizarre, the things that kept little girls entranced, but it was G-rated and Lisa was too stressed to care.

A low murmur of voices emanated from inside the principal's office but Lisa couldn't make out any distinct words. Kimberly had been in there for fifteen minutes now. What could they be talking about? Was the principal trying to appease Kimberly? Were they decrying Lisa's parenting skills?

At school, Lisa had been a model student. Solid grades. Always attentive and helpful. She knew the rules and stuck to them. Not because she necessarily believed in them. Some seemed downright silly—like the ban on brushing hair in the street. What was that about? How did the public maintenance of one's appearance bring the entire school into disrepute? No, she didn't quite understand the rationale for all of the rules but she stuck to them religiously. It was fear that made her obedient. The mere idea of detention or a visit to the principal's office was enough to send her stomach into nervous spasms. Beyond anything, she hated disappointing people—and she knew how disappointed her family and teachers would be if she broke the rules, even the stupid ones.

Now, having successfully avoided the principal's office for thirty-eight years, she found herself in the very situation she had dreaded. But if the death of her parents had taught her anything, it was that following rules didn't always keep you safe. Occasionally, life just reared up and bit you where it hurt, no matter how well behaved you were.

Finally, the door opened.

'Mrs Wheeldon, please come in. The girls can wait outside.'

Xanthe dawdled out the door. She'd obviously been crying, given the red rash around her eyes, and Lisa's heart gave way. 'Why don't you sit with the girls and watch the video?' Lisa patted the seat next to her.

'Yeah, Xanthe, come and look,' said Ava, shuffling along the seat to make room.

Kids. They could forgive and forget so easily.

Not like parents.

As Lisa took a seat in the principal's office, she glanced sideways at Kimberly, who looked like she was sucking on a sour lemon lolly. She seemed transfixed by the Aboriginal dot-painting on the wall and refused to meet Lisa's eye.

'Ladies.' Principal Valentic placed her elbows on the desk, fingertips touching. 'May I remind you of our school policy regarding discipline. At St John's, vigilante justice by either students or parents will not be tolerated. We do not take matters into our own hands. Am I making myself clear?'

'Yes, Principal Valentic,' said Lisa dutifully.

'Kimberly?' said Principal Valentic.

'Yes,' Kimberly snapped. 'Go on.'

'Right.' Principal Valentic put on her glasses. 'This matter does present ... *peculiar* challenges, posed by Ellie's delicate ... uh ... *situation*, with her mother being in absentia to care for her own mother.' She gave a sympathetic smile and Kimberly shot Lisa a look.

Please don't say anything! Please! Hate me all you like but don't sell Ellie out.

Lisa squeezed her thighs together. Kimberly opened and shut her mouth, and the principal continued. 'However, the fact is, we cannot accept violence of any kind towards another student—'

Lisa cut in. 'I've spoken to Ava, and she's very sorry for biting Xanthe. I've explained that she cannot bite anyone, whatever they say, and she understands that. It won't happen again, I promise you.'

Lisa took a deep breath to assess the reaction to her mea culpa. Principal Valentic nodded her approval. Kimberly sat stony faced.

'Excellent,' said the principal. 'And she will of course apologise to Xanthe.'

'Of course,' Lisa agreed, thinking that at that point she would probably have agreed to anything in order to get her precious daughter back in the principal's good books. That was the thing about children—their suffering, their pain, was always shared pain and suffering. If Ava was in trouble at school, Lisa felt it too. And it was the last thing she wanted for either of them.

'As for Xanthe,' the principal began. 'She understands that what she said to Ellie was wrong—'

'Although true,' said Kimberly under her breath but just loud enough for Lisa to hear.

'Did you say something?' asked Principal Valentic.

'Nothing at all, Jane. Please go on,' said Kimberly, waving her hand dismissively.

'Right, well, as per our restorative justice policy, Xanthe will also make an apology to Ellie. Does this approach satisfy everyone?'

'Yes,' said Lisa straight away.

Kimberly sighed. 'Let's just get on with it.'

The girls trooped in to the principal's office with heads bowed and shoulders slumped. When Principal Valentic spoke, they lifted their chins and gave her their full attention. Ava went first and delivered such a heartfelt and sincere apology to Xanthe 'for making her arm hurt so badly' that Lisa thought she might cry. Ava finished her speech by throwing herself into Xanthe's arms and clinging to her tightly. 'I'm really, really sorry and I'll never bite you or anyone again, even if you say really mean things.'

My sweet, sweet girl.

Then it was Xanthe's turn.

'I'm very sorry that I made you cry, Ellie. But Ava used to be *my* best friend, and now she's *your* best friend and that's made me feel very sad and upset.' Xanthe paused and looked to her mum for support but Kimberly was too busy inspecting her cuticles.

'Ellie, your mum is probably a really nice lady,' Xanthe went on, fidgeting at her zip pocket. 'But she never comes to pick you up, so I don't know …' she trailed off.

'She *is* a really nice lady,' said Ellie. 'She's the best.'

'Do you miss her?' said Xanthe.

'I do,' said Ellie. 'I just want her to come home.' Her voice started to quaver.

'I'm sorry. Please don't cry.' Xanthe looked in alarm to her mum, then Principal Valentic, then Lisa. 'Did I say something bad?'

'No, sweetie. No.' Lisa rubbed Ellie's back. 'She just misses her mum. That's all.'

'Right then. Are we done here?' Kimberly grabbed for Xanthe's hand and looked expectantly at Principal Valentic.

'Yes, you're free to go.' The principal stood. 'Let's hope our next meeting is under happier circumstances.'

Without a word to Lisa, Kimberly marched out of the office, dragging her daughter behind her. But at the door, Xanthe broke free of her mother's grasp and ran back to give Ellie one last hug.

'I really am very sorry.'

'It's all right,' sniffed Ellie.

'Xanthe!' called Kimberly from the hallway. 'Xanthe-Sienna. You'd better get here right now. Or you're going to be late to ballet. And you know what Miss Victoria is like if you're late. Now, where's Madison?' She tapped her foot.

Miss Victoria couldn't be half as scary as you.

After one last hug, Xanthe flew out the door. 'Coming, Mum,' she bellowed.

Ellie and Ava looked at each other and giggled.

'Right then, girls. I'll see you tomorrow.' Principal Valentic stood behind the desk, knuckles on the table.

'Goodbye, Principal Valentic. May god bless you,' they chanted before proceeding out the door, with Jemima trailing behind.

Lisa collected her handbag and headed for the door.

'Oh, Mrs Wheeldon, just one more thing,' called Principal Valentic. 'I hope you understand—children will be children.'

'Yes …' said Lisa uncertainly. What was the principal getting at?

'What I mean is—I suspect this won't be the last time we meet in this office. Once children perceive something different about one of their peers … Well, let's just say that children can be very cruel.'

Not to mention parents.

Lisa crossed her handbag across her body. 'I think as long as we're proactive and nip any negative comments in the bud—'

'I know you're doing your best.' The principal's eyes suddenly softened. 'But I've worked with children for twenty years.' She paused. 'Ellie deserves the truth … about her grandmother … and her illness.'

The truth? That wasn't the truth. How could she possibly tell Ellie what was really going on? That she'd been abandoned? That would crush her, and make Lisa no better than Xanthe. Besides, there was more to the story. There had to be. But she couldn't tell Principal Valentic that, and she certainly couldn't tell Ellie either.

Lisa walked out of the school in a daze, trying to process what Principal Valentic had said, while the three girls hopped about her like rabbits.

'Look, there's Xanthe and her mum,' called Ava, pointing down the street.

Lisa's breath caught in her throat. The last thing she wanted was to come face to face again with Kimberly. Fortunately, they were now too far away for that possibility. As the girls prattled away, Lisa kept her eyes on the mother and her two daughters. Madison trailed behind, while Xanthe slumped in Kimberly's arms—head buried in her mother's skinny neck and her hands moving up and down Kimberly's back in a gentle, stroking motion. After a few strokes, Xanthe kissed her mother's shoulder. The way Kimberly shimmied and shook her head, Lisa could tell she was irritated by the touch and was telling her daughter to stop. Xanthe buried her head again. This time, motionless.

Lisa felt tears springing to the fore. How could Kimberly be so mean?

Principal Valentic was right. A mother could do the worst—and still be loved by a child. But at some point, the child deserved the truth.

When Jeff finds her. When we have good news. That's when I'll tell Ellie.

CHAPTER TWENTY-ONE

Missy took a breath and stepped out of the train carriage and onto the platform. Every muscle and bone in her body ached from a journey that should have taken ten hours but had turned into fifteen. Fifteen hours of tossing, turning and pacing. Thoughts racing. In the end, she'd given up on sleep and watched for the kilometres to tick by. The lights in the carriage had dimmed, and if she concentrated hard, beyond her own reflection, she could pick out the occasional farmhouse in the distance. A glow of lights that suggested a small township. At 6 am, there had been an announcement. The train would be stopping for ten minutes in Taree. Missy took the chance to stretch her legs and use the toilet. It was grim. Paper everywhere. Wee on the seats. A disposal bin for needles next to the soap dispenser. Re-boarding the train, she passed a collection of passengers huddled on the platform and smoking furiously. Then, the train went nowhere and the ten-minute stop became a five-hour delay for some unspecified mechanical issue.

At least Ellie wasn't with her.

Missy yawned and stretched. She was here now, later than anticipated, but still, she was here, right on dusk.

She breathed deeply and took in the sky, all pinks and oranges and soft as sherbet. There was salt in the air. A sharp, vinegary smell. Craning her neck, she glimpsed the ocean beyond the train tracks and, rising up in the distance out of the water, the mountainous Muttonbird Island where the shearwaters flocked every spring to nest and raise their young before setting off again for the 4000-kilometre flight to the Philippines for mating. Missy's stomach turned. Home.

'Bye-bye.' It was the child she'd spoken with at the start of the trip. Behind, her mum stepped heavily out of the carriage.

'Bye-bye, sweetie. I hope you get to see that dolphin.'

'I'll give it a cuddle for you,' she said seriously.

'I would love that.' She knelt down and offered her hand for the little girl to shake. 'Thank you.'

And with that, she was gone, trailing behind a mother weighed down with candy-striped plastic bags and, Missy surmised, the burden of having wrenched a child away from everything she knew and loved, into an entirely new and uncertain world. But one she had to believe was safer. Definitely safer.

'You okay, love? Taxi rank's that way if you need it.' The station master, hands on hips, stood before her.

'No, I'm fine. Someone's meeting me.'

'Homecoming, eh? Nothing like it. No place like home.' He winked and headed back inside the ticket office.

No place like home.

Missy shivered and started walking. They'd agreed to meet at the park near the jetty. It would be quiet there now. Just a few joggers, a couple of surfers and the occasional fishing trawler heading out for the nightly catch. She'd messaged about arriving late.

As Missy neared the meeting point, her steps started to quicken.

There. Over on the park bench near the kids' playground. The back of that head. The angle at which it sat. The hair—a little more grey than she remembered. But still, it was nearly as familiar to her as Ellie's.

'Mum!' Missy couldn't help herself. She ran, dropping the suitcase out of her hands. At the bench, she fell into the arms she knew and loved so well.

'Missy, love. Let me look at you. Gawd, I've missed you.' Terri leant out and her eyes appraised her. 'You look absolutely knackered.'

'I'm okay.' Missy sat beside her mum. Definitely a little older. A little heavier. Wrinkles she hadn't noticed when they said goodbye six years ago. But still—that same smell. The smell of *her.* Missy couldn't even begin to describe it. Just like every home had its own distinctive scent, so too did her dear old mum. It was home.

'Did you make sure you weren't followed?' asked Missy, looking about nervously.

'Missy,' she scolded. 'I'm not a fool.' She took her daughter's hand and squeezed it. 'Where's Ellie? Is she all right?'

'She's fine,' Missy confirmed. 'For your own sake, it's better you don't know where, just in case …' she trailed off.

Terri squeezed again. 'I'm not afraid, if that's what you're worried about. You got photos?'

Missy produced her phone. 'Here.' She started flicking through images. Ellie eating spaghetti with a big tomatoey grin, riding her bike with legs splayed out from the pedals, kicking a soccer ball with intense concentration.

'Oh gawd, when did she get so big?' Terri said in wonder. 'She's an absolute doll, Miss. An absolute bloody doll.' Her mum wiped her eyes. 'Every night, I say a prayer to whoever might be listening.' She raised her eyes skyward. 'And I pray with all my heart that I get to see my baby granddaughter, at least one more time before I die.' Terri started to weep quietly.

'Oh, Mum,' said Missy, burying her head into Terri's shoulder. 'I'm so sorry. You don't know how sorry. I stuffed up so bad.'

Terri sniffed, wiping her nose with a tissue. 'Now, don't you go saying silly things like that, my girl. It's not you that's to blame. It's *him*.' She spat out the words with venom, anger taking over her sadness.

'He's been around?'

'Once. Said he just wanted to talk to you. I told him I had no idea where you were and that if he came around again, I'd call the police.' She stopped suddenly and dropped her eyes, fiddling with the tissue.

'What?' asked Missy. 'What else happened? You need to tell me, Mum. I need to know what I'm up against here.'

'The bastard took her photo. The one you sent on her fourth birthday. I had it framed and being the bloody idiot I am, I had it near the front door and the bastard took it.' Terri curled her fingers nervously against her thigh.

So he knows what Ellie looks like ...

'Okay,' Missy nodded, trying to hide her own growing unease. 'Anything else ... Mum?'

'When he left, I watched him ...' she began nervously, still unable to meet Missy's gaze. 'I watched him right to the car ... and ... and I saw it.' She stopped again.

'Saw what, Mum. Please.'

'I think ... I think he had a gun,' she whispered. 'Down his back ... I saw it through his shirt ... That shape.'

Missy sat back, her mind spinning. They were all in grave, grave danger. A gun?

'Oh, Mum, I'm so sorry.' She buried her head in her hands.

'Don't you worry about me. I'm a big girl. I can take care of myself.' Terri clutched her arm. 'Miss, it's you I'm worried about. It's too dangerous. You shouldn't be here. Go back to Sydney. It's a big city. He won't find you. You and Ellie are safe there.'

Missy shook her head violently. 'No,' she said firmly. 'No, no. I can't just sit there and wait for him to come and find us. I have to know what he's up to. I have to work out what to do. How to protect us.'

'What about the police? Maybe they could help?'

Missy gave her a look. 'Yes, because they were so great last time,' she spat out the words and felt immediate guilt as Terri recoiled. 'Sorry, Mum, it's not you I'm cross with ... It's just ... it's not like he's actually done anything yet. He hasn't really threatened us. You didn't *actually* see the gun. What could they arrest him for?'

Terri dabbed her nose. 'So what *are* you going to do, love?'

'I'm going to watch him. See who he's hanging out with, whether he's gone straight back into it. Try and get something concrete that I can give to the cops as a tip-off. Get him put away again.'

Terri nodded. 'Okay … okay.' From under her cardigan, she produced a roll of bills. Missy tensed. It had to be at least three grand. 'This is everything I've got, darl. But it should at least keep you going for a few weeks.'

'Mum, please, no. You can't.'

'I can,' she said firmly, pressing the notes into Missy's chest and looking round furtively. 'Take it, quick, before anyone sees; and I've rented a car for you, just like you asked—over in the parking lot.' She inclined her head and pressed the keys into her daughter's hands.

'I won't let you down.' Missy pocketed the cash and wrapped her arm around Terri in a tight, fierce hug.

'Ellie,' Terri whispered. 'Don't let Ellie down.'

CHAPTER TWENTY-TWO

Jared drummed his fingers against the table and looked about the café. 'So what's this guy's name? The celebrant?'

'Peter.' Jamie checked her phone. 'Peter McCluskey.'

'Hope he's not late to the wedding.'

'He's not late. Yet. We're early.'

Jared had rearranged an appointment with one of his most important clients for this meeting with the celebrant—something he rarely did. 'I'll give this guy two minutes. Then I'm out of here. All right?'

Jamie nodded and went back to her phone. They'd agreed to meet at a café that was exactly halfway between both of their offices, leaving them both equally inconvenienced. For a Tuesday morning, it was quiet. At 10.30 am, the morning buzz had dropped off. Most city workers would now have eyeballs glued to their computers, or be seated around oversized conference tables for meetings. That's where Jared wanted to be. Wedding planning was not his thing and he couldn't quite understand the joy that women got out of it. Jared didn't mind organising a party. That was fine. That was great! Food, booze, music—terrific. Like that little thing he'd organised in their courtyard for Jamie—that was fun to put together, even though she'd come home too late to really enjoy it. But weddings were different. They seemed to come with a much longer and more tedious list of things to organise. Jared just wanted to get married and get out of Sydney. He couldn't stop thinking about the kid. Ellie. Whenever he least expected it—during meetings, out cycling, shaving in the morning—her face would pop into his head and a chill would settle over his stomach. Was she the child, he thought? Could she be? Surely she wasn't?

He simply couldn't bring himself to answer. He couldn't even complete the questions in his head! And he sure as shit wasn't brave enough to talk about it with Jamie. If she found out, she would dump him for sure. And he wouldn't blame her. If they could just hurry up, get married and get out of Sydney, he might have a chance of getting away with it all.

'Do I even need to be here?' Jared finished his cappuccino and fidgeted with his phone.

'Yes. Peter said you had to come. There are papers to sign. Official ones.' Poor Jamie. She looked stressed and Jared knew he was being a prick. So far, in the ten days since the proposal, he'd successfully dodged all the appointments—for flowers and cake and string quartets—all the stuff he really didn't give a shit about. The least he could do was be a bit grateful. Show a little interest. Or she might start to think he didn't want to get married at all. It was weird—he'd gone from being ambivalent about getting married, to suddenly really wanting it. He got it now. He'd taken Jamie for granted, and it had taken the prospect of losing her to make him wake up and smell the fucking coffee.

'How about another coffee?' said Jared. 'My shout.'

Jamie's eyes brightened. 'Great! Skim cap, thanks.' She smiled, and Jared felt like even more of a prick. It was so easy to make her happy.

'I'll order.' As Jared went to stand, Jamie grabbed his hand and pointed at a man in a suit walking towards them.

'That's him,' she whispered to Jared. 'The coffee can wait.'

Jared followed her gaze. 'He looks like a fucking real estate agent,' he hissed. In Jared's experience of weddings, which was growing lengthier by the year as mate after mate said goodbye to bachelorhood, celebrants fell into one of two categories: middle-aged ladies in flowery dresses who waxed lyrical about the power of love, or second-hand car salesmen-types like this guy, who spoke like they were doing the hard-sell on marriage. Where were the magisterial types? Why couldn't a wedding celebrant simply be a person of gravitas and uncomplicated sincerity? If Jared could have been bothered, he would have looked into getting a judge to do it. In the end, though, he figured it didn't really matter who married them. As long as they ended up with the right piece of paper at the end of the ceremony, the piece of paper that said they were legally married, it didn't really matter which clown presided over the ceremony. Just as long as he or she was qualified to do it.

'Just give him a chance.' Jamie stood and straightened her skirt while Jared jammed his hands into his pockets.

'Jamie?' The man in the suit raised his eyebrows.

'Yes. I'm Jamie.' She shook his hand. 'And this is my fiancé, Jared.'

'Peter McCluskey. Call me Pete. It's a pleasure to meet you both. And congratulations on your engagement.' The celebrant stood formally, with his hands by his side, reminding Jared of an undertaker standing by a coffin. 'May I be so bold as to take a look at the lovely ring that I spotted on your hand, Jamie?'

She held out her hand and Peter whistled. 'Woo-ee, she's an absolute beauty.' He winked at Jared. 'Set you back a few pay packets, eh, Jared.'

Ugh. What a bozo.

As they sat down, Peter signalled for the waiter and Jared leant to whisper in Jamie's ear. 'I fucking hate this guy.'

'Shh. He's all I could get at short notice,' she whispered back as Peter inspected the menu.

Jared held up a finger. 'One chance,' he mouthed.

'Well, hello, fine sir,' Peter boomed to the approaching waiter. 'It's a cappuccino for me.' He looked at Jamie and Jared. 'And for the lovebirds?'

'Skim cap for me,' said Jamie brightly.

'Nothing for me,' said Jared.

Peter went to hand back the menu but held it mid-air. 'On second thoughts. Let's upgrade that cappuccino to a *mug*accino.' The waiter scribbled down the order. 'Nothing like living dangerously, eh,' he said with a wink to Jamie.

'Oh god,' Jared groaned under his breath as Peter cleared his throat.

'Now, let's roll the tape back to the very start of this epic love story.' He put his palms flat on the table. 'I want details.

How you met. Your first kiss. His special ticklish spot.' He pointed at Jared. 'And her favourite Hugh Grant movie. Details, people, give 'em to me.'

'Well, um,' Jamie muttered. 'There's not a lot to say.'

'Of course there is. Every wedding comes with its own, unique love story. And I want to know YOURS!' He pointed with two hands and two fingers in the pistol position.

Jared gave Jamie a look. *Where did you get this guy?* He had a vague recollection of Jamie sending him a link to McCluskey's website, which he'd probably deleted. Big mistake.

'Umm … I'm not sure where to start,' said Jamie.

Peter leant back. 'All right. I sense a little shyness here. That's all right. That's all right. Entirely okely-dokely. I get it all the time with my newbies. So, let's start with the basics. How long have you been dating?'

'Four years,' said Jared.

'Actually, it's six.' Jamie touched Jared lightly on the arm. 'Don't you remember? 2012? The London Olympics? We were watching the opening ceremony at the pub.'

'Yeah, of course I remember when we met.' Jared gestured to the celebrant. 'But he asked when we started dating.'

'We dated from the start, didn't we?'

'But it was only casual for the first couple of years.'

'Really? Casual?'

'We both saw other people in the first couple of years after we met, don't you remember?' said Jared, frowning.

'Ummm … no. We didn't.' Jamie looked at him incredulously. 'At least, *I* didn't.'

'People. People.' Peter held up his hands in the truce signal. 'Forgive and forget. Forgive and forget. All ancient history now.' He tapped Jamie's hand. 'After all, the ring is on *your* finger, Jamie. No one else's. Isn't that right, Jared?'

Jared grunted his assent.

'There we go. Let's all kiss and make up, shall we? It wouldn't be a wedding without a few little tiffs here and there. Kiss! Kiss!' he commanded them. Sensing he wouldn't stop until the required act had been performed, Jared gave Jamie a perfunctory kiss on the cheek.

'Excellent, excellent.' McCluskey reached under the table for his briefcase. 'How about we get going with the paperwork. Neutral territory. Call me Switzerland if you like.' He winked. 'Now, this is your notice of intention to marry. It is the legal document that has to be submitted at least one calendar month before the wedding. And as you are marrying on April ninth—' he checked his watch '—and today is March eighth I must stress the importance of getting this right the first time. One chance and once chance only.' He held up his finger. 'The answers you give today must be true and correct. All right?'

McCluskey's expression had become more serious and Jared squared his shoulders. This was more like it. The legalities. Excellent. Paperwork and documentation were his forte. Lawyers lived for it.

The first few questions were straightforward—names, addresses, dates of birth, identification details—and Jared answered confidently. In work mode, the celebrant was tolerable. Business-like. Seeking clarification of spelling where needed, but otherwise to the point. If he could behave like this at the wedding, perhaps everything would be fine.

'Nearly there. Just a couple more, I promise.' He looked over his glasses at them both. 'Though these ones are slightly more personal … and a bit unusual.'

'Fire away,' said Jared.

'Are you two related in any way?' said Peter.

'To each other?' Jamie laughed.

'I'm sorry,' said Peter. 'It is something we have to ask, legally.'

'Of course we're not related,' said Jared, looking a little peeved. 'Next question.'

'Any previous marriages?'

'No,' they said together.

'So, no children then?'

'No,' said Jamie firmly.

Jared said nothing.

Shit! Where did that question come from?

'Jared?' said Peter expectantly.

'I don't understand what that has to do with anything,' said Jared hotly.

'It's just a question on the form, buddy. I don't make them up,' said Peter.

'It's an invasion of privacy!' said Jared, his voice rising. His left leg started to jiggle uncontrollably, the way it always did when he felt circumstances getting beyond his control. 'I won't answer it.'

Peter looked from Jared to Jamie and put his pen down. 'You know what? I'm going to make a visit to the little boy's room.' He rose. 'Coffee,' he said by way of explanation. 'Does it to me every time.'

Jamie waited until Peter was out of earshot before clasping Jared's arm. 'What is wrong with you? It's just a question! Answer it!'

Jared twirled an empty sugar sachet in his hands. 'I don't want to,' he said sullenly.

'Sometimes, you're a real idiot. You know that?'

Jared folded his arms. 'The government gets far too much access to personal information,' he muttered.

'What are you talking about? You don't have any children! How does answering that question tell the government anything?'

'It tells them that I don't have a child.'

'You *don't* have a child!' Jamie threw up her hands.

Jared looked out the window and refused to meet her gaze.

'You don't have a child, do you, Jared?' Jamie sounded uncertain.

Jared kept his mouth set in a hard line.

'Oh my god. That's it. You have a child. Oh my god. Oh my god.' Jamie fanned her face with her hand. 'I think I'm going to faint.'

She started gasping for air as Jared looked at her and, seeing her distress, put his arm around her shoulder. 'Breathe. Breathe, Jamie.'

She shrugged off his arm. 'How could you not tell me? How could you?'

'It's not what you think,' said Jared miserably. 'I don't know for sure.'

'You don't know? How is that even possible?'

Jared looked out the window again and drummed his nails against the table. 'You remember Melissa?'

'The girl you dated before me?'

Jared nodded. He'd been thinking about her a lot lately. They'd met during Oktoberfest, in Munich, when Jared was twenty-eight. She'd accidentally spilt a beer stein over him and there was a photo, somewhere at home, of him looking like an extra from *The Sound of Music* in his khaki lederhosen and forest-green Tyrol hat. He had his arm slung around Melissa and it was dangerously close to her bosom, which was displayed to absolute perfection in a corset-like dirndl. She looked like a naughty milkmaid but her face was sweet and open. She was a pre-school teacher from some small town in the state's north and it had taken her two years to save for the trip, her first overseas. Sweet, uncomplicated and given to laughing easily, Melissa was unlike any other woman he'd ever dated before and Jared fell for her. Hard. Against all odds, their romance had survived the holiday and continued back in 'the real world'.

After two years, it ended. Abruptly.

'When we broke up, Melissa was pregnant.' Jared played with the teaspoon, flipping it back and forth so it made a chinking sound against the saucer.

Jamie swallowed. 'Why didn't you tell me?'

'I behaved like a dick. Told her I didn't want it. That we weren't ready. Couldn't afford it. That a baby would ruin our careers.' Jared sighed. 'Basically, all the things a woman really wants to hear when she's pregnant,' he said sarcastically.

'Then what happened?' Jamie asked faintly.

'I don't know.' The teaspoon was now tap-dancing on the saucer. 'She disappeared. Told me to never call again.'

'But you did, didn't you?'

He shook his head despondently. 'I was scared, and heart-broken.' As Jared gave the saucer a particularly hard whack, the whole thing cracked, sending the cup rolling across the table. As Jamie caught the cup, Jared rubbed his temples. 'I ruined everything,' he moaned.

'What about the baby?' Jamie whispered.

'I'd presumed she didn't have it. That she ... took care of it.' Jared kept his head down. 'But I don't know for sure. After Ava's party, when I first met Ellie at Lisa's place, I just wondered ...' he trailed off.

'If she could be your child.' Jamie finished the sentence and clapped her hand over her mouth. 'Oh my god,' Jamie breathed and looked squarely at Jared. 'That's why I felt like I knew her. Your eyes, they're exactly the same. And Melissa ... Missy. Ellie's mum's name is Missy.'

'Holy shit.' Jared started rocking backward and forward. 'I didn't know that. Melissa's mum used to call her Missy for short.'

'But how could she? Why would she? Do you think she?' Jamie's words tumbled out of her mouth, premature and unformed.

Jared rubbed his eyes. 'I have no idea,' he said wearily.

'Hey, folks, sorry for that brief intermission.'

Oh shit. The celebrant was back. McCluskey adjusted his tie as he lowered himself into the seat. He took in Jamie and Jared's distraught faces.

'Houston, I think we have a problem,' he said.

Jamie nodded. 'I think we do.' She placed her palms flat on the table. 'Jared has just informed me that he may have a child from a previous relationship.' She spoke evenly, with no emotion in her voice and for a brief moment, Jared felt nothing but admiration. Jamie really was quite extraordinary in a crisis. No wonder that crazy boss of hers loved her.

'You say *may* have a child,' said Peter slowly. 'What does that mean?'

'It means it's a possibility, but not a certainty,' snapped Jared.

Jamie gave him a look. 'Six years ago, Jared ended a relationship with a woman who was pregnant. He asked her to terminate the pregnancy.' She took a breath. 'But recent events suggest she may have gone ahead and had the baby. We're yet to confirm this, though,' she added quickly.

Peter leant back. 'Riiiiight,' he said slowly. 'But you know.' He tapped the form. 'For the purposes of this document, it doesn't actually matter.'

'What do you mean?' Jared leant in as Peter put the paper in front of him.

'See here.' Peter pointed. 'It's only asking if there are children from any previous marriages. And you weren't married, were you?'

Why the hell didn't you say that earlier?

'No,' said Jared firmly. 'Definitely not married.'

'All right, then. Legally, we can complete this form today, and as your celebrant I strongly advise you do that. Time is not on our side.' The celebrant signed with a flourish and passed the form to Jared. 'This notice of intention to marry is valid for eighteen months, so if you do decide to postpone, you might still be able to use it.'

At the mention of the word 'postpone', Jared stopped writing and looked at Jamie. Would she want to call it off, after what he'd just told her? It was a massive bombshell after all. It could ruin everything and maybe it would. Shit, he didn't want that. Jamie really was a terrific girl.

Jared slid the form towards her and though Jamie signed without hesitation there was something stilted about her movements.

Maybe she would be okay with it? After all, they still didn't know anything for sure. They certainly didn't know if Ellie was his.

His child.

It was the first time he'd been able to admit the full scope of the possibility—that Ellie was, possibly, his daughter and that for some reason, Melissa had seen fit to return her to his life, albeit via Jamie's sister Lisa.

The idea was so strange. So unlikely. So out of character for the Melissa he knew. Virtually impossible, really. And now that he had, mentally at least, conceived of the possibility and expressed it out loud, he saw how ridiculous it was. He'd panicked. With her dark hair and pointy chin, Ellie had reminded him so starkly of Melissa. And those blue eyes—it was just like looking in the mirror.

But so what?

So what if there was a physical resemblance? That's probably all it was. The Melissa he knew would never do anything as weird as abandon her own child. She was a pre-school teacher for god's sake.

Nope. It was panic. Pure and simple. Pre-wedding jitters. That's all. And hopefully that's how Jamie would see it. He couldn't let this ruin the wedding. He wouldn't. A DNA test or even a simple blood test would put him in the clear and then they'd be able to move on with their lives and get married. No secrets. A fresh start in Dubai. Easy. Jared smiled. He felt better than he'd felt in days. Lighter. It was good to be free of his secret and he now felt faintly ridiculous for having been so freaked out about it.

'Okay, folks, well that's all we need for today.' Peter started collecting his things and putting them into his briefcase. 'I'll be in touch in a week to let you know that everything's been approved. And then we'll start talking about readings and vows and all the fun stuff.' He raised his eyebrows. 'That's if it's still going ahead.'

Jared shook off the celebrant's remark and stood to shake his hand. 'Thank you, Peter. You've been a great help.' He was sincere. Sure, McCluskey was a bit of a tool but he'd been very useful in terms of helping Jared to unburden himself.

Jamie didn't move. In fact, she hadn't moved or said a word since signing the document. She was staring into space and she kept staring as McCluskey waved and left the café. Clearly, convincing *her* that everything was okay was going to be harder than Jared thought.

'Jamie. Jamie.' He sat down and tugged at her arm. 'What's wrong? Why aren't you moving? You didn't even say goodbye!'

She turned to him slowly. 'We have to find her.'

'Who? Melissa?'

Jamie nodded.

'Whoa! Hold on. Let's back up here for a moment.' Jared took Jamie's hand. 'Melissa would never abandon her own child. I'm sure of it. Look, I'll take a blood test. A DNA test. Whatever! I'm sure it will prove that Ellie's not mine.'

Jamie shook her head sadly. 'That's not enough.'

'How so?'

'Maybe Ellie's not your child. We don't know. And you're right, we can do a test to see. But your child might still be out there. Maybe Melissa's a single mum, raising your kid out in the suburbs somewhere. Can you really live with not knowing?'

Jared clasped his other hand over the top of Jamie's. 'You don't understand. You weren't there when she left. She never wanted to see me again. She hated me for what I said. Don't you think I've caused her enough trouble already without suddenly popping back into her life?'

Jamie was incredulous. 'But surely you want to know if you're someone's dad?'

'Well, actually ...'

'You cannot be serious!' Jamie wrenched her hand away from his.

'I don't think there is a baby.' The thought popped into his head like a shooting star. *Yes, yes. That was it*. This was his escape argument. 'You don't know Melissa. Yes, she hated me when she left but she wasn't insane. She was a very good, very decent person.' Jamie went to speak and Jared held up his hand. 'No, no. Hear me out. If Melissa had gone ahead and had the baby, she would have told me. I have absolutely no doubt about that. The fact that she didn't tell me means there's no baby! It's logic—pure and simple.' He clasped his hands, content with the argument he'd made. Circumstantial, yes. But convincing? Definitely.

'You don't know for sure.' Jamie banged the table.

Okay, so maybe not quite as convincing as he thought. 'In my heart, I know for sure.' Jared put a hand to his chest and used his most sincere voice.

'That's not enough.' Jamie collected her handbag.

'Wait, please, Jamie. Can't we talk about this?' Jared caught her hand.

'I need some time to think.' Shaking off his grip, Jamie strode from the café and didn't look back.

Jared's head dropped. Who was it that said honesty was the bedrock of relationships?

Whoever it was, they were wrong.

CHAPTER TWENTY-THREE

On the way back to the office, Jamie dawdled. As long as she was by herself she could exist on a plane where the last hour of her life had not actually occurred.

She paused at shop windows, pretending to admire the shoes, the clothes, the décor—whatever was on display. But she actually couldn't see a thing. Her brain was too full of Jared and his disclosure for her to think of anything else. At one point, she realised she'd been staring for five minutes at a heartrate monitor in a pharmacy window. She looked around, hoping no one had noticed her zombie-like trance. She needed to pull herself together or she would find herself in a psychiatric facility.

A child? Jared a father? Ellie's father?

It was all too much to take in.

Could she still marry him? Did she even want to?

Jamie shook her head. She was getting too far ahead. She had always prided herself on being a methodical thinker but in the space of five minutes, she'd gone from signing a notice of intention to marry, to contemplating calling the whole thing off.

She needed to slow down and take things step by step.

Back at work, Jamie flipped open her laptop and typed in *Melissa, pre-school teacher, Sydney.*

One hundred and eighty-four thousand results.

Damn! She would need more information from Jared if she was going to track this woman down.

Ben poked his head around the door. 'Angel's ready for you in the conference room.'

Jamie clenched her fingers. Oh Christ! The meeting where she was supposed to present her business plan for Spin and a plan for her own consultancy. The presentation was ready to go in her laptop, but mentally she wasn't prepared at all. Normally, she liked a few minutes before a major meeting to collect herself. Check her make-up and confirm the presentation was all in order.

There was no time for any of that.

'Of course. Just need a minute,' muttered Jamie as she unplugged her computer and gathered a few random papers sitting on her desk that she *thought* might be relevant to the meeting.

'Are you okay?' Ben was still at the door. 'You seem a bit stressed.'

'I'm fine. Fine,' she said a tad too brightly. 'Had an extra coffee this morning. And you know how that makes me a little—' She fluttered her hands about. 'Now, have I got everything?' She looked desperately about her desk and then stood.

'You'll be fine.' Ben's hand in the small of her back was a shock. A pleasant zap of electricity. 'You've got this,' he murmured and propelled her towards the doorway.

For a millisecond, she believed him.

For once, Angel was sitting. There was no one else in the conference room and the emptiness of the eleven other seats only served to double Jamie's nerves.

'You're late.' Angel glared over the rims of leopard-print reading glasses.

'Sorry, sorry. Just got caught up at—' *A meeting with our wedding celebrant where Jared declared he may have a love child.* 'Oh, never mind.' Jamie waved her hand. 'I'm very sorry to keep you waiting.'

'Well, let's hope it was worth the wait.' Angel's voice was cold. It wasn't like her. Jamie's nerves were now spiralling out of control as she fumbled with the power cord to plug her laptop into the projector.

'Here, let me.' Ben leapt to her side and took the cord from her hands. She gave him a grateful smile.

'Well, let's begin.' Jamie stood as her first slide came up on the projector screen.

Forward Strategy for Spin Cycle: Developed by Jamie Travvers

She had another presentation on the laptop as well, titled *Opportunities for PR Consultancies in Dubai* which she would deliver second. At the end, Angel would give her unbiased opinion on which strategy had the most potential.

'I thought you were going to present a business plan,' said Angel sharply.

'I ... I ... er ... I am,' Jamie stuttered. 'This is a strategy. A plan.'

Angel sighed. 'A forward strategy is not a business plan, Jamie. I thought you knew that.'

'I'm sorry, but I thought you wanted big-picture stuff. Where I want to take the company. Understand my vision for what Spin Cycle can be.' Jamie's fingers trembled. She felt Ben take a protective step closer.

He cleared his throat. 'Angel, if I can just step in there. I helped Jamie put this presentation together and I think you'll find it contains all the information you're looking for—cash flow, projected growth, earnings and expenses— it's all there, if you just give Jamie a chance.'

'Very well then. Continue.' Angel leant back in the chair and closed her eyes, which is what she did when she wanted to concentrate.

Thank you, Jamie mouthed to Ben. He nodded and clenched his fingers into a fist as if to say *Be strong. You can do this.*

But she couldn't.

The figures swam before her eyes and the words seemed nothing more than meaningless squiggles and dots. Jared's revelation had completely thrown her. How could she concentrate on work when her entire relationship was on the line?

As Angel grilled her on the specifics of each plan—'How do you account for 8 per cent growth for Spin in the coming financial year?' 'Name the top five PR consultancies in Dubai and explain how yours will be different?'—Jamie felt the room becoming more stuffy.

After the fifth question about the impact of technology on the 'PR space' in both Dubai and Australia, Jamie collapsed into a chair.

'I can't do this,' she whispered.

'What did you say?' Angel leant forward. 'Why are you sitting?'

'I'm not feeling very well.' Jamie put her head between her knees.

'Here, have this.' Ben touched her shoulder and pressed a glass of water into her hands. Jamie gulped gratefully.

'Jamie, I don't know what's going on with you but quite frankly, on the basis of these presentations, I don't think you're qualified to run anything more than a game of bingo, let alone operate *my* business, or your *own*.' Angel removed her glasses. 'I expect more from you.'

'I'm sorry,' said Jamie weakly. 'I've got a lot on my mind.'

Angel huffed. 'If you're talking about this hare-brained wedding of yours, I have no sympathy. You're in PR. Event organisation is our bread and butter.'

'Please, just one more chance.'

Angel stood and rested her knuckles on the table. 'All right. I'll give you one chance to redeem yourself.' She paused. 'The Nala show. It's happening in four weeks, April seventh, and it's all yours.' She rapped her knuckles. 'You put on the best fashion show Australia's ever seen and I'll give you a choice—either take over here at Spin, or go to Dubai with my blessing, and a personal introduction to an old friend of mine who happens to be the General Manager of Dubai's tourism corporation.'

Jamie thought quickly. April seventh. Two days before her wedding day.

She sucked in a breath. 'I'll take it.'

CHAPTER TWENTY-FOUR

Usually, Lisa looked forward to Tuesday afternoons and the forty-five minutes of peace that came from Ava and Jemima being ensconced in their ballet class while Lisa read her book or checked her phone or ducked out for a coffee, like all the other mothers usually did. The grey and dingy waiting room was always deserted and relatively quiet except for the background sounds of tinkling piano tunes and Miss Tenille shouting, 'Princess toes. I want Princess toes, my precious little *primas*.' Princess toes meant pointed toes, and the reference to primas was of course to prima ballerinas. It made Lisa giggle. Prima ballerinas they were not! For all Miss Tenille's exhortations to the girls to demonstrate elegance and grace, the sound that emerged from the classroom more closely resembled that of a stampeding herd of pygmy hippos. The more loudly she demanded ethereal lightness, the more loudly they stomped. Today was no exception. As the thuds grew louder and more violent, Lisa found Ellie's hand creeping into her lap.

'What are they doing in there?' The little girl's eyes were round and slightly frightened.

'It's all right, darling. They're just dancing. But not very well.' She inclined her head conspiratorially. 'Don't tell them I said that.'

Ellie nodded seriously.

Lisa had tried to get her into the same ballet class as Ava and Jemima but there wasn't a single place to be had—Scott and Lisa obviously weren't the only parents happy to pay $50 a week for the privilege of allowing their daughters to stamp around a room for half an hour and fail miserably in their efforts to emulate graceful butterflies.

'I'm sorry I couldn't get you into the class.' Lisa squeezed her hand. 'We'll try again next term.'

'It's okay,' said Ellie doubtfully.

'No really, I will try.' The little girl gave a worried frown. Maybe she didn't actually want to do ballet? Ellie was so polite, it was sometimes difficult to know exactly what she wanted—so different to Ava and Jemima who bellowed their demands on a minute-by-minute basis.

'But only if you want to, Ellie. How about you have a trial lesson and if it's a bit scary, you don't have to do it. Okay?'

'Will you be there?' Ellie asked.

'Of course. If you want me to be.'

'Okay,' said Ellie happily. 'That sounds good.' She swung her legs under the seat.

Not for the first time, Lisa marvelled at Ellie's resilience. She was such an easygoing child and she'd fit into the family with far more ease than Lisa had expected. There was something calming about her presence. Certainly, it had changed the dynamic between Ava and Jemima. Normally, the competition for Scott and Lisa's attention came down to a battle of who could yell the loudest. Now, the girls were competing for Ellie's attention and they'd quickly discovered that she didn't respond to being shouted at, as that tended to send her into Lisa's protective arms. But she did respond to gentility and quiet requests for games. Of course it probably wouldn't last. The novelty of Ellie would soon wear off, Lisa wasn't naïve enough to expect any different. But still, for ten days of relative peace and quiet, the introduction of a new family member had been well worth it. Besides, it would only be for a short time. Jeff had seemed confident of getting results. Lisa may as well enjoy the marked improvement in her children's behaviour, even if it was only temporary.

For a moment, the music and the stomping stopped and the waiting room was quiet. Ellie leafed through a tattered picture book out of the bedraggled collection of toys and puzzles in the corner, specifically put there for bored siblings of the primas. Then she sighed and closed it.

'Lisa, can I ask you something?'

'Certainly, sweetie. What is it?'

'Where's my mummy?'

Lisa's stomach clenched. 'You know where she is. She's gone away, for work.'

'But where?'

'I'm not exactly sure of the name, but it's a long way away. Overseas. That's why it's taking a little while for her to get back.'

Ellie bit down on her trembling lip. 'When will I get to see her?'

'At some point, darling. You'll definitely see her again at some point.'

Lisa put her arm around her and felt the child shaking in her arms. This was too much. The truth was that Missy's note had been so vague that Lisa had no idea if and when Ellie would see her mother at all, but she sure as hell wasn't going to break the child's heart. Besides, deep down, she had to believe that Ellie *would* see her mother again. Jeff would find Missy and somehow they'd convince her to come back for Ellie—she was such a gorgeous child who'd clearly been well loved. Obviously, something had gone catastrophically wrong, but what? She made a mental note to text Jeff and see if he'd made any progress. Nearly a week had passed since the meeting, and there'd been no news at all.

After a few minutes of Lisa stroking Ellie's back, the little girl's shaking had slowed to large and irregular sniffles. Lisa offered her a tissue and Ellie blew obediently.

'Are you okay, darling?'

'Yes,' she said in a shaky voice.

'You know we're so, so happy that you're with us, don't you?'

Ellie nodded.

'Give me a hug.' Lisa opened her arms and Ellie climbed into her lap and buried her head into Lisa's chest. She was still so small. Lisa felt terrible.

'Can you give me something?' Ellie's voice was muffled.

'Anything, darling. What would you like? A chocolate? I think I've got one in here somewhere—' But as Lisa reached for her bag, Ellie caught her face gently between her two hands and locked eyes with her.

'Will you promise me that I'll see her soon?' Ellie's eyes were so infinitely blue, they reminded Lisa of a midday summer sky.

'Yes, definitely. Cross my heart and hope to die,' Lisa said solemnly, feeling the sickly sensation of knowing she'd just committed to something she had no absolute certainty of achieving.

Mothers clutching coffee cups and wrangling tired, bored siblings started drifting back in. Soon, the pygmy hippos would stampede into the room like a giant flood of creaming soda with their pink leotards and even pinker faces, reddened from too much wild stomping.

Lisa quietly read to Ellie the picture book she'd been leafing through earlier. It was the story of a little girl who had two left feet but loved to dance. Ellie was entranced and Lisa made a second mental note to check again whether she might be able to join the ballet class earlier than term two.

On the last page, Lisa's phone rang. A number she didn't recognise.

'Lisa, is that you? It's me, Ben. Jamie's assistant.'

This was strange. Why was he ringing her? They'd met once or twice but Lisa was quite sure she'd never given him her number. 'Ben, what's wrong?'

A beat of silence. 'Something has happened to Jamie.'

Lisa froze. 'What is it? What's happened? Is she all right?' For Ellie's sake, she tried to keep the panic out of her voice, but she could see she was failing as the little girl's face darkened.

'She's all right. She's safe. She's here at work.' Ben paused. 'But she had a disastrous meeting with Angel, and I think something happened with Jared earlier, with their celebrant.'

'Where is she now?'

'Crying in her office.' Ben hesitated. 'I've tried talking to her, but she says she only wants you.'

'Of course,' Lisa said efficiently, not betraying the whirl of thoughts in her head. Scott was at work, which meant she'd have to take the girls. Not ideal. But Jamie never cried, she always said she'd used up her lifetime's supply of tears when their mum and dad died, and she rarely asked for help, which meant she must really need it. 'I'll be there right away.'

As Lisa hung up, the little primas swarmed in and filled the grey room with colour and excited chatter.

Like slippery little fish, Ava and Jemima threaded through the crowd and tried to pile onto Lisa's lap, where Ellie was still sitting.

'Girls, girls. Wait. Please.' Lisa stood up, causing all three to tumble off.

'Mummy,' Ava grumbled. 'I just wanted a cuddle.'

'I'm hungry,' whinged Jemima. 'I want dinner, NOW!'

Ellie just waited.

'Girls, get your jackets on.'

Lisa helped Jemima while Ellie helped Ava.

'Aren't we going home, Mummy?' said Ava.

'No, darling. We're off to visit Aunty Jamie.'

'Yay,' the three girls shouted in unison, and as they trooped towards the door, Lisa thought how much easier life would be if everyone remained a child forever.

Five pm and the city traffic was grid-locked. Based on Ben's excellent directions, Lisa knew they were only two blocks from Jamie's office. But in front of her was a sea of red tail-lights.

'Mummy, I'm hungry,' grumbled Ava from the back seat.

'Here, darling, share these.' Lisa reached into the glove-box and produced the packet of Pringles she kept in there for emergency situations.

'Chippies,' Jemima cheered as her sister carefully doled them out.

Lisa went back to day-dreaming out the window as the girls munched away happily. The footpaths were fill-ing with office workers on their way home and everyone was so smartly dressed. Sharp suits, skinny ties, pin-point high heels, beautifully tailored skirts. Lisa took in her own attire—loose jeans, canvas sneakers, and a grey sweatshirt. It was strange to think she had once belonged to this well-dressed tribe. When was the last time she'd worn high heels? Did she actually own any? She had a vague recollec-tion of some dust-encrusted, black suede pumps in the far reaches of her wardrobe, but possibly they were a pair of Scott's work socks, accidentally thrown into the wrong spot. All her work clothes were a size too small now. Even though she'd lost all the baby weight from Jemima, she'd had to accept that her two, four-kilo darlings, had forever altered the shape of her rib cage.

'You wouldn't bloody believe it,' whispered Lisa under her breath as she spotted a free car spot outside of Jamie's build-ing. It was a sign. Jamie must really need her. There was an actual sign designating the spot a loading zone, but Lisa figured that with three children in a station wagon she'd be able to make a good case to any skulking parking rangers.

'You said a rude word, Mummy,' chirped Ava from the back seat. 'You said *bloody*. Daddy's not allowed to say that word.'

'I didn't swear, darling. I said … um … *ruddy*, not … er … that other word.'

'What does ruddy mean, Mummy?'

'It's something that's red,' said Lisa, craning her neck to reverse park into the spot.

'So, a fire truck isn't red, it's a *ruddy* fire truck?' questioned Ava innocently.

'Not really, darling,' said Lisa, feeling herself descending into one of those parental rabbit holes that seemed to have no end. 'It's a bit hard to explain, and look! We're here at Jamie's work. Let's go.'

As they piled into the lift, Lisa texted Ben to let him know of their arrival and when the doors opened, he was there to greet them in Spin's glamorous foyer.

'Hi, Lisa.' Ben gave a grim smile before kneeling down to the girls. 'Hello, ladies, I'm Ben,' he said brightly and offered each child a high-five. 'I've heard a lot about you guys and I've heard you all really hate chocolate biscuits.'

'Noooooo,' said Ava, smiling. 'We love them.'

'Well, that's just as well because I have a whole packet in the kitchen. Who wants to come with me?'

'Me!' The girls threw up their hands in unison, their eyes as sparkly as the pristine glass walls around them.

'Thanks, Ben,' said Lisa gratefully as he led them towards the oversized doors emblazoned with the Spin Cycle logo.

'This way, ladies.' As Ben headed left, he gestured to Lisa to go right. 'Down that way,' he said, pointing discreetly.

What a thoughtful man, thought Lisa, to refrain from mentioning Jamie's name knowing that if he did, the girls would demand to see her straight away.

Things must be bad.

Lisa crept down the hallway, looking timidly over the tops of work stations and through office doorways. Although she'd never been there before, the place was gut-churningly familiar in the way that all offices tended to be. Whirring computers, grey carpet, the woody smell of paper, coffee-stained mugs on desks. She shivered. No, she didn't miss this.

As she approached the final door on the left, Lisa could hear sniffing and sobbing.

Jamie?

Lisa was so well acquainted with the sound of Ava and Jemima's crying that she didn't even need to see their faces to know which one would be soaked in tears—Ava screeched like a scalded cat, while Jemima bellowed like a calf separated from its mother.

This cry was different. She hadn't heard it since their parents' death, and the two of them had clung together with Jamie wailing like a wounded animal.

'Jamie.' Lisa rushed through the door. 'What's happened?'

Given the redness around her eyes, she'd obviously been crying for a long time. It was as if caterpillars had stamped tiny angry feet all about her eyebrows.

Jamie rose from the chair shakily, then half-collapsed into Lisa's arms. 'It's all a disaster,' she moaned, raising the volume of her crying to a new level that Lisa would have described as 'speared elephant'.

'There, there,' Lisa rubbed her back the way she did when Ava declared she was about to vomit. 'Everything's going to be all right.'

'No, it won't,' sniffed Jamie. 'It's all buggered up.'

'Hon, I'm sure it's going to be fine.'

'You weren't there!' Jamie fixed Lisa with an accusatory glare.

'Where wasn't I?'

'My meeting with Angel. It was terrible. She told me I couldn't run a bingo competition, let alone my own business—or hers.'

'But you did so much preparation for that meeting.' Lisa had seen the PowerPoint. She'd even helped Jamie with the figures about cash flow, profit and loss.

'I know!' Jamie cried. 'But Jared put me off.'

As Jamie filled her in on the meeting with the celebrant, Lisa felt shock coursing through her body, causing her feet and toes to tingle.

'So you're saying Jared *may* have a child.' Lisa slumped into a chair across the desk from Jamie.

'Possibly.'

She paused. The idea was almost too bizarre to say out loud. She'd never *adored* Jared, that much was true, but he was a smart man—far too smart to be unsure as to whether he had fathered a child or not. She'd heard of people being in denial about impending parenthood, but this went beyond that—it bordered on wilful ignorance. And the next bit was even harder to fathom.

'And the child ... could be Ellie?'

'Yes. No ... I don't know. I mean, they look alike.'

'But that doesn't really prove much. I mean, my postman looks a bit like a hound dog, but I'd never suggest he was related to one.'

'Unless you wanted to extinguish all hope of ever receiving another letter.' Jamie smiled weakly.

'Might not be a bad thing,' said Lisa gloomily. 'All we get are bills.' She looked out the window. The lights in the offices across the street were starting to come on. The city was prettier at night. The dull grey of concrete and bitumen gave way to sparkling lights against inky blackness. Usually, it made Lisa happy to see the city putting on her shimmery dress, but tonight she just wanted to bundle up her three little girls, race back to the safety of their own home and shut the door. Things had settled. Ellie was happy. Lisa was loving the extra little person in their life. The house was noisy and chaotic and Lisa was actually enjoying it immensely. But this? It was too much.

'I mean, it might explain why Ellie's mother left her with you,' said Jamie thoughtfully.

'But if Jared's her dad, why didn't she take Ellie straight to him?'

'Because she knows Jared and knows he's a man-child who would try to shirk the responsibility. This way, he can't really ignore her, can he? I mean, Ellie's *living* with you.'

'Maybe. But how would she have found us?'

'Oh, Lise, you're so innocent,' Jamie smiled. 'There's this thing called the internet. Makes it really easy to find people. Facebook. Relationship status. Would have taken her five minutes to work out who Jared was dating and who I was, and my family, my friends. All of it!'

'But there are privacy settings that stop people you don't know from seeing all that. I'm sure Scott showed me how.'

'I work in PR. Nothing's private. I'm an open book.' As Jamie swivelled nervously in her chair, Lisa leant forward and locked eyes with her.

'So, photos of the girls, their parties, that beach holiday we had together last year—that's all open to anyone to see?'

Jamie nodded.

'Oh, god.' Lisa clapped her hand over her mouth. 'That photo of me in the bikini just after Jem was born and my tummy's all jelly and wobbly, you don't have that one up there, do you?'

Jamie reddened. 'Your tummy wasn't *that* bad.' She cleared her throat. 'Anyway, I think you're missing the point. It's really Ellie we should be worried about.'

Yes, Ellie. That dear, sweet, loving, intelligent little girl. She couldn't possibly have half of Jared's genes. She was far too nice! Not that Lisa would say that to Jamie. The guy might have been a lying snake in the grass, but he was still her sister's fiancé. For the moment.

'Ellie says her dad died. And I know she wouldn't make that up,' said Lisa.

Jamie sighed. 'That poor child has obviously been lied to about a lot of things. You really think her mother wouldn't lie about this?'

'You sound like you *want* Jared to be Ellie's father.'

'And you sound like you *don't* want to find out,' said Jamie.

Lisa paused. 'I've hired a private investigator to try and find Missy.'

'You hired a what?'

'An investigator. People do it all the time,' she said stiffly.

'People on TV shows! Not people who live in the suburbs and never take pens from hotel rooms because they think it's stealing.'

'It *is* stealing. You don't pay for them.'

'Oh, Lise, it's factored into the price.'

'Well, hiring a PI is perfectly legal, but that's all beside the point because I haven't heard back from him since last week. He obviously hasn't found her yet or he would have told me something,' said Lisa.

'You know you really shouldn't sound so happy about that,' Jamie admonished.

'I know.' Lisa hung her head. 'And I know she hasn't been with us long but she's become like part of the family. I don't think I'm ready to lose her.'

'Well, I don't want to lose Jared, but Ellie deserves her mum.' Jamie tapped the desk. 'And I deserve the truth! And certainty. I want to know who I'm marrying and where I'm going to be working. And I don't know anything at the moment.' Jamie threw her hands up in exasperation and started weeping again quietly.

Lisa felt her heart give way. Poor Jamie. She was really suffering. As different as the two sisters were, Lisa completely understood her sister's need for certainty. 'Hon, please don't cry. You know Jared really loves you.' She thought it was the most reassuring thing she could say, but it only seemed to make Jamie cry harder.

'I ... pink ... ruddy ... dove ... Ben.' Jamie was sobbing now, which made her words almost impossible to make out.

'What are you saying, hon? Something about Ben having a pink and ruddy dove?' That word again. Lisa wished she'd never said it to Ava; now it was all she kept hearing.

Jamie lifted her head. 'I think I love Ben,' she moaned, before dropping her forehead to the desk again.

But before Lisa could respond she noticed a figure at the door, surrounded by three littler figures. Ben and the girls. Had he heard Jamie's declaration? Fortunately, her head was again buried in her arms and she didn't notice the party in the doorway until Lisa spoke. 'Ben! Girls!' she said brightly. 'Did you have fun?'

As Ben stood behind them, Ava prattled on and on about the chocolate biscuits and the soft drinks and all the cake in the kitchen. Finally, she drew breath and Lisa leapt at the chance to speak. 'Sounds like a wonderful time, so, girls, please thank Ben.'

'Thank you, Ben!' the girls chorused.

'Ben, I think you should go now. It's getting late. We'll be fine from here,' said Lisa reassuringly.

'You sure?' He looked at Jamie, who was wiping her eyes with tissues and smearing mascara across her entire face in the process.

'Yes, yes,' said Lisa confidently. 'All under control. Jamie will come home with us.'

'All right,' said Ben slowly. 'But at least let me help you all into the car.' He smiled at Lisa. 'My sister says she never goes anywhere because it takes longer to get the kids in and out of the car than the outing itself.' He knelt down in front of Jemima. 'Climb aboard,' he said, allowing her to climb onto his back.

'What about me?' complained Ava. 'Why don't I get a piggy-back?'

'You will,' said Ben easily. 'I'll take Jem to the lift. Then you can have a go while we're going down, and then it'll be Ellie's turn in the street. Fair?'

Ava nodded and jogged compliantly behind Ben as he horsey-galloped towards the lift, causing Jemima to squeal in delight. God, no wonder Jamie was in love with him. Even though they'd only met briefly, Lisa already had the feeling that Ben was the most thoughtful man, aside from Scott, that she had ever encountered. And he would make an incredible father, she marvelled, before turning her attention back to Ellie, who hadn't followed the others, but was looking carefully at Jamie's mascara-stained face.

'What's wrong?' The little girl put her arm around Jamie's shoulder. 'Are you okay? You seem really sad.'

Lisa felt her heart melting.

'I'll be fine, Ellie,' said Jamie, patting her arm. 'I'll be fine.'

CHAPTER TWENTY-FIVE

For the average human, one week may have been a short time in which to overcome a significant personal trauma but, in public relations, time passed like dog years; for Jamie, one week had provided ample time for her to get past the shock and hatch a plan. It was complex, intriguing and involved a black wig. In other words, a chance for Jamie to act out a long held fantasy, while also getting to the truth about Ellie.

Checking her reflection in the rear-view mirror of the car, Jamie was quite pleased with what she saw. The wig of straight, black, shoulder blade-length hair gave her a sense of mystery that her normal dirty-blonde curls could not. Hardly anyone at work knew that she had curls, for every morning she ironed them into submission. Straight hair was far more sophisticated and Jared agreed. He referred to her bathroom routine as the 'transformation of the woolly mammoth'. In their early dating months, after they spent their first full night together, he'd actually been quite shocked to wake up and find himself sleeping next to a girl who looked nothing like the one he'd gone to bed with. A straightening iron was the first personal item Jared had allowed her to keep at his place. Now, wearing the wig, Jamie wondered why she'd wasted all that time straightening when she could have simply popped on someone else's hair in five seconds flat.

'I really think this is a bad idea,' said Lisa, watching as Jamie tucked in a rogue curl.

'Nonsense. It'll be fine. She'll never guess who I am.'

'But all this lying,' said Lisa miserably. 'I don't like it.'

'It's not you who's doing the lying. It's me.' She swivelled round to the back seat. 'And Jems.' She winked at her niece, chomping on a milk arrowroot biscuit. 'Isn't that right, little daughter?'

'Yes, *Mummy*,' said Jemima with a big grin. She thought it was a tremendous lark. Aunty Jamie playing dress-ups with that wig, and Jemima having to pretend that Aunty Jamie was actually her mummy. It was just like the mummies and daddies games she, Ava and Ellie played at home, except that this time, she was not being forced to be the family dog, Bosco.

Jamie checked her make-up one last time and slid on a pair of white plastic oversized sunglasses. She looked a little ridiculous. Nothing like her usual self. Perfect!

'There must be another way,' said Lisa, leaning on the steering wheel.

'There's not, so don't worry. It'll be fine.' Jamie patted her arm soothingly. She was embarrassed about her mini nervous breakdown the previous week, which was completely out of character. Thankfully, her sister hadn't mentioned her little outburst about Ben. How mortifying! Of course she wasn't in love with her assistant. It was just a minor case of cold feet—in fact lightly chilled feet, if you like. It was only natural, given the speed of her engagement and the shock of Jared's possible parenthood, that she would waver at some point. And that was all it was. She loved Jared. She'd invested five years of her life in him. She couldn't throw that away because of a couple of speed bumps. But she did need to know the truth. That was reasonable, wasn't it?

At first, Jared had been reluctant to provide any clues at all—but Jamie insisted the only way forward for their relationship was full disclosure. Finally, Jared had started to talk more openly about Melissa—her looks, her hobbies, her personality, her family, where she went to school and uni. All of it. His recall of her was actually quite startling and he seemed to warm so enthusiastically to the topic that it was quite difficult to get him to stop. After a full two hours of *Melissa this* and *Melissa that*, Jamie finally had to hold up her hand.

'Okay, I've got it,' she'd said, pacing about the kitchen while Jared sat mournfully on the couch.

'What are you going to do?'

'*We* are going to find her and find out what happened.'

Jared had looked aghast. 'I can't. She hates me. She said she never wanted to see me again. There's no way she'll talk to me.'

Jamie had thought for a moment. 'Maybe not to you, but she might to me. Especially if she doesn't know who I am.'

Thanks to the load of information Jared had supplied, the process of finding Melissa took just a few clicks, and there she was—a photo of her at the Kid's Biz Kindy Christmas party. It was Melissa, Jamie had no doubt. Based on Jared's description of a buxom brunette with a nose ring, it had to be her. Though now, she wasn't just an employee of the preschool, she was its director.

But she still had the nose ring.

She wasn't Jared's type at all. It was so strange, how one man could be attracted to two such completely different women, and here they were about to come face to face.

Of course, Lisa had been dead against the idea. Such a rule follower.

'Jamie, you can't! You'll get caught. You said yourself that Melissa's probably been stalking you on Facebook. She'll know you right away. Let me get Jeff to investigate her. It's what I'm paying him for after all.'

'I need to see this woman for myself.' Jamie had been firm.

'But it doesn't make sense,' Lisa kept saying. 'Why would Jared's former girlfriend give her child to me?'

'Why would anyone give their child to you?' was Jamie's rather tactless reply. She hadn't meant it that way. 'I mean— why would anyone give their child to a virtual stranger?'

Lisa had got the point. One way or the other, they needed to find out firstly whether Melissa had given birth to Jared's child, and secondly, if that child was Ellie. The hows and whys of it all could come later.

'Ready to go, kiddo?' Jamie winked at Jemima and hopped out of the car.

'Yes, Aunty—oops, I mean, Mummy.' Jemima clambered out.

Without doubt, Jems was the weak link of the plan. Relying on a three-year-old to maintain a lie for more than five minutes was like relying on a puppy to be a seeing-eye dog. It *could* work, but there was a high chance of failure and the puppy could barely be held responsible.

But Jemima *seemed* to grasp the seriousness of the situation, her appreciation of its gravity no doubt helped along by the promise of a Barbie doll. The deal was—if she could 'pretend' (lying was a naughty-step offence in the Wheeldon household) that Aunty Jamie was her mummy during a visit to a new kindy, then she could have the new Crystal Palace Barbie doll.

Say no more. Jemima was in. She'd happily disown her own family if it meant getting that new doll.

But as Jamie stood at the entry to the kindy, her legs felt weak. What was she actually going to *say* to Melissa?

Hi, how are you? Do you have a kid? Can I see the kid?

They weren't exactly the type of questions one would ask at a tour of a prospective kindy. Actually, what the hell did a parent ask at one of those things?

From inside the kindy, she could hear high-pitched screams of terror, as if one of the kids was being stretched over a rack and stabbed with knives.

Jamie must have trembled a little because Jemima squeezed her hand. 'Don't worry. My kindy sounds like that too.'

'Thanks,' whispered Jamie as she rang the doorbell and stood back.

The kindy itself was in an area of Sydney known as the Hills District, part of the suburban commuter belt on the

city's fringes. It had taken them forty-five minutes to drive
there and as Jamie passed row after row of tightly packed
project homes with bikes and station wagons in the drive-
ways she felt slightly ill. She put it down to a mixture of
nerves about meeting Melissa and a slight fear that even
though her marriage was imminent, she was nowhere near
ready for a life of cutting crusts off sandwiches and pushing
swings.

Lisa, though, was unconcerned, and hummed along to
the radio as they sped through suburbia. She had embraced
family life with such a full and open heart. For the first time
in her life, Jamie felt envious of her sister's maternal desires.

Holding Jemima's hand, Jamie buzzed on the door to the
kindy, which looked very much like every other blond-brick
house in the street, except for the tall, child-proof fence surrounding it on all sides.

The door opened with a whoosh.

'Welcome to Kid's Biz!'

It was her, Melissa, beaming a big, friendly grin as
she reached down to shake Jemima's hand. 'Hi, Verity.
Welcome to Kid's Biz. I'm Melissa.'

As part of the 'pretend' game, Jemima had insisted on
choosing her own name, which of course, she based on her
favourite television fairy. 'Hi, Melissa,' said Jemima. 'Can I
go play?' Without waiting for an answer, she ran off to the
closest group of children, huddled around the biggest box of
Lego Jamie had ever seen.

'And you must be Georgina?' Melissa beamed again. She
was prettier than in her online photos. And slimmer too.
Her scoop-necked T-shirt showed just a hint of the fulsome
cleavage beneath but not too much as to worry the kindy

mums, nor give the kindy dads too much of an eyeful. Her dark curly hair was partly constrained by a colourful headscarf, but it sprang free joyously from behind—an explosion of corkscrews and ringlets.

'Yes. I am Georgina,' said Jamie rather robotically. 'Thank you for letting us see your kindergarten.'

'Our pleasure. Looks like little Miss Verity knows her way around a Lego table, so how about I show you the rest of the kindergarten while she's busy?'

They visited the outdoor play area, then the kitchen, followed by the school-preparation room for the four-year-olds and lastly the toilets, where Jamie marvelled (inwardly) at the size of the seats. Such tiny little bottoms these kids had! And the taps at knee height—so cute! Melissa kept up a running commentary about the kindy's philosophy of education and their staff ratios and usual daily routine etc, etc. Jamie didn't remove her sunglasses, concerned Melissa might work out who she was. Every so often, she would look at Jamie quizzically and ask if she had any questions, which Jamie didn't. At least, not about the kindergarten. In her mind, she was shouting *Are you the mother of my fiancé's child? And is that child Ellie?* But no actual words came out of her mouth which she could tell Melissa thought was a bit odd.

The tour was coming to an end.

'Mel, should we start putting out the things for morning tea?' asked one of the other kindy workers.

'Sure, I'll be with you in a sec. Just wrapping up now.'

Suddenly, Jamie's bladder felt incredibly full. She was going to lose her chance to ask anything! As Melissa led her back to the Lego table, she thought desperately.

'I'm pregnant!' she blurted out.

Melissa turned, slightly startled. 'Congratulations,' she said, and turned again for the Lego.

'Nearly eighteen weeks,' Jamie called to her back.

Melissa turned and glanced at Jamie's sleek black dress and four-inch Jimmy Choos. She had to go to work straight after the kindy visit and although she was prepared to don a wig to play 'Georgina', she wasn't prepared to go the whole way and dress 'mumsy' even though Lisa had offered her a pair of canvas shoes and her baggiest jeans. Ugh!

'Really? Eighteen weeks? Well, you look amazing. You don't look at all pregnant.' Again, Melissa turned her attention to the children.

'Well, you know, we all carry these things differently,' Jamie said. 'I'll bet you were tiny.'

Melissa turned slowly. Her face darkened. Even her curls seemed to droop. 'I've never been pregnant,' she said quietly, her shoulders slumping.

'Oh, I'm so sorry. I mean, you're just such a natural with the children, I just assumed you'd had some yourself.' Jamie covered her mouth with her hand. It wasn't the answer she was expecting. Never been pregnant? That was a lie, wasn't it? But she seemed so sincere.

'It's all right,' said Melissa wanly. 'You weren't to know.' She fidgeted with her fingers. 'Actually, I was pregnant once, but only for a few days.' Her eyes misted over.

'Oh no. You miscarried?' Jamie whispered.

Melissa nodded.

'I'm so, so sorry.' Jamie put her hand on Melissa's forearm. 'I never should have asked.'

'No, it's okay,' said Melissa, wiping her eyes. 'It was a long time ago, and I never think about it anymore.' She paused. 'I guess you just caught me off-guard.'

'I really am terribly sorry.' And she was. In that moment, she felt like ripping the wig from her head and telling Melissa everything but she suspected that might only cause more hurt.

'Really, it's all right.' She gave a weak smile. 'I'm engaged now.' She held out her hand to show off the modest diamond solitaire on her finger, which was about one-third the size of Jamie's. 'My fiancé is dead keen to start a family and until we do, I've got all these little ones to take care of.' She gestured to the children around the Lego table. 'I'm sort of like their second mum.'

Jamie squeezed her arm. 'They're lucky to have you,' she said sincerely.

'No,' said Melissa. 'I'm lucky to have them.' She paused. 'And hopefully, we'll soon have Verity with us too?'

'Yes, yes,' said Jamie hastily. 'I'll let you know by the end of the week.'

'Verity,' Melissa called. 'Verity.' Still no response. Jemima studiously added more blocks to her Lego tower.

Oh shit. She's forgotten her name is Verity. Don't ruin it now, Jems!

'Has she had her hearing checked?' said Melissa, frowning. 'You know you can get it checked for free at this age.'

'Yes, yes. It's all fine. She just gets very focused on what she's doing. You know how it is.' Jamie tapped Jemima on the shoulder. 'Come along now, sweetie. Time for us to go. Say ta-ta to Melissa.'

'But I'm not finished,' said Jemima defiantly.

'C'mon, darling, we have loads of Lego. How about I buy you some more on the way home? But only if you come now.' Jamie tugged at the reluctant little girl.

'All right.' She threw the remaining blocks back in the bucket and stomped towards the door with her arms folded.

'Thank you again,' said Jamie, taking one last look at Melissa's kind face.

'Really, it was a pleasure.' She waved at Jemima. 'Bye-bye, Verity.'

'What?' said Jemima rudely.

'You say "pardon", *Verity*. Isn't that what I, *your mother*, always tell you.'

'Oh, right.' Realisation dawned into a smile on her face. 'That's right, *Mummy*!'

As Melissa closed the door, she gave them a strange look and Jamie hurriedly tottered down the footpath, pulling Jemima along behind her. She didn't look back, worried that Melissa might put two and two together and chase her down, shouting *Fraud. This woman's a fraud!* Maybe Melissa would even rip off the wig. It was so obviously not her real hair.

But the kindy door remained closed and no one came running.

Around the corner and out of sight, Jamie hurriedly opened the passenger door for Jemima to climb in the back seat of Lisa's car.

'How was it? Was it her? Does she have a child? Is it Ellie?' Lisa was pale with anxiety as she wrapped herself around the driver's seat to talk to Jamie.

'Hold on, hold on. Just let me get Jem sorted and I'll tell you everything.'

Finally, with Jemima buckled, Jamie fell with relief into the car. She turned to Lisa, whose knuckles were turning white from clutching the steering wheel so tightly.

'It was the right person.' Jamie took a breath. 'But, she doesn't have a child. Any child. That pregnancy with Jared was a miscarriage.'

'Oh, thank goodness.' Lisa closed her eyes.

'What do you mean? The poor woman's still distraught over it.'

'Of course,' Lisa said quickly. 'A miscarriage is awful. But it does make things easier for you and Jared.'

'And means you get to keep Ellie for longer.'

Lisa reddened. 'Yes, well there is that too.' She blinked rapidly. 'But I do want to find Ellie's mum. I do.'

Jamie took in Lisa's ongoing blinks. Her sister was good at many things, but lying wasn't one of them.

'You don't want to find her, do you?' Jamie demanded.

'Of course I do,' Lisa shot back. 'What kind of monster would I be if I didn't want a child to be with their mother?'

Jamie softened. 'You'd be the kind of monster who's fallen in love with a child that's not theirs.' She paused as Lisa hung her head. 'It's not a crime, you know,' she said softly.

'Until Ellie came along, I didn't realise how much I wanted another child.' Lisa lifted her head. 'She completes our family.' She paused. 'I don't want to lose her.' Her voice cracked and she rubbed her temple. 'It's all a mess.'

Poor Lisa. She only ever wanted to do the right thing by everybody, which usually meant her needs came last. For her to say what she actually wanted meant she must actually want Ellie a great deal.

Jamie squeezed her sister's shoulder. 'It's all right, Lise. You've done all you can. Let's just leave it in the hands of your investigator. If Missy can be found, he'll find her.' She smiled. 'And besides, I've got a wedding to plan and I'm going to need my matron of honour's every spare minute to make this the best damn wedding Sydney has ever seen.'

'You said *damn*, Aunty Jamie,' piped up Jemima from the back seat. 'That's a swear word!'

'No, it isn't! A dam is like a pond. Animals drink out of it.'

Lisa put the keys in the ignition. 'You're going to make a great mum one day.'

'How's that?' asked Jamie.

'You've got an answer for everything.'

'And if I don't, I make it up,' she said gleefully. 'I do work in PR you know.'

But as they sped away, with the project homes receding into the distance of the rear-view mirror, it occurred to Jamie that she still had no answer for one very big question ...

What to do about Ben?

CHAPTER TWENTY-SIX

Missy lowered the camera. It was heavier than she was used to, mainly because of the zoom lens she'd bought with some of her mum's money. She massaged her shoulder and leant her head on the steering wheel. Stalking Kyle was exhausting, not to mention tedious, confusing, stressful, disappointing and, occasionally, downright frightening. Finding him had been depressingly easy, just a matter of driving by a few of his old mates' places and hanging out until he turned up, which he eventually did, at Deano's.

After three weeks of trailing him, Missy knew for certain he hadn't changed. Hadn't changed at all.

His days held a monotonous regularity. Wake at eleven, stroll out onto the porch dressed in nothing but footy shorts for a breakfast smoke. Sit, and watch the smoke curl into the air before pulling out a phone. Text messages. Endless text messages. Go back inside. Emerge again round one to accept a pizza delivery. Do some weights in the back-yard with Deano in the afternoon, then back inside to wait for the procession of snake-hipped men with hooded, ferrety faces to make their nervy approaches to the door. Kyle, ushering them inside, his eyes roving with suspicion about the street as he shut the door. Leave the house after midnight with Deano in a hotted-up ute and head down to some local dive to drink until dawn and do it all again.

If prison was about rehabilitation then it had been a 100 per cent failure for her stupid ex.

What had he been doing in there? Exercising, by the looks. He'd bulked up. All that free time in jail. There seemed to be a new tattoo on his neck. Thanks to the zoom lens she was able to zero in on it from three hundred metres away. Some kind of snake, wrapped about a sword.

Missy had clicked away.

She now had more than a thousand photos, and a few bits of video too. All that time sitting in the car had given Missy plenty of opportunity to put together a plan. To her, it was obvious. Kyle had picked up exactly where he left off and, at some point, he would come looking for them. What was he waiting for? Maybe to re-establish himself? Get some money together to pay for the search? There would be a reason, and while Missy wasn't quite sure what it was, she knew in her heart that the only way for her and Ellie to be safe was to see him back in jail.

Evidence was what she needed, but without something substantial Kyle would be in and out of jail far too quickly. It had to be something decent. Something solid, and while Missy had successfully compiled what looked like a compelling circumstantial case, she knew she needed more. But how to get it without getting too close?

While Kyle was an idiot, he wasn't completely brainless. All the dealing happened behind locked doors, drawn curtains, and lowered blinds. Occasionally, it seemed to take place at the pub as well, but if the police were called there, which they seemingly were on a regular basis, Kyle always managed to leave it two minutes before they arrived. He was a cat, always landing on his feet, cheating real trouble.

She sighed and tapped the steering wheel. It was only 10.30 am. No sign of movement at Kyle's. Missy turned on the radio and allowed her thoughts to wander. Where would Ellie be right now? What would she be doing? It was only when Missy's eyes weren't trained on the view-finder that she allowed herself to think of her daughter. Her body ached for her. The loneliness of what she was doing. It was twenty-six days since she'd kissed her goodbye at the party. Twenty-six.

Missy shook her head and sat up straighter, her eyes drawn to a sudden burst of activity at Kyle's front door. It was him, Kyle, and a man she didn't recognise and hadn't seen arrive. Their conversation was heated. Angry. When Missy checked through the lens she was met with Kyle's eyes, burning with rage. She felt winded. She knew that look and what it meant. Resuming focus through the view-finder, her fingers trembled too badly to keep it still. She lowered the camera. The other bloke was smaller than Kyle. Much smaller, and younger too. One of his minions, perhaps.

The argument had moved out onto the front lawn. Kyle shoved the younger man hard and he staggered back on the grass, falling to the ground. Standing over him, Kyle gesticulated wildly, threatening, and the other man cowered in fear, hands raised over his face, bracing for a blow.

Kyle reached behind his back.

Missy gasped.

A gun. Dark and shiny as a snake, Kyle brandished it in front of the smaller man's face. Was he crying? Missy thought she could see a slick of moisture. Her heart thundered. What could she do? Yell? Scream? Toot the horn? Sure, it might stop Kyle but it would put her in the gravest of danger, not to mention blow her cover completely.

Missy slid down in the seat, and clenched her fingers into fists. Over the dashboard, she could still just see Kyle's torso. His finger went to the trigger and he cocked the gun at the minion's forehead.

Missy's stomach caved and she sucked in a breath.

By the heave in the younger man's shoulder, she could tell he was sobbing, begging for his life.

Seconds ticked by.

Slowly, Kyle lowered the gun.

Missy exhaled.

Scrambling to his feet, the younger man staggered to his car, fell into it, and careered down the street. Missy caught a glimpse of his face—pale and distraught. She looked back to Kyle, who was waiting and watching. Looking about, his gaze landed on Missy's car.

She froze and sank lower in the seat. Her chest hammered away. Had he seen her? Would he come to check?

After what felt like the longest few seconds of Missy's life, a door slammed. Silence. He'd gone back inside.

Slowly, Missy turned the ignition. Staying low in the seat, she drove down the road without looking back once and it was only once she'd turned out of it that she allowed herself to take another breath.

Where was she going? She had no idea. She just needed to get away. Collect herself and work up the courage to go back again.

Missy's eye flicked to her rear-view mirror. What was that flash of colour? She was jumpy. Addled. Feinting at shadows. She checked again and this time computed what her eyes had seen. Blue and red lights flashing. Not at her, surely. She checked her speedo: 55 km/hr.

The lights flashed again and this time when Missy checked, she saw the police constable pointing at the side of the road and mouthing the words *Pull over.*

Missy flicked the indicator, her chest going tight again.

No, no, no.

She wasn't ready for police. Not yet. She needed time to think. Get her composure back and figure out the next step. She didn't trust them, and she had good reason not to.

Stopping on the side of the road, Missy tensed her hands on the wheel and debated whether to get out of the car or stay inside. *Inside*, she elected. *Less threatening that way.*

Through her side mirror, she watched the constable approach slowly. She wound the window down.

'Is there a problem?' she asked casually.

The constable leant down. 'Both your tail-lights are out.'

'Oh, right. Sorry. It's a rental car. I'll take it back straight away.' She went to wind the window back up but the constable put his hand out.

'Just a minute there. I'll need to check your driver's licence.'

A pause. 'My licence? Sure.' Missy reached for her handbag under the passenger seat and she sensed the constable's eyes flicking over the extended camera lens. 'I'm taking photos of the local wildlife. Those shearwaters are just incredible, aren't they?' Her voice was high-pitched and squeaky. She cleared her throat, and rifled through her wallet, pretending to look for a licence.

'Hmmm ... that's strange. I must have left it in the hotel room.'

The constable's mouth was set in a grim line. 'You understand that under NSW law, you must carry a licence while operating a motor vehicle.'

'Yes, I am. Really, I'm sorry. I won't do it again.' Missy felt sweat starting to sprout from her forehead.

The policeman studied her. 'Do I know you?'

Missy shook her head. 'No. I don't think so. I'm from Sydney.'

'Name and address?' He pulled out a notebook and pen.

'Missy Jones,' she said in a low voice, trying desperately to keep the quiver out of it.

'Sorry?' The constable cocked his head.

'Missy Jones,' she said more loudly. 'Sixty-four Abner Road, Daceyville.'

The policeman sauntered back to the patrol car and Missy watched him in the mirror. Punching her details into an onboard computer. She glanced out the side window. Traffic in the lane next to her had slowed. Rubberneckers wanting to find out what was going on. What had that young woman done wrong? Thank god it wasn't them. Not this time.

Missy tightened her grip on the steering wheel.

In a minute, the constable would be back. He'd want to know why she was driving without a licence. Why didn't she exist on his system?

Her foot hovered above the accelerator. Fight or flight? Her jaw tightened.

Too late. The constable was back. Frowning. He leant down. 'I'm sorry, Miss, but you'll—'

Missy stared straight ahead. 'I want to talk to Detective O'Dea.'

The interview room had been painted—that was one difference—bright white now as opposed to the eighties-inspired lime green. The desk was the same, though. Peeling laminate, no doubt picked at by the thousands of nervous hands that had sat exactly where Missy's were sitting now, clasped loosely. They'd be watching her. The all-seeing camera in the top right corner was still where she remembered it.

The door opened with a rush of air. Missy kept her eyes forward until the detective was seated in front of her.

O'Dea had a sheaf of papers. He always had a sheaf of papers, and Missy had come to perceive them as some kind of safety blanket for the conscientious detective. He wasn't a bad man. Not really.

'So, it is you,' he remarked, straightening the file before him. He studied her. 'I thought we'd never see you again.'

Missy shifted in the chair. 'I can assure you, Gary, the feeling was entirely mutual.'

'How's your daughter, Ellie isn't it?' The detective's eyes narrowed. He was a dad, as Missy recalled. Three kids, all much older than Ellie. Didn't mean you stopped worrying, he'd told her once.

'She's fine. Growing.'

With the file now perfectly straight, the detective nodded, clasped his hands and looked her directly in the eye. 'Missy, I have to ask—why the hell are you here?'

'You know he's out.'

'We know.'

'And he's gone straight back into it.'

O'Dea's eyes narrowed. 'How do you know?'

'Because I'm doing what you should be doing,' Missy exploded. 'Watching him.'

The detective shook his head. 'You know you shouldn't be doing that.'

'Well someone should,' she shot back and reached for the camera. 'You know he nearly killed someone today. He has a gun.'

O'Dea blinked. 'You have photos of that?'

Missy shook her head and kicked herself for having lowered the lens at the pivotal moment. 'No, but I've got plenty of other stuff. The scumbags he's hanging out with, all the comings and goings.' She handed it over and watched O'Dea's expression as he clicked through the photos.

'Missy, this is dangerous.' His voice was grave, his eyes still trained on the screen. 'What if he sees you?'

'He hasn't so far,' said Missy stubbornly. 'You need to arrest him again. Now. It's all there.' She pointed to the camera.

O'Dea sighed and rubbed his temples. 'Missy, you know it's not enough.'

'Then I'll get more!'

'And I'll have to arrest you for interfering with police enquiries,' he said wearily. 'You need to let *us* do the work.'

'What? Like you've done so far.' Missy couldn't keep the sarcasm out of her voice.

O'Dea paused. 'I shouldn't be telling you this, but ... we're onto him.'

'But you weren't there this morning. No cops at all and a man nearly got killed!'

The detective clasped his hands. 'Kyle is on our radar, believe me ... but so are plenty of others.' He leant in. 'We've got someone on the inside ... Deep undercover, and this time we're going to chop the head off this snake. I know last time, there were ... mistakes ... but not this time. This time we're going to get them all, the whole ring, and get them good.' O'Dea's eyes zeroed in on hers. 'But if he gets the slightest inkling that you're here and you're watching him, it could undo every little bit of work we've done so far.' He tapped the table. 'You have to leave it with us. You have to leave Coffs and let us do the job, and I promise we'll get it right this time.'

'Why should I trust you, after what happened?'

O'Dea ran his fingers through his hair, which Missy now noticed had thinned considerably since she last saw him. 'I know we stuffed up ... but it's different now. My team ... they're clean, I promise you.'

Missy sat back, her mind exploding with thoughts. O'Dea was asking her to trust him, with her life, and with Ellie's. Could she do that again? The whole reason she'd come to Coffs was to see if Kyle had changed and, if he hadn't, to make sure he couldn't hurt them. The job wasn't done. Far from it. Kyle was more dangerous than ever. Could she rely on the police to put him away, to keep her and Ellie safe? Did she even have a choice? O'Dea was clear about her staying out of it—she didn't doubt that he'd charge her if he had to—and there was also the small but important fact that her money was running out. The hotel was a dive, but even dives cost money. Missy needed to get back to work if she wanted to eat. She also needed to see Ellie ... Twenty-six days. Jesus.

Missy looked into the detective's grey eyes.

With a torn heart, she spoke. 'Okay,' she sighed. 'Okay. I'll go ... but on one condition.' She held up a finger. 'You have to give me your word that you won't let him out of your sight. As soon as you get what you need, you have to pick him up.'

'I promise.' O'Dea nodded solemnly. 'On the lives of my kids ... I promise. We'll get him.'

CHAPTER TWENTY-SEVEN

Finally, the humidity of February and March had given way to the more comfortable climes of April. Autumn was Lisa's favourite season in Sydney—still warm, but not sticky. It really was the perfect month for getting married and Lisa experienced a little shiver of delight as she thought about her sister's upcoming wedding, which was now only three days away. She would miss her dreadfully when she moved to Dubai, but if this was what Jamie wanted then Lisa would back her all the way. One upside—it did present an appealing travel opportunity. Lisa had heard Dubai was fantastic for young families and she'd opened a new savings account to get their travel funds started. So far, there was $200.

Interrupting Lisa's thoughts, Principal Valentic tapped loudly on the microphone and caused it to squeal in protest. The groans of parents and children were instantaneous and audible. In response, the principal frowned and raised her hand in the air without saying a word. Silence spread like a ripple, and soon the entire school was quiet and every student had their hand raised. Lisa checked to see if the other parents were doing it too but their hands remained firmly in their laps.

She settled back into the hard, plastic chair, Jemima wriggling into her lap, and looked about the hall. The faded photograph of Queen Elizabeth, wearing her ball gown and crown. A small crucifix hanging over the stage and brownwood honour rolls engraved in gold paint with names of the school's captain and outstanding achievers. In front of her was a sea of navy-checked tunics, shirts that needed tucking in, falling down socks and scuffed shoes. If Lisa closed her eyes, she was ten years old again and back in her own primary school, for her school assemblies had been exactly the same. Even the design of the seats hadn't changed—that curved plastic that pinched everyone in the back. Yet there was something comforting in the discomfort. It was all very familiar. At least her legs weren't sticking to the seat in the way they had been over the past few weeks.

'Thank you, girls and boys. Now let us stand for the national anthem.'

As the kids rose to their feet, excited tittering broke out again and prompted a rash of shushing from teachers sitting guard on both sides of the hall. This time, the parents around Lisa stood too. There weren't many—maybe thirty or forty or so, which wasn't a bad turnout considering it was 2.30 pm on a weekday when most parents would be at work. The active-wear mums were there, of course, sunglasses on heads and ponytails momentarily at ease. They'd given her warm waves of welcome on the way into the hall, which gave Lisa a flicker of confidence. Heather had kissed her on the cheek as if they were long-lost friends. Finally, Lisa felt like she was fitting in and finding her feet. Ellie and Ava were happy, and after the ridiculous escapade to the pre-school where Melissa worked, Lisa had given herself permission to take a break from worrying about the search for Ellie's mum. After all, Jeff was investigating. If Missy were to be found, the professional would find her.

'Girls and boys, YOU are the ones in charge of your bodies, so if you are talking then you have made a choice and it is a bad choice,' boomed the principal.

The tittering stopped and the singing of the anthem began. Lisa was confident with the first verse but found herself mumbling the second. Whoever sang the second? She'd almost forgotten there *was* one.

She sat down and pulled out a packet of sultanas for Jemima to guzzle while the Year Six class performed a role-play about bullying.

'Take a stand, lend a hand,' they shouted at the end, fists pumping the air. They looked a bit too angry, Lisa decided, but Principal Valentic was effusive in her praise.

'Thank you, Year Six. You have reminded us that St John's is a 100 per cent bully-free zone.' She paused. 'What are we, St John's?'

'A 100 per cent bully-free zone,' shouted three hundred and fifty children with gusto.

Next were the merit awards. Lisa had gleaned from Ava and Ellie that two awards per class were given at every assembly. She leant forward. Hope sprouted in her stomach like a germinating seed. She had a feeling something great was about to happen for the Wheeldon family. It was their turn for some good luck, wasn't it?

The kindy awards came and went without mention of Ava's name. Never mind. There was still a chance.

'Now, let's move on to Year One.' Principal Valentic peered over her glasses, a wad of certificates in her hand. 'And the first certificate goes to ...' she paused. 'Ellie Jones, for being a kind friend to all, and achieving ten out of ten on her spelling test. Ellie, you are a reading whiz, says your teacher Mrs Booth.'

Spontaneously, Lisa started to clap. Loudly. She felt her heart growing too big for her chest. She was so proud of the little girl making her way quietly to the stage. From where she was sitting, she could also see Ava, grinning madly and waving.

My gorgeous girls. My beautiful, beautiful girls.

'Excuse me,' said Principal Valentic sternly. 'But there is to be no clapping until ALL the awards have been read out.' She removed her glasses and fixed Lisa with her stare. 'Parents included.' All three hundred and fifty children were now glaring at her. Lisa tried to sink further into the seat and hung her head behind Jemima's back.

Oh gosh, how embarrassing.

Lisa looked around. She was the only one who'd clapped, but there was a woman holding her phone in readiness to take a photo of Ellie.

Good idea, thought Lisa, rummaging in her handbag. It was in there somewhere, among the muesli bars, spare undies and wet-wipes.

Ah, there. She retrieved the phone and snapped a picture of a beaming Ellie standing proudly on the stage, holding her certificate. Lisa waved but Ellie seemed not to see her at the back of the hall.

Guess who got a merit award? she texted to Scott, before attaching the photo.

She looked around again and Heather gave her a wink of congratulations that Lisa returned by mouthing *Thank you*. Next to Heather, the woman in the hat and sunglasses was still taking photos.

Bit odd to take so many photos of someone else's child.

As Lisa tried to get a better look at the woman's face, she quickly lowered the phone as if embarrassed to have been caught.

'Mummy, more 'tanas,' wailed Jemima, flinging the empty box to the ground and earning another disapproving look from Principal Valentic.

Lisa again rummaged in her bag, hoping to find a stray pack of sultanas. Her daughter's dried-fruit habit was really getting out of control—two packets a day!

In the depths of the bag, she discovered a small packet of roasted fava beans that her daughter dived upon like a starved seagull. Once Jemima had settled back and was munching away happily, Lisa turned around again.

The woman who'd been taking the photos of Ellie was gone.

Lisa tried to focus on Principal Valentic, who had now moved on to Year Two but she found it impossible to concentrate, especially when there was no chance of another Wheeldon being called.

Who was the woman taking photos?

In the midst of foraging for Jem's snack, Lisa hadn't had a chance to get a good look.

But why was she taking shots of Ellie? And why did she leave so quickly?

The assembly was only open to parents and grandparents, though there was no one to actually check ID on the way in. But how would anyone outside of the school know it was happening? It had to be another school mum. But who?

The intrusive trill of a mobile phone interrupted her thoughts.

Someone forgot to put their phone to silent. How embarrassing.

The phone got louder. Three hundred and fifty pairs of eyes swivelled to the parents sitting at the back.

Why don't they switch it off, really and truly.

'Mummy, your phone's ringing.' Jemima held it up.

Oh bugger, I must have passed it to her when I was looking for food.

Lisa snatched quickly at the phone and started frantically pressing buttons to switch it off.

'Hello? Hello, Lisa? It's Jeff,' said a voice at the other end of the line.

Oh, great. She'd managed to answer it.

'I can't talk right now. I'm in an assembly,' Lisa hissed into the phone.

'Wait! Don't hang up. I've found something out about Missy. I've got appointments today but can you meet me tomorrow night? I'll text you the address?'

'Yes. Fine.' Lisa hung up, double-checked the phone was on silent and quickly read the message from Jeff.

Meet me tomorrow at Nitecap, 6 pm. J

The assembly closed with the singing of the school song and Lisa milled out the door with the other parents. She needed to find Heather, and ask her if she knew the mystery woman in the hat and sunglasses.

There she was, over by the statue of Mary. Clutching Jemima's hand, Lisa sidled up to her.

'Heather, hi.'

'Lisa, darling. Congratulations!' Heather kissed her enthusiastically on the cheek. 'An exciting assembly for you! That little Ellie seems to have made quite the first impression.'

'She's a special little girl.'

'Now, don't be modest,' said Heather, giving her a gentle dig in the shoulder. 'She could never have got that certificate if it weren't for you and Scott. Not with that mother of hers.' Heather sniffed. 'I mean, where could she be?'

'I'm not sure about that,' Lisa mused. The more she got to know Ellie, the more evidence she saw of a child who'd been extremely well loved, well educated and well disciplined, which made the whole situation all the more puzzling. It was something she couldn't quite put into words and she wasn't about to try in the milieu of mothers who were now moving at slow speed towards the school gate from where they could collect their little charges.

'Any update from Jeff?' Heather enquired.

'Actually, we're catching up tomorrow night. He says he has something for me,' said Lisa.

'Where are you meeting?'

'Some bar called Nitecap? I've never heard of it, but he says it'll be quiet at that time.'

Heather nodded. 'It's one of his go-to places. They do a really fabulous Negroni. You must have one.'

Lisa had zero intention of drinking a cocktail. She was nervous enough as it was. What had he found out?

The investigation had taken longer than expected, and with each week that passed, Jeff had sent her apologetic text messages to let her know he was still looking. *No rush*, she'd told him. Quite frankly, she was a little bit relieved at the blow-out. Jeff worked for a flat-rate fee, a thousand bucks for a 'find', so there was no danger of Lisa receiving a nasty bill that she had no hope of hiding from Scott. No, the longer Ellie stayed with them, the more torn Lisa became about finding her mother, because finding her would mean losing Ellie and Lisa had come to love the little girl as her own. Saying goodbye would be a wrench. But then again, as Scott had reasonably pointed out, they couldn't just keep her indefinitely. At some point, people were bound to ask questions.

Lisa touched Heather's arm. 'Say, who was that mother sitting next to you in assembly? I couldn't quite see her properly.'

'The one in the cap? No idea. I barely gave her a second glance, but I don't think I know her.'

'Really? You've never seen her before?'

'I don't think so. She looked quite young, so I assumed she might be one of the nannies, you know, sent along by a guilt-stricken parent in case of an award.' Heather stopped. 'Why do you ask?'

'She was taking photos of Ellie, and it struck me as being a bit odd. I just wondered if she might ...' Lisa trailed off. 'Did you see a nose ring?'

'I wasn't really looking. Let me ask the girls. They might have been paying more attention.'

'Please, don't.' Lisa put her hand on Heather's arm and looked around, concerned someone might be listening. But the other mothers were too wrapped up in discussions about homework (too little) and the dreadful inadequacy of the infant playground. A fundraiser was needed. Stat!

'Why not? It might have been her. It might have been the woman I saw at the carnival.' Heather frowned. 'Don't you want to know?'

Well, sort of. I think so. I don't know. Maybe not. Oh, god. What kind of terrible person am I to deprive a child of their parent?

Lisa sighed. 'All right. You can ask the girls if they know her.' She squeezed Heather's elbow. 'But please don't mention me or Ellie.'

Heather winked. 'Leave it with me.'

As Lisa monitored Jemima playing hide-and-seek with another three-year-old, Heather worked the crowd like a silent vacuum cleaner, moving from mother to mother with quiet, information-sucking efficiency. Within minutes she was back and breathless with excitement.

'The woman's a complete Jane Doe. No one knows her. How odd!'

But before Lisa could say another word, the school bell went and the gates opened, bringing with it a tsunami of children sweeping over the waiting parents and spilling out into the street where a line of cars was already waiting to whisk them off to swimming and ballet and karate.

Only Lisa remained still, like a statue, sensing that if she were to move an inch she might get swept out to sea.

CHAPTER TWENTY-EIGHT

Missy pulled her hat down and checked over her shoulder. No one following. Thank goodness. She'd got too close. Far too close. It was silly. Selfish. Getting that close could only put Ellie in danger and she'd worked so hard and sacrificed so much to ensure her little girl's safety. Now was not the time to lose it.

She scurried down the street, past the newsagent and butcher's, all operating as usual as if it was just another day. Slowly, Missy felt her heart rate returning to normal. She checked once more. There was no one following and the adrenaline that had been pumping through her veins was now nothing but a trickle. She let the tears come. Her sunglasses were large enough so that no one would see. She was free to cry and cry she did.

Her little girl! Her precious little girl, walking so confidently onto that stage in front of all those children and parents! Missy had never felt more proud, or envious. When she heard Lisa break into spontaneous applause it was all she could do to not join in. It should have been her, Missy, being the embarrassing mum. Instead, she had settled for taking a photo—a poor substitute—but she had to do something to express the thump of maternal pride in her heart.

What a silly, silly thing to do! Lisa had noticed her, and the fact that she had noticed was both reassuring and frightening. Reassuring, for it told Missy that Lisa had accepted Ellie as her own—she was watching her as a mother did, seeing and sensing anything of possible threat to the child, including the sight of a complete stranger taking Ellie's photo. But at the same time it was frightening, because Lisa's expression told Missy she thought it strange. At any moment, Missy expected her to stand, point at her and shout: *It's you. You are the terrible mother who abandoned this poor, wonderful child.* But Lisa wasn't the type to make a scene. Missy knew enough of her to know she was too sensible for that. After all, Ellie was in no imminent danger, so Lisa would wait—and that was Missy's chance to escape, a chance she took, bumping knees with the other mums as she bumbled her way out of the ceremony, her heartbeat roaring in her ears.

This was not the time to be exposed.

The police hadn't arrested him. Not yet. Every day she rang and hounded O'Dea, and every day he promised the same: *We're very close, trust me. Just a little bit more time. We have to nail them. All of them.*

When Missy hung up, she was angry. And not just with the police. How had she ever got caught up with such a dangerous loser? It was the biggest mistake of her life, and she'd known that from the minute he looked at their little girl, still waxy with vernix, and laughed. 'She looks like a monkey,' he'd jeered over the cooing midwives. In that moment, Missy knew that Ellie was the best and worst thing she had ever done. Best—for Ellie was hers to love and cherish. Worst—for it meant she would forever be tethered to Kyle.

What had she been thinking? How had she ever fallen for him? Over the years, Missy had asked herself the question time and again. But the answer was never satisfactory. She was young—just nineteen when they'd met at the Hoey Moey, Coffs Harbour's most dodgy pub. Her, an apprentice hairdresser looking for nothing more than a few laughs to go with her Vodka Cruisers. Him—slightly older, with confidence bordering on arrogance, intoxicating green eyes and hair the colour of deep, rich soil. Why hadn't she asked more questions? Demanded to know who the parade of visitors were that came to his house in the middle of the night? Why he never seemed to have a real job, just bits and pieces here and there that didn't quite explain the volume of cash he always had in his wallet?

It seemed so obvious to her now, but back then she was young and in love and by the time she thought to ask, she was two months' pregnant and Kyle's arrogance had taken on a menacing edge. Every minute of the day, he wanted to know who she was with, which clients she'd seen at work, which friends she'd had coffee with, who she'd spoken to on the phone. She told him he needed to back off. Let her breathe.

I'm only asking because I love you. I don't want to share you, he would say angrily, to which she would tell him he needed to trust her.

I don't trust anyone.

Any hope she'd had that Ellie's birth might improve things quickly evaporated. If anything he was worse. He started to check her phone, her emails, insisted that if she wanted to go anywhere with Ellie, then he had to come too.

Kyle wasn't just clingy and controlling, he was also stupid and dangerous. All it took was one look at tiny baby Ellie, lying in a hospital bed with wads of tape around her little finger to make up Missy's mind. What kind of idiot could think it a good idea to take a four-month-old on a motorbike ride?

I was only going down the street and back! She was loving it.

Sure, right up until the point Ellie tumbled off and had the top of her little finger severed in the process.

In that moment, Missy hadn't screamed or cried as she wanted to. What would be the point? She'd been asleep when the accident happened, catching up after another restless night of feeding Ellie, and blamed herself for the injury as much as her stupid boyfriend.

In the hospital corridor, she told him she was leaving, that she would tell the cops he was responsible for the maiming of their daughter. She and Ellie would go and live with Terri.

No, you won't. Checking to make sure no one was watching, he'd pressed her up against the wall, hand to her throat, and hissed the words into her ear. *Because if you do, I'll come for you, and I'll make sure our precious little girl loses much more than just a finger.*

When he let go, Missy had run to the ward bathroom and vomited. She'd stayed there, thoughts tumbling and turning, until her daughter cried—a small, pained cry—and, in that hospital toilet, Missy found her resolve. Ellie needed her. For the sake of this innocent child—her own flesh and blood—Missy needed to make a plan.

Back at home, she started watching Kyle closely, making notes and hiding them. On the rare occasions that Kyle left the house, she set Ellie up in her bouncer, and turned the rooms upside down, searching for anything that might be incriminating. It wasn't that hard. In fact, it was depressingly easy. The wads of cash under the floorboards, a stash of pills in the safe with his date of birth as the combination. With every discovery, Missy kicked herself for having been so naïve, so blind to what was so clearly happening under her nose.

After two months, she was ready. Kyle was becoming more erratic. He had to go to the Gold Coast, he said, just for the day, but she wasn't to leave the house. He would call her to check. As she waved him goodbye, she dropped her hand quickly to hide the tremble in her fingers. This was her chance. Strapping Ellie into the pram, she walked the four kilometres to the police station, and in the grim interview room she told O'Dea everything she knew, on the strict condition of anonymity. If Kyle ever found out, there was no telling what he would do to her and Ellie. The detective listened intently. At the end, he'd collected his papers and thanked her. Kyle was already on their radar, but with her information, they could now make an arrest.

True to his word, O'Dea and his men pounced on Kyle as soon as he walked in the door. They made a show of arresting Missy too, just to deflect any suspicion. Later that night, she walked out of the police station under an inky midnight sky, a familiar face waiting for her.

'You're safe now, love,' said Terri, putting Ellie into her arms and absorbing Missy's sobs. The relief was overwhelming.

Missy was free, or at least, she thought she was. Two months later, in the baby aisle of the supermarket, a hooded figure shoved at her shoulder.

'He's watching you. And the kid. And when he gets out, he's going to take what's his. He knows what you did ...'

At first, Missy thought she imagined it. She was still sleep deprived after all, thanks to Ellie's continual night feeding. But as the hunched, grey shoulders sauntered away, Missy knew it wasn't her mind playing tricks.

Kyle knew. He knew she'd dobbed him in. He was still watching her through his loser mates and when he served his time, he'd come for her, if not sooner.

Clutching the trolley for support, Missy headed robotically for the checkout. O'Dea had promised complete confidentiality. He'd given his word and failed her.

Later at the police station, with Missy still shaking from shock and anger, he promised to get to the bottom of it. If there were any corrupt cops in Coffs, he'd find them. She could see he was genuinely shocked.

Whatever.

She didn't trust him, or any of them anymore.

It was time for her and Ellie to disappear.

Draining her bank account for the final time, Missy bought a one-way train ticket to Sydney. Onboard, with the kilometres clattering by, she swore into the downy hair on Ellie's still-forming scalp that she would devote her life to keeping her safe. She hadn't even told her own mother where they were going.

It was how it had to be.

For six years she'd been so careful. Never getting close to anyone. Never signing anything. Never using anything but cash. It was exhausting, trying to stay hidden in an electronic world. But they'd managed, until now, and Missy's faith in the world had been a little restored. She still believed it was a dangerous place, but it wasn't dangerous for everyone. It certainly wasn't dangerous for the children of St John's—a school so trusting that it openly displayed its school calendar on the internet, telling the world that assemblies were every Thursday at 2.30 pm and then throwing open the doors to whoever turned up. People like Missy. People like Kyle, who she knew, if he had any clue about Ellie's whereabouts, would simply turn up and take her, or worse.

But here was the thing. He didn't know where Ellie was. Only she did, and on the off-chance Kyle found Missy, she sure as shit wouldn't tell him anything.

She was safe with the Wheeldons and Missy couldn't jeopardise that. Not until Kyle was back behind bars.

Missy tugged at her collar and jammed her hat down. She'd got too close, turning up to the assembly at St John's. Now was not the time for making mistakes.

Back at the hotel, she stared at her reflection in the bathroom mirror. What she was about to do simply had to be done and probably should have been done earlier. Now, there was no choice. She was going back to work. Her boss would never allow her to wear a cap and, at this point, anything she could do to keep her identity a secret was worthwhile, just in case Kyle managed to somehow come looking. This was a small sacrifice. It was only hair. So what if she had been growing it for the past five years? It would grow back, eventually. That's what she always told clients who were unsure about making a radical change.

She pulled her hair back into a ponytail, picked up her scissors and just above the nape of her neck, cut the whole thing off. She looked at it, in her hand.

Just dead cells, nothing more.

The biology of hair was the first thing they'd been taught at college. *That's why it doesn't hurt to cut*, the teacher had explained. *Hair isn't like skin, it's just dead cells*, and that's how Missy had treated it until Ellie was born. When her baby girl emerged with a shock of dark hair, Missy had nuzzled her nose in it, feeling the incredible softness of the strands that had grown within her womb.

As Ellie had grown into a little girl, the nightly brushing of hair had become their ritual, one hundred strokes every evening before bed that transformed Ellie's hair from a bird's nest into a shining sheet of silk. It had never been cut. The ends of Ellie's now waist-length hair were the same cells with which she had been born—the ones that had grown within Missy. There had been times Ellie had asked for a cut, the length annoyed her and the knots were endless, but Missy always resisted. In solidarity, she had agreed that as long as Ellie didn't cut her hair, neither would Missy—a promise she had now broken.

She removed the hair elastic and started snipping. The back was hard to reach. She would use the clippers for that. An edgy undercut would suit the platinum blonde she was about to become.

Two hours later, Missy took a final look in the mirror. Under her feet were hanks of dark hair, and in the confines of the small bathroom the chemical smell of peroxide was almost overpowering. She gripped the basin.

She was barely recognisable. Even to herself. Except for one thing.

Missy took a breath. Her fingers fumbled. Slipping and sliding. She tried again. *Bugger. Slipped. Wait. Nearly got it. Just a little bit more. There.*

The nose ring made a tinkling sound as she dropped it down the sink.

She looked again at her reflection.

Bare-faced. Bleached and stripped back. She barely recognised the woman staring back at her.

Perfect.

CHAPTER TWENTY-NINE

'Four major catastrophes, Jamie.' Ben's face was creased with worry.

'Talk to me,' Jamie ordered, removing the headset through which the director was screaming at the DJ to get his dirty equipment off the white, lacquered runway. *Your fucking turntable is turning my runway to shit.*

'Okay, well, first of all, the globes in the strobe light have blown and the lighting technician's gone AWOL.' Ben held up a second finger. 'Two of the models had a bender last night and haven't turned up. Also, the editor of *Shopping Madness* is refusing to get out of her car until we guarantee a front-row seat. And lastly, Nala says her *assistant*—' Ben used his fingers to quote the word '—who I think is actually her best friend's boyfriend, is saying the music needs to be louder and so Nala wants to know if that's possible.' He removed the pencil from behind his ear and held it expectantly over his notebook. 'What do we do?'

'Walk with me,' Jamie said to Ben, striding through the plethora of half-naked women standing around racks of clothes. Fashion shows were always terrible for one's body image and Jamie always emerged from them with a new resolution to hit the gym twice as hard. She saw Ben look sideways. 'Hey, buddy,' she snapped. 'Eyes on me, thanks.'

'Sorry,' he muttered. 'It's just a little distracting.'

Jamie stopped at the fire exit and pointed to the door. 'Outside here is where you'll find the sparkie—it's where all the tradies hang out for smoko. As for the models, I've actually got a couple of extras on standby.' She leant in. 'I always have back-ups. Models are flakier than pastry. Two drinks and *pffft*, they're in bed for days. The downside of zero per cent body fat.' Jamie took out her phone. 'Just call Miriam at the agency, and she'll send them over. I'll shoot you her number.' As she tapped her phone, Jamie kept talking. 'As for the *Shopping Madness* princess, give her my spot and I'll watch from backstage. And on the music issue, tell Nala's *assistant*—' Jamie quoted the air '—to go fuck himself.'

Ben's eyes widened. 'Really?'

'No!' Jamie cried. 'Of course not.' She put her hand on Ben's arm. 'Just leave Nala to me. I'll calm her down.'

As the minutes ticked by, Jamie's nerves began to mount. This was it. This was her final chance to prove her worth to Angel and get her approval to either take over at Spin or get her blessing for the Dubai venture. But Jamie wasn't the only one with everything on the line. This was Nala's first catwalk parade, and possibly her last, given the cut-throat nature of the Australian fashion industry. She'd put all the money she had into the show (which actually wasn't much at all) and begged Angel to produce something that would establish her as a fixture on the Australian fashion landscape.

Angel was hooked, both by the challenge and by Nala's clothes, which were a modern vibe on the African tribal trend and made women look exactly how they wanted to— sexy and elegant. Nala herself was a total sweetheart—a fashion-school graduate for whom everything was 'stellar', as in *Ooh, that dress is stellar on you* or *That collar is just, like, stellar, right?*

Yes, Jamie's client was as starry-eyed as her favourite word. But her *assistants* (there seemed to be about five of them) were dope-smoking douchebags.

Jamie found Nala at the feet of a six-foot glamazon, madly performing last-minute touches to a floor-length, black maxi-dress, shot through with leopard print.

Stunning.

Jamie knelt down beside her. 'Hon, I hear there's a problem with the music.'

Nala removed three pins from her mouth. 'Jamie, you know I think everything is looking like, so stellar, but Justin thinks the music is maybe a teensy-weensy too soft.'

Jamie nodded. 'Well, you tell Justin that because of the neighbours, this venue has noise restrictions.'

'Of course,' said Nala, nodding earnestly. 'Completely understand.'

'But—' Jamie held her hand up. 'Because I know the manager, we'll boost the music during the show to just over the legal level, so you tell Justin it's going to be plenty loud.'

Nala nearly knocked Jamie to the floor with her enthusiastic hug. 'You're the best.'

Jamie rose and straightened her skirt. 'My pleasure, hon. You are going to shine like a star.'

Nala squealed. 'My first show.'

'Enjoy it, lovely.'

Jamie felt a firm hand on her waist. Ben. Still frowning. 'We've got another major problem.' He guided her away from Nala and behind a black curtain where it was quiet.

'What is it?' Jamie felt her nerves re-doubling. Whatever it was, it was serious.

'The singlets for the drummers haven't arrived,' he whispered urgently. 'The supplier thought the show was tomorrow and he hasn't even started on them!'

To make Nala's show really pop, Jamie had organised a crew of African drummers to kick it off with a walk down the catwalk and through the crowd. Jamie had heard them in rehearsal and knew the effect would be extraordinary. To top it off, they'd be wearing cool, black singlets with the word 'Nala' emblazoned in white across them.

Shit.

As Jamie visualised the crew of drummers, a thought popped into her head. 'The guys in the drumming crew are all pretty hot, right?'

'I dunno. I guess so.'

Jamie frowned. 'C'mon, Ben. Don't go all macho on me now.'

Ben set his mouth in a line. 'Yes. Objectively, they are hot.'

'Okay, well let's have them do it topless.'

'No singlets at all.'

'Nothing,' said Jamie triumphantly. 'But I want the make-up artists to get their coal sticks and slash the word Nala across each guy's chest.'

Ben nodded slowly. 'I think that'll work.'

'Course it will.' Jamie knew she sounded more confident than she felt. 'Now you go see if the drummers are up for it. And if they're a bit shy, promise them an extra hundred bucks for getting their kit off.'

Ben saluted and disappeared into the crowd, while Jamie moved on to checking the lighting. Two minutes later, Ben was back and breathless.

'They're all fine with it, except the guy who plays the rain shaker thing.'

'What's his problem?'

'He's on Jenny Craig.'

'Jenny Craig?' Jamie's mind boggled and an image of a chubby guy rattling a shaker came into her head. In her mind, the shaker and tummy wobbled in unison. It wasn't pretty. Jamie tapped her foot. 'The rain shaker guy just plays at the start and finish and kind of bobs around while the drummers do their thing.'

Ben nodded. 'Yeah, it's pretty basic. Anyone could do it.'

'Anyone could do it,' said Jamie slowly, a smile spreading across her face.

'No, no.' Ben started backing away. 'You can't make me.'

'But I can,' said a familiar voice.

Jamie whipped around to find Angel, looking like a magnificent cassowary in a royal blue-and-black kaftan from Nala's collection.

'Angel,' said Jamie, flustered. 'I thought you'd already been seated.'

'Oh, sweetheart, it's such a bore out there. Much more exciting here, behind the scenes with all the beautiful people.' Angel raised her eyebrows at one of the passing, shirtless drummers. 'And, of course, I wanted to make sure everything's going to be 100 per cent perfect.' Her gaze narrowed on Jamie.

'It certainly is,' chimed Ben. 'Jamie has everything sorted.'

'Of course you do,' cried Angel. 'Mwah, mwah.' She kissed the air between Jamie and Ben. 'Toodle-oo! See you on the other side.'

They waited till she'd wafted into the distance before speaking.

'She scares me sometimes,' said Jamie, staring after her boss and half-expecting her to magically reappear at her side.

'She scares me all the time,' said Ben, wandering away and untucking his shirt.

'Where are you going?' called Jamie.

'To get changed of course.' He gestured to his navy suit. 'I like to get a little more comfortable when I'm African drumming.'

Jamie laughed as the director bawled in her ear. *Places NOW, everyone. Five fucking minutes till showtime.*

The show was a blur. For most of it, Jamie stayed by Nala's side but the young woman was in a zone of her own, flouncing skirts, straightening collars and rolling sleeves with such studious determination that Jamie didn't dare interrupt. If backstage was a cyclone of women getting furiously dressed and undressed (worse than a Gucci sample sale) then Nala was the eye of the storm—calm and serene. So under control was she that Jamie at one point left her side to peek from the wings at the audience. So many open mouths, it was like being at a dentists' convention. From the minute Ben kicked off the show with a shake of the rainmaker, the audience was hooked. It was like a musical waterfall that quickly gave way to a thumping African beat, taking the crowd from delight to unbridled energy. The beat was primal. Exhilarating. Jaded was a fashion trend that this crowd wore well, but as the drummers threaded their way through the seats, chests rippling under the effort of pounding their instruments, every single black-clad figure in the audience sat up straighter. Feet tapped. Hands clapped. The crowd was in the palm of Nala's hand—and not a single garment had hit the runway.

As the drummers subsided, the DJ's driving electronica beat took over and the first model hit the catwalk, striding out in a glorious chiffon dress, patterned in earth tones of burnt orange and deep auburn. So light and airy was the material that the model appeared to float down the runway, like a falling autumn leaf.

The applause thundered.

Applause for the first frigging dress.

It was unheard of, and as Jamie had gone to squeeze Nala's shoulders in congratulations, she'd stopped. The young woman hadn't seen any of it, too focused was she on the next model and the one after that, and the one after that. She would watch it back later, Jamie reasoned, leaving her be.

The show was nearly over now. The DJ had switched the music into an up-tempo party groove and the models were pulling on swimsuits, preparing for their final pass.

Jamie held her breath. The finale was the most technically complex part of the show, requiring the models to walk through a wall of water. It had worked well in rehearsal— water had fallen on cue like a spontaneous rain shower. But none of the models had actually walked through it—wet hair and streaky mascara one hour before the show would have sent the make-up artists into a meltdown.

The waterfall was a risk. A huge risk.

And cue the water, said the director in Jamie's earpiece.

Nothing. Not a single drop. Dry as a drought.

Make it fucking rain. NOW! he roared.

And the heavens opened.

Barefoot and bikini-clad, the models loosened for the final pass, dancing down the runway and then luxuriating in the water for a second, before flicking their hair (stray droplets hitting the front row) and slinking their way back, skin glistening as if they'd been coated with diamond dust. Backstage, the girls whooped and hollered as they dived for the towels.

The parade was done but there was one thing left to do.

Jamie pushed Nala into the wings. 'Go, go. It's your turn.'

Stunned by the spotlights, the young woman covered her eyes and squinted into the light. The crowd erupted and Nala skipped to the end of the runway, kicking at the puddles like an excited kid.

Jamie scoured the crowd. There was Angel, beaming. The editor of *Vogue*, shouting *Bravo*. Even the cranky editor of *Shopping Madness* was stamping her feet.

Jamie exhaled and felt arms encircling her waist and lifting her into the air.

'You did it.' Ben twirled her around and pulled her in tightly for a hug. He was still shirtless, his muscles warm and firm beneath Jamie's hands.

'That was amazing,' he whispered into her ear, tickling her cheek with his breath. '*You're* amazing.'

Jamie drew back and then moved in again to kiss him full on the mouth. A firm kiss. Lips pressed together. She broke away.

'I'm sorry,' Jamie began, shaking her head. 'We can't do this. I'm getting married in—'

'I don't care.' Ben pulled her back in and this time the kiss was soft and tender. Their tongues met and Jamie felt desire, cresting like a wave within her. She wrapped her arms around his neck and Ben pressed into her.

'Ooh I say, I thought the runway show was fabulous, but like I say, the real fun always happens backstage.' Angel stood with her hands on her hips and winked as Ben and Jamie sprang apart. 'Come here, my darlings. Aunty Angel is so, so proud of you.' She wrapped Ben and Jamie in a hug, her germ-phobia momentarily forgotten. 'You two are a wonderful team.'

Finally, the three-way hug ended, but the trio remained holding hands and grinning like idiots at each other. Then, Angel reached into the swathes of her caftan and produced two business cards.

'These—' she stopped for dramatic effect and held them aloft '—are for you, my dear.'

Angel handed over the cards and Jamie quickly scanned them.

On the first was the Spin Cycle logo. *Jamie Travvers, Spin Cycle, Managing Director.*

The second bore a logo she didn't recognise.

Issam Al Mazouri, Chief Executive Officer, Dubai Corporation for Tourism and Commerce Marketing.

'I don't understand,' said Jamie.

Angel put her arm around Jamie's shoulder and leant in to whisper in her ear. 'I'm giving you a choice, my dear. Stay or go. You have my blessing for either.'

A choice. That must have meant she passed the test with flying colours!

Jamie hugged her boss and kissed her cheek. 'Thank you, Angel.'

'Is there room for one more or is this a Spin-employees-only affair?' Jamie felt a tap on her shoulder and turned to face Jared, smiling widely at her. She winced at the word 'affair'.

'Great show, babe.' Jared pulled her in for a perfunctory kiss on the cheek. 'Very proud of you.'

'You came,' she said lamely, suddenly remembering that she'd casually mentioned the show to him before he'd left for work.

'Of course I did. Couldn't miss the last big shebang, could I?' He smiled easily at her. Ever since the Melissa debacle, Jared had been on his best behaviour. When Jamie had confessed to tracking her down, he hadn't been angry like she thought he might be. Instead, he was relieved and almost wistful.

'How did she seem, when you saw her?' he'd asked.

'She seems happy,' Jamie had told him. 'She's obviously great at what she does and she's an absolute natural with the kids …' She trailed off, unsure what to say next.

'But what?'

Jamie sighed. 'I think she's sad that she hasn't had a child.'

Jared had nodded and for the rest of the night was uncharacteristically quiet. He didn't even check his phone. Not even once.

'I'm sorry I didn't tell you,' he'd whispered to her in bed, before rolling away. But Jamie had lain awake for hours, mulling over the events of the day and Jared's odd reaction.

She had accepted his apology. What choice did she have? Ellie was not his child. There was no child. They were free to marry, no strings attached. But what she hadn't anticipated was his sense of disappointment. Anger that she had gone behind his back, she could understand. Relief that there was no child could also be expected. But not this sad disappointment, this sense that he was not really sorry for having withheld such material information from Jamie, but extremely sorry over the way he'd treated Melissa and her pregnancy all those years ago.

With models and photographers still milling about, Jared took Jamie's hand. 'Let me take you out for dinner, to celebrate.'

'That's my job, isn't it?' Angel protested, taking her other hand.

'As much as I would love to take you both up on your offers, I actually already have an appointment to go to.' Jamie squeezed both their hands. 'I'm sorry.' She'd have to tell Jared about Angel's generous offer later.

'What could possibly be more important than celebrating the hottest show of Fashion Week with your *boss*, your *fiancé*, and of course your darling *assistant*.' The way Angel winked as she emphasised the words made Jamie feel queasy. The woman was incorrigible.

'Oh, it's just the hairdresser.' Jamie tried to sound nonchalant. 'But I've already put it off twice and the wedding is just two days away now. I really need to go.' She looked at the three puzzled faces surrounding her.

'Well, if you must, darling.' Angel wafted her hand around. 'Don't want you looking like a tramp on your *big day*.' She turned to Ben and Jared. 'Looks like it will be just us three, then. Shall we?'

'What?' Jamie was aghast. 'You're all going without me.'

'Why not, darling?' Angel hooked one arm through Ben's and the other through Jared's. 'We've got so much to talk about.'

CHAPTER THIRTY

Lisa stepped timidly into the bar. Jeff had suggested it, and Lisa had been too flustered in the school assembly to think of an alternative. But, a bar? Was that really the appropriate place for meeting with one's private investigator? Particularly a bar that was dimly lit and scattered with private booths and sort of screamed SEX.

What would Scott think if he could see her now? On her way out of the house, he'd kissed her on the forehead and pressed fifty dollars into her hands. 'Enjoy the drinks! Have one on me,' he said cheerfully. 'Shame you can't stay longer. You might have made some friends.'

Poor, unaware Scott. He really had no clue. Lisa had to bite on her lip to stop herself from spilling the beans. Lying gave her a stomach-ache. In Scott's mind, Lisa's night involved making a brief appearance at the kindy mums' drinks night, and then heading to Jamie's hairdresser where her sister planned to have a trial run of her 'do' for the wedding.

But, here she was, walking into a sexy bar to meet with a very good-looking man—objectively speaking, the whole linen/sherbet colours thing didn't really do it for Lisa. She was more a jeans and polo shirt kind of woman—all to discuss an investigation she hadn't even cleared with her sweet husband.

Lisa let her eyes grow accustomed to the dim lighting. There was Jeff, in the corner and pastel as ever, completely at odds with the dark tones of the leather banquette that seemed to hug around him. Lisa waved nervously. God, this was worse than a first date, if the butterflies in her stomach were anything to go by. Fingers-crossed she didn't run into anyone she knew. That would be an absolute disaster. How would it look? Her, a married woman, meeting in a sexy bar with a Don Johnson lookalike?

'Lisa! Hey!'

She wheeled around, heart in her mouth.

'Heather, what are you doing here?' Lisa clutched a hand to her chest.

'Thought you could use some back-up.' Heather gave a little wave to Jeff. 'And I'm absolutely dying for a little Negroni. I tell you. Out of this world.'

'Ladies, a pleasure to see you as always.' Jeff rose and gave Heather a kiss on the cheek. Lisa went to shake hands but Jeff drew her in for a kiss as well. He smelt good. Very good. Lisa swooned a little. Maybe pastels weren't all bad.

'Oh! Right. Thanks, Jeff. How are you?'

He slid back into the banquette and frowned. 'I wish I had better news for you.'

'Why? What is it? Have you found Missy? Is she all right?' Lisa slid so far to the edge of the leather seat that she had to grab hold of the table to stop herself from falling right off.

Jeff gave her a look and, at that moment, Lisa noticed he wasn't quite his usual suave self. Perhaps it had been camouflaged by the dim lighting but now that Lisa was closer, she could see a ring of grey around Jeff's normally sparkling blue eyes. The linen shirt had gone from *artfully crushed* to *been in the dirty laundry too long* and he was pale, in places, a dead giveaway for a spray tan that needed a top-up. He shifted in the seat. 'Look, I'm just going to say this straight out.' He clasped his hands together and focused on the coaster in front of him. 'I can't find her.'

'But you were so confident. I don't quite understand.' Lisa turned to Heather, who gave a *don't ask me* shrug.

'It happens occasionally, usually when people have a good reason to not want to be found. It's not impossible to completely disappear you know.'

'And that's what's happened here?' Heather demanded.

'Maybe,' Jeff conceded. 'But I do know one thing for certain, which is why I brought you here.' He looked from Heather to Lisa. 'I'm not the only one looking for her.'

Lisa inhaled. 'Why? Who else is looking?'

Jeff picked up the little plastic stick in his drink and started to swirl it. 'I ran a check on the address you gave me, the one in Daceyville, and I couldn't get anything that related Missy to the place, but I did find out that the house is owned by a man by the name of Igor Ivanov.'

'Igor Ivanov,' Heather repeated with a snort. 'Next you're going to tell us he's Russian mafia.'

Jeff gave her a look. 'Please! Keep your voice down.' He looked about the empty bar before continuing. 'Anyway, I knew the name was familiar so I asked around a bit and it turns out he's also put out the feelers to track down the woman who was renting his granny flat, and more specifically, her daughter.'

Lisa felt bile rising into her throat. 'Is this man ...' she swallowed hard. 'Is he dangerous?'

Jeff put the stick into his mouth and started to chew on it. 'I don't think so.'

Heather sniffed. 'That's hardly reassuring. Is he a criminal or isn't he?'

'Let me put it this way,' he began slowly. 'There was a time Igor Ivanov was very active in the underworld, but he's an old man now. Over eighty I believe.'

'But mafia bosses don't just retire, do they? It's not like they have pension plans and a super fund. Either they get killed, or they go to jail. Isn't that how it ends?' insisted Heather.

Lisa sat back, with a feeling of having been punched in the gut.

Is she trying to make me feel better or worse?

'Not always,' said Jeff mildly. 'The smart ones, and there aren't many of them, get out of the game, enjoy their millions and let the young bucks take over.'

Lisa found her voice. 'But I don't get it. What would this Ivanov man want with Missy? Or Ellie, for that matter? She's just a little girl.'

'Who knows?' Jeff shrugged. 'Maybe they're related. Maybe Missy's his lover. Maybe Ivanov is Ellie's dad? I've got no idea. Missy Jones is a complete Jane Doe. She could be anyone to him.'

Lisa slumped back in the banquette. It was utterly ridiculous. One minute, Jamie had her believing Jared could be Ellie's father, and now, Jeff was trying to convince her it could be an eighty-year-old mafia boss, possibly retired.

'Anyway,' said Jeff miserably. 'I just thought you should know.'

'Right, well, thank you for that information. I think we'd best be going.' Lisa rose and tugged on Heather's arm.

'Wait! What are you doing? Aren't we at least going to have a cocktail?'

Dropping Heather's arm, Lisa headed for the door. She needed to get outside. She needed air. Space. An environment that didn't contain leather. Or pastel linen.

Outside, she leant against a telegraph pole and closed her eyes.

'Are you going to faint? Tell me if you're going to faint because I need to be ready.'

Lisa opened her eyes to find Heather with her knees bent and her arms outstretched, ready to catch her.

'I'm not going to faint,' she said weakly. 'But I might be sick.' She rubbed her stomach.

'Here!' Putting a hand into the small of her back, Heather led her over to the gutter. 'This will have to do.'

Lisa turned around. 'It's all right. I'm not actually going to be sick. I just feel very, very queasy.'

Heather nodded. 'I had that when I was pregnant with Savannah and the only thing that would fix it was hot chips.' She held her finger up. 'That's exactly what we need. Wait right here.'

Lisa stayed in the gutter and watched after Heather as she disappeared down the street into a local greasy spoon. She put her head in her hands. What the hell was she going to do now? If she told Scott, he'd want to go straight to the police and maybe that was the right thing to do. Except, as Jeff pointed out, Missy had proved almost impossible to find. Ellie would be put straight into foster care, which would mean everything that they had done to this point would have been a complete waste. Besides, there was also Jamie's wedding to think of. The girls were pants-wettingly excited about the prospect of being flower girls. If Scott and Lisa went to the authorities now, it would forever tarnish the wedding, and not just for the girls, but for Jamie as well. She'd be devastated if Ellie was wrenched from the family at the eleventh hour. She'd grown as fond of the child as Scott and Lisa were.

Heather was back with two buckets of chips. She thrust one into Lisa's hands and started munching.

'Oh my god, I'd forgotten how good these things were! They're, like, better than sex!' Heather spoke through a mouthful of hot and greasy potato.

Lisa took a bite. They *were* good. Straight out of the deep fryer judging by the way she was now having to pant with her mouth open. 'How long has it been?'

'What? Since the sex or the hot chips?' Heather munched away. 'Actually, it's about the same for both. And let's just say you need nearly two hands to count the years.'

'Really?' said Lisa, flabbergasted. 'You mean you and Henry never …'

'Dip ourselves in hot oil and get salty? Not much.' She grinned and picked up another chip. 'Speaking of husbands, what are you going to tell yours about Igor Ivanov?' Heather rolled the 'r'. 'It kind of changes things, don't you think. I mean, you guys might actually be in a bit of danger.'

'Maybe,' admitted Lisa. 'But while you were off getting the chips, I had a chance to calm down and think things through.' She licked the salt off her fingers and brushed her hands together to remove any excess. 'Jamie's wedding is in two days. Ellie's a flower girl and she's just so excited about it that I can't imagine depriving her and if I tell Scott now, he's going to want to go straight to the police.'

'Maybe you *should* be going to the police?'

Lisa shook her head. 'Think about it. We've managed to keep Ellie safe for nearly six weeks. What's a couple more days.' She shrugged nonchalantly. 'Piece of cake.'

Heather's eyes widened. 'Lisa Wheeldon, look at you. Acting all renegade. I'm impressed.'

Lisa took another chip and held it up in the air. 'Watch and learn, my friend.' Quickly, she put the hot potato in her mouth. She didn't want Heather to see just how badly her fingers were shaking.

CHAPTER THIRTY-ONE

Normally, the hair salon was Jamie's happy place. Decked out with chandeliers, pink velvet chaise lounges and up-lighting that removed all evidence of 'fine lines' (AKA: wrinkles) it was the place where she was transported, for an hour or so every week, into a world of pampered luxury. There, she felt a little bit Marie Antoinette—minus the whole cake-entitlement attitude. But tonight, sitting in the chair with half her hair wrapped in little pieces of aluminium foil that made her resemble a beauty-obsessed alien, she felt nothing but antsy. The salon was too quiet. Her favourite hairdresser, Kristy, had come in especially to do the trial of Jamie's wedding 'do and the salon owner was long gone, leaving just the two of them and a great big silence that Jamie was busy filling with anxious thoughts.

What will Angel say about me? And how will Ben feel after all the excitement of the show and—she shuddered as she thought of it—*the kiss?*

It didn't help that Kristy seemed to be matching her mood. Jamie had never seen the girl so fidgety and nervous. After the thousandth 'Sorry'—this time for dropping a piece of foil in Jamie's lap—Jamie swivelled in the chair. 'Kristy, is everything okay?'

'All fine,' she muttered and gently swivelled Jamie back into position to continue the bleaching.

'I know you've never done foils for me before, but seriously, it's no reason to be nervous.' Jamie gave what she hoped was a reassuring smile. 'It's not like it's for my wedding or anything,' she joked.

Kristy smiled weakly. Jamie went back to leafing through a magazine but the words were a messy blur in her racing mind.

'I like your new hairdo,' Jamie said casually. After three years of near-weekly appointments, she knew Kristy well enough to know the hairdresser wouldn't like a big fuss being made of the new, platinum pixie-cut she was sporting tonight. For as long as Jamie had known her, Kristy had tended to hide behind a curtain of heavy hair which was nearly waist-length and a deep, expensive brown, the colour of antique furniture. The short blonde crop was a radical change, but it suited her wide eyes and swan-like neck. She had transformed from Nana Mouskouri to a modern-day Twiggy.

'Thank you,' said Kristy, without lifting her head to acknowledge the compliment. 'I just felt it was time for a change.' She tilted Jamie's head into the required position. 'What time is your sister coming?'

Jamie checked her watch. Five to eight. 'Should be here any minute.'

The comb slipped from Kristy's hand and clattered to the chequerboard floor. 'I'm so sorry.' She covered her eyes and clutched her stomach. 'I'm not feeling so well.'

Jamie reached down for the comb. The girl was awfully pale. More so than usual. And dark circles shadowed her large, blue eyes. Jamie passed her the comb and patted her hand. 'Maybe you should go home? We can do this another time.'

Kristy fixed her gaze. 'Your wedding is less than forty-eight hours away! And I can't leave you like this ...' She gestured to Jamie's head, and as they considered the aluminium-alien hairstyle before them, the tension eased and Jamie let out a small giggle.

'I guess not.'

She went back to the bridal magazine. Statuesque Barbie dolls looking soulfully into the camera. Serenely happy.

At that moment, the black lacquered door to the salon swept open and in bustled Lisa. 'I'm sorry I'm late, Jamie. The girls took forever to eat their dinner tonight.' She pulled a face. 'Always the way when you're in a hurry.' She kissed Jamie on the cheek. 'Love the hair.' She winked at the mop of foil on Jamie's head. 'Setting a new wedding trend, I see.' Lisa sank into the lounge and kept babbling. 'A friend of mine once got foils and it turned her hair a Trump kind of orange! She was absolutely devastated ... not that your hair will go orange, I'm sure.' Lisa beamed.

Jamie looked at her with irritation. 'What is wrong with you? You sound like a chipmunk on acid and your eyes are like marbles. Where have you been?'

'Ah ... um ... Nowhere. Just home, like I said,' Lisa stammered.

Jamie sniffed, nose in the air. 'You've been eating hot chips,' she said accusingly.

'Me? Hot chips? No way.' Lisa shifted on the couch and rearranged her legs.

'I can't wait until this wedding's over and I can eat again,' muttered Jamie. 'Anyway.' She turned to Kristy. 'This is my sister, Lisa, and Lisa, this is my hairdresser extraordinaire, Kristy.'

'Sorry, how rude of me.' Lisa leapt up. 'Lisa Wheeldon.' She extended her hand. 'Jamie raves about you, so it's wonderful to finally meet.'

'She's talked a lot about you too.'

As Kristy went to shake, Jamie noticed the hairdresser's hand was trembling, as was her sister's.

What the hell is wrong with these two? I'm the bride. Aren't I the one who's supposed to be nervous?

'Hopefully, she's only told you the good things,' said Lisa, over-effusively.

'Yes, only the good,' Kristy spoke in a hoarse whisper.

'Oh, you poor thing.' Lisa threw her arm around Kristy's shoulder. 'You sound like you've got this dreaded flu that's going round at the moment. Half of St John's seems to have been wiped out with it. Not my girls, thank goodness.' Lisa rummaged around in her bag. 'I always carry a Lemsip, just in case.' She foraged some more. 'And usually some throat lollies too.'

'Oh, no, no, no, no.' Kristy started backing away. 'I'm fine.'

'Oh my god, you two!' Jamie exploded. 'Can you please start acting normally. I've got the stress of the wedding to deal with and I really don't need you two and your ...

weirdness.' She went back to the magazine and flicked furiously, in silence, for a few seconds. As Kristy went back to the foils, Jamie looked up from the page.

'I told you my sister was a born mother, didn't I?' She winked, wanting to let Kristy know that she wasn't really cross, just a little stressed.

Kristy nodded strangely. 'She is.' Her voice was a whisper.

'I know you don't want me to talk, Jamie, but are you sure we should be doing this tonight?' Lisa looked from Jamie to Kristy. 'The poor girl does seem rather unwell and we can postpone to tomorrow, can't we? It's only hair, after all.'

'I said the same thing.' Jamie shrugged. 'But Kristy says she's okay and I don't think she wants me walking out of here with a half-bleached head. Right, Kristy?'

'Yes, that's right. I'm fine.' Kristy busied herself about Jamie's hair while Lisa got up from the lounge, restless, and peered into the mirror.

'Ugh! More wrinkles.' Lisa squinted. 'I swear it's children that make you old. Not actual, you know, ageing.' She retreated back to the lounge and picked up a magazine. 'No wonder I never come to the hairdresser. No offence, Kristy.'

'None taken.'

'Do you have children, Kristy?'

This time it was the scissors that dropped to the floor. A flustered Kristy dropped after them and scuffled about under Jamie's chair. 'Sorry,' came the muffled apology.

'If you apologise one more time, I'll have to lacquer you into submission with this.' Jamie held up a can of hair spray.

'Sorr—'

'Kristy!'

'All right. But I am … you know. That word.'

'I know.'

Lisa resumed flicking through the magazine. 'So, do you, Kristy?'

'Do I what?'

'Have children?'

Jamie lifted her eyes to observe Kristy in the mirror. She was interested in the answer. Usually, when she came to the salon on a Saturday morning she used it as a debriefing session and unloaded all the news and events of her week onto Kristy's calm and quiet shoulders. But the young woman had never volunteered information about herself, and Jamie got the impression she appreciated that Jamie did not pry.

'No, I don't.' Kristy spoke the words so forcefully that it seemed almost a shout compared to the hoarse whisper.

For a few seconds there was silence, while Jamie and Lisa exchanged looks and Kristy focused on mixing the putty-coloured paste being smeared onto Jamie's hair.

'My sister doesn't mean to be nosy,' Jamie explained. 'She just loves talking about children. I'm sorr—'

'Hey!' In the reflection, Kristy pointed the brush at her. 'I thought we weren't using that word.' She smiled and tension eased out of the room like a deflating balloon. Kristy squeezed Jamie's shoulders. 'Just going to mix more colour. I'll be back in a sec.'

As Kristy headed out the back, Lisa slid into the chair next to Jamie's. 'Hey, I forgot to ask about the big show. How did it go?'

'Oh my god, I completely forgot. The first reviews would be online. Quick! Pass my phone.' Lisa handed it over and Jamie started scrolling and tapping madly, navigating to the Fashion Week coverage on the *Shopping Madness* website. If anyone was going to unload on Nala, it would be them. A front-row fiasco was all the ammunition they needed; Jamie had seen editors take vengeance for less.

Heart in her mouth, Jamie read the headline aloud. '*New Aussie Designer Hits the Perfect Beat.*'

Lisa clapped her hands together. 'They loved it! Yay!'

'Listen to this.' Jamie kept reading. '*In a high-octane show that transported the audience to the plains of Africa, Nala wowed the fashion crowd with a debut collection that marks her as THE Australian designer to watch. From the opening drumbeat (how hot were those drummers, BTW?!) right to the final rain shower, we were completely mesmerised by the whole production—props to Jamie Travvers for putting on one hell of a show! But back to the clothes. Chic and sexy, these are the looks that every woman will be wanting to wear. The only question is—can we wait till next summer? Might be best to put your name on the wait-list now for one of those lust-worthy maxis, because trust us, this is a designer we'll be talking about for years to come.*'

Lisa flung her arms around Jamie's shoulders and squealed. 'You did it! I'm so proud.'

Stunned, Jamie slowly disentangled herself from Lisa's embrace so she could re-read the article. 'Gosh. I can't quite believe it,' she said slowly.

I need to talk to Ben. I should be sharing this with him.

Kristy was back with a fresh bowl of grey peroxide for Jamie's hair, but sensing she'd interrupted something she stopped and cleared her throat. 'Lisa, I've only got a few more foils to do on Jamie here, so while I'm doing that, do you want to talk me through what you're after for the wedding?'

While Lisa and Kristy talked chignons and top knots, Jamie let her mind wander back to the show and the way Ben had kissed her. Just thinking about it made her stomach squirm. It was everything a great kiss should be—soft yet passionate, full of desire, and something else— caring. It was a really loving kiss. She couldn't remember the last time Jared had kissed her like that. Maybe in their early dating days, but those were so full of alcohol and lust that she couldn't really remember much kissing at all, or whether Jared had the capability to kiss her like that. It just wasn't him. He saw kissing as being an early stop on the journey to somewhere much more important—sex. When he did kiss her now, it was a bit rushed and forceful. Certainly, it made her feel wanted, but not cherished. *Ugh.* This was driving her crazy. All this thinking about Ben. In two days, she'd be married to Jared and wouldn't have to see Ben or think about his beautiful, soft lips ever again.

Never, ever again.

Jamie felt tears tip-toeing into her throat. Oh god. If she moved to Dubai, she really wouldn't see Ben again. She'd been so busy working on the wedding and the show to really stop and think about it. But now, the reality of life without him played like a sad, slow-motion movie in her brain. His cheeky smile. His stylish pocket squares. The way he brought her a coffee every morning. The way he consoled her when a client was being particularly difficult. The way he got her jokes, and didn't even roll his eyes at the really terrible ones. And the way he was with Lisa's girls. He'd be an amazing dad one day. Oh. My. Goodness. He was breathtaking. Jamie sucked in a sob.

'Are you okay, Jamie?' Kristy put a concerned hand on her shoulder.

'Are you about to vomit, hon? Should I get a bucket?' Lisa got into a crouch, ready to bolt out the back.

'No,' Jamie croaked. 'Just feeling a bit overwhelmed. Lost myself in the emotion, that's all.'

'Hon, you'd be forgiven for that. You've had a massive few weeks.' Lisa patted her arm. 'How about I run next door to the bottlo and get us some champers? Maybe this yummy thing called moscato? It's delicious and pink, and it's low-alcohol. Might take the edge off.'

'Great idea, Lise. I think I deserve it.'

'Back in a jiffy.' And before Kristy could mutter her assent, Lisa had disappeared out the door and into the night.

For the next two hours, the three women sipped champagne from tea cups (it was all the salon had) and discussed everything from the state of the nation's politics (dreadful) to the new hunk on *The Bachelor* (was he in it for love or fame?) and of course the latest exploits of Ellie, Ava and Jemima. Lisa had the other two in stitches over Jem's latest bad habit, which was to pull down her underpants in the shops, pull up her dress and announce loudly to passing shoppers, 'I have a front bottom,' as Lisa quietly died of embarrassment and vigorously pulled the clothing back into its rightful spot.

'So, will the girls be part of the wedding?' Kristy asked casually after the mirth had died down.

'Yes, of course!' Jamie cried. 'I couldn't not have my darling nieces by my side on my big day.'

'They're going to be so cute!' said Lisa, taking another sip of champagne. 'Though I hope Jem doesn't do her undies trick while walking down the aisle.'

'She won't,' groaned Jamie. 'You know what she's like.'

'I do know what she's like. And that's the problem.'

'I'm sure she'll be fine,' said Kristy, putting the finishing touches to Jamie's hair. 'Little kids understand when things are important. That's what my mum tells me,' she added quickly.

'Well, she's right,' said Lisa, tipping her cup towards Kristy. 'Like Ellie, this little girl who's staying with us at the moment. She's just an amazing child—a flower girl as well. Anyway, last week, I thought I'd lost Mum's earrings.'

'The pearl ones?' Jamie asked.

'Exactly,' Lisa nodded. 'Anyway, the girls were being no help at all, until I explained to them that they were very special earrings that belonged to my mum. And you know what Ellie did? She got out a torch and got down onto the floor and searched under every bed and couch and chair in the house.'

'And did she find them?'

'Yes!' said Lisa. 'She's just the most lovely child. The more I get to know her, the more I love her.'

'She is a great kid,' Jamie agreed.

'It must have been so, so difficult for her mother to … ah … well, to do what she did. I mean, Ellie's just so amazing, and I don't know how anyone could bear to part with her.'

Jamie noticed Kristy had stopped pinning her hair and was staring at Lisa, her eyes full of tears. 'Hon, are you okay?'

Kristy sniffed. 'I'm fine,' she said, wiping her eyes hastily. 'Just a tough week. Lots going on.'

'I hear you, girl. I hear you,' said Jamie.

'Is there anything we can do to help?' Lisa leapt from the chair and squeezed Kristy's shoulder.

'No,' she sniffed. 'You've already done enough.'

Slightly puzzled, Lisa hugged her. 'But we haven't done anything.'

'Just you being here … and caring,' said Kristy, her voice muffled by tears. 'That's everything.'

In the mirror, Jamie raised her eyebrows at Lisa as if to say *I don't know what the hell is going on* and Lisa gave a small shoulder shrug back that said *I don't either, but let's just go with it.*

Poor girl. All Jamie really knew about Kristy was that she was from the north coast, which presumably meant no family locally, and possibly only a few friends. Even though she'd never lived anywhere else, Jamie could see how Sydney was a tough city for newcomers. Perhaps that was Kristy's problem.

'How about a cup of tea?' Lisa disentangled herself from Kristy. 'I think we've probably had enough moscato for one night. It's nice at first, but then it's a bit like drinking fairy floss.'

'That would be lovely,' said Kristy, adjusting her spiky fringe and dabbing any remaining wetness from her cheeks. 'I'm sorry, Jamie. Let's finish you off.' She tilted Jamie's head forward and started sliding bobby pins into her hair to create the 'loose-but-done' hairstyle that Jamie had requested.

After a few minutes, she stopped. 'All right, you can look now.' As Kristy reached for a hand mirror, Jamie stared at her reflection. The style was perfect. Her hair was pulled softly from her face so that a few tendrils skimmed her cheeks, and it had been secured with an easy twist at the back of her head from which gentle curls tumbled down her back.

Back from the kitchenette and holding two cups of tea, Lisa audibly sucked in a breath. 'Oh, it's gorgeous ... Your curls, I haven't seen them in years.'

'Hold on. Just stand up for the finishing touch.' As Jamie stood, Kristy took the tulle veil with its scalloped edge of sparkling beads and slid the comb gently into the crown of Jamie's head, bringing the front of the veil down over her face. Now, Jamie's world was misted white, as it had been in the bridal shop. She peered through the netting at herself. *Oh my god.* She was really a bride. Feeling her knees starting to weaken, she clutched Kristy's arm for support.

'Holy shit,' she breathed.

Lisa laughed. 'I don't think that's quite what a bride is supposed to say.'

Kristy giggled nervously. 'Do you like it?'

'Oh, I love it!' She let go of Kristy's arm. 'It's just a lot to take in.'

Kristy nodded. 'I hear you, Jamie. I hear you.'

After a few more minutes of inspecting the hairdo and discussing logistics for the day, Kristy removed the veil and Jamie breathed a sigh of relief. She checked her watch. Nearly 10 pm. Goodness, it was getting late. She couldn't wait to get home and find out how the dinner between Jared, Angel and Ben had gone.

As Kristy tidied, Jamie and Lisa collected their things and carefully folded the veil into its white suit bag. After profuse thank yous to Kristy, they were nearly out the door when Lisa stopped.

'Say, Kristy, we never talked about the girls' hair for the wedding.' She pulled a face. 'I'm hopeless at doing it, and you're such a star, I don't suppose you'd mind doing three quick French braids on the day?'

The colour drained from Kristy's face and she stumbled a little, reaching for the door handle to keep herself upright.

'Oh gosh, you poor thing, you're exhausted,' said Lisa, rushing to keep Kristy propped up. 'We've kept you far too long. We can talk about the girls later. Tomorrow maybe? I could bring them in for a little trial?'

'No,' Kristy croaked. 'No, please, I'm sorry. But I don't do hair for children.'

'Sorry?' said Lisa, as if she'd simply misheard.

'I can't do it. I'm sorry. Please don't ask me.' The girl suddenly looked very young and vulnerable. 'I'm just …' she trailed off.

'Kristy, it's fine,' said Jamie firmly. 'It's really no big deal. I'm sure Lisa and I can manage a couple of plaits between us, can't we, Lise?'

'Of course,' Lisa stammered, still slightly stunned by Kristy's strange reaction.

'I'm so sorry,' said Kristy miserably. 'But … um …' She looked about the salon desperately, as if the chandeliers might be able to tell her what to say. 'Well, you see … Cosima, the owner here, really doesn't like having children in the salon. And I get a bit nervous around them, so … And. Oh!' She clicked her fingers. 'Just remembered that I have another appointment straight after yours, so, you know, I don't really have time …'

Jamie knew a lie when she saw one, and the way Kristy wouldn't meet her eyes confirmed her suspicions. But it wasn't worth calling her out. The last thing Jamie needed was to put Kristy off-side. She might back out of the wedding altogether and Jamie couldn't cope with that. The woman was a magician with hair. So what if she was a bit funny about kids. The idea of trying to tame the locks of a little wiggling, jiggling three-year-old made Jamie nervous as well. 'Honestly, it's fine, Kristy. You've already gone out of your way to help, staying back so late and all. We really appreciate it, don't we?' She shot a look at Lisa, who had finally managed to close her surprised mouth.

'Yes. Don't worry about the children.' Lisa patted Kristy's arm. 'Just wait till you become a mother, that'll cure you of the nerves.'

Kristy looked pained. 'Maybe,' she said softly and opened the salon door for the sisters.

Their goodbyes said, Jamie and Lisa walked slowly into the quiet street.

'What was that all about?' said Lisa.

Jamie shrugged. 'I have no idea. Kristy is a total mystery woman. She's a bit of a floater, I gather. Only does Saturdays at Cosima's, and odd days here and there at other salons. Keeps to herself a lot, I think. She's been away recently but thank god she's back for the wedding. She came in especially for tonight.'

'She seems a bit haunted by something,' said Lisa thoughtfully.

'I guess we all have a few skeletons, when you think about it.' Jamie looked into the inky sky, the stars shining like miniature glitter pots, and thought of Ben kissing her. She shivered. Her skeleton certainly needed to stay in the cupboard. She needed to forget Ben and move on to her life with Jared. It was madness at this late stage to be having thoughts of another man when she was about to get everything she wanted. She picked up the pace. She needed to get home. See Jared. Forget Ben.

'In a hurry to get home to the fiancé, are we?' said Lisa, lagging a couple of feet behind.

'Something like that,' Jamie muttered, before stopping. 'Sorry. Here.' She held out her hand to Lisa, then tucked it under her arm, appreciating her sister's warmth.

The bedroom had a distinct odour of beer and garlic. They must have gone to Angel's favourite Vietnamese place, thought Jamie, as she slid under the covers. Despite the less-than-appealing smell emanating from her husband-to-be, she moulded herself around his strong back and slipped her arm onto his chest. Jared stirred and squeezed her hand.

'Good night?' he asked sleepily.

'Shhhh. Go back to sleep,' she whispered, nestling into his neck.

Jared belched. 'Sorry,' he sighed, rolling onto his back. 'That boss of yours made me eat too much food,' he groaned. 'I'm still full.'

'You didn't have to go.'

'Angel insisted. The woman does not take no for an answer.'

Questions swirled through Jamie's head. *What did you talk about? Did you talk about me? What did Angel say? What did Ben say? Is he in love with me?* But she resisted the urge to ask anything, particularly the last question.

'They really love you there.' Jared shifted onto his side and faced Jamie. Her muscles tensed.

'Angel doesn't want you to leave.' Jared paused. 'Neither does Ben.'

'They just don't want to do the mountain of work that'll hit them when I leave.' Jamie stared at the ceiling but felt Jared's eyes on her.

'I don't think it's that ...' He rolled onto his back and joined Jamie in looking upwards. 'They think—' he started, then stopped. 'Why didn't you tell me about Angel's offer to hand you the reins at Spin?'

Jamie curled her fingers. 'I didn't want you to think I had any doubts about Dubai.'

Jared sighed. 'You could have told me. They think you're something really special. Not just a great boss, or a great employee. It's more than that.'

'That's what they said?'

'No. But I could tell.'

Jamie rolled onto her elbow and looked directly at Jared. 'Well, I don't need Angel or Ben to tell me I'm special, because I have you.' She ran her finger down Jared's chest. 'And I know you think I'm special.' Before he could answer, she leant over and kissed him full on the mouth. A passionate kiss designed to erase all thoughts of Ben. But as her tongue explored the familiar terrain of Jared's mouth, she could visualise only one thing.

Ben.

Jared broke away. 'Babe, I'm really tired, and stuffed full of food ...' he apologised, before rolling away from her.

'Night then.'

As Jared took up the gentle, regular breathing that told Jamie he was asleep, she pressed her hand into his warm back. What was she doing, thinking of Ben when the man she loved was right here? And that was the point. He was here, warming her bed, ready and willing to marry her.

Ben was a fantasy. Jared was her reality, and he was a wonderful reality. Together, they would have a fabulous life in Dubai. Tomorrow, she would officially refuse Angel's offer to take over at Spin.

Jamie slipped her other hand onto Jared's chest. When she closed her eyes, the vision that came was of herself in the veil, the white cloud falling over her eyes. And she slept.

CHAPTER THIRTY-TWO

Missy leant on the broom, suddenly overcome with exhaustion. Normally she found sweeping therapeutic which was fortunate in her line of work. But tonight, the broom was lead in her hands and she kept noticing stray hairs that the bristles of the broom had missed.

All that lying to those two lovely women! It was totally exhausting and guilt-inducing. How could she have possibly imagined that she could cope with this charade, physically or emotionally?

At first it had seemed easy. Two months ago now, the day Jamie dropped that brightly coloured bit of paper in the salon, Missy thought all her Christmases had come at once.

'Jamie, Jamie, you dropped something,' Missy had called after her from the door of the salon. But Jamie was already in her car and roaring off into the traffic. Missy studied the invitation.

Ava's turning 5! it exclaimed in big pink letters, festooned with balloons. Ava was the niece Jamie had raved about. There was a time and a date and a mobile phone number for Lisa—the sister Jamie had also raved about for her amazing mothering skills. The two had a special bond, Jamie had explained, because of their parents dying and Lisa assuming the guardianship role. 'She got me out of the group home. I'll never be able to thank her enough for that. The care system in this state is seriously broken,' she had railed. 'I mean, I know a lot of foster carers are genuinely amazing, but some are seriously dodgy. I mean, could you put a child at risk like that? I couldn't even do it to a pet.'

That's who Ellie needs to be with. That's who'll keep her safe.

Missy checked the date for the party—February 27. Kyle would get out of jail on the first of March. The timing was perfect. A party would be the ideal cover for dropping Ellie straight into the Wheeldons' life. Of course, there'd be hiccups. The Wheeldons would be shocked, no doubt. They were so normal and what Missy was about to do was so strange. Then there was Ellie. How would she convince her daughter to go along with it all?

For a start, she needed to know more about Lisa Wheeldon. Was she really the mother that Jamie claimed? Missy had to see for herself before she could entrust her with her most precious possession. From idle salon chit-chat with Jamie, she knew that Lisa had two daughters—Ava was at St John's and Jemima was in pre-school. Lisa was a self-employed bookkeeper because it gave her the flexibility she needed to be there for the kids. It was good information, but not enough. Missy needed proof.

She soon had it. With small children, a mother tended to be strikingly predictable in her routines and Lisa was no exception. Morning was school drop-off. Afternoons were pick-ups. Three days a week they went to the playground near St John's. Fridays were swimming lessons for both girls. Two days, Jemima was at pre-school. And on the other three days, Lisa kept her busy with gymbaroo and art class and supermarket shopping. After a couple of weeks of watching them, Missy came to realise that it wasn't necessarily the routine that was important, though that would be helpful to Missy's plan, it was the small moments that gave her pause for hope—the way Lisa constantly showered her girls with kisses and always knelt down to talk to them. The way she held their hands so firmly when they crossed roads. The way she'd spoken calmly but firmly to Ava when she'd pinched Jemima and made her cry. But, moreover, it was simply the way she looked at her girls with so much love in her eyes. It moved Missy to tears, for she recognised it as being the same way she looked at Ellie. Yes, putting her daughter into this woman's hands was the right thing, but *asking* her to care for Ellie wasn't the way to do it—no loving mother in their right mind would agree to take in a stranger's child if there was the merest hint of danger. Missy couldn't give Lisa a chance to say no. Besides, the risk to the Wheeldon family was minimal, Missy would see to that. What was the saying—it was better to seek forgiveness than ask permission? This was the way it had to be done.

Missy slumped into one of the salon chairs and startled at the pale, platinum blonde staring back at her. The colour wasn't her. It wasn't her at all, and as soon as all of this was over she would be going straight back to her natural brown.

As soon as Kyle is arrested …

She took a breath. O'Dea said they were close. Just a couple more days, he reckoned. But in the meantime, Missy wasn't to worry. They had Kyle and his cronies under 24/7 surveillance. He wouldn't be going anywhere.

That might have been comforting for O'Dea, but as far as Missy was concerned, she wouldn't relax until Kyle was behind bars. While ever he was free, he was a risk to her and Ellie. Her daughter was safer with the Wheeldons, for now. But how long would it be? Anyone could see that Lisa Wheeldon was getting attached. Had Missy's plan gone too well? How would Lisa manage when Missy decided it was time to re-enter her daughter's life?

As she stared into the mirror, it occurred to her that in giving her precious little girl to a near stranger, she had thought only of her own sacrifice. Not once had she thought how that stranger would feel when it was time to give her back.

CHAPTER THIRTY-THREE

From the outside, the house was dark and quiet. At the door, Lisa removed her boots and tip-toed inside, carefully turning the door handle until it closed with a soft click. But as she walked further down the hall, she stopped. Voices, coming from inside their living room. It was nearly 11 pm. Surely everyone was asleep? She would kill Scott if he'd let the girls stay up this late on a school night, and less than two days out from Jamie's wedding. The last thing she needed to deal with was over-tired, hyper-excited little girls. The emotion levels would be off the charts!

She strode into the living room, ready to admonish, and stopped at the couch.

Her husband was snoring softly, the TV remote hanging loosely from his hand. She glanced briefly at the screen. *NCIS* was it? One of those cop shows that he claimed to enjoy but almost always sent him to sleep within twenty minutes.

Gently removing the remote from his grasp, she felt a wave of love for her husband. He was such a good man. A decent and kind man. She wished her parents had met him. They would have approved. Scott and her dad could have gone to the rugby together, and talked cop shows. Every Tuesday night of her childhood, her dad had commandeered the TV remote to watch *The Bill*—his favourite TV show, despite Lisa and Jamie's claims that police with silly hats and no guns were 'lame'. Scott loved the show too. He would have been like the son her father never had, not that he ever expressed a particular desire for one. But still, a son-in-law would have added an extra dimension to her parents' lives, as would the addition of grandchildren.

Tenderly, Lisa pressed her lips against Scott's forehead. She hated the idea of not telling him about Igor Ivanov, but it would only be for forty-eight hours. After the wedding, she'd tell him everything and they'd decide what to do, together.

Scott snuffled and blearily opened his eyes. 'Hey, you're home. How did it go?'

'All fine.' She patted his shoulder. 'Everything all right here?'

He yawned. 'Just the usual Melbas. Eight of them tonight, from memory.'

She and Scott had a running joke that every night at bedtime their children staged more farewells before bed than the famed Dame Nellie. The excuses were many and varied—water, extra hugs, another kiss, a scary shadow, another wee, a strange noise, itchy pyjamas, too hot, too cold, a very important story that could not wait until the morning. The list was endless and now, Scott and Lisa simply referred to them collectively as *the Melbas*.

'Might just go check on them and then head up to bed.' Lisa rose.

'I'll join you.'

Helping him up, Lisa kept hold of her sleepy husband's arm as they walked back down the hallway to the girls' room.

'Bit like practice for the wedding.' Scott started humming a wedding march. He'd volunteered to walk Jamie down the aisle.

'Make sure you go nice and slow and keep a good hold of her. She's just as likely to trip in those crazy high heels. I remember my feet after our wedding. They were killing me, and my shoes were flat! I really don't understand why women put themselves through the agony.'

'And that, my darling, is one of the reasons I married you.' Scott squeezed her arm. 'You are a podiatrist's dream come true.'

They stopped at the door, the light from the hallway spilling into the room and illuminating the three small bodies before them.

'Is it considered poor form at a wedding for the flower girls to completely steal the show?' Scott inclined his head towards the three white dresses, hung up on the outside knobs of the girls' wardrobe, pressed and ready to be worn for Saturday.

'Being outrageously cute is fine, I think, but if they start a brawl over who gets to hold the rose petals, that's another matter.'

In the bedroom, Scott kissed each of the girls in turn—
Ava, then Jemima, then Ellie. Lisa followed suit and paused
in front of Ellie's assembly certificate, stuck with blu-tack to
the wall above the girls' chest of drawers, where they tended
to put up all their awards.

'We stuck it up tonight.' Scott adjusted the doona around
Ellie. 'She was so proud of herself. So different to the scared
little girl we met at the party.' He stood, still with his eyes
on Ellie. 'It was the right call, Lise, to look after her. You
were right.'

'I hope so,' Lisa began. 'I mean, I still don't quite know
how this is going to end …' *With a Russian mafia boss on our
doorstep?*

'Whatever happens, I think we've done a good thing, and
Ellie's been good for our family. I don't know what I was so
worried about.'

Quickly, Lisa switched off the hall light, casting the room
into darkness that covered the rising flush in her cheeks.

Just forty-eight hours, she told herself. *Then, you tell him
everything.*

CHAPTER THIRTY-FOUR

As far as a last day of freedom went, this one had been pretty shit, thought Jared, as he fiddled with the straw in his glass. For a start, there'd been a bunch of loose ends to tie up at work, which was probably a full day of work in itself, but on top of that, Jamie had him running all over town like a blue-arse fly, doing last-minute wedding errands. At home, she'd nearly bitten his head off. Apparently, the vintage hire car company had called him a week ago to confirm the booking but he'd never rung back. 'Thankfully, they rang *me* this morning to double-check.' She'd thrown up her hands. 'It's the one thing I asked you to take care of. One thing! I know you've got a lot to finish up at work, but I need you to snap out of that and put your head in the game.'

She was right. His head wasn't in the game. But it wasn't because of work. There was something else he needed to do before the wedding, and it had nothing to do with vintage hire cars.

'Thanks for meeting me.' Jared's fingers shook and he dropped the straw back into the ice. Christ, he was nervous.

'I have to admit, it does seem an odd thing to do the night before your wedding.' Melissa smiled, took a sip of her gin and tonic and looked out the window to the city lights below. 'But I'm glad I came. It's really beautiful.'

Not as beautiful as you.

'You should see the view from my room,' he joked and Melissa punched him lightly in the arm.

'I'm not going anywhere near your room.'

The bar Jared had suggested was on the top floor of the hotel where he was staying with his best man for the night. Overlooking the Harbour Bridge and the Opera House, there were no better views in Sydney. Below, ferries with strings of fairy-lights chugged across the water and in the west were the remnants of the sunset, fading out to violet and indigo.

'I know. I probably should be out at a club or something, enjoying my last night of freedom.' Jared took a paper serviette off the bar and started scrunching it. 'But I had to see you. To apologise.' He went on, now breaking the serviette into small pieces. 'I was such a dick when we broke up.'

Melissa nodded. 'You were.'

Jared grinned. 'I was.' He paused and looked up, the smile fading as he gazed into her soft, hazel eyes. 'But I think I've realised that I was scared.'

Melissa sighed. 'I think you were too. And so was I,' she added.

'Yeah?'

'Yeah, of course.' She ran her hand across her headscarf. 'I mean, I was only twenty-six, and pregnant, and we weren't married. And then to lose the pregnancy. It was all a bit of a mess.'

'But I was older. I mean, I was thirty, for crying out loud. I should have known better.'

'You were a young thirty.' She smiled and looked out the window. The bar was starting to fill now with corporate-types in greys and black and within an hour it would be chock-full of suits celebrating the arrival of the weekend. In her floral dress with its large swirls of pink and green, Melissa was a breath of fresh air.

'I was so in love with you.' Jared touched her knee. 'I don't think I've loved anyone the way I loved you.'

When he'd heard her voice on the phone, it had been like a jolt, taking him straight back to the past. Suddenly, he remembered. He remembered everything. The softness of her hair, the gentle roundness of her body, the smoothness of her skin and the musicality of her laugh. That she had agreed to meet for a drink was a surprise and he still couldn't quite believe she was here in front of him.

'Why are we here, Jared?' Melissa frowned. 'I've moved on, and you clearly have too. Gosh, you're getting married tomorrow. What's the point of all this? Things worked out the way they did for a reason. It just wasn't meant to be.'

'The baby, you mean?'

'I mean everything. Our timing was just off.'

'Was that all it was? Off timing?'

Melissa groaned. 'Oh, Jared, I don't know. And I don't think it matters. All I know is you can't go back.'

But you can't always forget.

'I should probably go.' Melissa reached for her handbag and Jared watched her, feeling as if his past was a train pulling out of the station and taking him to a place he did not want to go—a place where he would never see Melissa again.

'Please, don't.' He reached for her arm but somehow his hand managed to connect with her bottom, which caused her to jump and fling her hand across the top of the bar, sending both their drinks flying.

Within seconds a waiter arrived to mop up the mess and provide reams of paper towel for Jared and Melissa to dry off.

She laughed out loud, a sweet sound that sliced through the din of the bar.

'Oh my goodness,' she giggled. 'You look like you've wet yourself.'

He looked at her, smiling at him widely and warmly and in a way that made him want to kiss her.

Suddenly, Jared understood. He didn't love Jamie in the way he'd loved Melissa, which was instinctual and impossible to repress. The way he felt about Jamie was more clinical—their being together was so right, on paper. Their compatibility was through the roof. The relationship made rational sense and after several years of dating in your thirties, marriage was the logical next step. It was what people did and it was what Jared wanted because he was restless. He wanted to know *what came next* in life and he didn't want to get left behind.

But they weren't the right reasons to marry.

Jamie deserved more. She deserved to be loved in the way he'd loved Melissa, at least the way he'd loved her until she fell pregnant.

What a freaking mess!

Jared looked at his sodden pants. 'Oh man, I'm going to have to change.'

Melissa's giggle tapered off. 'And I really should go. Gavin's expecting me.'

'Your fiancé?'

'Yes.'

'When's the wedding?'

'We haven't set a date yet.' She dipped her head in slight embarrassment. 'We're still saving.'

'Congratulations,' he said sincerely. 'He's a lucky guy.'

'I know,' she said with a wry smile. 'He knows I'm one in a million.'

They both stood. 'You are.' Jared leant in and kissed her on the cheek. 'Thank you for coming.'

Melissa stood back and looked at him. 'I'm not sure it's helped you any.'

It has in ways you'll never know.

Together, they walked towards the lift, and as the doors closed on Melissa's smiling and beautiful face, Jared had the strong sense that he knew exactly what he had to do.

He pulled out his phone to text his best man, Roger, a mate from school. They were due to meet in half an hour for a 'last supper'.

Mate. Not feeling the best so I'm going to have to cancel on dinner and the rest. See you in the morning.

Roger's reply was quick.

Geez you're a soft cock! But who am I to argue with the groom. Later, dude.

Jared pressed again for the lift and scrolled through his contacts to 'J'. How was he going to do this? Not over the phone. He wasn't that much of a prick. He could go home and see her face to face. Do it like a man. Only problem was that Lisa would be there. She was going over to keep Jamie company and watch some kind of lame movie. No. This had to be strictly between him and his fiancée.

Back in the room, Jared started pacing.

Eventually, he stopped at the desk. There was a pen and paper. He could write a letter. That might be okay. Kind of old-fashioned. Add a bit of sweetness to what would otherwise be a bitter pill to swallow. But how would he get it to her? He started pacing again, up and down, and finally stopped at the window.

Ben.

Ben would be arriving at the hotel early in the morning to collect Jared and Roger for the wedding ceremony (he was the only guy Jamie would trust to act as chauffeur). He was the man for the job. The way he'd talked the other night at dinner, any fool could tell he had feelings for Jamie that went beyond the strictly professional. He could deliver the letter and provide a shoulder for Jamie to cry on.

Jared started writing.

CHAPTER THIRTY-FIVE

Was it normal for the bride's hairdresser to be more nervous than the bride? Jamie leant back over the basin as Kristy fumbled with the lid of the shampoo bottle.

'Everything all right, Kristy?'

'Oh fine. Just haven't had my morning coffee yet. You know how it is,' she trilled and followed up with a nervous laugh.

Jamie frowned. Clearly the hairdresser's mood had not improved since Thursday night. Jamie knew for a fact that Kristy didn't drink coffee. She'd told her so during one of their first appointments, and it was a disclosure Jamie remembered because she simply couldn't imagine life without caffeine. Why would Kristy lie now? Jamie settled back into her chair and closed her eyes in the quiet of the salon which, at 6 am, was still officially closed to the general public. It was just her and Kristy. And it was time for Jamie to stop being so concerned about her hairdresser's nerves—she had butterflies of her own to worry about.

This was it. Her wedding day. A morning that had dawned as bright as a daisy. Jamie yawned. Last night, Lise had come over for a pad thai and a rom-com but she'd left early, leaving Jamie to get a good night's sleep ahead of *the big day*. The idea was good in theory, except that Jamie could not sleep. She tossed and turned, thoughts twisting and turning until her brain felt like a ball of wool being played with by a cat. In her mind, she went through the checklist of arrangements. Flowers? Confirmed. Caterers? Confirmed. Cars? Confirmed (no thanks to Jared). Cake? Confirmed. Musicians? Confirmed. Place cards? Confirmed.

It was all done. Her excel spreadsheet was a sea of pink—the colour she always used for events once arrangements had been checked and double-checked. Having ticked off the logistics in her mind, Jamie let it wander into the unknowns. How would Angel behave at the wedding? Would she be formal and stiff, like she was at Jamie's work farewell yesterday where she shook her hand and wished her all the best for her future in Dubai, as if they'd only known each other for five minutes? Or would she be weird and gregarious, like normal? And what about Ben? He'd also been a bit strange at the farewell. Probably because of the kiss, she supposed. Not that he seemed embarrassed; if anything, he was overly chirpy, patting her on the back and telling her how okay everyone at Spin would be after she left. The whole affair had the sense of a disappointing anticlimax. In her mind, she had visualised Ben and Angel begging her not to leave and saying they could not live without her. What she had not been able to visualise is how she would respond to their pleas. In reality, Angel had been true to her word. She'd left the decision to Jamie and Jamie had chosen Jared, and Dubai.

Suddenly, Jamie became aware of a burning sensation on her head. The temperature was turned up to boiling point, scalding her scalp. Jamie leapt from the chair.

'Ouch! Oh hell,' she yelped, frantically fanning at her steaming locks.

'Oh god, I'm so sorry.' Kristy dropped the nozzle and nearly flew over the chairs to help.

'What is wrong with you?' said Jamie crossly. The last thing she needed on her wedding day was a red raw scalp.

Nor do I need an overwrought hairdresser, she thought as Kristy burst into tears.

'Please don't cry.' Jamie put her hand on Kristy's shoulder. 'Honestly, it's okay. I'm fine.' The intense burning sensation on her head was settling to a warm tingling as she led Kristy to the chaise lounge. 'Now, please tell me what's wrong.'

'I can't,' said Kristy.

'You can,' said Jamie calmly. 'It doesn't have to be specifics.' She handed Kristy a tissue. 'You'll feel better if you let it all out.'

Kristy blew her nose and took a deep breath. 'A few years ago, I made a bad decision. A really, really bad decision.' She started shredding the tissue into tiny pieces. 'And I've been paying for it ever since.' She took a deep breath. 'But I'm trying to fix it. And I'm scared out of my mind.'

Jamie watched Kristy clenching and unclenching her fists and leant in to give her a hug. 'The right thing to do is always the hardest.'

The right thing is always the hardest.

Jamie repeated the words in her head.

The right thing is always the hardest.

I can't marry Jared. I'm in love with Ben.

As she tightened her embrace around Kristy, Jamie felt her eyes growing hot. Now that she'd admitted it to herself, it seemed so obvious. She was doing the wrong thing. How could she have denied it for so long? Ben was her soul mate. He was the first person she thought about in the morning and the last person she thought about at night. He was her favourite person to hang out with, work with, laugh with, simply *be* with. Yes, he was a friend. Her best friend, and until recently she had not thought of him as anything more, but that was simply because *more* hadn't been in the realms of possibility, until he kissed her and confirmed he wasn't gay.

The right thing is always the hardest.

She'd been in PR for too long. She'd become so good at massaging 'the truth' that she couldn't even see a falsehood when it hit her in the face. She and Jared were living a lie. She didn't really want to marry him and she had a feeling he probably felt the same.

Jamie clung to Kristy and sniffled. After a few seconds, she felt the younger woman stiffen.

'Hey, are *you* okay?' Kristy leant back to take in her teary client.

'I'll … be … all right,' she stammered, then took the used tissue from Kristy's outstretched hands to wipe her own nose. 'But I need to fix something as well and it's going to be awful.'

All the guests. All the presents. All the arrangements she'd so carefully made and triple-checked.

But it would be easier to undo all of that than to undo a bad marriage.

'Let me fix you first.' Kristy gestured to the basin as Jamie remembered the suds in her hair.

She nodded. 'Can't go setting the world to rights like this, I suppose.' It was only 6.30 am. Why make Jared's day any worse by waking him at the crack of dawn? She would wait and let Kristy rinse out her hair before making any calls.

Jamie settled back into the chair and this time, as Kristy ran her fingers through her hair, she could detect a surety that hadn't been there before. She closed her eyes and let her mind fill with visions of Ben. Ben smiling. Ben winking. Ben frowning at the computer. Ben … Ben … Ben …

'Ben!' For a minute, Jamie thought she was still dreaming. She blinked. Nope. That was definitely Ben's face leaning over hers. Eyes crinkled from his serious frown. He was so close she could feel his warm breath on her cheek. He quickly took a step back.

'Sorry, but when I arrived here you were asleep and the hairdresser said you'd had a rough morning and that I should just leave you for a few minutes—'

'Sorry, Jamie, I hope you don't mind,' said Kristy from the chaise.

'But, Ben, what are you doing here?' Jamie cut in.

'I need to talk to you.' He looked around the salon. 'Privately.'

'There's no one here but Kristy,' Jamie pointed out.

Ben shifted his weight nervously.

'How about you guys go out the back? There's a staff kitchenette …' Kristy trailed off as Ben grimly took Jamie's elbow to help her out of the salon chair.

'You're scaring me. What is it?' said Jamie.

Ben was flushed as he led her out the back. She'd never seen him look so serious. In the kitchenette, he squared her up against the sink. 'I have two things to tell you.'

'Bad news?' Her stomach sank.

'Yes.'

'What is it?'

'Jared's gone.'

'What do you mean Jared's gone?'

'Well, we planned to get up early for a game of golf before the wedding, but when I went to Jared's room I found this under his door.'

From his back pocket, Ben produced an envelope, marked simply *Jamie*. 'Then I got a text from him saying I should take the note to you straight away.'

Fingers trembling, Jamie unfolded the small piece of paper, written on hotel letterhead.

Dear Jamie,

This is the hardest letter I've ever had to write, but I know it's the right thing and I think, deep down, you know it is too.

I can't let you marry me.

When I asked you, I did mean it. We're a good match, you and I, and we'd been together so long that it seemed the logical next step. I was happy to be marrying you. Or, I thought I was.

But then Ellie came into our lives and for me it dredged up all these old memories of Melissa and how it truly feels to be passionately in love with someone.

I don't think we've been that way for a while, if ever. When we met, I think I was still in love with her. Maybe I still am. Anyway, you deserve better. And I'm pretty sure you're going to find it. I'm sorry for mucking things up.

Love, Jared

For a moment Jamie felt shock, but it was brief compared with the immense feeling of relief that sheeted over her. For the first time in weeks, she felt free. Unburdened. Exhilarated.

'Are you okay?' asked Ben.

'I am,' said Jamie, calmly folding the note. 'But you said you had two things to tell me. I've got the first.' She held up the letter. 'Now what's the second?'

Ben frowned. 'You can't marry Jared.'

'Why?'

'Because I love you,' said Ben without hesitation, taking a step towards Jamie. 'I love you so much that it's killing me. And I don't know what's in that letter he sent you but you deserve better. So much better. You deserve someone who appreciates you, someone who feels like they've won the lottery when they're with you. Someone who loves your mind and your sense of humour and the way you never give up on anything or anyone.'

Jamie closed the gap so they were nearly nose to nose. 'Funnily enough, Jared agrees with you.'

'But what about you?' Ben breathed.

'I think,' she said slowly, 'that I need to be with someone who is respectful, intelligent and thoughtful. A man who understands, deeply, and shares my passion for terrible reality television.' She took a breath. 'Ben Chambers, I think I am madly in love with you, and you are exactly the man I deserve.'

Cupping her face in his hands, Ben drew her in for the kiss Jamie had been waiting her whole life to have. Urgent yet sensual. Soft yet passionate. A kiss born of true love and desire. Swinging her around, Ben leant Jamie against the wall and ran his hands lightly over her breasts. From her throat escaped a lusty moan and she circled her arms around Ben's waist until she could feel he wanted her as much as she wanted him. As his hand reached for the top button of her shirt, she squeezed his shoulder.

'Ben,' she whispered. 'We're in a hairdressing salon.' She giggled quietly as realisation broke across his face and he looked around as if emerging from a dreamy sleep.

'Oh shit, so we are.' He took her hand. 'Let's get out of here.'

But as they went to leave, the sound of an angry, guttural voice coming from the main part of the salon stopped them in their tracks.

Ben put his finger to his mouth in a shushing motion.

'You give me what I want and no one will get hurt.' It was a man, and he sounded threatening.

While Kristy's reply was inaudible, Jamie could tell from the tremor in her voice that she was terrified.

Her skin crawled. A hold-up. The salon was being robbed.

Ben beckoned her back from the doorway. 'You stay here,' he whispered. 'I'm going to take a look.'

Jamie shook her head furiously. 'No.' But before she could say anything else, Ben had taken a couple of steps towards the doorway, then returned to her side, his face white.

'He's got a gun.'

'Call the police,' she hissed.

'I don't have my phone.' Ben's face contorted. 'Do you?'

Missy felt the room was spinning and she reached for the wall to hold her up.

'What are you doing here?' Her mouth was full of cotton.

'You really thought I would be so stupid as to get caught *again*?' Kyle gave a mocking laugh. 'Turns out you can learn *new* tricks in jail, like how to make friends, friends in high places. Friends who are only too happy to let you know when your ex has been in town, visiting the pigs.'

'You knew I was there in Coffs?' Missy gasped.

Kyle sneered. 'Course I did. And I have to say I'm a little hurt you didn't come and say hello. And then you left, without saying goodbye to anyone, 'cept your good mate, O'Dea. But that's what you don't get, Miss. My buddies are more powerful than yours. That dickhead detective lives in la-la land.'

So that's why he hadn't been arrested. There was still a mole in the Coffs cops and O'Dea had no idea. No wonder Kyle was always one step ahead.

'How … how did you find me?' Missy staggered backwards and gripped the reception desk for support.

'Turns out your Russian landlord and I have a few mates in common.' Kyle grinned like a shark. 'He was worried about you. Put out a few feelers. Such a pretty little hairdresser. So young to be a mum on her own.'

Mr Ivanov? The harmless old Russian was actually a criminal? That's why he'd been so secretive.

'What do you want?' Missy exhaled.

'What do you think I want?' Kyle's mouth twisted.

'You can't have her.'

'You're going to pay for what you did.'

'I'll never let you find her.'

Kyle held out the gun, allowing the salon lights to glint off the handle. 'Right now, I don't think you have a choice.' He sneered. 'Now where is she?'

'She's somewhere safe. Somewhere you'll never find her.'

'Oh, I think we both know that's not true.' He was getting closer and with each threatening step, Missy felt weaker and weaker. Kyle had bolted the front door. No chance of escape through there. But where was Jamie? Where was the guy who'd come to see her? Maybe they had their phones on them and were calling the police? Missy looked around desperately. Jamie's handbag was still under her chair, but maybe the guy had his mobile in his pocket? She squeezed her hands into a fist. All she had to do was hold on. Just for a few more minutes. As long as she could keep Kyle talking, the police would surely get there in time.

'C'mon, Missy. We both know you're going to tell me, sooner or later.'

He was now so close she could smell him, a stomach-churning stench of stale cigarettes and sickly sweet after-shave. The barrel of the gun hovered near her chin and Missy stretched her neck away.

The tap at the door made them both jump and as Kyle whipped around, Missy took the chance to scoot over to the other side of the salon.

'Who's that?' he growled.

Oh shit. It's Lisa.

'No one,' Missy said quickly. 'Just a client. Ignore it, and she'll go away. I promise.'

But quick as lightning, Kyle checked through the blinds. 'Well, lookie here.' He gave an oily grin. 'If it isn't Daddy's little girl.'

Lisa tapped on the door and tried the handle again. 'Well, that's strange,' she said to the gaggle of little girls holding her hand. 'Jamie was supposed to be here at six, so I'm sure they're in there.' She tried to peer between the closed blinds. 'Looks like the lights are on, so let's just give her a minute.'

'Will Aunty Jamie have her wedding dress on?' Ava jumped excitedly from one foot to the other.

'No, darling. She'll get dressed back at her own place, after her hair's done.'

'Are you going to have your hair in a bun, like a princess?' asked Jemima.

'Something like that,' said Lisa distractedly, searching for signs of life within the salon.

'You're already as pretty as a princess,' said Ellie seriously, squeezing Lisa's hand.

'Thank you, darling.' Lisa looked down at the solemn little face in front of her. She hadn't planned on bringing the three girls to the salon, but they'd woken so early, so full of excitement for the big day that Lisa felt it only fair to include them. She knew Jamie would love to have them around her, with all their energy and vibrancy. It would make the salon into a bit of a party. Lisa had explained to them that the hairdresser wouldn't have time to do their hair, and the girls didn't care. They'd be happy to watch Mummy and Aunty Jamie have theirs done. It was all terribly, terribly thrilling!

'Where are they?' muttered Lisa, reaching for her phone. But as she rummaged through her bag, the door magically swung open and the girls piled into the salon.

'Get in here quick.'

Lisa swivelled in the direction of the snarling voice and felt her stomach lurch as a swarthy man wielding a gun sprang towards the girls and bolted the door behind them.

For a split second, she froze, before her mothering instinct kicked into gear.

'Ava. Jemima. Ellie. Come here,' Lisa ordered. Bewildered by their mother's stern tone and the sight of a strange man with a gun, the girls cowered into Lisa's side.

'I don't know who you are, or what you're doing here, but you should just take what you want and leave.' Lisa's voice was cold.

'Oh, I will, lady. I will.' Kyle lowered the gun and shoved it into the back of his jeans. 'Ellie,' he said in a crooning voice and knelt down. 'Baby girl, do you remember me?'

A pain went through Lisa's chest as Ellie clutched her leg more tightly. 'Lisa, I'm scared,' said the little girl.

'Who are you?' Lisa demanded.

'Ellie,' said a soft voice behind them. Kristy. As Lisa turned, Ellie released her leg and flung herself into the arms of the pale-faced hairdresser.

'Mummy,' she squealed. 'You're back.'

'Yes, honey,' Kristy murmured. 'I'm back.'

'Wait.' Lisa tried to sort through her confusion. 'Kristy? You're ... you're Ellie's mother.'

Kristy nodded.

'But your name's Kristy, not Missy.'

'I'm sorry, Lisa. I'm Missy. It was for Ellie, all to keep her safe,' said Kristy desperately.

'And who is this man?'

'I'm Ellie's dad,' said Kyle, taking another step closer.

'No, you're not,' said Ellie in a determined voice. 'My daddy's dead.'

'Well, actually, sweetie—' started Missy.

'Is that what you told her?' Kyle's voice was cold and angry. 'That I was dead?'

'What should I have told her?' retorted Kristy. 'That you were a low-life criminal who traded in people's misery for a living—'

'You little bitch—'

As Kyle lunged, Lisa threw her handbag in his direction and flung herself over Ava, Jemima, Ellie and Missy which sent them all tumbling to the ground. Keeping her head buried and her eyes tightly closed, Lisa heard scuffling and male grunts for a few seconds until there was a loud crack, a high-pitched squeal and then silence.

'Ben, get the gun,' said a calm and authoritative voice.

Lisa knew that voice! It was a voice she loved. She opened one eye to find Jamie standing over an unconscious Kyle with a hairdryer in her hand. As she opened a second eye, she spotted Ben, scurrying for the gun which lay just out of Kyle's reach.

'Lise! Girls! Are you okay?' Jamie rushed over as Lisa picked herself and the girls off the floor.

'Yes, yes. We're fine. What about you? What did you do?'

'Oh, I just whacked that dickhead over the head with this,' said Jamie airily, wielding the hairdryer. 'I'm pretty handy with these things, you know.'

'You could have been killed!' cried Lisa.

'So could you! And the girls!'

In the background, Ben was dialling triple zero. 'Hello, yes, this is an emergency. There's been an armed hold-up at the hair salon on …'

Suddenly, Lisa felt exhausted. She had no idea what had just happened, except that Ellie's mother was Jamie's hairdresser and her father appeared to be some sort of criminal who was now unconscious on the floor. And for some unknown reason, Ben had been there to help save the day.

'What just happened, Mummy?' Ava's eyes were as big as saucers.

'I'm not really sure, darling, but all that matters is that we're okay.'

'Is that Ellie's mummy?' Ava pointed. Behind them, Kristy cradled and rocked Ellie like a baby and the little girl had a contented smile on her face, as if she had finally found peace.

Without a shadow of a doubt, Lisa knew the answer in her heart.

'Yes, darling. That's Ellie's mother.'

CHAPTER THIRTY-SIX

Eleven Months Later

Lisa yawned and contemplated rolling over. But the very idea of it made her feel tired. With her stomach the size of a beach ball, rolling would be a three-step process—grab hold of stomach, roll onto back (groaning), then shift bottom so as to re-gather momentum for the final push onto the other side. Oh, it was all too hard. Instead, Lisa lay where she was and moved the only part of her body that didn't feel heavy—her eyelids. She opened them and looked at the clock.

Oh hell! 9.59 am. Surely not. She blinked again and patted for the spot where Scott's thigh usually lay.

Empty!

He was up and hadn't thought to wake her?

Everyone would be arriving in precisely—she checked the clock again—precisely one minute! Catastrophe.

Lisa threw off the doona and summoned her heavy body to leap out of bed. She needed perky-dolphin pace. Instead, her body gave her slow-moving-slug and literally groaned, involuntarily, in protest. Seriously, she was not conscious of emitting noise but now, every time she bent to pick up a toy or put on shoes, her body transmitted a sound from deep in her throat. A bit like the sigh a leather couch made when someone sat on it, only deeper, and more pained.

She was a suffering sofa.

Rummaging through her wardrobe, Lisa pulled out the only items that a) were clean and b) still agreed to accommodate her burgeoning body. That meant leggings with a hole in the knee and an extra-large T-shirt from a corporate team-building day eight years ago. She checked her reflection. *There is no 'I' in team*, the mirror shouted back at her.

But there's an 'I' in failure, Lisa muttered to herself.

It was four years since she was pregnant with Jemima and her brain had conveniently wiped all memory of the hard bits. All that remained in there was a highlights package, like the best bits of a footy game that showed the home side scoring glorious tries. She remembered the delight of feeling the baby kicking, the cute way it got hiccups from amniotic fluid and the mind-blowing amazingness of seeing her little being on the ultrasound screen, like a little ghost-baby in outer-space. But for every cute baby kick and ultrasound, there was a dropped ball or a fumble that the highlights reel had conveniently left out. Pregnancy was combat sport. And right now, Lisa was losing.

How had she managed to forget the difficulty of the final month? She was nearly ten months pregnant. Lisa had done the maths. Forty weeks did not equal nine months—that was simply another myth designed to trick women into this unfortunate state of being—it was nine-and-a-half. And if the baby was late, it was nearly ten months, which is what she was now!

Why had she ever agreed to host *a party* in her over-abundant state?

Lisa knew exactly why.

It was Ava. She'd been so desperate for a sixth birthday party and after the shemozzle of her fifth, Lisa didn't have the heart to refuse her. Besides, it would be a small affair this time. Just family and one or two of her closest little friends. Still, even the smallest of parties required a modicum of effort. Guests, however few in number, needed to be fed, watered and entertained.

At the top of the stairs, Lisa paused again for one final, side-on check in the mirror. Certainly the team-building T-shirt was less than flattering (elephant-trapped-in-a-tent was the image that came to mind) but gosh her belly was ridiculously large. Lisa raised the T-shirt and ran her fingers over the creamy white skin. So tightly was it stretched across the expanse of baby, it made the blue veins stand out like rivers on a map. She exhaled. It was miraculous, really, to think that just centimetres beneath her fingertips was a living, breathing, baby boy, quite capable of living life on 'the outside' but content for the moment to stay in his tummy home.

The baby was one week overdue. 'Cervix is tight as a clam,' the obstetrician had announced far too jovially at her last check-up. This kid wasn't going anywhere in a hurry.

Lisa caressed her belly one final time before letting the dreadful blue T-shirt drop like a curtain over her wondrous miracle.

Clutching the handrail, Lisa made her way slowly down the stairs, running through a checklist in her mind of all that needed to be completed. *Cake? Iced and in the fridge, ready to go. Food? All prepared, just needs to be put on platters. Decorations? Put up last night. Toilet? Clean.*

Actually, she was in pretty good shape. If last year had taught her anything, it was that—

'SURPRISE!'

Lisa clutched the railing with one hand and her stomach with the other as the baby reacted to the noise with a particularly violent karate kick.

'Oh my goodness! You're all here.' Lisa sucked in a breath. 'Already.'

'Course we are.' Jamie let go of Ben's hand and ascended several steps to take Lisa's hand. 'Oh lord, take a look at you, woman!' Jamie leant back as if struggling to fit Lisa's girth within her field of vision. 'You're like a beached whale that took a wrong turn and ended up at an Anthony Robbins conference. That T-shirt is dreadful!'

'Thanks, Jamie. You really know how to make a girl feel great.'

'Hey, I'm not the one who nearly slept through her own party.'

'Ava's party, you mean.'

'No. I don't,' said Jamie pointedly, gesturing to the blue and white balloons and bunting now strewn about Lisa's living room.

'Oh no!' she groaned. 'Did Ava decide she wanted a *Frozen* party after all? Now the cake's all wrong and—'

'No, silly.' Jamie squeezed Lisa's hand and led her down the stairs. 'This party's for you. It's your baby shower,' she said proudly. 'I know gender-stereotyping is so last century and all, but seriously, I can't have my nephew schlepping around in all his sisters' pink hand-me-downs.' Jamie rejoined Ben at the foot of the stairs and he put his arm comfortably around her shoulder. 'And besides, my very able assistant did most of the work, including bribing Ava into sharing her party. A promised trip to Luna Park did the trick.'

She kissed Ben on the cheek and he looked at her with such devotion that Lisa nearly averted her eyes. Every time she saw Ben and Jamie together she felt like doing a happy dance. It was thrilling to see a couple so happy with each other and so in love. To think her sister had come within hours of marrying the wrong man—it sent a chill down Lisa's spine. Ben was the man for her sister. They were partners in life, and in business, a fact that lit a pilot light of jealousy in Lisa's heart, for much as she loved Scott, she knew that working with him would be a sure-fire ticket to the couch of a relationship counsellor. There were some things couples simply weren't meant to do together. But Jamie and Ben seemingly knew no obstacles to their partnership. Since Angel's departure, they'd taken Spin from strength to strength. Certainly Jamie bore the title of Managing Director but as she was so fond of telling everyone, she was nothing without her right-hand man, the man who also happened to be the love of her life. (Of course, she kept the second bit from clients. Sleeping with one's assistant sounded so much worse than it actually was.)

Lisa clinched Ben and Jamie in a three-way hug. 'I love you guys.'

'Ow.' Jamie pulled away. 'Your stomach's squashing me.'

'What she means is—you look fantastic, Lisa.' Ben gave her a kiss on the cheek.

'Always on the job, this guy. Massaging truths everywhere.' Jamie looked hungrily at Ben. 'Never stops,' she murmured.

'Oh you two should get a room. You're making me blush.'

Lisa moved away as Ben and Jamie started nuzzling like randy thoroughbreds. A flutter went off in the lower part of Lisa's tummy—not the baby but something far more basic. It made Lisa blush to even admit it—but she was feeling hornier than a viking's helmet. The same thing had happened when she was pregnant with Ava and Jems, and apparently it was common for many women. One of mother nature's little jokes, she supposed, to raise a woman's libido just as it became nearly logistically impossible to make love, with the tummy and everything.

'You know you want it, don't you?' whispered a sultry voice into her ear. Lisa swung around to find Heather looking very pleased with herself.

'Heather, hi! Thank you so much for coming,' stammered Lisa as she leant in for a kiss.

'Oh, you look like you're gagging for it.' Heather clapped her hands.

'What do you mean?' said Lisa, taking in the leopard-print singlet-top that had squeezed Heather's breasts into juicy, mountainous perfection. Oh it was unbearable! Now the pregnancy hormones were turning her into a lesbian.

'The cake of course! What else?' Heather took her over to the kitchen table. 'I remember simply dying for sugar when I was about to give birth to Savannah-Rose.' She stood proudly in front of the most gorgeous cake Lisa had ever seen—three-tiered and coated entirely with the most delicately piped white rosettes.

'Oh, it's even nicer than my wedding cake!' Lisa gasped.

'Pierre outdid himself this time.' She leant in. 'And under all that buttercream is the richest, most moist dark chocolate mud cake you've ever tasted in your life.'

At the word 'moist', Lisa lost it and the two women groaned in unison.

'It looks utterly delicious.' She hugged Heather tightly, trying to ignore the feeling of squished boobs against her own rapidly expanding bosom, until a thought struck her. 'But where's the cake I made for Ava?'

Heather sniffed. 'Hon, that cake you made last year made even the dog sick.' She put a consoling hand on Lisa's arm. 'It's about knowing your strengths, babe. I make a mean martini but I cannot make a cake to save myself, so I call in the experts and give precisely zero shits about doing so.' She made an 'O' with her fingers.

Lisa giggled. This was what she loved about Heather, the fact that she was entirely unapologetic for who she was. Together, they'd developed a Friday afternoon ritual of congregating at Heather's house for 'drinkie-poos' where they would workshop the highs and lows of the week over peach Bellinis. Now that the drinks were non-alcoholic, in deference to the pregnancy, Heather had renamed them 'pussy-tails'—cocktails for pussies. But the tradition had continued and Lisa could always rely on her friend to launch an outrageous rant about a particularly frivolous first-world problem … *Lisa, you will NOT believe this but Net-a-Porter had the hide to charge me GST on my new Prada bag because it cost over $1000. That's an extra 10 per cent! I can't believe the unfairness …* and on she would go for a few more minutes, gradually slowing down, like a wind-up toy in need of another wind. *Oh god, I'm a self-entitled bitch, aren't I?* is how she would end, to which Lisa would calmly nod her agreement and the conversation would move on with a clinking of glasses. *Cheers to self-awareness,* Heather would say. *My Buddhist therapist says it's the pathway to enlightenment. But she's so fucking zen about everything.*

'You're hilarious and I love you,' said Lisa dreamily, draping herself over Heather, who stiffened in response.

'Your baby just kicked me in the boobs.'

'Oh gosh, I'm sorry.'

'No sweat, hon. The silicone softened the blow.' And off Heather sailed in the direction of the cutlery drawer. 'Getting a knife so we can gorge on this thing,' she called over her shoulder.

As Lisa ogled the cake (Heather was right. She did need it. If she couldn't have sex, then excess sugar would have to do) she felt a warm little hand creep into her own.

'Ellie, sweetie.' Lisa gave her a quick hug and took in her pale, solemn face. 'Darling, what's wrong?'

'I'm worried about your tummy,' she said seriously.

'It's a bit of a worry to me too, hon.' Lisa patted it. 'But I know it'll get smaller when the baby's born.'

'But how will he fit through your belly button?' said Ellie, closely inspecting Lisa's mountainous girth.

'Who told you that?'

'Ava did. She said your tummy button opens up like a little door and the baby just pops out like a lolly coming out of a machine.' Ellie frowned. 'But your baby is so big, there's no way he could get through such a small hole.'

'Oh, honey.' Lisa leant down and put her arm around Ellie's shoulder. 'That's not quite how it works.'

'Then how does it work?'

'How does what work?' Missy was holding a tray of sausage rolls, which she offered to Lisa.

Oh, Missy! Just in the nick of time.

Lisa rose, put her hand on Missy's shoulder and leant in. 'I think someone needs a little chat about the birds and the bees.'

Missy nodded, a small smile playing at her lips. 'I think I can manage that.' She took Ellie's hand. 'What do you want to know, El?'

'Mummy, how will Lisa's big baby get out of her belly button?'

'He won't,' said Missy matter-of-factly. 'He'll come out of her vagina.'

At the mention of the 'V-word', Lisa clutched the bench, but Ellie simply said, 'Ooooh,' as if everything now made perfect sense.

'El, why don't you go play with Ava and Savannah-Rose? I think they're outside, playing pin-the-needle-on-the-cloth-nappy.'

'Okay, Mummy.' And off she trotted like a little, obedient lamb.

'Such a special little girl,' said Lisa, gazing after her.

'I know, right?' Missy sighed. 'Especially with such a loser for a father.'

Thanks to the hair salon showdown, Kyle was now ten months into a fifteen-year jail sentence for attempted kidnap. Happily, the courts took a particularly dim view of parolees who dived straight back into crime and then tried to take a child at gunpoint. Kyle would be well into his forties before he could wear anything but green tracksuits and even when he got out, Missy was confident he would do no harm to her or Ellie. Not if he valued his own life. In that regard, old Mr Ivanov had proved particularly useful. Through the post office box, Missy had sent newspaper clippings from the trial which detailed the terrifying events of the hair salon confrontation. Obviously, Mr Ivanov got the message, for one day on her way to work a dark car pulled up beside Missy and from within the murky darkness came a familiar Russian voice. *Missy*. But with Mr Ivanov's accent it sounded more like *Meesy*.

'*Meesy*, my dahlink. You and your *myshka*. You no worry. I take care of your ex. That scum. *Pfft*.' With a small spit, the window wound up again and the black car roared away, leaving Missy with heart palpitations that soon slowed into regular beats. From digging around, she'd learnt that Ivanov was a much bigger deal than Kyle in the criminal world, and if he said Missy and Ellie weren't to be touched, they wouldn't be. Even Kyle wasn't dumb enough to take on a Russian mafia boss.

'Missy, at some point you have to forgive yourself.' Lisa patted her back. 'We all make mistakes and you have more than made up for yours by being the best mother I know.'

Missy's face brightened. 'You mean that?'

'I do,' said Lisa confidently. 'You know, if it wasn't for you and Ellie I wouldn't be having this baby.'

Missy looked puzzled. 'Lise, even I know enough about the birds and bees to know that babies aren't made by little girls and their mums. This is all your and Scott's doing.'

'I know that, silly.' She gave Missy's arm a playful flick. 'But what you showed me is that a mother's love is endless.

It doesn't have to stop at two children. The heart grows to accommodate all it needs to.'

'So, you'll still have time for Ellie and me when little Master Wheeldon comes along?' Missy looked nervous.

'Of course I will,' she said, wrapping Missy in the warmest hug she could muster. A hug she hoped said *You are like family to me*.

'Coming through, ladies!' At the sound of Heather's very loud and commanding voice, Lisa and Missy sprang apart. The woman was wielding the largest knife in Lisa's cutlery drawer and her grin was so wide it appeared to glint off the blade. 'Cake time, kids!' she bellowed in a voice that triggered a stampede of footsteps into the kitchen.

As Heather started lighting the candles, Lisa took in the faces around her. Scott, valiantly trying to put his arm around her non-existent waist. Ben and Jamie canoodling. Ava, Jemima, Ellie and Savannah-Rose gazing expectantly on the cake with the candle-flame making their big eyes shine even more brightly than usual. Missy, smiling and looking into Lisa's eyes in a way that made her feel they were part of a secret club that only they would ever understand. A club where it was understood that a perfect mother was not one who produced Instagram-worthy parties, or dressed their children in a way that made them look at home in a Ralph Lauren catalogue. No. The perfect mother was the one who loved her child with all her heart and did whatever was necessary to keep them safe. Simple as that.

'All right, how about we have Ava and Lisa blow out the candles together?' Heather stood back. 'Though I'm not quite sure where you're fitting air into that body of yours.'

Lisa took as deep a breath as her squeezed lungs could muster, and blew with all her might. As the flames flickered, there was a watery splat on the floor.

Everyone looked down.

'God, don't tell me the dog got into the other cake again,' Heather groaned and peered more closely. 'Wait! Why are my Manolos wet! And yuck—they're slimy. Lisa—you didn't, did you?'

As a searing pain went through Lisa's belly, hot and sharp as a blade, her grip on the knife tightened. 'Wait, I'm okay. Just give me a second.' She doubled over, puffing and panting and telling herself to visualise the pain as the Harbour Bridge, rising to a peak, then falling away. Everyone watched her, open-mouthed.

The pain had gone. Lisa stood up, knife at the ready. 'All fine. Just one of those super-intense phantom pains—a Braxton Hicks I think.' She waved the blade airily at the concerned faces surrounding her. 'All fine. Now who wants some—' She gripped the bench again. 'Cake. Oh no. Actually. Wait.' Another contraction gripped her belly, even more intense than the first. 'Nope, sorry. Not a Braxton Hicks after all.' She put the knife down and doubled over again. 'Ava, honey,' she gasped from below the bench. 'Next year, I think you're going to be sharing your birthday with another little Wheeldon.'

Scott was at her side, white as the icing. 'Oh gosh. You mean—'

Lisa grinned weakly as the contraction started to fade. 'I do. My hospital bag's next to the bed, hon,' she called as Scott scooted up the stairs.

'Shit, Lise. Is there anything we can do?' Jamie rushed to her side as the pain began to mount in her belly again.

'Just stay and look after the girls,' she exhaled.

'I'll stay too,' volunteered Missy.

'Me as well,' said Heather.

Leaning on Ben and Jamie, Lisa staggered into the garden as Scott charged ahead to start the car.

'Oh wow, so on this day next year you'll be celebrating your baby boy's first birthday and Ava's seventh,' said Ben in amazement.

'How the hell are you going to manage that, Lise?' said Jamie, opening the car door for Lisa to lower herself into the seat. 'Two parties on one day.'

As another contraction took hold of her stomach, Lisa looked at the concerned faces above her. 'I have no idea,' she said, smiling widely through the pain. 'But I can't wait to try.'

ACKNOWLEDGEMENTS

Writing these acknowledgements is a 'pinch-me' moment. It is such a thrill and a privilege to be in a position of being able to express my overwhelming gratitude to the many people who have helped bring *After the Party* into the world. You have made my dreams come true!

Firstly, to editor and writer extraordinaire Kim Swivel. Kim, I asked you for a manuscript assessment and you gave me an annotated manuscript, along with a full report. Such a generous gift! The story wouldn't be what it is now without your initial input.

Finding a publisher is a bit like blind dating—sometimes you have to kiss a lot of frogs to find 'the one'—but with Jo Mackay, the moment we sat down together, I knew my book had found 'the one'. Your support and encouragement has given me much needed confidence, and your insightful feedback has made this into a much better book. Many, many thanks.

Johanna Baker—I don't know how many unsolicited manuscripts come across your desk, but thank you for spotting mine in the pile, and for being its first 'champion'. I struck the lottery when you laid eyes on this story, and loved it.

To the wider Harlequin/Harper Collins family—James Kellow, Sue Brockhoff, Darren Kelly and all in sales, marketing, publicity and design—you have been so warm in your welcome and generous in your enthusiasm. A special shout-out to the cover fairies for giving me the smashed cupcake of my dreams, and also to the editorial team—co-ordinator Annabel Blay, editor Alex Craig and proofreader Annabel Adair—for the gentle yet attentive editing. It wasn't half as scary as I was expecting!

Writing can be a solitary business, but what I have discovered is that there is a community of writers out there who are warm, witty and wise. I am so pleased to be among your ranks. Thank you for the inspiration and solidarity. Also, to the readers and booksellers of this world: you are a special bunch, and I thank you for making this book a possibility.

To my 'real-life' friends, right through from school days to mother's group and now. You are my loveliest cheer squad and I thank you all—especially my 'mum' friends, who are the inspiration behind much of the material in this book.

One of life's great blessings is to have an extended family that you not only love, but really, really like spending time with. Sade, Tim, Muz, Jack, Jen and all my darling nieces and nephews—I love you all, I appreciate your support and I love hanging out with you.

Mum and Dad—I wish every kid in this world had parents like you! You have been my biggest and most biased supporters, always believing more in me than I have myself. You taught me what it is to be a reader. You put books in my hands and when my reading was obsessional, you (rightly) told me to put them down and engage with the world. I love you very much and know I can never repay you, but I'll keep trying!

To Ruby, Sasha and Lucy—you are my sun, moon and stars, my sunshine and my clouds, my rain and my rainbows. I adore you, even when you don't finish your dinner. I think you're proud of me, and maybe you have learned that dreams can become reality, even when you're really, really old, like me!

Finally, to Sam (now I really am crying). Spilling that drink on you all those years ago was the best klutzy move I ever made. I love our little life together because it is big in the ways that matter. I could not and would not have done this without you. Thank you for holding my hand.

Turn over for a sneak peek.

the end of cuthbert close

by
CASSIE HAMER

Available April 2020

CHAPTER ONE

Bring a plate!

The three little words sat so cheerily at the bottom of the invitation.

So simple, so innocuous, so friendly.

So deceitful.

Because it wasn't just a plate, was it, thought Alex O'Rourke as she removed a tray of shop-bought spinach and cheese triangles from the oven. After all, any old clown could turn up to a party with a piece of dining-ware. She had a million plates and platters that did nothing more than collect dust in her kitchen cupboard. They'd love an outing to a party!

She started stabbing at the formerly frozen pastries with a spoon.

'Hmmm … something smells good.' Alex's husband, James, sauntered into the kitchen and peered over her shoulder. 'Did you make these?'

He went to pick up a triangle and Alex tapped his hand away. 'Of course I didn't make them.' She stabbed again to make divots in the golden pillows.

'What are you doing? You're ruining them. They're perfect. Stop it.' James put out his hand to shield the defenceless triangles.

'They're *too* perfect,' said Alex. 'No one will ever believe I made them. Maybe if I just burn them a little …' She went to open the oven door but James stood in front of it, arms folded.

'No one cares if you bought them from a shop. You have twins. A full-time job. The neighbours don't expect pastry made from scratch.'

Alex looked at him. Her sweet, supportive husband, trying to be so millennial, while completely failing to understand that some things never changed, like the meaning of that god-awful phrase *bring a plate*, which meant today what it had always meant – that a plate of homemade food was to be produced (exceptions could be made for foodstuffs by a celebrity chef. A Zumbo cake, for instance, could be forgiven) and, as keepers of the social diary, the responsibility for such provision lay in the hands of the woman of the house.

Bring a plate was the phrase that time forgot.

'It's all right for you,' Alex grumbled. 'No one expects you to cook from scratch.'

'But I would have, if you'd asked me. Remember my meatballs?'

Alex nodded. 'Impressive balls.' She tapped her nose. 'And you've given me an idea.' She smiled and kissed his cheek.

'Glad to be of service.'

Alex set about loading the triangles onto a platter, humming happily.

'Er, so what is this idea?'

'I'll tell them that I specifically asked you a week ago to make the meatballs, but you forgot, so rather than having the neighbours go hungry, I ran out and picked up a box of spinach triangles from the supermarket.'

James frowned. 'But that's a lie. You never asked me. If you had, I would have made them.'

'They won't know that. And because you're a man, they'll think nothing of it.'

'But these people are our friends. Cara? Beth? They wouldn't judge you.'

Alex thought of the women who lived in the houses to their immediate right. Beth, two doors up, an incredible homemaker and mother extraordinaire, and Cara, right next door, who managed to be both strong and fragile as she negotiated parenthood all on her own.

'You're right. Cara and Beth would understand.'

'But the rest?'

Alex sighed. Her husband's desire to see the best in everyone was endearing and exhausting. 'They're neighbours. We smile, we wave, we say hello and we get together once a year. They don't know what happens in my house and I don't know what happens in theirs. The one little insight they get is through what I bring to the party. And you know what they see when a full-time working mum turns up with a plate of frozen pastry?'

'A woman with an actual life?'

Alex gave him a look. 'They see a woman who's put her work in front of her family, values convenience over health, is a little bit stingy, isn't quite coping, and doesn't really care if other peoples' arteries become clogged with trans fats.'

'They get all of that from a plate of pastry?' James looked crestfallen.

'You have no idea.' Alex wearily covered the steaming parcels with a sheet of aluminium foil. 'Here, you can carry them out. It'll look more like your fault that way.' She handed over the platter and checked her watch. 'Where are the boys?'

'They're out front playing with Henny.'

Alex whipped around. 'You left them alone, unsupervised, with a three-month-old guinea pig?'

James shifted his weight uneasily. 'They won't hurt her. They love her to death.'

'That's what I'm afraid of. Have you seen the way Noah hugs her?' Alex strode towards the driveway and cursed inwardly. How could she and James have been wasting time discussing pastry when their little boys were potentially monstering a poor, defenceless guinea pig. If any harm had come to Henny, Alex knew exactly which three little words to blame.

Bring a plate.

* * *

Beth Chandler poked the last of the licorice tails into a prune and stood back from the bench to survey her collection of edible mice. So cute, with those little musk lollies as eyes. Twenty-two, she counted – that would be enough for the kids of Cuthbert Close. What was the collective noun for a group of mice? A nest? Yes, nest. A nest of mice for the nest of kids in her street. Perfect.

'These aren't for the party, are they, Mum?' Twelve-year-old Chloe sidled up beside her.

'What do you mean? The prunes are seedless, if that's what you're worried about. None of the kids could possibly choke.'

'It's not that.'

'Then what is it?'

Chloe bit her lip. 'It's that they're kind of gross.'

'Rubbish. Kids love my mice. We had them at all your parties when you were little.' Beth wiped her hands on the tea towel.

'But that was before we knew they were made from prunes.' Chloe picked one up and held it between her finger-tips like a piece of toxic waste. 'Only old ladies eat prunes.'

Beth did a quarter turn and drew herself up. 'What rot. Prunes are for everyone. They're full of fibre and vitamin K and they're as sweet as a lolly.'

Chloe dropped the mouse back to the tray and wiped her hands down her sides. 'They're disgusting.'

'What's disgusting?' Ethan sat up from where he'd been lying on the couch and removed his earbuds.

'Mum's made the prune mice,' said Chloe.

'Yeah, sure.' Ethan went to put the buds back in.

'No, seriously. They're here.' Chloe wrinkled her nose.

'Oh, Mum, you haven't, have you? They are all shades of wrong.' Ethan leapt up. 'Remember the effect those things used to have on me? I'd be on the toilet for days after my birthday.'

Beth started to wash up the pots and pans that had accumulated during her preparations for the neighbourhood party. As well as the mice, she'd elected to make a range of other treats for the kids, figuring that as she was one of the few stay-at-home mothers in the close, she had the most time to give. And besides, she did enjoy cooking.

'That's a complete lie, Ethan Chandler. You were not.'

Her son came to the sink and put his hands on her shoulders. At seventeen, he'd well and truly outstripped her in the height department. 'Mum, please tell me there's going to be something else for the kids to eat at this thing. It's not just prune mice, is it?'

'Of course not,' said Beth in a huff, wriggling out of her son's condescending grasp and opening the fridge door. 'Look, there's fruit kebabs, mini quiches and cheese-and-vegemite sandwiches.' She'd even used her star-shaped cookie cutter. 'Healthy *and* delicious.'

Chloe and Ethan exchanged glances.

'Mum, it's a party. The food's supposed to be ... like ... good, you know?' said Ethan.

'Yeah, like chips and pizza – that kind of thing.' Chloe leant her elbows on the bench.

'I think I know what little children like to eat, thank you very much. I'm not sure if you've forgotten, but I actually raised two of them, and anyway, Cara's little Poppy loves my vegemite sandwiches and Alex's little boys will love the mini-mice. They look just like that new guinea pig of theirs.'

'You really think a kid wants to *eat* their pet?' Ethan shook his head and Chloe giggled.

'They wouldn't be— Oh look, never mind. It's too late now to do anything else, and besides, your father's going to be cooking up some sausages, so there'll be plenty of food if no one likes what I've made.'

Ethan exhaled with relief. 'Phew. Those beef ones are pretty good with heaps of sauce.'

Beth went to open her mouth but thought better of it. They'd find out soon enough that the sausages were of the chicken variety – so much lower in saturated fat than beef or pork.

'Speaking of Daddy, has anyone seen him?'

Chloe smirked. 'I think *Daddy* is in the garden.'

Beth glared and handed her the tea towel. 'Thank you, Chloe. You can finish the washing up for me.'

The near-teenager took it sullenly. 'What's the point in having a dishwasher if we never use it?'

Beth held up a finger. 'Ah, but that's where you're wrong. We have two dishwashers. They tend to moan quite frequently and they cost a lot of money to run, but we just can't bear to get rid of them. You never know, *one* day they might just do the dishes without an argument.' She went to kiss her daughter lightly on the forehead, but Chloe feinted and ducked.

'This family sucks,' she said under her breath.

Beth stopped, stung. This was not her sweet little Chloe. The child who, less than a year ago, had insisted on kissing her at least ten times a day and never walked anywhere without her hand slipped into Beth's. Where had it all gone so wrong? Hormones? Or something more … Was this somehow Beth's fault? Maybe she'd coddled her children too much? Held them so tightly that now they were springing, like elastic bands, away from her. Beth hurried out of the kitchen and towards the front yard, hoping neither Chloe nor Ethan would notice the flush in her face or the heat in her eyes. But, of course, how could they notice, when her son was too busy nodding away to the music between his ears and her daughter was caught up in cursing the unfairness of her life.

Beth stood at the top of steps, breathed deeply and repeated the mantra she'd started using when Ethan was only a few weeks old, though back then they didn't call them mantras, just sayings.

This too shall pass.

She closed her eyes. Usually it gave her a sense of peace.

This too shall pass.

But maybe that was the problem. Everything was passing, just too quickly for Beth to keep up.

She breathed deeply one more time and opened her eyes. Living in the 'bulb' end of the cul-de-sac gave her a good overview of the length of the street. The party was beginning to take shape. Lanterns and fairy lights going up. Neighbours pulling out deckchairs and tables.

She made her way towards the garage and stood at the door.

'Oh, there you are.'

Inside, through the gloom, she could just make out her husband in the corner of the garage, frowning over his phone, the lines on his face accentuated by the screen's eerie glow.

'Everything all right?'

Max looked up, surprised, and quickly stuffed the phone back into his pocket. 'Oh, nothing. Just a couple of issues at work. Tony couldn't find some keys for an open house. No drama.' He came towards her through the dim light. 'Everything set for the party?'

Beth made a face and put her hands on her hips. 'Chloe and Ethan say the food I've made is all wrong and none of the kids will eat it.' As she spoke, her stomach contracted with nerves. Perhaps the children had a point. Maybe kids of today had different tastes. More sophisticated. Salmon sushi seemed to be a staple food from what she saw of children at the local food court.

'Just ignore them,' said Max. 'What does it matter? This party's more about the catch-up than the food. The kids probably won't eat anything anyway. They'll just scoot up and down the street like they always do.'

Beth folded her arms. It was all very well for him to tell her not to worry, all he had to do was wheel out a barbecue and throw some sausages onto it. The difficulty level of that was close to zero, certainly much lower than making mice out of prunes.

'I don't want the neighbours to think I don't care. I did promise to provide for the children.'

'And you are.' Max stopped ferreting about under the surfboards and stood still. 'You need to stop worrying. You always do this and you should know by now that it's always fine.' He glanced down again. 'Now where the hell did I hide the barbecue tongs.'

Beth coloured. Max had given her similar pep talks before every one of the kid's birthday parties, events that always brought her panic levels to fever pitch. For a stay-at-home mother, a child's party was a little like a performance review, or a grand final – the culmination of so many hopes and dreams, for the child, that is. But Max was so easygoing, he always treated it like just another day, albeit with a few extra kids involved. No biggie. Beth told herself it was good for her – the laissez faire approach. He was the yin to her yang. The ebony to her ivory. Usually, his pre-party spiels served to reassure her, but this one in the garage sounded more like a rebuke and she was glad of the gloom to cover her flush.

'Will you set up the barbecue on the Pezzullos' lawn?' The house at the end of the cul-de-sac had been vacant for months, thanks to George's job transfer to Singapore.

'Sure, whatever you think,' he said, still ferreting through boxes.

'I think it's the best spot, out of the way.'

'Hmmm …' Max murmured.

'Are you listening? I said—'

'Here they are!' Max held up the tongs with a self-satisfied grimace, like a dog holding up a bone. 'Now, we're set.'

* * *

'Who wants to try a chicken wing?' Cara Pope stopped at the doorway to the living room as two heads swivelled around to face her. 'Meeeeeeeeeee!' Her daughter, Poppy, leapt up from the piano stool and ran towards the kitchen.

'Hey, little girl, you come back here and finish your scales.' Cara's mother spoke with a rapid-fire delivery.

'Ma, please. It's been nearly an hour.' Cara entwined her fingers behind her back. 'She needs a break, and the party's about to begin.'

Joy bent down to collect her handbag and a pile of sheet music from under the piano. 'You are too soft with that girl,' she grumbled in Korean, which is what she always did when she didn't want Poppy to understand. 'Practice makes perfect.'

Cara bit her lip. 'Come and eat something.'

In the kitchen she found Poppy smacking her lips and wiping sticky soy sauce off her lips. 'Can I have another one?'

Cara smiled and picked up a tissue. 'Just one, or there won't be enough for the party.'

'Little girl, you should wait for your elders.' Her mother tapped Poppy on the shoulder before prodding at a wing.

'Try one, Ma,' Cara encouraged.

Joy picked up a wing and sniffed it before taking a small bite. 'Good,' she said, chewing. 'They need more gochujang.' Her mother went to reach for the fermented chilli paste.

'Wait, Ma. These are for the neighbours. The annual street party. Remember I told you? Poppy's going to wear the hanbok you had made.'

Poppy nodded. 'It's very pretty, Halmi. Thank you.'

Her mother let go of the chilli sauce. 'Then it is okay.'

Cara exhaled. 'Would you like to stay, Ma? You're very welcome.'

'Will the lawyer be there?'

'Alex? Yes, and you know Beth, the one who's married to the real estate agent.'

Her mother cocked her head. 'She is the one who asks for my kimchi recipe?'

'That's her. She loves your kimchi.'

'She has a very clean house.' Her mother grunted with approval, her eyes flicking to the dishes piled high in Cara's sink. 'I will not stay for this party. Your father will die of hunger if I am not home to feed him. So hopeless.' She shrugged and sighed. 'What can you do.'

Cara suppressed a smile. Her father had been the one who suggested she stay for the party. *She is too much in this new house*, he'd complained on the phone. Joy always made him ring to let Cara know she was on her way for Poppy's piano lesson, as if she expected the little girl to be ready and waiting with hands poised on the keys for her arrival. *Your mother needs to get out more. She loves this place like a baby, almost like she loves that church. So much praying. I think she will be the first Australian-Korean saint.*

'Oh, okay, Ma. That's a shame you can't stay.' She paused and contemplated how to phrase what she was about to say. 'They'll be closing the street soon, and I would not want you to be delayed …'

Her mother's eyebrows shot up. 'Closing the street? Woh, these people and their parties. So strange. Why would you want to eat in a street when you all have nice houses.' Her gaze went to the peeling wallpaper above the piano. 'Some are nice.' Clutching her bag more tightly, she patted Poppy on the shoulder and headed for the hallway. 'Goodbye, little girl. Practice your scales twice every day.'

At the front door, she went to remove her slippers and slip her shoes back on.

'Need some help?' Cara bent down to pick up the shoes.

'Who do you think I am? An old lady?'

Ignoring Cara's outstretched hand, her mother instead reached for the wall to steady herself, putting her hand right near the wedding photo of Cara and Pete. Joy's gaze went to it, and she shivered, blessing herself, as she always did.

'Such bad luck.' She shook her head and gave Cara a look that asked her for the thousandth time why she chose to stay in the broken-down old cottage that was saddled with no dishwasher, and the curse of a death of a man in his prime.

Cara kept silent.

Shoes on, Joy was out the door in a hurry. No goodbyes. No *I love you*. Not even a *See you next week*. Just gone.

'Bye, Ma. Thanks for the lesson,' Cara called, and her mother waved without turning around. Further down the street, she could see Beth and Max, setting up the barbecue on the Pezzullos' front lawn, and Alex's twins playing in the driveway with their new guinea pig.

Waiting for the little lawnmower engine of her mother's ageing Daihatsu sedan to come to life (Joy believed in good appliances over good cars) Cara allowed herself to shift focus from the street and back to the photo of her and Pete. She stepped closer, rubbing a speck of dust off his grey-green eyes, then flinched as the car emitted a tinny beep of fare-well. Her mother's way of saying goodbye.